African Women Narrating Identity

This book examines the complexities of women's lives in Africa and the transnational spaces of Europe and North America through the literary works of key African women writers.

Using a postcolonial analytical framework, the book highlights the commonalities of African women's identities and experiences across national, ethnic, linguistic, and religious boundaries in Africa and in western settings. It collates the multi-regional narratives of key African women writers who convey how women's lives are shaped by social, economic, and political factors at home and abroad. It also illustrates the intersection of ethnicity, class, and gender that flows through all the texts examined. Unlike existing works that explore African women's fiction, this book uncovers the transformation from postcolonial themes of nationhood to global modalities of post-independence writing through the lens of gender. The book engages with feminist expression through broad themes including religion, war, and ethnic conflict, women's status in society, tradition and modernity, and local and global tensions.

A unique approach to literary criticism of Anglophone African women's writing, this book will be of interest to scholars and students in the field of African Literature, African Studies, Women's Literature, Postcolonial Literature, Cultural and Ethnic Studies, and Migration and Diaspora Studies.

Rose A. Sackeyfio is an Associate Professor in the Department of Liberal Studies at Winston-Salem State University, USA. She is also the author of *West African Women in the Diaspora* (Routledge 2021), editor of *African Women Writing Diaspora* (Lexington 2021), and co-editor of *Emerging Perspectives on Akachi Adimora-Ezeigbo* (Lexington 2017).

Routledge Studies in African Literature

Autobiography, Memory and Nationhood in Anglophone Africa
David Ekanem Udoinwang and James Tar Tsaaior

Mazisi Kunene
Literature, Activism, and African Worldview
Dike Okoro

Nigeria's Third-Generation Literature
Content and Form
Ode Ogede

African Women Narrating Identity
Local and Global Journeys of the Self
Rose A. Sackeyfio

For more information about this series, please visit: www.routledge.com/ Routledge-Studies-in-African-Literature/book-series/RAL

African Women Narrating Identity

Local and Global Journeys of the Self

Rose A. Sackeyfio

Routledge
Taylor & Francis Group

LONDON AND NEW YORK

First published 2024
by Routledge
4 Park Square, Milton Park, Abingdon, Oxon OX14 4RN

and by Routledge
605 Third Avenue, New York, NY 10158

Routledge is an imprint of the Taylor & Francis Group, an informa business

British Library Cataloguing-in-Publication Data
A catalogue record for this book is available from the British Library

ISBN: 9781032395388 (hpk)
ISBN: 9781032395401 (pbk)
ISBN: 9781003350200 (ebk)

DOI: 10.4324/9781003350200

Typeset in Sabon
by Deanta Global Publishing Services, Chennai, India

This book is dedicated to my Ancestors, without whose guidance and blessings I could not have completed this work.

I also dedicate this book to my grandchildren, Chiyo, Zora, and Miles, who bring me joy and a celebration of life by just being...

Contents

Part I

Feminist Perspectives from the African Continent

Introduction
Literary Herstories of African Women's Lives

African Women Narrating Identity: Local and Global Journeys of the Self is a volume of eight critical essays that interrogate the complexities of women's lives in Africa and the transnational spaces of the West. The work collates the multi-regional voices of important women writers to form a tapestry of authentic representations of women's experiences as they navigate the gendered realities of womanhood in Africa and abroad. Part I of the book presents four writers from each of the four regions of Africa whose works engage women's experiences within local spaces in society. The diverse regional focus in Part II moves beyond Africa to foreground narratives of immigrant women's lives from a diaspora perspective. The fictional works in the volume span the Colonial, Postcolonial, and twenty-first century landscapes to unfold a kaleidoscopic portrait of women that grapple with gender norms in ways that reconfigure their identity in society. African women's writing from the four corners of the continent resonates the commitment to:

> create works that decry the deteriorating material conditions of life in the postcolony, exposing their countries' self-seeking oligarchical regimes, sorely underfunded educational and social service infrastructures, and limiting patriarchal social frameworks.
>
> (Kroll, 2010: 137)

Pioneering African women writers in English are Ghana's Mabel Dove Danquah and Adelaide Casely-Hayford who began writing decades before the mid-1960s when Ama Ata Aidoo published the dramatic work *Dilemma of a Ghost* (1965). However, African women's literary history accords the genesis of women's writing to Flora Nwapa with the 1966 publication of *Efuru* as a groundbreaking novel. From the inception of Anglophone African women's fiction from the mid-1960s until the present, female authors unfold their stories of African women who contend with patriarchal norms that entrench gender inequality within social, economic, and political spaces in the lives of women. The legacies of colonization rendered a massive blow to women's status across the continent, and although great strides have been made in the post-independence era, African women's lived experiences belie the need for social transformation to uplift women as full participants in

DOI: 10.4324/9781003350200-2

society. Despite greater access to education along with expanded opportunities for many women throughout Africa, cultural norms and expectations continue to erect barriers that may constrain women's development and confine them to the margins of society. Through fictional works, African female authors unfold postcolonial perspectives that constitute *herstories* as literary history of the African novel by women.

African Women Narrating Identity: Local and Global Journeys of the Self aims to highlight the ways in which African women writers narrate women's experiences through a broad range of thematic exploration of compelling forces in society such as religion, war and ethnic conflict, women's status in society, tradition and modernity, and local and global tensions. The fictional works that are set in the African Diaspora uncover the modalities of transnational identities that resonate hybridity and otherness for African female migrants in the global spaces of the twenty-first century. The intersection of ethnicity, class, and gender flows through all the works examined along with feminist expression as a unifying theme. An important feature of the volume is the inclusion of diverse women's narratives and perspectives that provides rich insight across national, ethnic, religious, and linguistic communities in Africa and beyond.

Obioma Nnaemeka traces the development of African women's writing in "From Orality to Writing: African Women Writers and the (Re)Inscription of Womanhood." She highlights the transition from women's oral expression to writing by highlighting the centrality of oral performance in the lives of African women throughout the continent:

> In African oral tradition, women were very visible not only as performers but as producers of knowledge, especially in view of oral literature's didactic relevance, moral(izing) imperatives and pedagogical foundations. Researchers in the field of African oral tradition have documented the active participation of women at professional and nonprofessional levels, in the crafting, preservation and transmission of most forms of oral literature.
>
> (1994: 138)

Further, Nnaemeka documents diverse examples of women's poetry, songs, and dirges, throughout Africa that mark rites of passage rituals such as birth, weddings, and death ceremonies. She asserts that women's participation is imperative and integral to the socio-cultural and spiritual nexus of indigenous societies in ways that intersect with the matrix of African womanhood across the continent.

Kenyan writer and activist Micere Mugo corroborate Nnameka's assertions when she attests:

> African women have always dominated the African Orature tradition as cultural workers, storytellers, singers, dancers, riddle posers, dramatists

and so on. As creators, educators, guidance counselors, family historians, (which is a common arrangement in horizontal social formations), women artists become, so to speak, the collective memory and stream of consciousness that links a specific social unit from one generation to another. The woman artist combines this role with those of mother, aunt, grandmother and at times big sister. The woman artist sits at the heart of a community's well-being and fans the fire at the hearth of its imaginative furnaces, especially those of its youth.

(2012: 74)

Nnameka and Mugo echo similar sentiments that convey the centrality of women's voices to sustain the fabric of African communities in the past and the present. The fact that Mugo and Nnaemeka are from east and west Africa, respectively, supports the convergence of women's perspectives across regional boundaries on the continent.

African women's participation in oral performance is thus a precursor to the transition to writing as well as a historical framework of women's creative expression in both African and eventually foreign languages. Nnameka skillfully reconstructs the trajectory of women's written expression that may be interpreted as a consequential development of literature despite women's late entrance onto the Anglophone African literary landscape a decade later than male writers that emerged during the mid-1950s. Prominent women authors express their indebtedness to women in their local communities whose stories stirred their imaginations in the creation of compelling fictional works in the twentieth and twenty-first centuries. For instance, Flora Nwapa, one of the godmothers of African literature, recalls the knowledge and inspiration she gained from the stories she heard as a child in her natal village of Ugwuta in southeastern Nigeria. Ama Ata Aidoo infuses Ghanaian folklore in her dramatic works in *Dilemma of a Ghost* (1965) and *Anowa* (1970).

Alongside folklore, important women writers have also integrated spiritual traditions and mystical elements into their fictional works in ways that invigorate women's writing in the past and the present. Flora Nwapa's *Efuru* (1966) and *The Lake* Goddess (1995) represent the divine female principle within Igbo cosmology that may empower women devoted to water goddess. Further, Buchi Emecheta's *The Joys of Motherhood* (1979) is well known for the inclusion of folklore and indigenous spiritual traditions of her Igbo community in Nigeria. East African writer Rebekah Njau recounts oral narratives of Kenyan women in *Kenyan Women and Their Mystical Power* (1984) and *The Hypocrite and Other Stories* (1977). Zulu Sofola draws upon Igbo women's spiritual roles in *Queen Omu-ako of Oligbo* (1989). In recent years, leading African-futurist author Nnedi Okorafor has infused strong elements of Igbo spiritual traditions into her imaginative works of speculative fiction. For example, in *Lagoon* (2014), Okorafor's otherworldly heroines are powerful figures that display superhuman powers that resemble Igbo mythical water goddesses.

The multi-vocal framework of *African Women Narrating Identity, Local and Global Journeys of the Self* brings together diverse representations of women's identities that inform the literary historiography of African women's fiction. African women's writing is a wellspring of creative expression that re-imagines the Anglophone literary tradition that began in the mid-twentieth century with first-generation male writers. Scholars of African literary studies have critiqued works such as Achebe's *Things Fall Apart* (1955), Cyprian Ekwensi's *Jagua Nana* (1961), and *Jagua Nana's Daughter* (1986) for projecting stereotypical and one-dimensional images of female characters. Wole Soyinka's highly celebrated *The Lion and the Jewel* (196 2) and *Death and the King's Horseman* (1975) have also been scrutinized for negative images of African women. Carole Boyce Davies in "Maidens, Mistresses, and Matrons: Feminine Images in Selected Soyinka Works" contends that "a feminist reading of Soyinka reveals enough female stereotypes to suggest a definite sexist bias against women" (1986: 76).

Naana Banyiwa-Horne asserts that:

a close look at the various images of African womanhood provided in the literature reveals that, to a considerable extent, depictions of African women in the literature by African women writers differ from the images presented by their male counterparts.

(1986: 119)

She examines *The Concubine* (1966) by Elechi Amadi and observes that the novel "provides a perspective that is male and limiting" (120). The feminist perspectives expressed in African women's fiction re-configured monolithic images of females, and similar to the critiques by Boyce-Davies and Horne, Nfah-Abbenyi emphasizes the difference in the depiction of women by women authors: "Female characters...are portrayed not in stereotypical subservient, unchanging roles, or in roles that are deliberately limiting. Instead, they come alive as speaking subjects and agents for change" (1997: 151). The fictional works of Achebe, Soyinka, Armah, Amadi, Ekwensi, and other prominent male authors represent a dominant trend of the period although there are exceptions as the genre has evolved.

Theoretical approaches to African women's writing include postcoloniality, feminist perspectives, and Afropolitan aesthetics. The fictional works span the mid-twentieth and twenty-first centuries in ways that expand the discourse on postcolonial writing broadly, and specifically the development and contributions of Anglophone African women's writing. African women have added their voices to the literary landscape in ways that interrogate conventional questions that plague postcolonial perspectives such as transformative impact of colonialism on the social, economic, and political landscape of the African nation-state, as well as individual responses to the European encounter. In his editorial article, "New Directions in African Literature: Building on the Legacies of the Twentieth Century," noted literary critic Ernest Emenyonu recalls that:

> African literature served in the 20th century, especially the second half, as a forum for addressing and redressing issues of education and mis-education in and about Africa: a forum for dismantling myths and distortions about Africa by the outside world.
>
> (2006: xi)

Further, Nana Wilson-Tagoe explores implications of the bridge between twentieth- and twenty-first-century African writing defined by the emergence of the global economy at the turn of the century. She poses important questions about global themes that have come to dominate African literature over the past two decades. She asks:

> in these transnational imaginary landscapes where we can locate a modern African literature that continues to link nation, culture and narrative, yet that centers on traumas of national collapse, trans-national movements and an increasingly global focus in social and economic relations?
>
> (2006: 94)

The novels studied in this book represent a synthesis of theoretical perspectives that address the complexities of the post-independence era into the contemporary age of global transformation.

Feminist-inspired literature provides an important link to connect twentieth-century African women's literature to the global era of African writing, and Chimamanda Ngozi Adichie's *Purple Hibiscus* (2006) and Sefi Atta's *Everything Good Will Come* (2005) were exemplary in this regard. These works are thus pivotal in the evolution of the genre because:

> Sackeyfio observes that: third generation Nigerian writers have extended conventional themes from the 1960's and 1970's to include coming of age, modernity, religious conflict, the failure of the democratic government, and the attendant pejorative impact upon the individual in society.
>
> (2015: 267)

These works are important because they are written by African women, about women's experiences in new ways that reconfigure the African novel as well as the image of women in society. Moreover, Iniobong Uko avers that: "the coming of age of African literature is identifiable by the true and pragmatic feminization of the literary vision as a way of correcting absurd female images in African literature and culture" (2006: 82).

Leading critic and scholar, Carol Boyce Davies codifies feminist perspectives as:

> African feminist criticism so far has engaged in a number of critical activities which can be conveniently categorized as follows: 1) Developing the canon of African women writers: 2) Examining stereotypical images of women in African literature; 3) Studying African women writers and the development of an African female aesthetic; and 4) Examining women in oral literature.
>
> (1986: 13–14)

Finally, Molara Ogundipe Leslie presented the commitment of the female writer: "the woman writer has these two major responsibilities; first to tell about being a woman; secondly, to describe reality from a woman's view, a woman's perspective" (1987: 5). The literary history of African women's writing has lived up to these tenets in the twentieth and twenty-first century in ways that unsilenced women from the margins to the center of African literary production.

Afropolitan aesthetics forms another layer of critique to guide readers, scholars, and critics' research on African women's writing. The term gained currency through Taiye Selasie's controversial essay "Bye Bye Babar" in 2005. It has become a seductive catch phrase to describe sophisticated, globe-trotting, multi-lingual African elites who people western settings of mobility and fluid identities. Many critics convey troubling concerns about Afropolitanism's essentialist framing that ignores masses of African immigrants whose diaspora lives are marked with adversity, otherness and alienation, and worse, massive loss of life between the watery boundaries of Africa and Europe. The best feature of Afroplitanism is that it usurps tropes of victimhood and other stereotypical representations of African émigrés to provide a nuanced rendering of diverse African people and their experiences in the world. Chimamanda Ngozi Adichie's *Americanah* (2013) is examined in Chapter 8 and provides a sustained engagement with the misleading use of Afropolitanism's claims of universal congruity and uniformity across socio-economic strata within the multi-regional mix in the global landscape.

Regional Perspectives

West Africa is markedly overrepresented in the historiography of African literature that spans generational categories within literary discourses by scholars and critics of the genre. Canonized works of classic fiction represent the inception of Anglophone African writing within a postcolonial framework of world literatures. Since the 1950s, writers from the region have generated an outpouring of creative artistry, and women are prominent in this corpus, along with renown literary figures of this generation.

Beginning in the 1930s with Ghana's Mabel D. Danquah and Adelaide Casely-Hayford, women's literary expression in West Africa grew to include a host of female writers such as Efua Southerland, Ama Ata Aidoo, Flora Nwapa, Mariama Ba, Buchi Emecheta, and Amma Darko among others, to pave the way for later generations of artists to stand on their shoulders in the literary world. Since the turn of the century, Nigeria has remained prominent in the African literary landscape, and Pious Adesanmi and Chris Dunton situate Nigeria as a locus of creativity by third-generation African writers who fall into this category because they are born after 1960 during the period of independence throughout Africa (2005: 14–15). In "Nigeria's Third Generation Writing: Historiography and Preliminary Theoretical Considerations," Adesanmi and Dunton assert the "numerical superiority of Nigerian writers within the continental equation" (14-15). At first glance, this statement appears audacious, although it is authentically grounded in the prolific outpouring of contemporary African literature. Both female and male authors from Nigeria have taken the lead in the production of award-winning and critically acclaimed works that are published in western settings that confer accessibility to a wide audience. Most exciting is the prominence of Nigerian women authors such as Chimamanda Ngozi Adiche, Sefi Atta, and Chika Unigwe who excel on the African literary stage through their highly successful fictional works.

Prominent first-generation African women writers usurped the dominance of masculinist fictional narratives in the creation of successful works of feminist expression such as Flora Nwapa's groundbreaking *Efuru* (1966). Buchi Emecheta's oeuvre is pivotal in the representation of women's transcontinental experiences in Nigeria and in London. Emecheta's semi-autobiographical diaspora novels include *Second Class* Citizen (1975), *In the Ditch (*1972), and *Head Above Water* (1986). Through her iconic works, *The Bride Price* (1976), *The Slave Girl* (1977), and *The Joys of Motherhood* (1979), Emecheta vividly depicts Igbo gender norms and customs that restrict women's equality among the Igbo community in Nigeria. These works are significant because they represent women's perspectives on a range of issues within a postcolonial context.

Senegalese writer Mariama Ba's *So Long a Letter* (1979), originally written in French, evokes feminist synergy that established her contribution to the evolution of African women's fiction in the late twentieth century. These early works codify canonical status as feminist-inspired literature as well as the representation of theoretical underpinnings of postcolonial writing.

In West Africa, Ghana is also a site of important literary production, and among a constellation of writers, Efua Sutherland is distinguished as a pioneering figure through her enormous contribution as a dramatist, creative artist, and activist. Renowned poet Kofi Anyidoho asserts that when she died in 1996, "Africa lost one of its most remarkable daughters of the twentieth century" (2007: 235). Her literary corpus is impressive and includes several dramatic works: *Playtime in Africa* (1960), *The Roadmakers* (1961), *The*

Marriage of Anansewa (1975), and *You Swore an Oath, Vulture, Vulture* (1968) among many others. In her role as a foundational author who carved a place in the African literary canon, she created pathways for a host of Ghanaian writers to follow in her footsteps from the mid-twentieth through the twenty-first centuries.

In 1965, Ghanaian playwright, novelist, and poet, Ama Ata Aidoo published her classical debut work: *Dilemma of a Ghost*, followed by *Anowa* in 1970, and two successful novels, *Our Sister Killjoy* (1977) and *Changes, a Love Story* (1991). Aidoo's works reposition women's voices at the center of their narratives to assert their awareness and resistance to gender imbalance, racial dynamics, the dark period of enslavement, diaspora identities, and pressing issues of postcolonial dissonance among Ghanaian subjects at home and abroad. In her often-cited essay, "The African Woman Today," Aidoo is clear in highlighting the legacy of colonialism in shaping the status of African women:

> Much of the putting down of women that educated African men indulge in and regard as "African culture" is a warmed-up leftover from colonization. European colonizing men (especially Victorians) brought with them a burden of confusion; first about their own women, and then about other women-all of which was further muddled-up by the colonizer's fantasies about the sexual prowess of both African men and women.
>
> (1998: 47)

Amma Darko's contribution to Ghanaian women's writing includes her novels in English that explore the lives of Ghanaian women within multi-local settings such as urban and rural Ghana and Germany. Her most well-known works are *Beyond the Horizon* (1991), *Faceless* (1996), and *The Housemaid* (1998). The women characters in these novels represent the ways in which African women navigate gender inequality, socio-economic barriers, and the challenges to their survival in Europe. Ghanaian women's writing drew significant attention in the twenty-first century with the emergence of a younger generation of authors such as Nigerian-Ghanaian Taiye Selasie in her debut novel *Ghana Must Go* (2013). The work received critical acclaim as a vivid rendering of a Ghanaian family in the throes of immigrant angst in America, disconnection to Ghana and to each other across multiple geographical spaces. In 2016, Yaa Gyasi rose to prominence through the publication of the sweeping multigenerational epic *Homegoing* that traces the lives of the descendants of two Ghanaian half-sisters through several generations in America. The work is significant as historical fiction expressed through the spatio-temporal dimensions that capture the complexities of transformation from Ghanaian origins to diaspora identity. *Transcendent Kingdom* (2020) is Gyasi's second novel that examines racial identity, drug addiction, and loss within a splintered Ghanaian family in the USA. Other Ghanaian women writers are rising to the challenge of representation and visibility in the publication of the *God Child* (2019) by Nana Oforiatta Ayim and *His Only Wife* (2020) by Peace Adzo Medie. Both novels display the emerging talent of young writers that craft new narratives of women's experiences in the global age.

Other notable authors from west Africa are Calixthe Beyala, Zaynab Alkali, Aminata Sow Fall, Rebecca Njau, and Zulu Sofola. Collectively, the fictional works include both Anglophone and Francophone writing that constitute a dynamic and vibrant literary tradition that reconfigures the African novel.

The global age witnessed a dramatic shift in Nigerian/African writing through the emergence of leading female authors who presently dominate the African literary stage. Global mobility is mirrored in the production of arresting contemporary themes that intertwine new forms of postcolonial realities in the lives of African women. Akachi Adimora Ezeigbo's compelling woman-centered narratives form a bridge between women's first-generation fictional works and contemporary Igbo women's writing in novels such as *The Last of the Strong Ones* (1996) and *House of Symbols* (2001), followed in 2002 by *Children of the Eagle*. Ezeigbo's *Roses and Bullets* (2011) chronicles Igbo women's participation in the Nigeria-Biafra War as a form of "writing back" to male authors of the first generation of postcolonial Anglophone African writing that depicted unfavorable and stereotypical women characters.

In the early twenty-first century, Chimamanda Ngozi Adiche's *Purple Hibiscus* (2003), *Half of a Yellow Sun* (2006), and the 2013 epic *Americanah* vividly foreground women's perspectives that link postcolonial themes in the period after Nigeria's independence with the political legacies of instability that emerged during the 1990s through a gendered lens. Sefi Atta's *Everything Good Will Come* in 2005 and *Swallow* (2008) also form a literary bridge between conventional interrogation of the postcolonial landscape and the examination of twenty-first-century challenges to social, economic, and political stability in Nigeria. Since her independence from Britain in 1962, the burgeoning nation suffered the calamitous Nigeria-Biafra Civil War from 1967 to 1970 whose legacy haunts the political landscape till the present through pervasive ethnic tensions. The late twentieth century ushered an era of dictatorship lasting for ten years beginning in 1983 with the first of three political coups in the nation and the attendant economic fragility caused by Structural Adjustment interventions, the World Bank, IMF, systemic corruption, and repressive political environment.

Nigerian women were disenfranchised and marginalized as a continuation of their eroded status during the colonial period. As a mirror of existential realities in the twentieth and twenty-first centuries, vivid fictional works such as Adichie's *Purple Hibiscus*, Atta's *Everything Good Will Come* and *Swallow*, and Unigwe 's *On Black Sisters' Street*, among others, shed light on Nigeria's deeply troubled history from a female perspective. In these works, women's lives in urban spaces are fraught with the pressures of post-independence fractures within the political, economic, and social matrix that impede women's equality and routes to empowerment. These novels distinctly convey the ways in which Nigerian women navigate the complexities of modern life in a changing world. The works illustrate how multiple forces in society shape women's identities in the effort to surmount the barriers to their autonomy and restricted opportunities for success in the twentieth century as well as the global age.

Nigerian women's literary history is thus a chronicle of fictional works that express postcolonial realities beyond local settings to describe journeys abroad in search of education and greater opportunities. Adichie's *Americanah* is representative of this trend through the confluence of thematic focus on Nigerian immigrants driven into global spaces that may offer upward mobility and success. Helen Oyeyemi is the author of *The Icarus Girl* (2005), *White Is for Witching* (2009), *Boy, Snow, Bird* (2014), and in 2021, *Peaces*. As a master storyteller, her fictional works are haunted by magical realism, re-worked fairytales, and dark-themed flavor. Unomah Azuah contributes to Nigerian women's fiction with the publication of her novel *Sky High Flames* in 2005. She has edited a stunning collection of narratives by members of the LGBT community in Nigeria that brings to light the severe homophobia and victimization in society.

In 2019, Bernardine Evaristo captured the literary spotlight as the winner of the Caine Prize for *Girl Woman, Other* that maps the intersecting stories of women from Africa and the diaspora in London. Finally, award-winning writer Aminatta Forna, of Sierra Leonean heritage, is the author of four novels and a memoir *The Devil That Danced on the Water: A Daughter's Quest* (2002). From Cameroon, Imbolo Mbue's *Behold the Dreamers* has received critical acclaim as her first novel about Cameroonian immigrants in America.

The overwhelming success of African women writers in the global age parallels the continued focus on Diaspora/Immigrant fiction as part of a larger interdisciplinary interrogation of global mobility of African people in the Humanities and Social Sciences. As a reflection of life, African women's writing mirrors the continent's rich and diverse ethnic communities, geographical, religious, and linguistic multeity.

South African women writers have made their mark in the annals of Postcolonial writing from the region in ways that parallel Nigeria's prominence in West African literature. South African literature owes its development to the trauma of Apartheid, and the nation is an important site of literary intervention to subvert oppression and to achieve social justice and racial equality. Apartheid and Post-Apartheid literature are imbued with a broad range of political themes such as the experiences of exiles, refugees, and prisoners. Issues of race haunt the literary landscape, and Black South African women authors examine gender in ways that echo women's writing from across Africa and the Black world.

Among South African writers, Bessie Head is the most well-known, and her iconic novel *A Question of Power* (1974) is a richly textured work that fuses autobiographical elements of her troubled life. Her novels *Maru* (1971), *The Collector of Treasures* (1977), and *Serowe: Village of the Rain Wind* (1981) explore women's experiences of displacement, gender inequality, and the challenges to survival in Botswana. Diedre Byrne charts the contributions of an array of female writers from South Africa in "A Different Kind of Resistance: An Overview of South African Black Women's Writing." An important autobiographical work is *Call Me Woman* (1985) by Ellen Kuzwayo that historicizes pivotal moments of resistance against Apartheid. Maggie Resha published *My Life in the Struggle* (1991) that recounts her political activism during the 1950s and 1960s. Another important writer is Miriam Tiali, whose work *Muriel at Metropolitan* (1975) is the first novel to be published by a Black woman in South Africa, and like other successful writers, her works are historically authentic and politically charged.

Along with the pioneering work of Bessie Head, Byrne acknowledges Sindiwe Magona, Zoe Wicombe, and others for their texts that describe women's lives under Apartheid. Magona's *To My Children's Children* (1990) and *Forced to Grow* (1992) are vivid accounts of everyday lives marked by adversity and political oppression expressed through a gendered lens. Byrne highlights the prevalence of autobiography as a form of resistance writing that resonates Juliana Makuchi Nfah-Abbenyi's articulation of "African Women's Writing as a Weapon." According to Nfah-Abbenyi:

> African women seek to create spaces for themselves. They do so by rewriting conventional literary forms, by questioning a combination of the multiple oppressive conditions both traditional and specific to their post-colonial heritage in a constantly changing post-colonial context, a context that therefore positions their challenges sometimes alongside, but mostly beyond the limits of Western feminism and within postcolonial theoretical practice.
>
> (1997: 149)

African women's writing is thus a subversive act through the re-inscription of womanhood that un-silences women to voice their truth to patriarchal structures and a plethora of postcolonial realities in the global age.

The realism of autobiography is compelling in its impact, and pervasive in Black women's writing cross-culturally in the past and the present. When assessing the significance of these texts, Byrne highlights "the use of historical detail as a method of expressing political resistance. This technique creates the impression that the facts of oppression, on their own, constitute an attack on it" (1994: 23). Within a historical context, these ideas resonate with the eighteenth-century slave narratives by women that represent the origins of African diaspora writing. Two of the most well-known nineteenth-century works are Harriet Jacobs' *Incidents in the Life of a Slave Girl* (1861) and Mary Prince's *The Life of a West Indian Slave* (1831). The slave narrative genre served a similar function as Apartheid literature by women through vivid rendering of the brutality of racial and gender oppression, women's resilience, and the triumph of the human spirit in the effort to survive.

In the southern region of the continent, Zimbabwean women writers have distinguished themselves alongside their South African sisters. Well-known talented women include Tsitsi Dangaremgba, NoViolet Bulawayo, Yvonne Vera, and Petina Gappa among others. Tsitsi Dangaremgba's *Nervous Conditions* (1998) is a Postcolonial classic and part of a trilogy that includes *The Book of Not* (2006) and *This Mournable Body* (2018). Tsitsi Dangaremgba is the first Black woman from Zimbabwe to publish in English. NoViolet Bulawayo emerged onto the literary stage with the publi-cation of the critically acclaimed *We Need New Names* in 2013. The novel is a gripping account of Zimbabwe's decline into social, economic, and politi-cal chaos under the brutal dictatorship of Robert Mugabe through a gen-dered lens. The work spans Zimbabwe and the diaspora setting of Detroit Michigan in the USA as the young female protagonist comes of age to experi-ence cultural hybridity and alienation. Yvonne Vera is the author of five nov-els before her death in 2005. Her fiction describes the experiences of women in Zimbabwe sin works such as *Nehanda* (1993), *Without a Name* (1994), *Under the Tongue* (1996), and *The Stone Virgins* (2002). Petina Gappah is the author of two novels, *A Book of Memory* (2015) and *Rotten Row* (2016). This overview of writers from Zimbabwe is by no means exhaustive and their works are a major contribution to the literary corpus of women's fiction from the Southern region of the continent.

Among writers from East Africa, Kenyan author Grace Ogot's *The Promised Land* (1966) ushered a vibrant tradition of resistance literature conceptualized by Lennox Odiemo-Munara in "Women Re-writing East Africa" to interrogate the complexities of women's experiences in Kenya. Grace Ogot's fiction includes *Land Without Thunder* (short stories) (1968), *The Graduate* and *The Other Woman,* both published in (1980), and *The Strange Bride* in (1983).

The development of East African Women's writing illustrates intertextual-ity in Postcolonial fiction from all the regions of Africa, and Odiemo-Munara unequivocally asserts:

> Women's voices of the late twentieth century to the present dynami-cally confront the intricate questions of patriarchy, politics, culture/ tradition production and formulation, among others. They aim at (re) defining the East African woman in the exercise of power and authority in the society, and in the process see to her active participation in the public sphere.
>
> (2010: 2)

The evolution of East African women's writing echoes their sister story-tellers throughout the continent, to interrogate the legacies of the colonial encounter and the marginalization of women in the socio-cultural, economic, and political spaces in society. Although East African women's literature may be underrepresented in the international arena as compared to the prominence of West and Southern Africa, the latter years of the twentieth century into the global age have produced an appreciable number of female authors that have emerged on the literary stage.

Throughout East Africa, women writers are known primarily through national or regional exposure, and in 2010, in "New Visions, New Voices: Emerging Perspectives in East African Fiction, Njeri Githire notes that "the underrepresentation and invisibility of East African women in the African literary canon is disquieting" (2010: 183). Refreshingly, the twenty-first century has thrust East African women into the literary spotlight through the prestige of the Caine Prize in African writing beginning with Yvonne Ahiambo in 2003, Monica Arac de Nyeko in 2007, and Leila Aboulela in 2000.

Other distinguished authors are Rebecca Njau who is known for her works *The Scar* (1965), *Ripples in the Pool* (1975), *Kenyan Women Heroes and Their Mystical Powers* (1984), and in 2003 *The Sacred Seed*. Her works foreground the experiences of women who grapple with patriarchy, and "traditional" norms and customs as a connecting thread to African women's writing from other regions of the continent.

Muthoni Likimani's first and second novels *They Shall Be Chastised* and *What Does a Man Want* were both published in 1974. *Passbook Number 47927: Women and Mau in Kenya* (1985) is included in this volume and remains her most well- known work about women's participation in the struggle for independence. This work is yet another illustration of African women (re)writing history to foreground women's immense but underrepresented contributions to resistance movements during the colonial era in Africa. Another notable writer from Kenya is Margaret Ogola who published three novels: *The River and the Source* (1995), which traces the lineage of four Kenyan women; *I Swear by Apollo* (2002); and finally, *Place of Destiny* (2005). Ugandan author and politician Mary Karooro Okurut's contribution to East African women's literature begins with *The Invisible Weevil* (1998) and *The Official Wife* (2003). She is also the founder of the Ugandan Women Writers Association FEMRITE.

The contemporary age in East African writing brings to the stage a new generation of important writers such as Kenya's Yvonne Adhiambo Owuor, Maaza Mengetse from Ethiopia, along with Igiaba Scego and Cristina Ali Farah from Somalia. Owuor's *Weight of Whispers* (2003) is the winner of the Caine Prize in the same year. In 2014, she published *Dust*, and in 2019, her second novel *The Dragonfly Sea* (2019) that was received with critical acclaim as it portrays a woman's journey beyond the shores of Africa to infuse global perspectives.

Maaza Mengitse's *The Shadow King* (2019) is called "A Gorgeous Meditation on Memory, War and Violence" by *The New York Times* book reviewer Michael Schaub. The book is a work of historical fiction about the participation, strength, and resilience of women during the Italian invasion of Ethiopia during the 1930s. Mengitse's debut novel *Beneath the Lion's Gaze* (2010) was named one of the 10 best contemporary African books by *The Guardian*. The novel *Adua* (2016) by Igiaba Scego spans Somalia and Italy through the voice of a beautiful woman whose dreams are dashed against the trauma of racial exclusion and sexual exploitation in Italy. Another memorable work by a Somali writer is *Little Mother* (2017) by Cristina Ali Farah. The book weaves a tale of Somali women immigrants displaced by war and their attempts to reconstruct their identities in Europe and America. The increasing body of fiction by East African women is thus long overdue and the emerging perspectives in the new millennium are compelling representations of African women's lives in the past and the present.

North African women writers have claimed their space among women's literary traditions throughout the continent although Islamic influence pervades creative expression through Arabic language and culture. Throughout the twentieth century and the global age, writers from Egypt, Morocco, and Tunisia dominate literary production in the region.

African women's writing has historically been driven by the impulse to "write back" to colonial intrusion by Europeans, nationalist energies, masculinist literary traditions, and indigenous norms and customs that may impede women's development and empowerment in society. In all periods of North Africa's history, class differences have defined women's access to education so that communities of elite women have been educated as well as experiencing varying degrees of autonomy, employment, and participation in the public sector, especially in Morocco and Egypt. Broadly speaking, despite less access to education than women from sub-Saharan Africa, women's writing throughout the Maghreb upholds traditions of "writing back" expressed through the overlay of discourses that examine Islamic conventions such as veiling, seclusion, and restrictive codes of behavior.

Literary works in Arabic and French increased during the middle to late twentieth century, and writers such as Amina Arfaoui examine polygamy in her short story, "The Gramophone" published in 1987. Writing from Egypt, Salwa Bakr's 1992 short story "Worms in the Rose Garden":

> can be read as an expression of resistance against the increasing influence of newly wealthy societies that may have eschewed rules for enforced segregation and veiling, yet have not in any meaningful adopted liberal attitudes toward women.
>
> (Nowaira et.al., 2009: 43)

North African women have also written about pressing issues such as Female Genital Cutting, and Sudanese author Buthanyna Khadyr Mekky's disquieting story titled "Rites" exposes women's painful experiences that is juxtaposed with the sexual pleasure of males. Women's emotional and physical trauma pervade this piece through Mekky's vivid rendering of women's plight, and the challenge in eradicating the practice in society.

Writing in French, iconic Algerian author, poet, playwright, and filmmaker, Assia Djebar is widely read and taught throughout the world through translated publications. Djebar's classic works span the twentieth and twenty-first centuries to reconfigure Arab women's identity. *Fantasia: An Algerian Cavalcade* (1985) and *A Sister to Scheherazade* (1987) assert feminist themes of resistance against patriarchy and the French colonial intrusion in Algeria that began in 1830. *Children of the New World: A Novel of the Algerian War* (2005) chronicle Algeria's War of Independence (1954–1962) through the lens of gender.

Nawal El Saadawi's literary corpus is renowned in world literature and her works examine the lives of Arab Muslim women in her native country, Egypt. Her death in 2021 marks the loss of a pioneering and courageous voice for women's empowerment and freedom from oppressive patriarchal structures and assault on women's bodies as a cultural norm. Saadawi's life and works created a legacy of radical feminist energy and Susan Arndt in *The Dynamics of African Feminism: Defining and Classifying African Feminist Literatures* (2002) denotes Saadawi as a radical feminist writer because in some of her works, the female protagonist takes the life of her male oppressor.

As a dissident writer, Saadawi has published more than 40 books; among them, her most well-known and widely taught novel is *Woman at Point Zero* (1973). Other notable works of both fiction and non-fiction are *The Hidden Face of Eve* (1980), *God Dies by the Nile* (1984), and her autobiography, *Daughter of Isis* (1999). Writing in Arabic, many of her works have been translated into English as well as over 30 other languages. Her contribution to women's progress includes her work as a medical doctor, psychiatrist, and her activism against Female Genital Mutilation (FGM), which was banned in Egypt in 2008 after over 50 years of protesting the practice. Saadawi's works explore oppressive norms and customs within a matrix of multilayered themes of patriarchy, sexual violence, religious hypocrisy, and political issues that entrench marginal status of women in Egyptian society.

Among authors from the Muslim regions of northeast Africa, Leila Aboulela's novels represent Sudan's most successful contribution to women's literary production. Aboulela's novels, *The Translator* (1999) and *Minaret* (2005), merit inclusion among North African women's creative expression through interrogation of Muslim identity, patriarchy, nationalism, and matters of religious faith such as veiling and codes of conduct in Egypt and the Sudanese diasporic landscape. Her novels share intertextual elements with Arab Muslim women as well as with contemporary sub-Saharan African women's works through vivid narratives of political upheaval, displacement, hybridity, and gender dynamics within a spatio-temporal nexus. The *Translator and Minaret* engages Sudanese diasporic themes as women navigate disparate realities across national, ethnic, and religious boundaries.

The volume opens with Egypt's Nawal El Saadawi to examine "Radical Feminist Synergy and Sexual Exploitation in Saadawi's *Woman at Point*

Zero and God Dies by the Nile" (Chapter 1). The novels convey the intersectionality of patriarchy, religion, and politics to inhibit women's equality in Egyptian society. Women are central figures throughout the works, and in *Woman at Point Zero*, a female reclaims her autonomy to reinscribe feminist expression of her *selfhood*. In *God Dies by the Nile*, a woman becomes the moral center within a corrupt system of injustice against the females in her family. *Woman at Point Zero* and *God Dies by the Nile* are feminist novels that display women's awakening to agency in the face of death, loss, and utter powerlessness in society. The allegorical and thematic constructions of the novels are emblematic of women's oppression as a trope that appears throughout texts within Saadawi's immense literary corpus.

Chapter 2 illuminates the complexities of women's lives in Botswana through the artistry of Bessie Head in *Maru* (1972). Head's portrayal of female characters reveals much insight into multilayered elements of intra-ethnic discrimination, racial exclusion, and gender oppression. The chapter examines the cancerous nature of caste and class through an allegorical tale of romance and intrigue as expressed in *Maru*. Salient themes that link the works are independence, patriarchy, and sisterhood among women. Head has infused autobiographical elements in *Maru* in similar ways to *A Question of Power*.

Kenyan author, Muthoni Likimani's work is the subject of Chapter 3 titled "Sisters in Arms: Women's Resistance in Muthoni Likimani's *Passbook Number 47927*" as a work of historical fiction. The chapter looks at the portrayal of Kenyan women's participation in the Mau Mau Revolution in Kenya during the 1950s. Analysis of the novel complements the feminist themes that appear in other works included in the volume by highlighting Kenyan women's strength, resilience, and enormous sacrifices in support of the nationalist movement for independence during the mid-nineteenth century. The chapter penetrates the inner world(s) of women at war with powerful forces of destruction to themselves as well as their nation.

In Chapter 4, the gendered spaces of poverty and tragedy in Amma Darko's *Faceless* unfold themes of exploitation, disruption in the family and society, and unfavorable outcomes as women's bodies are sites of trauma and pain. Women and children lead impoverished lives as disposable bodies in the slums of Accra in Ghana. "Postcolonial Disjunctures and Urban Spaces in Amma Darko's *Faceless*" highlights the ways in which the confluence of social, economic, and political forces mangle women's lives in the struggle to survive insurmountable odds. Despite the dark themes that haunt the text, women exhibit agency to rescue themselves from the margins of society.

Chapter 5 foregrounds the Sudanese Muslim diaspora in London and Aberdeen to highlight themes of religious faith and women's identity in Leilia Aboulela's *The Translator* and *Minaret*. Aboulela's works are important representations of Islamic influence on women within Northeast Africa. The chapter connects women's Muslim identities across national borders where commitment to religious practice motivates new forms of diaspora transformation among women from Sudan. Unlike much of contemporary diaspora fiction that narrate experiences of racial otherness and hybridity in the west, Aboulela foregrounds the centrality of religion as a binding thread of women's experiences in the cosmopolitan space(s) of London and Aberdeen. This chapter unveils women's cultural transformation through the representation of transcultural Sudanese females that move beyond the challenges of racial otherness in Europe to experience new expressions of their identity through Islamic faith, relationships with males, and memory of home. In both works, Aboulela presents women's adherence to Islam in ways that counter monolithic and stereotypical portrayals of subordinate and silenced Muslim women.

Chapter 6 focuses on NoViolet Bulawayo's *We Need New Names*, and the work is a vivid rendering of the shattered innocence of Zimbabwean youth in post-independent Zimbabwe. This chapter illustrates that childhood innocence is a casualty in the marginalized world of Robert Mugabe's Zimbabwe during the 1980s that is marred by social, economic, and political injustice. The novel charts the life of the female protagonist to unfold a bildungsroman experience that spans Africa and America. This chapter demonstrates how childhood innocence gives way to a new form of splintered existence in America that juxtaposes the *divided self* of the protagonist. The young female at the center of the novel matures in America as the stage for disjointed awakening to a new and conflicted identity.

In Chapter 7, Igiaba Scego's *Adua* is examined in "Black Venus Dreams and the Migrant Body." The work is a skillfully etched portrait of otherness and hybridity in the Somali diaspora of Italy. Scego's artistry emerges through a lucid and compelling account of the ravages of diaspora life for an African woman migrant. This chapter engages the multi-vocal narration of the transnational encounter in Italy to frame the postcolonial discourse of the twentieth century into the global age. Through Scego's insight, the vulnerable status of immigrant women is highlighted in the quest for new identity as women experience local and global tensions in the diaspora setting. The Italian imperial "gaze" captures the ethos of Somali journeys into uncharted vistas of the Italian diaspora-scape.

In the final chapter of the volume, Chimamanda Ngozie Adichie's highly successful *Americanah* is investigated in "Afropolitan Energies in the Twenty-First Century: Immigrants, Dreamers, and Marginalized Others" in Adichie's *Americanah*. The lifestyles of African émigrés have been articulated as a new way of being African within transnational settings through the lens of *Afropolitanism*, understood by some writers and scholars as a phenomenon that represents a unified and universalistic assimilation into western life for African immigrants. This chapter argues that essentialist constructions of *Afropolitanism* are not universalistic because they reflect the lived experiences of a particular sub-set of African Diasporans that collapses the multiple, diverse, and contested spaces of other African subjectivities into a singular narrative. *Americanah* is a critically acclaimed fictional work that refutes the assertions of Afropolitanism because it captures the complexities of immigrant experiences that are problematic and disjointed. Adichie's

Ifemelu evolves throughout her journey and conveys her experiences from a woman's perspective. The portrayal of conflicts, hybridity, and marginalization of female and male characters is realistic and oppositional to glowing descriptions of success, acculturation, and transnational identities across national boundaries in the west.

Finally, the volume celebrates the artistry of representative writers from across the African continent to form a tapestry of women's literary history in English through a feminist lens. *African Women Narrating Identity: Local and Global Journeys of the Self* illustrates how African women speak their truth to the world to (re)imagine their identities in the past and present, in Africa and in Western settings. The collective voices of women authors narrate the ways in which powerful forces in society enmesh females within interlocking forms of oppression. The combination of local and global perspectives of African women authors contributes insight and realism as women write *herstories* in their fictional works:

Gendering the Narrative.

Since the mid to late twentieth century, women writers throughout the African continent have broken barriers to convey popular and unpopular notions of Feminism. During the second wave of Feminism in the late 1970s, non-white women have reconfigured the notions of what it means to be a feminist and a number of prominent women writers and scholars have distanced themselves from the term over several decades. A colorful example is the prolific author Buchi Emecheta saying she is a feminist with a small "f." Another forerunner of Anglophone African women's writing is Ama Ata Aidoo, and in her iconic essay in 1998 "The African Woman Today," she contextualizes the debates over the relevance of Feminism for African women and for herself as a writer:

> Currently, the debate about African women and feminism is quite heated. It is common to hear feminism dismissed as a foreign ideology, imported into Africa to ruin good African women. It is also easy, and a trap we fall into occasionally, to feign a lack of interest in this discourse, or to airily main that "we don't need feminism because we had strong women for antecedents. Many of us have declared at one time or another that African women were feminists long before feminism. Certainly, from the male camp, the chorus is that African women do not need feminism...When people ask me rather bluntly every now and then whether I am a feminist, I not only answer yes, but I go on to insist that every woman and every man should be a feminist-especially if they believe that Africans should take charge of African land, African wealth, African lives, and the burden of African development. It is not possible to advocate independence for the African continent without also believing that African women must have the best that the environment can offer. For some of us, this is the crucial element in our feminism.

> (Aidoo, 1998: 46–47)

Aidoo's powerful sentiments are borne out in the diverse characterization of women in the fictional works examined in this text. Interestingly, her ideas are timely, relevant, and theoretically viable in the analysis of the authors writing about women's lives throughout the continent as well as those who are transnational subjects in the global age. Aidoo's thoughts are deeply linked to postcolonial concerns and issues and since postcolonial critique spans the colonial period before independence and extends to the twenty-first century. Her inspirational ideas about Africa's future and questions of women's potential contribution emerge in the fiction explored in this volume. Africa's development is tied to social, economic, and political equality for women as partners with men in society. Emecheta and Aidoo are among the first generation of distinguished female writers from Africa and their views appropriately introduce Feminism as a theme in this volume. Their ideas resonate strongly in the portrayal of women protagonists, and the diverse representation of women's lives is a strong expression of Feminist aesthetics.

In the postcolonial era, a cursory look at women's commitment to feminism throughout African nations and abroad demonstrates that among activists and writers, African women have far outshone their activist sisters in supporting the cause of feminism. The overview of women writers from diverse regions throughout Africa discussed earlier shows that they have published an enormous body of fictional works that tell the African story from a woman's perspective. It is necessary to note that in the twenty-first century, an explosion of female literary figures based in the west has claimed center stage as opposed to authors based on the African continent as part of the local and global politics of the publishing industry. A major aim in publishing this book is to showcase important African women's writing through regional as well as geo-spatial diversity. It is unfortunate that the machinery of the publishing industry is a reflection of global hegemonic structures that undermines the publishing, exposure, and overall success of writers that live on the African continent.

In looking at the four authors in Part I that live on the African continent, and the literature they have produced, clear trajectories of feminist literary expression emerge, and in Chapter 1, Nawal El Saadawi is both a literary and a political activist of international renown. Since she joined the ancestors in 2021, the world has lost one of the most important feminist activists in the world. Her literary oeuvre are classics of feminist fictional as well as non-fictional publications. *Woman at Point Zero* and *God Dies by the Nile* stand out among the authors in the entire volume, and her contributions to women's empowerment extend far beyond the literary world.

Bessie Head's *Maru* is, on the surface, a fairytale odyssey into the stratified world of Botswana. Although Head was also an activist against Apartheid in South Africa in the years prior to her exile, her sad and difficult life is infused in the autobiographical works she published, especially *A Question of Power* and *Maru*. In the creation of *Maru*, readers may glimpse many feminist attributes in the portrayal of strong and intelligent women who resist the patriarchal structures that subordinate them personally and professionally. In the novel, leading females do in fact "lead" in their professional spaces of competence. These kinds of images were unusual in South African writing during the period. An interesting feature of *Maru* is the evolution of agency as women push against the institutions and restrictions that silence them in society. Further, Likimani's *PassbookF47937 Women and Mau Mau in Kenya* deserves more literary attention and critique as a strong contribution to anti-colonial histories, Kenyan fiction, and women's writing. The multivocal work is about women's enormous support for the Mau Mau rebellion, and their roles were entirely feminist in their ideology, activities, agency, and intelligence. This is a historical example of indigenous feminism that was never called feminism.

As a postcolonial work, Likimani has (re)membered Kenyan women's strength, which counters early accounts of the Mau Mau uprising written by male authors. The work's postcolonial themes resonate with the ideas expressed by Ama Ata Aidoo about feminist ideals being intrinsic to nation-building and to Africa's development. The profiles of women's activities, strategies, courage, and sacrifices are a testimony to their patriotic zeal in support of the anti-colonial movement. Likimani asserts that the Mau Mau fighters could never have survived without the support of Kenyan women. In Ghana, Amma Darko's *Faceless* sheds light on the ravages of urban life in postcolonial Ghana. Through the lens of gender, the work is a critique of government policies that cripple the economy with women and children being crushed at the bottom of society. The plight of street children informs the novel although strong women characters emerge in the work and collectively work to solve their problems. The novel usurps patriarchal control over the lives of young girls whose bodies are exploited for economic gain.

The four novels in Part II also underscore women's capacity to evolve beyond the restrictions of society in the African diaspora spaces of America and Europe. As transnational subjects, both the authors and the women they write about navigate the frequently unwelcoming spaces of *difference* as women of color. From the vantage point of the African diaspora, women are constantly gazing, looking back and (re)membering the bits and pieces of their past African selves. Positionality shapes the fluid and shifting nature of their identities and they must figure out their new place in the world for themselves. Race, class, and gender project new and uncomfortable identities for them when skin color repositions them as marginalized *others*.

Aboulela illustrates the "figuring out" part through adherence to Islam as the core of Muslim women's identity in Europe. Najwa in *Minaret* and Sammar in *The Translator* evolve Islamic Feminist moorings that anchor them against diaspora angst and hybridity. Both works are very subtle but powerful in their message about the importance of faith and the presentation of non-stereotypical images of Sudanese Muslim women. Igiaba Scego's *Adua* reconstructs a Somali woman's journey in the Italian diaspora-scape. As a middle-aged woman, the protagonist reflects on the trauma of the past and how she moved beyond it to recover a sense of control over her life and belonging to her Somali community. Postcolonial ruptures in Somalia pushed her into a world where her body is objectified in painful ways. She has the opportunity to return home that becomes a critical dilemma for postcolonial subjects. The same issue of an immigrant returning to Africa is explored in NoViolet Bulawayo's *We Need New Names* although Darling, the protagonist, has not come to terms with her African "self" at the end of the novel. The postcolonial themes overshadow feminist aesthetics in this work that traces the coming-of-age journey of a ten-year-old girl from a ravaged environment in Zimbabwe. Finally, Adichie's Ifemelu is the strongest figure to embody notions of women's empowerment and agency. She starts out as a lonely, splintered figure who transforms into an educated, polished professional who does return to Nigeria and to the man she loved from her youth. Ifemelu's journey mirrors Adichie's success as a commanding presence in the literary world. Finally, *African Women Narrating Identity: Local and Global Journeys of the Self* is a celebration of African women's stories about their lives within diverse spaces throughout the continent and beyond.

Works Cited

Aboulela, Leila. 1999. *The Translator*. New York. The Black Cat.

———. 2005. *Minaret*. New York. The Black Cat.

Achebe, Chinua. 1958. *Things Fall Apart*. London. Heinemann.

Adesanmi, Pious and Chris Dunton. 2005. "Nigeria's Third Generation Writing: Historiography and Preliminary Theoretical Considerations". *English in Africa*. Vol. 32, No. 1, New Nigerian Writing. pp. 7–19.

Adichie, Chimamanda Ngozi. 2003. *Purple Hibiscus*. Chapel Hill. Algonquin Books of Chapel Hill.

———. 2007. *Half of a Yellow Sun*. New York. Alfred A. Knopf.

———. 2013. *Americanah*. New York. Alfred A. Knopf.

Aidoo, Ama Ata. 1965. *Dilemma of a Ghost and Anowa*. Essex. Longman.

———. 1991. *Changes. A Love Story*. New York. The Women's Press.

———. 1997. *Our Sister Killjoy: Or Reflections of a Black-Eyed Squint*. New York. Longman.

———. 1998. "The African Woman Today". *Sisterhood Feminism & Power From Africa to The Diaspora*. ed. Obioma Nnaemeka. Trenton. Africa World Press. pp. 39–50.

Amadi, Elechi. 1966. *The Concubine*. London. Heinemann.

Anyidoho, Kofi. 2007. "Dr. Efua Sutherland (A Biographical Sketch)". *The Legacy of Efua Sutherland: Pan-African Cultural Activism*. ed. Anne V. Adams and Esi Sutherland-Addy ed. London. Ayebia Press. pp. 7.

Ardnt, Susan. 2002. *The Dynamics of African Feminism: Defining and Classifying African Feminist Literatures*. Trenton. Africa World Press.

Arfaoui, Amina. 2009. "The Gramophone". *Women Writing Africa: The Northern Region*. Vol. 4. ed. Sadiqui, Fatima, et al. New York. The Feminist Press. pp. 259–265.

Ata, Sefi. 2004. *Everything Good Will Come*. Northhampton. Interlink Books.
———. 2008. *Swallow*. Lagos. Farafina.
Ayim, Nana Oforitta. 2019. *The God Child*. London. Bloomsbury Circus Plc.
Azuah, Unoma. 2005. *Sky High Flames*. Maryland. Publish America Press.
———. 2016. *Blessed Body: The Secret Lives of Nigerian Lesbian, Gay, Bisexual and Transgender*. Jackson. The Cooking Pot Publishers.
Ba, Mariama. 1972. *So Long a Letter*. London. Heinemann.
Bakr, Salwa. 1992. *Worms in the Rose Garden. Ajin al Fallaha (The Peasant Woman's Dough*. Bulgaria. Prosveto.
Banyiwa-Horne, Naana. 1986. "African Womanhood: The Contrasting Perspectives of Flora Nwapa's Efuru and Elechi Amadi's The Concubine". *Nagambika*. ed. Carol Boyce Davies and Anne Adams Graves. Trenton. Africa World Press.
Byrne, Diedra. 1994. "A Different Kind of Resistance: An Overview of South African Black Women's Writing". *JSTOR Primary Sources*. Vol. XXXII, No. 2. pp. 22–26.
Dangaremgba, Tsitsi. 1998. *Nervous Conditions*. London. The Women's Press.
———. 2006. *The Book of Not*. Minneapolis. Graywolf.
———. 2018. *This Mournable Body*. Minneapolis. Graywolf Press.
Darko, Amma. 1995. *Beyond the Horizon*. London. Heinemann.
———. 1998. *The Housemaid*. Portsmouth. Heineman.
———. 2003. *Faceless*. Accra. Sub-Saharan Publishers.
Davies, Carol Boyce and Anne Adams Graves. 1986. ed. *Nagambika. Studies of Women in African Literature*. Trenton. Africa World Press.
———. 1986. "Introduction: Feminist Consciousness and African Literary Criticism". *Nagambika. Studies of Women in African Literature*. ed. Carol Boyce Davies and Anne Adams Graves. Trenton. Africa World Press. pp. 1–23.
Djeba, Assia. 2005. *Children of the New World: A Novel of the Algerian War*. Trans. Marjolijn de Jager. New York: Feminist Press.
———. 1993. *A Sister to Scheherazade*. Trans. Dorothy Blair. Portsmouth, NH. Heinemann.
———. 1993. *Fantasia: An Algerian Cavalcade*. Trans. Dorothy Blair. Portsmouth, NH. Heinemann.
Ekwensi, Cyprian. 1961. *Jagua Nana*. London. Heinemann.
———. 1986. *Jagua Nana's Daughter*. London. Heinemann.
Emecheta, Buchi. 1972. *In the Ditch*. London. Heinemann.
———. 1974. *Second Class Citizen*. New York. George Braziller.
———. 1976. *The Bride Price*. London; New York. Allison and Busby; George Braziller.
———. 1977. *The Slave Girl*. New York. George Braziller.
———. 1998. *The Joys of Motherhood*. London. Heienemann.
Emenyonu, N. Ernest. "New Directions in African Literature: Building on the Legacies of the Twentieth Century". *New Directions in African Literature*. Vol. 25. Trenton. Africa World Press. 2006. pp. xi–xiv.
Evaristo, Bernadine. 2019. New York. Grove Press.
Ezeigbo, Akachi. 1996. *The Last of the Strong Ones*. Lagos. Vista Books.
———. 2001. *House of Symbols*. Lagos. Oracle Books.
———. 2002. *Children of the Eagle*. Lagos. Vista Books.
———. 2011. *Roses and Bullets*. Lagos. Jalaa Writers Collective.
Farah, Cristina Ali. 2011. *Little Mother*. Bloomington. Indiana University Press.

Forna, Aminata. 2002. *The Devil That Danced on the Water: A Daughter's Memoir*. London. Harper Collins.

Gappa Petina. 2015. *A Book of Memory*. London. Picador.

———. 2017. *Rotten Row*. London. Faber and Faber.

Githire, Njeri. 2010. "New Visions, New Voices: Emerging Perspectives on East African Fiction". *Transition An International Review*. Vol. 102. pp. 182–188.

Gyasi, Yaa. 2016. *Homegoing: A Novel*. New York. Vintage Books.

———. 2020. *Transcendent Kingdom*. New York. Alfred A. Knopf.

Head, Bessie. 1971. *Maru*. London. Heinemann.

———. 1974. *A Question of Power*. Oxford. Heinemann.

———. 1977. *The Collector of Treasures*. London. Heinemann.

———. 1981. *Serowe: Village of the Rain Wind*. London. Heinemann.

Jacobs, Harriet. 1861. *Incidents in the Life of a Slave Girl*. Wayland, MA. L. Mary Child.

Kroll, Catherine. 2010. "Domestic Disturbances: Women's Cultural Production in the Postcolonial Continuum". *Research in African Literatures*. Vol. 41, No. 3, Special Issue: Southern African Literature/Guest Editors Peter W. Mwikisa et al. pp. 136–146.

Kuzayo, Ellen. 1985. *Call Me Woman*. London. Women's Press.

Likimani, Muthoni. 1974. *They Shall be Chastised*. Nairobi. East African Literature Bureau.

———. 1974. *What Does a Man Want*. Nairobi. East African Literature Bureau.

———. 1985. *Passbook Number 47927: Women and Mau Mau in Kenya*. Houndmills and London. Macmillan Publishers Ltd.

Magona, Sindewe. 1990. *To My Children's Children*. Claremont. David Philip.

———. 1992. *Forced to Grow*. Claremont. David Philip.

Mbue, Imbolo. 2016. *Behold the Dreamers*. New York. Random House.

Medie, Peace Adzo. 2020. *His Only Wife*. Chapel Hill. Algonquin Books.

Mekky, Buthayna Khadr. 2009. "Rites". *Women Writing Africa: The Northern Region*. Vol. 4. ed. Sadiqui, Fatima, et al. New York. The Feminist Press. pp. 315–319.

Mengiste, Maaza. 2010. *Beneath the Lion's Gaze*. New York. W.W. Norton & Company.

———. 2019. *The Shadow King*. New York. W.W. Norton & Company.

Mugo, Micere. 2012. "The Woman Artist in Africa Today: Critical Commentary". *Writing and Speaking from the Heart of My Mind: Selected Essays and Speeches by Micere Githae Mugo*. Trenton. Africa World Press. pp. 63–86.

Nfah-Abbenyi, Makuchi. 1997. *Gender in African Women's Writing: Identity, Sexuality, and Difference*. Bloomington. Indiana University Press.

Njau, Rebecca. 1984. *Kenya Women and Their Mystical Power*. London. Risk Publications.

———. 1965. *The Scar*. Moshi. The Kibo Art Gallery Press.

———. 1975. *Ripples in the Pool*. London. Heinnemann Educational Books.

———. 1984. *Kenya Women Heroes and their Mystical Powers*. London. Risk Publications.

———. 2003. *The Sacred Seed*. Coral Gables, FL. Horizon Books.

Nnameka, Obioma. 1994. "From Orality to Writing: African Women Writers and the (Re) Inscription of Womanhood". *Research in African Literatures*. Vol. 25, No. 4. pp. 137–157.

Nwapa, Flora. 1996. *Efuru*. London. Heinemann.

———. 1977. *Idu*. London. Heinemann.

———. 1992. *The Lake Goddess*. Nigeria. Tana Press LTD.

Odamtten, Vincent O. 1994. *The Art of Ama Ata Aidoo: Polylectics and Reading Against Neocolonialism*. Gainesville. University Press of Florida.

Odiemo-Munara, Lennox. 2010. "Women Engagement with Power and Authority in Re-writing East Africa". *Africa Development*. Vol. 35, No. 4. pp. 1–18.

Ogola, Margaret. 1995. *The River and the Source*. Focus Books.

———. 2002. *I Swear by Apollo*. Nairobi. Focus Books.

———. 2005. *Place of Destiny*. Nairobi. Pauline Publications Africa.

Ogot, Grace. 1966. *The Promised Land*. Nairobi. East African Publishing House.

———. 1968. *Land Without Thunder*. East African Publishing House.

———. 1980. *The Graduate*. Nairobi. Uzima Press.

———. 1980. *The Other Woman*. Nairobi. Transafrica.

———. 1983. *The Strange Bride*. Nairobi. Okoth Okombo.

Ogundipe-leslie, Molara. 1987. "The Female Writer and Her Commitment". *Women in African Literature Today*. Vol. 15. ed. Eustace Palmer and Eldred Durosimi Jones. Trenton. Africa World Press.

Okorafor, Nnedi. 2014. *Lagoon*. New York. Saga Press.

Okurut, Mary Karooro. 1998. *The Invisible Weevil*. Richmond. Fountain Books.

———. 2003. *The Official Wife*. Nairobi. Femrite Publications.

Owuor, Adhiambo Yvonne. 2006. *Weight of Whispers*. Nairobi. Kwani Truse.

———. 2014. *Dust*. New York. Vintage Books.

———. 2019. *The Dragonfly Sea*. New York. Alfred. P. Knopf.

Oyeyemi, Helen. 2005. *The Icarus Girl*. London. Bloomsbury Publishers.

———. 2009. *White is for Witching*. London. Picador.

———. 2014. *Boy, Snow, Bird*. London. Picador.

———. 2021. *Peaces*. New York. Riverhead Books.

Prince, Mary. 1831. *The Life of a West Indian Slave*. London. F. Westley and A. H. Davis.

Resha, Maggie. 1991. *My Life in the Struggle*. Johannesburg. Congress of South African Writers.

Saadawi, Nawal El. 1974. *God Dies by the Nile*. Trans. Sherif Hetata. London and New York. Zed Books.

———. 1983. *Woman at Point Zero*. Trans. Sherif Hetata. London and New York. Zed Books.

———. 1999. *A Daughter of Isis: The Autobiography of Nawal El Saadawi*. Trans. Sherif Hetata. London. Zed Books.

———. 1980. *The Hidden Face of Eve: Women of the Arab World*. Trans. Sherif Hetata. London. Zed Books,

———. 1985. *Memoirs from the Women's Prison*. London. Women's Press.

———. 1994. *Memoirs of a Woman Doctor*. London. Methuen.

Sackeyfio, Rose. 2015. "Recasting Sisterhood and its Ambiguities". *Writing Contemporary Nigeria: How Sefi Atta Illuminates African Culture and Tradition*. ed. Walter P. Collins III. Amherst. Cambria Press. pp. 41–58.

Schuab, Michael. 2019. "A Gorgeous Meditation on Memory, War, and Violence". *Delmar Public Media*. https://www.delmarvapublicmedia.org/arts/2019-09-25/the-shadow-king-is-a-gorgeous-meditation-on-memory-war-and-violence. Sept. 25, 2019.

Scego, Igiaba. 2016. *Adua*. New York. New Vessel Press.

Selasie, Taiye. 2013. *Ghana Must Go*. New York. Penguin Press.

Sadiqui, Fatima, et al. 2009. *Women Writing Africa: The Northern Region*. Vol. 4. New York. The Feminist Press.

Simatei, Tirop. 2005. "Colonial Violence, Postcolonial Violations: Violence, Landscape, and Memory in Kenyan Fiction". *Research in African Literature*. Summer Vol. 36, No. 2. pp. 85–94.

Sofola, Zulu. 1989. *Queen Omu-ako of Oligbo*. Buffalo. Paul Robeson Theatre.

Soyinka, Wole. 1962. *The Lion and the Jewel*. Oxford. Oxford University Press.

———. 1975. *Death and the King's Horseman*. London. Eyre Methuen. Ltd.

Sutherland, Efua. 1960. *Playtime in Africa*. London. Brown Knight and Truscott.

———. 1961. *The Roadmakers*. London. Neame Ltd.

———. 1975. *The Marriage of Anansewa*. London. Longman.

———. 1978. *You Swore an Oath, Vulture, Vulture*. Accra. Ghana Publishing Corporation.

Tiali, Miriam. 1975. *Muriel at Metropolitan*. Johannesburg. Raven Press.

Uko, Iniobong. 2006. "Transcending the Margins: New Directions in Women's Writing". *New Directions in African Literature*. Vol. 25. Trenton. Africa World Press. pp. 82–93.

Unigwe, Chika. 2009. *On Black Sisters' Street*. London. Jonathan Cape.

Vera, Yvonne. 1993. *Nehanda*. Basel. Baobab Books.

———. 1994. *Without a Name*. Basel. Baobab Books.

———. 1996. *Under the Tongue*. Basel. Baobab Books.

———. 2002. *The Stone Virgin*. New York. Farrar, Straus and Girioux.

Wilson-Tagoe, Nana. 2006. "Re-Thinking Nation and Narrative in a Global Era: Recent African Writing". *New Directions in African Literature*. Vol. 25. Trenton. Africa World Press. pp. 94–108.

1 Radical Feminist Synergy and Sexual Exploitation in Nawal El Saadawi's *God Dies by the Nile*

Nawal El Saadawi is Egypt's most accomplished woman writer who has achieved widespread international acclaim for her literary works. Her death in 2021 is a great loss to the literary world and her legacy resonates in African women's writing through feminist expression in Muslim women's fiction. This chapter examines the intersectionality of patriarchy and sexual exploitation that subjugates women in *Woman at Point Zero* (1975) and *God Dies by the Nile* (1974). Both novels convey the stark realism of women's plight in a male-dominated society to represent the ways in which women's lives are enmeshed within a web of interlocking forms of subjugation.

Saadawi's activism and commitment to Arab feminism, social justice, and freedom distinguish her as a controversial author who uses writing as a weapon against social injustice in Egypt. Nawal El Saadawi has contributed to the literary world through her prolific outpouring of writing as an expression of resistance to gender inequality and the struggle for women's empowerment in the Arab world and beyond. In the socio-political environment of the Arab woman's world, the frequently muted voices of women have found expression through the wellspring of Saadawi's artistic vision of awakened womanhood. Saadawi writes across genres of drama, novel, short stories, essays, and memoirs to ignite the flame of protest against the subjugation of Muslim women in the Arab world through religion, politics, and harmful customs.

Saadawi's writing conveys a radical and penetrating articulation of the experiences of females that represent a lifetime of advocacy for women's rights. In her role as a leading spokesperson for women, she is described as radical, dissident, and ultra-feminist. Her works have commanded critical acclaim that places her within a constellation of iconic feminist writers of her time such as Assia Djebar,[1] Ama Ata Aidoo,[2] and Buchi Emecheta[3] among others. The patriarchal society of Egypt has provided fertile soil for Nawal El Saadawi's activism and the struggle to defend women's sexuality from destructive practices such as female genital cutting.

Born in 1931, in a small village outside Cairo, Nawal El Saadawi was educated at the University of Cairo and became a writer, medical doctor, and psychiatrist. She has written over 40 books, and most notable among her works are *Woman at Point Zero* (1973), *The Hidden Face of Eve* (1977),

DOI: 10.4324/9781003350200-3

Memoirs of a Woman Doctor (1989), *Memoirs from the Woman's Prison* (1986), and her autobiography, *Daughter of Isis* (1999). Her works, both fiction and non-fiction, are widely taught in universities, especially, her classic *Woman at Point Zero* (1975).

In 1982, she founded the Arab Women's Solidarity Association which was eventually banned in 1991. Her activism against British colonization and the government of Anwar Sadat resulted in political persecution when she was imprisoned in 1981. She was released two months after his assassination. As a dissident writer whose works have criticized Islam and the political machinery of her nation, three of her books were banned and she received death threats from religious fundamentalist organizations that forced her to flee Egypt in 1988. While in exile in USA, she taught at many universities including Duke University, the University of Washington, the University of Illinois at Chicago, Spellman College, and many others.

Saadawi is well known for her activism to eradicate female genital cutting for over 50 years and the practice was officially banned in Egypt in 2008. She was a fearless and formidable writer who writes life into art in ways that speak to the marginality, subordination, and sexual exploitation of women in Arab Muslim society. In the introduction to *Emerging Perspectives on Nawal El Saadawi* (2010),[4] Ernest Emenyonu offers a succinct and compelling tribute to Saadawi's immense contribution to social justice and describes her as:

> an incurably courageous free spirit whose writings denounce political injustice, social corruption, and gender inequities in an era of "lethal" democracy; an ultra-feminist intellectual whose ideas are unalterably in conflict with the very pillars and foundations of absolute patriarchy; a fearless universal mouthpiece for marginalized womanhood; a writer whose message of "truth" is unbearable and offensive to men of fragile egos and twisted mindsets about the place of women in any world order.
>
> (2010: 3)

It is clear from experiences in her childhood that Saadawi is a born rebel and symbol of women's agency and resistance to prescribed patterns of inequality through restrictive forces in society such as patriarchy, religion, customs, and unfavorable norms for women and girls. Her autobiography, *Daughter of Isis*, was first published in 1999 and spans her life from infancy, her youth, training, and practice as a medical doctor. Her autobiography unfolds many compelling insights that fashion the seed thoughts of a rebellious nature. Her female identity is challenged by gender inequality, in early childhood that set the stage for activism throughout her life. Her mother taught her to read and write and she recalls learning how to write her mother's name next to hers. The vivid recollection of patriarchal intrusion is inscribed in her consciousness when her father removes her mother's name from next to hers and writes down his instead. He tells her, "It's God's will" (1999: 1). This was the first time she had heard the word God as she struggles to understand (and writes a letter to Him) asking why (He) treated her mother and father differently. Even as a child, Saadawi's rebellious nature is awakened by gender inequality and lower status of women in her society. Iniobong Uko affirms the early development of Saadawi's radical perceptions about entrenched gender roles:

> El Saadawi realizes early in life the disastrous consequences of marriage on the woman. She is worried but finds no answers to her questions. To her, the word marriage was steeped in as much mystery as the word God...El Saadawi's questioning of the Qur'an its treatment of women and apparent gender discrimination couples with the abhorrent practice of female circumcision, opens up a vista of rebellious reactions that have alchemized in her writings, speeches and publications to ensure female awareness of the oppression they experience.
>
> (1999: 98)

Saadawi states emphatically that:

> Ever since I took hold of a pen in my fingers, I have fought against history, struggled against the falsifications in official registers. I wish I could efface my grandfather Al-Saadawi from my name and replace it with my mother's name, Zaynab.
>
> (Saadawi, 1999: 30)

The psychological impact of her mother teaching her to write her name in Arabic suggests the (re)inscription of female identity, bonding with her mother, and valuing of herself that was etched into her psyche as a child.

In coming to terms with these realities: "the contradictions wreaking havoc on El Saadawi's young mind prompt her to opt for dissidence as a springboard for the re-inscription of female subjectivity" (Gueye, 2010: 166). She remembers her anger growing like a wellspring in her consciousness since her childhood. Her spirited sense of rebuttal to gender inequity continues throughout her young life as she displays unusual courage in the face of sexual harassment when riding the train to school. When she is touched inappropriately by males on the way to school, Saadawi recalls that:

> Sometimes I would turn around suddenly and slap one of them in the face. From where I got the courage to do this I do not know. I was a young girl of thirteen or fourteen, almost a child, but the anger of a child is the most powerful, the most pure, the most true of all angers. It accumulates in the body, multiplies over time, but it is like God, in that it gives birth only to itself.
>
> (1999: 206)

El Saadawi's rebellious energies and strong spirit emerge through activism while a student in secondary school. She remembers her anger growing like a wellspring in her consciousness since her childhood.

Whenever there was a demonstration, she could be found chanting and protesting, stamping the pictures of the King, the pashas, and the British under her feet (Saadawi, 1999: 261). In 1936, she became the only female student in her school who made speeches or wrote stories and articles. Later on, in medical school, she joined anti-colonial demonstrations against the British and sometimes was the only female amidst thousands of male students, infused with patriotic vision (Saadawi, 1999: 285).

Throughout her career, she has wielded her pen as a sword, and Sophia Ogwudu confirms that:

> El Saadawi's resistance is on many fronts; and in a social setting that expects that women should not have a voice, her protest voice rings out; in a social set-up which takes it for granted that all should accept the patriarchal mandate of woman's lower status as a human being, she exposes the fallacies and mis-conceptions of these assumptions where religion is used to buttress sexist stances, she challenges those aspects.
>
> (2010: 207)

In what is perhaps Nawal El Saadawi's most celebrated work of fiction, *Woman at Point Zero* is a feminist classic in women's literature. This canonical work squarely places El Saadawi among writers described as "activist 'mothers' whose…pathbreaking contributions to the empowerment of women in their home countries and on the broader world stage cannot be over-emphasized" (Browdy de Hernandez et al., 2010: 5). Brinda Mehta confirms that "Saadawi's work establishes the vital link between gender and creative dissidence by highlighting the urgency of narrative and cultural re-assertions in local memory wherein women initiate the necessary *nuschuzor* rebellion against patriarchal authority by becoming agents of change" (2010: 8).

In Susan Ardnts' *Dynamics of African Feminism* (2002), she classifies *Woman at Point Zero* as radical feminist literature because the protagonist kills a man (Ardnt, 85–86). In addition, the presentation of male characters is extremely negative, and "such texts argue that men (as a social group) inevitably and in principle discriminate against, oppress, and mistreat women. The men characters are 'by nature' or because of their socialization hopelessly sexist and usually deeply immoral" (Ardnt, 2002: 85).

El Saadawi expresses that Firdaus, the protagonist in *Woman at Point Zero*, displays more courage than herself and feels diminished by comparison. Firdaus, like Zakeya in *God Dies by the Nile* and Fathyaa the Murderess[5] in Saadawi's *Memoirs from the Women's Prison*, shows no remorse for taking the life of her male oppressor, and the author suspends moral judgment in the portrayal of women who have been pushed to point zero and who repel oppression in ways that may spell tragic outcomes. Saadawi developed a keen interest in women who commit murder, and in a 2006 interview with Sophie Smith, Saadawi states emphatically:

> Obviously, I am against killing, whether a man or a woman is the killer. However, in some cases, women have no choice. They are pushed towards killing by misery. Look at Firdaus for example (in *Woman at Point Zero*). She killed because she wanted to remain true to herself and because she did not fear death. She had no other choice. Some women kill because they have no alternative way of fighting back. As individuals they are weak. The answer to this is for women to mobilize and fight as larger, more significant political entities.
>
> (2006: 67)

Unlike Nawal El Saadawi, Firdaus exhibits a different type of courage in the face of her oppression. The inspiration for women's experiences in prison occurred during a period in Saadawi's career as a psychiatrist who treated women suffering from neurosis. She developed an interest to visit the Women's Prison in Qanatir in Egypt and became fascinated with the nature of incarceration for women. Saadawi wants to talk to Firdaus before she is executed for her crime, and Firdaus's first act of resistance is to refuse to see her. She has accepted her tragic fate and has chosen to remain in the space that she has created for herself. The space that defines her criminality denotes her use of agency in controlling her destiny. Firdaus's resistance can be traced to her early life because as Ramzi Salti succinctly observes:

> Firdaus is thus a woman without a home, without a support network. Throughout the novel, she cannot seem to find a space in which to belong. She leaves the domestic space early in her life, never to return. In addition, her marriage reinforces the notion that for her, home comes to represent an oppressive space. Upon her escape from domesticity, she establishes a new space for the novel—*the streets*.
>
> (1994: 158)

As Firdaus unfolds the story of her life, she affirms her spirited resolve to find her own path when she narrates to El Saadawi that:

> all my life, I have been searching for something that would fill me with pride, make me feel superior to everyone else, including kings, princes, and rulers. Each time I would pick up a newspaper and found the picture of a man who was one of them I would spit on it.
>
> (1983: 9)

These early expressions of feminist impulse capture the flavor of Firdaus's futile search for recognition in a society that stifles her success.

Firdaus's challenge to survive with dignity is tested when she is married off to Sheik Mahmoud who is over sixty while she is eighteen. Firdaus's refusal to endure abuse, domestic drudgery, and poverty leads her to choose a questionable path that results in her ultimate demise by the end of the novel. After a terrible beating, as a personal choice of resistance, she runs away to the streets, a space that represents freedom from the prison of her brutalized existence in marriage.

Sackeyfio[6] observes that Saadawi employs the same strategy as Assia Djebar in the classic *A Sister to Scheherazade (Ombre Sultane)* (1987) by presenting public space as a refuge for secluded or imprisoned women (2022: 8–9). Firdaus knows that her only hope for freedom and safety lies in running away into the streets. Throughout the novel, this action is repeated several times, the first of which is Firdaus' horror at the idea of an arranged marriage to a man in his sixties. Upon running into the street, her feelings echo Hajila's in *A Sister to Scheherazade* as she recalls: "When I looked at the streets it was as though I was seeing them for the first time. A new world was opening up in front of my eyes, a world which for me had not existed before" (Saadawi, 1983: 42).

Each time that Firdaus runs away, she escapes brutal treatment, exploitation, and violence at the hands of men. She runs into the streets a second time when her husband beats her with a heavy stick until the blood ran from her nose and ears (Saadawi, 1983: 47). Later in the novel, she is imprisoned by Bayoumi and forced into sex with him and other males, but she escapes again. For Firdaus, the cyclic patterns of escape from danger highlight women's vulnerability, even when they attempt to transform their lives. As public space, the streets become a site of freedom, resistance, and safety.

According to Saiti and Salti, Saadawi is a displaced person because:

> Throughout the novel, she cannot seem to find a space in which to belong. She leaves the domestic space early in her life, never to return. In addition, her marriage reinforces the notion that, for her, home comes to represent an oppressive space. Upon her escape, she establishes a new space for the novel-the streets...the streets are still the only space in the novel where she feels some kind of freedom. Life outside of the domestic space becomes liberating for her since the unknown, in many ways, may be better than the known misery she has endured at home.
>
> (1994: 158–159)

The inter-textual elements of *A Sister to Scheherazade* and *Woman at Point Zero* are striking as both women protagonists seek to move beyond the spatial boundaries through feminist agency. In the context of the Arab Muslim environment, both Hajila and Firdaus develop feminist consciousness of their plight that nurtures their resistance to subjectivity. The spatio-temporal dimensions of *Woman at Point Zero* codify the idea that women can find freedom, even if only temporary, in the public domain. Both women are willing to risk the dangers of the streets, as they become naked to the world and the vulnerability it poses for them outside the domestic sphere.

After repeated betrayals and exploitation by men that Firdaus encounters, she accepts a life of prostitution. As she recalls the unfortunate events that introduce her to the world's oldest profession, the unyielding power of men in Arab society is revealed because she has no control over her body or her future. Her choice of prostitution conveys her agency to control her sexuality and develop her independence. The realization that women can also attain power is explained by Sharifa, an older woman in the sex trade and her Madam, who describes the possibilities for women who sell their bodies:

> A man does not know a woman's value. She is the one who determines her value. The higher you price yourself, the more he will realize what you are really worth and be prepared to pay with the means at his disposal.
>
> (Saadawi, 1983: 58)

By the time Firdaus is twenty-five, she reflects upon her new life of independence and affluence as she asks herself:

> How many were the years of my life that went by before my body and myself became really mine to do with them as I wished?...Now I could decide on the food I wanted to eat, the house I wanted to live in, refuse the man for whom I felt an aversion no matter what the reason, and choose the man I wished to have, even if it was only because he was clean and well-manicured.
>
> (Saadawi, 1983: 74)

Years later, Firdaus admits to herself that she hated men even though she never doubted her integrity and honor as a woman. She thinks to herself: "all women are prostitutes of one kind or another" (Saadawi, 1983: 99). She prefers to be a free prostitute rather than an enslaved wife. Eventually, a pimp attempts to control her by taking a large amount of the money she earns. When he tells her there are only two kinds of people in the world, masters and slaves, she says she wants to be one of the masters. The pimp tells her that a woman on her own can never be a master, especially not one who is a prostitute (Saadawi, 1983: 104). This prompts her to attempt to leave, and when he attacks her, she kills him, thus revealing the price she pays for her independence. She remains true to herself till the end by preferring death as a form of freedom. Firdaus subverts male authority and exploitation of the female body by reclaiming control of her sexuality, demanding higher prices for her services, and choosing her male customers. Throughout the novel, Firdaus is gradually hardened by repeated sexual abuse by all the men in her life that begins in her childhood. By the end of the work, she achieves a measure of freedom from exploitation and experiences economic empowerment and feminist awakening although she loses her life in the process.

God Dies by the Nile is also a radical feminist novel that displays women's awakening to agency in the face of death, loss, and utter powerlessness within a feudalistic society, led by a man who is essentially God on earth. Women are central figures in Saadawi's works, and in *God Dies by the Nile,* a female is the moral center within a corrupt system of injustice against her family. The allegorical and thematic constructions of the novel are emblematic of women's oppression as a trope that appears throughout texts within Saadawi's impressive array of fictional works.

In *God Dies by the Nile* and *Woman at Point Zero*, Saadawi reveals the collusion of religious hypocrisy and sex, class dynamics and poverty, patriarchy and religion, and abuse and violence in the lives of women. Saadawi writes to achieve social transformation in society, and in an interview, "Conversations with Nawal El Saadawi" she states that "Feminism is very broad in the Arab world and includes issues of political, historical, cultural, personal, social, and religious significance" (Saadawi 56). She believes that politics and religion are intrinsically oppressive to women. Moreover, Brinda J. Mehta elucidates Saadawi's ideas on religion and patriarchy in "Excavating the Divine Feminine: Nawal El Saadawi's Creative Dissidence and Religious Contentions": Saadawi exposes the collusion between religion and patriarchy by stating that the latter receives its sanctified power from Islam, especially in terms of the regulation of gender and the subaltern status of women that is in violation of the Prophet's call for the equality of the sexes (2010: 11).

In looking at Saadawi's inspiration to write *God Dies by the Nile*, she states that the men and women in the work are not very different from people in her village because "In addition to the oppression of colonial rule at that time, women were oppressed by men in the family, in society and in the streets. Poor women were more vulnerable than rich women" (Saadawi *viii*). Letters from readers also affirm the realistic depiction of rural life at the time, and in 2006, Saadawi expresses that village life still resembles Zakeya's community (1974: *x*).

God Dies by the Nile is a clear example of radical feminist writing, and additionally, Arndt posits that male characters in these texts are "hopelessly sexist and deeply immoral" (2002: 85). Ardnt states emphatically that:

> In radical African Feminist texts the women characters suffer physical and psychological violence at the hands of men. In most texts the woman protagonist finally kills a man, who represents the violation of women's rights, and/or is killed by such men.
>
> (2002: 85)

Saadawi's works epitomize the salient features of this body of compelling feminist works that are vivid and realistic.

Written during a climate of political repression in Egypt, and like others among Saadawi's works, *God Dies by the Nile* was published in Lebanon. The title of the book as well as the portrayal of Islam raised an alarm and

Saadawi endured fierce criticism amidst accusations of heresy. Her publisher told her that God cannot die and changed the title to *Death of the Only Man on Earth*. Further, Isam M. Shihada confirms the significance of the title in capturing the insidious nature of patriarchy because:

> it is a metaphor for both patriarchy, class and religion. The title may also reflect Saadawi's intention to reveal the interplay between the political power of the ruling class, the oppression of women in rural Egypt and the misuse of religion.
>
> (2007: 163)

Much like the role of Islam in Egypt and other Muslim societies, the encroachment of Christianity in Africa during colonization has functioned as a means to subjugate and socialize women to accept their condition, remain obedient, and to serve a male God. In its civilizing mission, Christianity was intrinsic to European patriarchal dominance with deleterious effects on the status and role(s) of African women. Further, the narratives of African Americans during the centuries of enslavement in the Americas reveal massive sexual exploitation within the rural plantation system of the American south along with adherence to patriarchal Christian values. Religious hypocrisy and brutal treatment of enslaved women by slave masters is described in Fredrick Douglas's classic *The Narrative of the Life of Fredrick Douglas* (1845). Chattel slavery mandated African women's bodies as the sole property of the slave masters as a common feature of the system. Moreover, Egyptian society during the early to mid-twentieth century and beyond sustained great economic disparity and class division between the rich and the poor, with women at the lowest rung of society. In this way, women's bodies and their labor are commoditized both in Egypt and during the period of enslavement in America.

Incidents in the Life of a Slave Girl (1861) by Harriet Jacobs is also a classic text of immense literary and historical significance. Writing under the pen name of Linda Brent, the young protagonist describes her slave master's obsession to molest her when she becomes an adolescent. Intertextual elements of the works come into focus because the Mayor in *God Dies by the Nile* schemes and intimidates women in ways that echo Dr. Flynt's threats to kill Linda in *Incidents in the Life of a Slave Girl*. He makes plans to build her a cabin in the woods so that he can visit her and tells her that she is his property. Likewise, the Mayor in *God Dies by the Nile* resorts to coercion and manipulation to gain access to young women and force them to ultimately submit to his sexual advances. In *Incidents in the Life of a Slave Girl*, Linda Brent must resort to extreme measures to avoid intimacy with her master Dr. Flynt.

The Mayor and other wealthy male rulers of Kafr El Teen display moral degeneracy, hypocrisy, and lust that fuel their aims to defile girls and women. In both works, the powerful men are outwardly religious, projecting respectability and high social standing as leaders in their communities. Women and girls are virtually powerless and, in both works, males such as fathers and husbands are unable to protect them. As these texts reveal, despite differences in religious and cultural background, nationalities, and different geographical regions, the idea of men, power, and sex unites the works through the exploration of female sexuality as a tool of oppression.

God Dies by the Nile (1974) is Nawal El Saadawi's second novel whose female protagonist subverts the patriarchal order that consumes the lives of her family in a rural community on the banks of the Nile. In the town of Kafr El Teen, village (in)justice is meted out by the Mayor, surrounded by his male cohorts at the top of the governing hierarchy. These include Hamzawi, the Imam of the mosque, Ismail, the local healer and barber, and Sheikh Zahran, the Chief of the Village Guard. The men constitute a power unto themselves, and the impoverished peasant community is held in the grip of brutal corruption and blatant misuse of authority. Through strategies of manipulation, fear, and intimidation, they effect a reign of unbridled corruption and brute force to quell opposition from the villagers.

The men control the affairs of the community that include social, political, and religious activities. In a conversation with the Mayor, the Head of the Village Guard laughingly remarks that "Who would dare deny that we're just as much of a government ourselves" (Saadawi, 1974: 12). He regards their authority as equal to the government of Egypt. The inner circle of men protects and supports the Mayor, and they execute his authority through any means necessary. Alamin Mazuri and Judith Abala affirm the role of the men that assist the Mayor: "These three characters … act, in addition as sycophants and "court jesters" who form a protective wall around the Chief and provide him with the music of invulnerability of the patriarchal dispensation" (Saadawi, 1974: 20). The Mayor reflects on his dependence on these men because "Without them he could not rule Kafr El Teen. They were his instruments, his aids and his means for administering the affairs of the village" (Saadawi, 1974: 124). Sheik Zahran, in a conversation between himself and the village barber, remarks that "We are God's slaves when it's time to say our prayers only. But we are the Mayor's slaves all the time" (Saadawi, 1974: 69). Saadawi's repeated reference to *Gods* and men who behave like *God(s)* serve to heighten the all-consuming patriarchal authority in Kafr El Teen. The face of Islamic patriarchy is presented as unyielding, dangerous, and relentless in the ability to render women and indeed the peasant villagers totally powerless. Shihada confirms the elevated status of men when he states that: "in *God Dies by the Nile* we find that the Mayor is not only a symbol of class but also symbolically foregrounded as the ultimate god of patriarchy. He is perceived as a kind of demigod in the village" (2007: 169). In the novel, the presentation of women's lives that are controlled and warped by patriarchal religion and class status of males is disturbing because it mirrors the lived experiences of women and girls in Arab Muslim communities and throughout the world. The unshakeable power of men in *God Dies by the*

Nile is a formidable and terrible blight on gender relationships in the Arab Muslim world and beyond.

Early in the novel, as he speaks to the Mayor, Haj Ismail displays obsequious behaviors, and chooses his words carefully to avoid the insinuation that:

> Since the Mayor was the representative of government in Kafr El Teen
> … he was using his position to exploit the peasants, and to spend the
> money he squeezed out of them on his extravagant way of living, and
> his extravagant tastes in food, tobacco, wine and women.
>
> (Saadawi 17)

The Mayor's unjust authority is expressed in the following passage: "people like him, who live on top of the world, don't know the word impossible. They walk over the earth like Gods" (Saadawi, 1974: 70).

Further, Saadawi conveys the immutable power of the Mayor when Sheik Hamzawi describes the villager's fear:

> In their hearts they don't fear God. What they really fear is the Mayor.
> He holds their daily bread in his hands and if he wants, he can deprive
> them of it. If he gets angry their debts double, and the government
> keeps sending them one summons after the other. "Either you pay or
> your land will be confiscated". You do not know the mayor, Fatheya.
> He's a dangerous man, fears no one, not even Allah. He can do injustice
> to people and put them in gaol when they have done nothing to merit
> it. He can even murder innocent people.
>
> (Saadawi, 1974: 134)

These perceptions foreshadow the dark undertones of male dominance that shape the events in the novel where women are at the mercy of powerful and ruthless men. Later in the novel, as the Mayor contemplates how to overpower Zeinab, his inner reflection divulges a complete sense of impunity as he is accountable to no one in Kafr El Teen. Since the disappearance of her sister Nefissa, he consoles himself as he thinks:

> Who could find out about the things that had happened? He was above
> suspicion, above the law even above the moral rules, which governed
> ordinary people's behavior. Nobody in Kafr El Teen would dare suspect him. They could have doubts about Allah, but about him…It was
> impossible.
>
> (Saadawi, 1974: 124)

He has unwittingly appropriated God-like qualities with no thought of the consequences to those he exploits.

In stark and compelling realism, Saadawi unfolds a chilling tale of an ensnaring form of patriarchal tyranny and sexual exploitation through lustful machinations and the rape of young women in Zakeya's family. The subjugation of females is introduced early in the novel as Sheikh Hamzawi, in a flashback, recollects a discussion with the father of his wife Fatheya before they married. The extreme and rigid religious restriction of women's movements in public space highlights the subordination and helplessness of females in the novel. Sheikh Hamzawi recalls his expectations that his wife is:

> never to be seen elsewhere except twice in her life. The first time when she moved from her father's house to her husband's house. And the second when she left her husband's house for the grave allotted to her in the burial grounds.
>
> (Saadawi, 1974: 40)

He remembers that when time for the marriage approaches, Fatheya refuses to leave with Sheikh and hides atop the oven. Haj Ismail, the village Barber and Healer, is asked what to do and responds:

> Is that a question for a man to ask? Beat her, my brother, beat her once and twice and thrice. Do you not know that girls and women are only convinced if they receive a good hiding?…he climbed on top of the oven pulled her out by her hair, and beat her several times until she came down. Then he handed her over to Haj Ismail the same day she married the pious old Sheikh.
>
> (Saadawi, 1974: 40–41)

The idea of beating women into submission is repeated in the novel because the same experience happens to Nefissa who refuses to obey when told to go to the Mayor's house.

The unrestrained power displayed by men to physically assault and sexually abuse women are also demonstrated by Tariq, the Mayor's youngest son. He attends college and while visiting home in Kafr El Teen, he debates his mother on gender inequality in clearly hypocritical and sexist terms. As the son of his wealthy father, his arrogance and sense of entitlement to sexual favors from females from the peasant class are spelled out in glaring contempt. He asserts that: "the most precious thing they possess is their virtue" (Saadawi, 1974: 51). Tariq is unaware of the nature of his arrogance toward women, derived from class privilege, sexism, and double standards of morality. Mazrui and Abala note that:

> In spite of their ideological and institutional support, however, the dynamics of patriarchy are not mysterious to all. Its evils are, in fact, quite transparent to those who, like the wives of the bourgeoisie, are closest to its very center. Thus, even though the Chief's wife continues to submit to patriarchal authority, she is able to see the hypocrisy of

its ideology sooner than those who, like Zakeya, are a stage removed from its center.

(Saadawi, 1974: 21)

Consequently, his mother sharply rebukes Tariq by asking:

Where was your virtue hiding last week when you stole a ten-pound note from my handbag, and went to visit that woman with whose house I have now become quite familiar? Where was your virtue last year when you assaulted Saadia, the servant, and obliged me to throw her out in order to avoid a scandal? And where does your virtue disappear to every time you pounce on one of the servant girls in our house? Matters have gone so far that I have now decided to employ only menservants. Pray tell me what happens to your virtue when you are so occupied pursuing the girls on the telephone, or across windows, or standing on our balconies.

(Saadawi, 1974: 51)

Saadawi positions a female character as the moral center of the work to interrogate male supremacy in her home. It is one of the few instances in the novel when a woman speaks out at length. An important theme in the author's feminist agenda is to deconstruct the objectification of women, with the attendant attacks on their sexuality that belie underlying expressions of misogyny. The perceptions expressed by men about women's virtue and sexuality are blatantly hypocritical and reprehensible.

In addition to issues of morality and ethics, Saadawi resonates male attitudes about women's virtue in her short story "In Camera" an excerpt from *Death of an Ex Minister* (1987) when Leila Al Fargani becomes a political prisoner for calling the king stupid. While in prison, she is gang raped by ten men and "One of them, lying on top of her, had said: this is the way we torture you women—by depriving you of the most valuable thing you possess" (Saadawi 1200). Leila's act of resistance is aptly conveyed when even though:

Her body under him was as cold as a corpse but she had managed to open her mouth and say to him: You fool! The most valuable thing I possess is not between my legs. You're all stupid. And the most stupid among you is the one who leads you.

(Saadawi, 1987: 1200)

Her response negates male authority, brutality and moral corruption, and the entire patriarchal order with the king symbolically represented as *God*. These events represent connecting threads of inter-textual elements that appear in Saadawi's fictional works. Gueye corroborates Saadawi's mandate for gender equality when she asserts that "El Saadawi's philosophy of justice and equality leads her to reject patriarchal grounds of religion and scorn totalizing discourses that impede individual and collective freedom" (Saadawi, 2010: 161).

Moreover, the patriarchal system serves to maintain its honor through measuring, to some extent, virginity and chastity before marriage and the avoidance of extra-marital sex (Mazrui and Abala, 1997: 21). Thus, in *God Dies by the Nile* and the short story "In Camera," references to the most valuable thing that women possess articulate the social codes that dictate women's and the family's "honor."

The overlapping nature of patriarchy and sexual exploitation is at the center of *God Dies by the Nile* as Zakeya's family is destroyed by an intricate and complex set of events controlled by the Mayor. She is the sister of Kafrawi and her two nieces, Nefissa and Zeinab, fall victim to sexual abuse and impropriety by the Mayor. Through Zakeya's dilemma, Saadawi reveals women's inevitable entrapment.

Nefissa's plight unfolds in a vivid account of her being forced by her father to go to the Mayor's house, supposedly to work as a servant.

The Chief of the Village Guard is sent to collect her and to wear down her resistance by showing how worthless she is. He tells her, "you're a stupid girl with no brains. How can you throw away all the good that is coming to you? Do you prefer hunger and poverty rather than doing a bit of work?" (Saadawi, 1974: 27). She hides and refuses to go with him. Her father Kafrawi notes Nefissa's stubbornness at which Sheikh responds sharply "Then it's the girl who decides what is done in this household?" Kafrawi is powerless and asks the Sheikh what can be done if Nefissa refuses, to which he replies: "Is that a question for a man to ask?...Beat her. Don't you know that girls and women never do what they're told unless you beat them?" (Saadawi, 1974: 27). Kafrawi beats her several times until she comes down from hiding and is handed over to the Sheik. The sad plight of Nefissa is her eventual pregnancy and she runs away to another town. She does not appear again in the novel, but mysteriously, a baby is abandoned on the doorstep of Sheik Hamzawi and is adopted by his wife Fatheya. The baby symbolizes the offspring that result from the predatory sexual license of males in the patriarchal system of double standards for women and men.

Zeinab is Nefissa's younger sister who is also raped by the Mayor. Sadly, the Mayor makes it known that he wants her. Sheikh Zahran notes that "He's got strange tastes where women are concerned, and if he likes a woman he can't forget her. You know he's pretty obstinate himself. Once he sets his eyes on a woman he must have her, come what may" (Saadawi, 1974: 70). The men are described as knowing that the Mayor "burned with such desire for Zeinab that only death could put an end to it. Sooner or later, he was going to lay hands on her, for like all Gods he believed that the impossible did not exist" (Saadawi, 1974: 70). The Mayor's immorality has no boundaries and he is secure in the knowledge that the men who surround him will continue to procure young women for his pleasure.

Saadawi discloses the deeper layers of patriarchal control by unraveling the forced complicity of males in the subjugation of women in Kafr El Teen. Three male characters are ill-fated as part of the machinery of patriarchy, orchestrated by the Mayor, and implemented by his cohorts. In the same way that women and everyone in the peasant class must obey the dictates of the patriarchal order, males are also forced to act against women. First, a young man named Elwau is blamed for the disappearance of Nefissa. His alleged connection to Nefissa is literally a hatched plot of scapegoating, concocted by the Mayor. Elwau ends up dead and the blame falls on Kafrawi who is falsely accused and arrested. As the father of Nefissa, logical speculation suggests his motive in protecting his honor although everyone knows he could never kill anyone. The Village Guard states that "Kafrawi is not capable of killing a chicken…but when it's a man's honor at stake, anyone can kill" (Saadawi, 1974: 68).

To compound matters, Galal is Zakeya's son who returns to Kafr El Teen after many years. His offense in the village is that upon his return, he marries Zeinab who refuses to return to the Mayor's house. The Sheik has attempted all manner of schemes to force Galal to send Zeinab to the Mayor, all to no avail. Tension rises and the Sheikh comments: "The only way out he could now see was to get rid of Galal in one way or another. He had got rid of Kafrawi by arranging things in such a way that he was accused of a crime and ended in gaol." The circle of deception tightens and Saadawi foreshadows the dark events as the village is described as sinking "into a silence as still and profound as the silence of death" (Saadawi, 1974: 162).

The ominous events portend Zakeya's gradual awakening to the real import of forces beyond her control that devastate the lives of her loved ones. She says aloud that not only is her son Galal gone, but Kafrawi is gone as well, along with Nefissa and Zeinab is the only one left. Traumatized when Galal is taken away, Zeinab sells the Buffalo, and with the money goes in search of the prison where Galal is kept. This is an ill-omened journey that seals her fate to become ensnared by yet another predatory male and no one in Kafr El Teen ever hears from her again.

All of the women in the novel experience suffering, abuse, and terrible violence at the hands of men. Fatheya, along with her adopted child, is viciously killed by mob violence by superstitious villagers. The presence of a "child born of sin and fornication" is blamed for poor crops and any misfortune that befalls the village.

Zakeya is weighed down by the horrific cycle of loss in her family so that "the darkness of her mind is no longer the same" (Saadawi, 1974: 169), and she experiences an unnatural anger; "a terrible anger like the anger of some wild beast being hunted down" (Saadawi 1974: 169). Throughout the novel, she is cast as the moral center and, by the end of the work, she awakens to the realization that the Mayor is responsible for the tragic events that destroy her family. In a terrible act of vengeance, she kills the Mayor. As she approaches, he has no inkling of her intentions. When she attacks him:

He did not feel the hoe land on his head and crush it at one blow. For a moment before, he had looked into her eyes, just once. And from that moment he was destined never to see, or feel, or know anything more.

(Saadawi, 1974: 173)

She goes quietly to prison but feels no remorse. She says to a female prisoner that she has buried Allah "on the bank of the Nile" (Saadawi 75). The symbolism is unmistakable, and the irony lies in the fact that God cannot die.

In sum, both *Woman at Point Zero* and *God Dies by the Nile* capture the pernicious nature of patriarchy that may imprison poor women within a system of sexual violence and abuse. Their fates are sealed by a multilayered and complex environment that ruin their lives and from which there is no escape. The radical feminist themes in the work lie in women's resistance, and the foregrounding of female characters who interrogate immorality, cruelty, and hypocrisy of males. In *Woman at Point Zero*, Firdaus's feminist awakening fuels her determination to reclaim her autonomy by any means necessary through her understanding of the dynamics of sex, men, marriage, and money. In *God Dies by the Nile* the Mayor's wife, though powerless, speaks out to her son, in very sharp tones and indirectly to her husband about moral hypocrisy. Zeinab, after her marriage, invokes the religious tenets of Islam that forbid her to go to the Mayor's house because Allah forbids it. Fatheya accepts the innocence of an abandoned child against the wishes of her husband but pays for this decision with her life. Finally, Zakeya, like Firdaus in *Woman at Point Zero*, kills her oppressor with no remorse. These actions by women characters in both novels underscore larger issues such as abuse of power, patriarchy, religious hypocrisy, and sexual violence that destroy the lives of women. In writing *Woman at Point Zero* and *God Dies by the Nile*, Saadawi vividly conveys women's inequality in radical and extreme terms to reflect her commitment to social transformation. Both works stand among Saadawi's literary oeuvre that distinguish her as an outspoken feminist. Her creative artistry has carved a space in African women's literature as a brilliant and celebrated writer of enormous influence. *Woman at Point Zero* and *God Dies by the Nile* are unapologetic indictments of the suffocating and pervasive nature of Arab Muslim patriarchy that must recognize the equality of women and recant the religious misinterpretation that condemns women to subordinate status in society.

Notes

1 Assia Djebar is a renowned Algerian author of *A Sister to Scheherazade (1993)* and *Fantasia: An Algerian Cavalcade (1993)*
2 Ama Ata Aidoo is a distinguished Ghanaian dramatist, poet, and novelist. She is the first African woman to write a play in English with the publication of *Dilemma of a Ghost* in 1965. She is known as a Feminist writer.

3 Buchi Emecheta is a prolific Nigerian writer, distinguished as a forerunner of Anglophone African women's writing in the mid-twentieth century. Her most well-known novels are *In the Ditch* (1972), *Second Class Citizen* (1975), and *The Joys of Motherhood* (1979). She is renowned as an African Feminist.
4 *Emerging Perspectives on Nawal El Saadawi* (2010) is a comprehensive collection of critical essays on the works of Buchi Emecheta edited by Ernest Emenyonu.
5 Female character in Sadawi's *Memoirs from the Women's Prison* who is incarcerated for killing a man.
6 See Works Cited: "Muslim Women for Change: Celebrating Assia Djebar in." *Legacies of African Women Writers*.

Works Cited

de Hernandez, Browdy, et. al. 2010. "African Women in the Twenty-first Century". *African Women Writing Resistance; Contemporary Voices*. Madison. University of Wisconsin Press. pp. 3–11.

Djebar, Assia. 1993. *A Sister to Scheherazade*. Trans. Dorothy Blair. Portsmouth: Heinemann.

Douglas, Fredrick. 1845. *The Narrative of the Life of Fredrick Douglas*. Boston. Anti-Slavery Office.

Emenyonu, Ernest. 2010. *Emerging Perspectives on Nawal El Saadawi*. Trenton. Africa World Press.

Gueye, Khadidiatou. 2010. "'Tyrannical Feminity' in Nawal El Saadawi's Memoirs of a Woman Doctor". *Research in African Literatures*. Vol. 41, No. 2. pp. 160–172.

Horst, Adele S. Newson. 2008. "Conversations with Nawal El Saadawi". *World Literature Today*, Jan/Feb. Vol. 82, No. 1. pp. 55–57.

Jacobs, Harriet. 2008. *Incidents in the Life of a Slave Girl*. Penguin.

Mazrui, Alamin M. and Judith Abala. 1997. "Sex and Patriarchy: Gender Relations in *God Dies by the Nile*". *Research in African Literatures*, Vol. 28, No. 3, Arabic Writing in Africa, pp. 17–32.

Mehta, Brinda J. 2010. "Excavating the Divine: Nawal El Saadawi's Creative Dissidence and Religious Contentions". *Emerging Perspectives on Nawal El Saadawi*. ed. Ernest Emenyonu. Trenton. Africa World Press. pp. 7–33.

Ogwude, Sophia. 2010. "Woman in Resistance Writing: Nawal El Saadawi and Gender Politics" *Emerging Perspectives on Nawal El Saadawi*. ed. Ernest Emenyonu. Trenton. Africa World Press.

Pawar, Urmila. 2003. *The Weave of My Life*. Trans. by Maya Pandit. New York. Columbia University Press.

———. 2013. "Woman as Caste". *Mother Wit*. Trans. Veena Deo. New Delhi. Zuban.

Saadawi, Nawal El. 1974. *God Dies by the Nile*. Trans. Sherif Hetata. London and New York. Zed Books.

———. 1980. *The Hidden Face of Eve: Women of the Arab World*. Trans. Sherif Hetata. London. Zed Books.

———. 1983. *Woman at Point Zero*. Trans. Sherif Hetata. London and New York. Zed Books.

———. 1987a. "In Camera". *Death of an Ex-Minister*. London. Methuen.

———. 1987b. *Memoirs from the Women's Prison*. London. Women's Press.

———. 1994. *Memoirs of a Woman Doctor*. London. Methuen.

————. 1999. *A Daughter of Isis: The Autobiography of Nawal El Saadawi*. Trans. Sherif Hetata. London. Zed Books.

Sackeyfio, Rose A. 2022. "Muslim Women for Change: Celebrating Assia Djebar". *Legacies of African Women Writers*. ed. Helen Chukwuma and Chioma Opara. Lanham. Lexington Books. pp. 199–214.

Saiti, Ramzi and Ramzi M. Salti. 1994. "Paradise, Heaven and Oppressive Spaces: A Critical Examination of the Life and Works of Nawal El Saadawi". *Journal of Arabic Literature*. Vol. 25, No. 2. pp. 152–174.

Shihada, Isam M. 2007. "The Patriarchal Class System in Nawal El Saadawi's *God Dies by the Nile*". *Nebula*. Vol. 4, No. 2. pp. 162–181.

Smith, Sophie. 2007. "Interview with Nawal El Saadawi (Cairo, 29th January 2006)". *Feminist Review*. Vol. 85, Political Hystories. pp. 59–69.

Susan, Arndt. 2002. *The Dynamics of African Feminism: Defining and Classifying African Feminist Literatures*. Trans. Isabel Cole. Trenton. Africa World Press.

Uko, Iniobong I. 2010. "Re-Structuring Patriarchy: Iconoclasm in Nawal El Saadawi's *A Daughter of Isis*". *Emerging Perspectives on Nawal El Saadawi*. ed. Ernest Emenyonu. Trenton. Africa World Press. pp. 93–103.

2 Caste, Class, and Women's Identity in Maru by Bessie Head

Chapter 2 illuminates the complexities of women's lives in Southern Africa through the artistry of Bessie Head in her second novel *Maru* (1971). This chapter highlights Bessie Head's vision of social transformation through the intersection of caste, gender, and power dynamics in Southern Africa. Head's portrayal of female and male characters reveals much insight into multilayered elements of intra-ethnic discrimination, racial exclusion, and gender oppression. The chapter examines the cancerous nature of caste and class through an allegorical tale of romance and intrigue as expressed in *Maru*. Head's writing conveys the experiences of South African people whose lives reflect the trauma inflicted by ethnic identity and marginalization against the landscape of colonial oppression during the Apartheid era. Her novels and short fiction form a tapestry of hybridized spaces within local communities where women are most vulnerable.

Head's first two novels are *When Rain Clouds Gather* (1968) and *Maru* (1971). In 1974, *A Question of Power* was published as perhaps her most important work through the compelling chronicle of Head's inner struggle to reconcile the challenges she faced throughout her life. An autobiographical work, *A Woman Alone: Autobiographical Writings*, was published posthumously in 1991 as well as her first work of fiction, the novella titled *The Cardinals*. Much of Head's fictional works convey autobiographical elements in ways that parallel her troubled life in her native South Africa. As a bi-racial child, Head's difficult journey in life begins with her birth in the Fort Napier Mental Institution in Pietermaritzburg in 1936. Her mother was a wealthy divorcee who became pregnant by a black man, a union that was declared illegal by the South African government during Apartheid. In *A Woman Alone: Autobiographical Writings*, Head states that she is "a dark secret hidden in someone's closet, a person bereft of genealogical anchors, one with no frame of reference but herself" (Head, 1990: 3). She was rejected from her first foster home because of her skin color and was placed in a second foster home of a "colored" couple, Nellie and George Heathcote, but she eventually became a ward of the state. Head was neither accepted as a white nor a colored person, so her *in-between* status became a double-edged sword that cut deeply into her psyche. Eustice Palmer compares the outcast status of the Masarwa, "or 'Bushmen' who, like the Osu in nineteenth-century

DOI: 10.4324/9781003350200-4

Igboland, were considered too filthy to be fit for communion with their fellow human beings" (Palmer, 2008: 109).

Thus, Head's early life is characterized by otherness and unbelonging that cast a dark shadow over her entire life. As an adolescent, a missionary informed of her mother's identity along with insensitive and cruel fragments of her early childhood through the lens of racial outcasting (Sample, 2003: 3). In *A Woman Alone: Autobiographical Writings*, Head recounts:

> the missionary opened a large file and looked at me with a wild horror and said: "Your mother was insane. If you're not careful, you'll get insane just like your mother. Your mother was a white woman. They had to lock her up as she was having a child by the stable boy who was a native."
>
> (Head, 1990: 20)

Craig Makenzie underscores:

> the deep psychological impact induced by Head's early childhood and adolescent experiences: being wrenched away from her biological mother (which she must have registered in some profound subliminal way); her rootless, alienating years as a foster-child; her induction into the severe and unnatural milieu of an orphanage run by repressed religious women; her sense of inadequacy as a teacher and her hurried abandonment of this career; her struggle to survive in Capetown and Johannesburg in an era of increasing oppression by the State of people of color, oppression which included the promulgation and enforcement of a law that forebade sexual relations between people of different races-that made a person like Bessie, in fact profoundly illegitimate (in every sense of the word).
>
> (2004: 86–87)

Despite a life of discrimination, trauma, and emotional upheaval, Bessie Head possessed a great talent that was nurtured through her love of books. After high school, she earned a certificate in teacher education and taught for two years. Her writing career began with many journalistic pursuits during the early- to mid-1960s, and to escape the political and racial torment of South Africa, Head fled to neighboring Botswana in 1964. Unfortunately, as a refugee, she was treated poorly, with no passport, no employment, and no place to call home. Eventually, she became a member of a refugee community for two years that she called "a fearfully demoralizing way of life" (Head, 1990: 67). From her years in exile, Head stated that "nothing can take away the fact that I have never had a country; not in South Africa or in Botswana where I now live as a stateless person" (Head, 1990: 45). She was finally granted citizenship in Botswana in 1979.

Bessie Head's perception of her hybrid status within a rigid and racially corrosive environment colors her life path in unwholesome and traumatizing ways until her early death at 48 in 1986.

Bessie Head's life is mirrored throughout her fiction in ways that animate the adage, *art imitating life*. In this process, Head's painful experiences are reinscribed as *herstories* that express layers of trauma, rejection, and unbelonging in multiple sites of otherness. Mauren Fielding states that:

Bessie Head "had written through cycles of alienation and rejection in an effort to claim a space and, guided by a reverence for ordinary people living small "life dramas," had put down roots".

(2003: 8)

The novel evokes Head's experiences as an exile in Botswana beginning in 1964. The novel is a largely factual account of her life in Botswana that was written as a form of cathartic healing from the layers of trauma in her life that Maureen Fielding calls the "Literature of Trauma" in "Agriculture and Healing: Transforming Space, Transforming Trauma in Bessie Head's *When Rain Clouds Gather.*"

The protagonist Makhaya represents Bessie Head as a refugee fleeing political repression in South Africa. Like Head, Makhaya is seeking calm and serenity. Head writes:

My first novel is important to me in a personal way. It is my only truly South African work, reflecting a Black South African viewpoint. The central character in the novel, a Black South African refugee, is almost insipid, a guileless, simple-hearted simpleton. But that is a true reflection of the Black South African personality. We are an oppressed people who have been stripped bare of every human right. We do not know what it is like to have our ambitions aroused, nor do we really see liberation on an immediate horizon. Botswana was a traumatic experience to me, and I found the people, initially extremely brutal and harsh, only in the sense that I had never encountered human ambition and greed before in black form.

(Head, 1990: 24)

Gillian Stead Eilersen notes that in *When Rain Clouds Gather*, Bessie Head's "theme was the way changes in traditional family patterns, crop production and political status affect the lives of people, especially the women, and the traditional distribution of power" (1995: 96). While in Botswana, Head's work on a communal agricultural development project brings to light the relationship between agriculture and healing, social transformation, and collective energies to sustain life. Head's experience with farming as expressed in *When*

Rain Clouds Gather, resonates the significance of women connecting with the earth as part of African cultural traditions. It flows throughout Africa's cultural history through women's control of food production to sustain their communities. Moreover, women's participation in farming represents reconnection with the mystical elements of nature embedded in earth symbolism throughout Africa's diverse spiritual traditions that animate the female principle in nature and society. Since childhood, Bessie Head loved to grow things, and her return to the earthbound task of farming is not only therapeutic but serves as perhaps a return to a time in her life that was less traumatic as well as a return to a period in life where she felt grounded. Head was a stateless person in Botswana for thirteen years before being granted citizenship in 1979.

A *Question of Power* is Head's autobiography that unfolds the complexities of her inner journey of mental unrest as she battles the demons of trauma, apartheid, alienation, adversity, and layers of outcast status that began with her birth. Helen Kapstein asserts: "the trope of madness opens a range of transgressive border crossings, and allows her to shuttle between various identities, genders, sexualities, and nation states" (2003: 72). In the work, Head essentially recounts her recovery from a severe nervous breakdown in 1969 where she was hospitalized in a mental hospital for three months.

Head says of the novel:

> A *Question of Power* had such an intensely personal and private dialogue that I can hardly place it in the context of the more social and outward-looking work I had done. It was a private philosophical journey to the sources of evil. I argued that people and nations do not realize the point the point at which they become evil; but once trapped in its net, evil has a propelling motion into a terrible abyss of destruction.
>
> (Head, 1990: 15)

The protagonist Elizabeth represents Bessie Head in the novel and the madness she recalls mirrors a nightmarish rendering of encounters with two male figures, Dan and Sello. The interplay between Elizabeth and both men explores patriarchal behavior as they both try to destroy her in a psychic battle. In Wilhelm's "The Face of Africa," she interprets the significance of males thus:

> The men in A *Question of Power* who struggle for Elizabeth's soul are less important as "real" figures than they are as symbolic indices of the forces which threaten to full the half-caste woman in two, to separate her out into black and white components, or into soul and body, the opposing elements which would mesh her "normal" self.
>
> (1983: 3)

Head's volume of short stories, *Collector of Treasures*, represents her revival of the oral tradition in Africa. The stories are set against the background of village life that captures the flavor of African communal society in a bygone age. The lives of many women in the rural setting reflect the struggle to survive as a result of irresponsible men who abandon them and their offspring. As a focal point of the stories, Head explores the status and treatment of women, and Coreen Brown aptly notes that "for Head, the whole question of the impoverishment in human relations is caused by the abuse of power, it is women who, as the most vulnerable members of a patriarchal society, are the most likely victims" (Brown, 2003: 117). The portrayal of male characters is largely negative through descriptions of women's unequal status, gender,power dynamics and tragedy.

The work is comprised of thirteen stories that cover a broad range of themes such as love, migration, Christianity, myths, sisterhood, witchcraft, and tradition among others. In the stories, women's experiences feature prominently and, in some instances, women are shown to be complicit in their own victimization. Some of Head's female characters are depicted through their deeply flawed behaviors such as brazenness, uncaring attitudes, and sexual promiscuity. For example, in the title story "Collector of Treasures," a woman lands in prison for murdering her husband. The story "Life" displays the tragic end when a woman flaunts her promiscuity and is murdered by her husband.

Eilerson discusses Head's portrayal of males:

> Bessie is never more outspoken in her criticism of men than in *Collector of Treasures* though she does recognize the fact that the three stages through which rural African society passed during the last hundred years have in part been responsible for the shaping of most male attitudes. Traditional custom was intended to regulate the life of the whole society and generally it succeeded. But it was the women who paid the greater price for this: they were regarded as inferior, chattels even, while the men took their superior position for granted.
>
> (1995: 168)

However, Head achieves a measure of balance regarding male behaviors in the creation of characters like Paul Thebolo in "*Collector of Treasures.*" When Dikeledi, the protagonist, is sentenced to life imprisonment, he tells her not to worry about her children because he will raise them as his own and give them a secondary school education. Furthermore, the story "Hunting" includes a responsible married man who nurtures a wholesome relationship with his wife.

Bessie Head's works include a novella *The Cardinals*[1] (1993) that remained unpublished for thirty years. The work unfolds the romantic experiences of a woman who is a victim of emotional and material deprivation. She has developed psychic trauma that distorts her ability to navigate her surroundings in conventional ways. Finally, Head published *Serowe, Village of the Rain Wind* in 1981 and, unlike her other works, the setting is South Africa.

The book is based on interviews with villagers in early 1971. Head's last publication, *A Bewitched Crossroad* (1984), is a work of historical fiction that chronicles the social and political transformations in South Africa between 1800 and 1896.

Maru is Bessie Head's second novel that echoes her experiences of exile in Botswana that began in 1964. The autobiographical nature of the book provides compelling insight into intra-ethnic hostilities that Head asserts are no different from the racial hatred that fuels the evils of the Apartheid system. Bessie Head's entire life was encapsulated in the multilayered network of intersecting forms of oppression and marginalization in her nation. Her one-way exit from South Africa to Botswana was her attempt to liberate herself from the throes of Apartheid's deathly grip on the black race and the violent system that she so detested. Over time as the political situation worsened, Head recalls that one by one her friends fled South Africa for their safety. In one of Head's essays, "Social and Political Pressures that Shape Literature in Southern Africa," she recalls:

> I was born in South Africa and that is synonymous with saying that one is born into a very brutal world-if one is black. Everything had been worked out by my time and the social and political life of the country was becoming harsher and harsher. A sense of history was totally absent in me, and it was as if, far back in history, thieves had stolen the land and were so anxious to cover up all traces of the theft that correspondingly, all traces of the true history have been obliterated. We as black people, could make no appraisal of our own worth; we did not know who or what we were, apart from objects of abuse and exploitation.
>
> (Head, 1990: 12)

Out of this deep sense of anguish, Head attempted to escape from the history of Southern Africa "associated with so many horrors-police states, detentions, sudden and violent mass protests and death, exploitation and degrading political systems" (Head, 1990: 11). Ogunyemi acknowledges that "Head carried an enormous baggage with her from South Africa: racism, errant sexuality, insanity, poverty, statelessness, and a need to reinvent her genealogy" (2009: 139).

Maru essentially examines the nexus between caste, gender discrimination, and power dynamics within a village setting in Botswana. Among the four characters, the protagonist is Margaret Cadmore whose experiences of marginalization mirror those of Bessie Head. Dikeledi is an important character, along with Maru and Moleka who represent royal families in the social hierarchy of Dilepe. In this way, Head initiates a discourse between the oppressed communities and the nation as represented by Margaret and her encounters with Dikeledi, Maru, and Moleka who are elites in the village.

Margaret hails from the outcast ethnic community that was called Masarwa, a Tswana word used in the past as a pejorative appellation. They are also known by the derogatory terms "Bushmen," and worse, N-----s in the context of the novel. The appropriate names are the San or Khoisan peoples whose populations are spread across Botswana, South Africa, Zimbabwe, Zambia, Angola, Lesotho, and Namibia. Their status correlates with the lowest Hindu caste designation of people from communities formerly known as "Untouchables" who are now called Dalits in India. Moreover, the perceptions, low status, abuse, and exploitation of captive Africans during and after the period of enslavement in the Americas bear many social, economic, and political parallels.

Early in the novel, Head situates the perceptions of Masarwa:

> In Botswana they say: Zebras, Lions Buffalo and Bushmen live in the Kalihari Desert. If you can catch a Zebra, you can walk up to it, forcefully open its mouth and examine its teeth. The Zebra is not supposed to mind because it is an animal. Scientists do the same to Bushmen and they are not supposed to mind, because there is no one they can still turn round to and say, "At least a ____." Of all things that are said of oppressed people, the worst things are said and done to the Bushman. Ask the scientists. Haven't they written a treatise on how Bushmen are an oddity of the human race, who are half the head of a man and half the body of a donkey? Because you don't go poking around into the organs of people unless they are animals or dead.
>
> (Head, 1971: 11–12)

Moreover, this passage is a startling illustration of Head's concern with the roots of the subjugation of Africans by Europeans. There are many passages in the novel that capture perceptions of the Masarwa through the lens of ethnic hatred and rejection as part of Head's didactic focus in the work.

In Head's *A Woman Alone*,[2] she states:

> With all my South African experience I longed to write an enduring novel on the hideousness of racial prejudice. But I also wanted the book to be so beautiful and so magical that I, as the writer, would long to read and re-read it. I achieved this ambition in an astonishing way in my second novel, *Maru*. In Botswana they have a conquered tribe, the Basarwa or Bushmen. It is argued that they were the true owners of the land in some distant past, that they had been conquered by the more powerful Botswana tribes and from then onwards assumed the traditional role of slaves. Basarwa people were so abhorrent to Botswana people because they hardly looked African, but Chinese. I knew the language of hatred, but it was an evil exclusively practiced by white people. I therefore listened in amazement as Botswana people talked of the Basarwa whom they oppressed.

"They don't think," they said. "They don't know anything."

For the first time, I questioned blind prejudice:

How do they know that? How can they be sure that the Basarwa are
not thinking?

(Head, 1990: 91–92).

Head's research among the Botswana people revealed to her that the root
cause of oppression is the lack of communication, and she concludes:
"And so my novel was built up in blinding flashes of insights into an evil
that hung like the sickness of death over all black people in South Africa"
(Head,1990: 92).

Among the salient themes rendered in the novel, Bessie Head has woven a
vivid narrative of the ways in which ethnic discrimination, gender, and power
dynamics unravel to achieve social transformation in Botswana. Head's artistic vision has crafted a complex tale of romance as the backdrop for the more
serious issues that play out in the village of Dilepe. Maru and Moleka are
both powerful sons of chiefs as well as close friends who rival each other for
the love of Margaret who accepts a teaching post in the village. Dikeledi is
Maru's sister who loves his rival Moleka. The four characters symbolize the
prominent ideas in the work, and the romantic elements highlight the deep
fissures within a society divided by rigid stratification.

In Head's period of exile as a refugee in Botswana, she explores and interrogates prejudice among Africans, commonly referred to as "tribalism."

Head's focus on transformation of a marginalized individual is illustrated
through Margaret's unusual life in Botswana as the adopted daughter of a
white missionary. Margaret Cadmore bequeaths her name, sponsorship of
her education, and the repeated mantra: "One day you will help your people" (Head, 1971: 17). When her Masarwa mother dies in childbirth, the
missionary critiques the blatant disdain of her body by the Batswana nurses.
The hospital supervisor informs Mrs. Cadmore that no one wanted to bury
the dead body because she was an "untouchable." When looking closely at
the Masarwa woman's body, she observes:

The thin stick legs of malnutrition and the hard calloused feet that had
never worn shoes. She took in also the hatred of the fortunate, and that
if they so hated even a dead body how much more did they hate those
of this woman's tribe who were still alive. Maybe she really saw human
suffering, close up, for the first time, but it frightened her into adopting
that part of the woman which was still alive—her child.

(Head, 1971: 15)

She takes the infant home and thinks of her as "a real living object for her
experiment" (Head, 1971: 15). Margaret Cadmore was an amateur scien-
tist at heart who believed in the supremacy of environment over heredity
and imagines the possibilities: "Who knew what wonder would be created"
(Head, 1971: 15). Huma Ibrahim observes that:

Margaret is the archetypal example of experimentation, exile, and colonialism. She is cut off utterly from her own people after birth and is taken over by an individual, by a colonial administration, by an experimenter, and also by a set of differently expressed prejudices.

(1996: 99)

Margaret's sense of identity is confounded because the narrator notes "there seemed to be a big hole in the child's mind between the time that she slowly became conscious of her life in the home of the missionaries and conscious of herself as a person" (Head, 1971: 15). Her upbringing by Margaret Cadmore resulted in a person who simply could not be placed or defined through conventional means.

Years later as a child, Margaret becomes aware of her ethnic identity when she is told "that she was a Bushman, mixed breed, half breed, low breed or bastard" (Head 16). Early realization of her status is reminiscent of enslaved children on antebellum plantations in the American south who did not know they were slaves until around the age of six. Further, the narrator queries the appellative designation of Margaret's people:

Some time ago it might have been believed that words like "kaffir" and "n----r" defined a tribe. Or else how can a tribe of people be called Bushman[3] or Masarwa? Masarwa is the equivalent of "n----r", a term of contempt which means, obliquely, a low, filthy nation.

(Head, 1971: 12)

Margaret's sense of unbelonging is deepened because she speaks like a European which confounds those around her. Hybridity colors all her experiences and encounters with others since she does not embody the perceived attributes of the Masarwa. The in-between status she experiences is similar to the author who was never accepted among whites, the "colored" class, South African, Indian, or Botswana indigenes. Margaret's background also links with Head's life because her English mother, Bessie Amelia Emery, provided for her education that later became the foundation of her intellectual growth as a successful writer. Margaret endures painful bullying and ridicule from other children in school but manages great stoicism and resolve through it all:

if they caught her in some remote part of the school buildings during the playtime hour, they would set up a wild, jiggling dance: "Since when did a Bushy go to school? We take him to the bush where he eats mealie pap, pap, pap."

(Head, 1971: 18)

Margaret was actually spat upon as well: "If a glob of spit dropped onto her arm during the playtime hour, she quietly wiped it away" (Head, 1971: 17).

The effect of these disturbing events on Margaret's psyche is the development of an inner resolve to survive at all costs. Margaret develops a thicker skin and thinks to herself: "No one by shouting, screaming or spitting could un-Bushman her" (Head, 1971: 17).

Even in her young mind, she somehow understood the nature of the poisonous insults from others:

> An allowance for life had always been made for vicious people, who for too long had said the kind of things to helpless people which really applied to their own twisted, perverted hearts. Those who spat at what they thought was inferior were really the "low filthy people" of the earth, because decent people cannot behave that way.
>
> (Head, 1971: 19)

In its simple form, Margaret's analysis articulates the psychoanalytic theory of projection that "is involved in othering, where the other comes to represent the opposite of the self, often that which is disavowed in the self" (Rohleder, 2014: 1520–1522). Put simply, feelings and characteristics within oneself are attributed to someone else and the elder Cadmore helps to fortify Margaret against the stigma of her ethnic outcast status. As Margaret's life unfolds, she develops many inner qualities of resilience, and despite her marginalized existence, she excels academically through her passion for books. The solitary world of isolation becomes the soil for academic achievement, and eventually, Margaret becomes a primary school teacher as a successful "experiment" nurtured by her English benefactress.

Spatiality frames Head's portrayal of the abhorrent status of the Masarwa community when Margaret accepts a post as a primary school teacher in the village of Dilepe. Her education sets her completely apart from her people. After the senior Cadmore departs permanently to England, Margaret is on her own as she transitions to the distant rural location as the site of a new life marked by change. She crosses the boundaries of caste, socio-economic class, and gender norms for Masarwa women through her education. As an educated Masarwa, Margaret is both centered and marginalized. She is centered through the enormous power of English education and economic benefits. At the same time, she is marginal, because she is set apart from her own Masarwa community that is uneducated and perceived as backward (Katrak, 1995: 70).

Ato Quayson in *Oxford Street: City Life and the Itineraries of Transnationalism* frames the term "spatial traversal" that denotes the movement of individuals across spaces that initiates transformative energies in their lives. Although Quayson's coinage of the term lies within the context of modern African urban spaces, the idea of "space as the correlative of social relations" is appropriate and central to the analysis of social hierarchies within the Botswana rural environment of Dilepe (2014: 217).

These crossings by hitherto marginalized characters reconfigure their identities and their status in markedly different ways as potential sites of personal growth, empowerment, and expanded opportunities as well as the hope for social transformation of the nation-state. Although Margaret is a Masarwa, she rises to a higher social class in Dilepe because of her education that was provided by the senior Margaret Cadmore. Thus, Margaret begins a journey beyond the boundaries of her home with the elder Cadmore armed with the acceptance of her Masarwa identity. When she meets Dikeledi and is immediately asked about her background, she confidently replies "I am a Masarwa" (Head, 1971: 24). To this, "Dikeledi drew in her breath with a sharp, hissing sound. Dilepe village was the stronghold of some of the most powerful and wealthy chiefs in the country, all of whom owned innumerable Masarwa as slaves" (Head, 1971: 24). Margaret is unashamed of her ethnicity and Dikeledi had assumed she was a "colored." Ibrahim describes Margaret as having "a sense of dignity about claiming her identity back from the malaise that has surrounded her identity traditionally, but she is extremely passive, like a fairytale heroine, in terms of everything else that happens to her in the course of the novel" (1996: 100). The women become friends, an act which foreshadows the seeds of change in the social order of Dilepe. Olaogun states that:

> Margaret's insistence on declaring her ethnic background, together with the questioning of the caste custom by three notable members of Dilepe's ruling elite—Dikeledi, Moleka and Maru—constitutes the promise of a recognition of the society at large both by the mistreated Masarwa and their oppressors. This recognition involves a multiplicity of ironies on the part of the various characters and their situations in the society.
>
> (1994: 73)

Margaret's journey into otherness in Dilepe begins when she appears on the first day of school and encounters the dishonest and sexist principal Pete, who, like Dikeledi, also assumes she is "colored"[4] because of her appearance. Margaret, in true form, confidently replies that she is a Masarwa, which sends shock waves through his body causing an agitated state that leads to a cunning intrigue with Seth, the education officer. The two men can't believe that Margaret "could have gotten there on her own brains." "Someone was pushing her" (Head, 1971: 41). Sexism rears its ugly head when Pete tells Seth, "She can be shoved out." "It's easy. She's a woman" (Head, 1971: 41). Here, male power, and the abuse of that power, illustrates the deeply entrenched patriarchal attitudes that undermine female equality. Although the men want to be rid of Margaret:

> but the community, prejudiced though it is, has to recognize that she is the educator of their children. Despite Margaret's education, the males in charge have power to retain or dismiss her. The pettiness and

prejudice of the so-called "educated" males in charge of the school cast a negative light on what knowledge and education can accomplish, particularly against deeply ingrained and socially legitimized sexism.

(Katrak, 1995: 70)

Head introduces another unsavory male character, Morafi, the younger brother of Maru, to complete the trio of plotters against Margaret. In a discussion about Margaret, Morafi says:

"I really wonder what Maru is going to do about the problem of the Masarwa."

Things are moving ahead for this country, and they are the only millstone. I don't see what we can do with people who can't think for themselves but always need others to feed them. Mind you, they seem quite contented with their low, animal lives.

(Head, 1971: 44)

These comments are an appalling example of raw inhumanity as the Masarwa are not perceived as human. Pete orchestrates a plan to defame and unseat Margaret when he persuades a fourteen-year-old boy to "look directly into her face with an insolent stare: 'Tell me', He said. 'Since when is a Bushy a teacher?' The other children began chanting 'You are a Bushman'. It froze the whole school" (Head, 1971: 46). In the ensuing uproar, Pete intended to dismiss Margaret on the grounds that she is unable to control the class. His plan is thwarted by Dikeledi who rushes ahead of him into Margaret's classroom to restore order. Her agency and quick intervention interrupt the race, class, and gender oppression meted out by the principal and the education officer. Head illustrates women's potential for disruption of male power through Dikeledi's solidarity with a Masarwa woman, her outspoken resistance, and the fact that she becomes the principal of the school to replace Pete, whom the narrator refers to as "a traditional dog" (Head, 1971: 47).

In a sexist rant under his breath, Pete says, "'The bossy little bitch has buggered up the works,' he muttered over and over again" (Head, 1971: 46). All of the other teachers ridicule Pete's failed schemes and cowardice.

The transformative elements in the novel unfold through the actions of Moleka as one of the two powerful leaders of the wealthy ruling class in Dilepe. Moleka invites all the Masarwa slaves to eat with him, which is something unheard of within the rigidity of the caste system in the village, and the news spreads like wildfire among the people. Moleka's actions take a more dramatic turn in the social relations of Dilepe:

Moleka, who heard that the principal and the high-ups were planning trouble for the new mistress, could not make allowance for the slow removal of prejudice. He removed it all in one day. He told Seth, the education supervisor, that there was good food in his house on Sunday. When Seth arrived, he found all the Masarwas in the yard of Moleka also seated at the table. Moleka took up his fork and placed a mouthful of food in the mouth of a Masarwa then with the same fork fed himself.

(Head, 1971: 53)

Seth storms off in anger and vows to cut himself off from Moleka. The complexity of these events surrounding Margaret and other Masarwa people foreshadows the potential for social upheaval illustrated in the discourses of the power elite and the oppressed caste. Through the romantic intrigue and interplay between Margaret, Dikeledi, Maru, and Moleka, Head has created a vision of liberation from the prison of racism, caste, and gender inequality. Through her central characters, their romantic intrigues, and power dynamics, Head engages the evils of racial hatred and sexism although the work is ostensibly a romantic novella.

The male characters are the major figures that fuel the transformative energies infused within themes of racial hatred and oppression in Dilepe. Both Maru and Moleka are in love with Margaret while Dikeledi is in love with Moleka. The complicated and winding trail of events involves the treatment of Masarwa slaves, Margaret, and three totems of power; the school principal, the education supervisor, and Maru's younger brother. Maru's actions herald a new direction in the future of the village. Maru and Moleka enter a power play over Margaret that threatens their friendship and tips the balance of power in the community. The narrator notes that: "It was only Maru who saw their relationship in its true light. They were kings of opposing kingdoms" (Head, 1971: 34). Further, Maru reflects on the nature of his rivalry with Moleka: "Throughout this time, Moleka was the only person who was his equal" (Head, 1971: 34).

Head portrays Maru as having many positive qualities although he owns many Masarwa slaves. He is destined to become the paramount chief and is described as sensitive, emotional, intuitive, and idealistic. His lofty thoughts presage the possibility for change in the village hierarchy through egalitarian ideals.

In contrast, Moleka has a reputation as a womanizer in the village: "There was nothing Moleka did not know about the female anatomy. It made him arrogant and violent. There was no woman who could resist the impact of his permanently boiling bloodstream" (Head, 1971: 114). Both men are immersed in hidden intrigues and clever manipulation in order to win Margaret's love. Maru pretends to uphold the prevailing racist power structure of the village while he secretly plans to marry Margaret. He thinks of his love for her as the catalyst for a new and different world (Glover, 1990: 115). He states, "I was not born to rule this mess. If I have a place, it is to pull down the old structures and create the new" (Head, 1971: 68). Maru's love for Margaret grows deeply through admiration for her artistic talent as expressed in beautiful paintings of the village landscape. In a passionate outpouring of creative energy that drains her to the point of exhaustion, Margaret paints pictures that echo images from Maru's dreams as a mysterious connection to each other on a psychic level. Margaret's paintings convey a shared vision that animates Maru's optimism for a better future: He says: "Look! Don't you see! We are the people who have the strength to build a new world!" (Head, 1971: 108). He confides his romantic interest only to his sister and secretly arranges for a new home beyond Dilepe where he plans to live with Margaret.

The winds of change in the village are apparent when the three totems remove themselves from the scene which dismantles the power structure:

> Three bombs went off in Dilepe village, one after the other. First, Pete the principal fled. Then Seth the education supervisor fled. Then Morafi kept looking over his shoulder for two days and he also fled. No coherent explanations were ever given, except that the people who lived with them all thought they had suddenly lost their minds.
>
> (Head, 1971: 92)

The work ends on a high note as Head creates a "love conquers all" ending that evokes a fairytale quality. Instead of a formal proposal to Margaret, Maru essentially elopes with her much like a knight rescues a damsel in distress. Upon learning of Margaret's pregnancy and forthcoming marriage to Moleka, Margaret lapses into a depressed and death-like state: "A few vital threads of her life had snapped behind her neck and it felt as though she were shrivelling to death" (Head, 1971: 118). Margaret comes to life when Maru arrives and essentially carries her off. He tells her:

> We used to dream the same dreams. That was how I knew you would love me in the end. What could she say, except that at that moment she would have chosen anything as an alternative to the living death into which she had so unexpectedly fallen?
>
> (Head, 1971: 124)

Further, the idea that they were heading straight for a home, a thousand miles away where the sun rose, new and new and new each day" heralds a new beginning for the couple and for the Masarwa people in society. Glover suggests that "the final message of achievement in the book is not so much about the power of personal love as the socially liberating effect" (1990: 116) of the marriage on the caste distinctions and power structure of the village. The fact that Maru relinquishes the inherited role of paramount chief is unprecedented with far-reaching implications for change in the old order of social relations in Dilepe, but "When people of Dilepe heard about the marriage of Maru, they began to talk about him as if he had died" (Head, 1971: 126). Mckenzie argues that Head describes Maru's unselfish actions so that readers will perceive him favorably as a progressive agent of change since he "achieves change at the expense of leadership of his tribe" (54). However, for the Masarwa, "a door silently opened on the small dark airless room in which their souls had been shut for a long time" (Head, 1971: 126). In stark contrast:

> People like the Batswana, who did not know that the wind of freedom had also reached people of the Masarwa tribe, were in for an unpleasant surprise because it would be no longer possible to treat Masarwa people in an inhuman way without getting killed yourself.
>
> (Head, 1971: 127)

The suggestion of violence evokes Fanonian dialectics that may indeed shift the winds of change to achieve liberation for the oppressed in society. Maru succeeds on many levels, and despite the appearance of a simple love story, the complexities of racial and ethnic oppression, gender inequality, and power dynamics carry the message of human potential for social transformation. Ogwude aptly confirms the significance of Maru's abdication of leadership:

> Maru rejects his traditional rights of leadership and marries a Masarwa, convinced that no man should be the object of pity or the slave of another. For the apartheid system as well as for the perpetrators of oppressive tribal prejudices, these are recriminatory pictures. Indeed, by contrasting it with what is, the writer indicts the ugly South African machinery which desecrates human life on both the rural and urban fronts.
>
> (2002: 70)

In sum, *Maru* effectively critiques the evils of caste and gender bias in Botswana through the outcast status of the protagonist in ways that parallel Bessie Head's life as a refugee. Head was deeply affected by the unwelcoming experiences during her exile and in *Maru*, as well as in *When Rain Clouds Gather* and *A Question of Power*, the autobiographical narrative examines deep fissures in society that cause trauma and suffering, especially to women. Feminist perspectives strengthen the novel despite flawed characteristics of the heroine. Both Margaret and Dikeledi are educated although both women must battle gender discrimination in the school where they teach. Fortunately, resilience and agency to dismantle the male power structure are successful as Dikele's preemptive actions protect Margaret's job and eventually she takes on a leadership role as principal of the school. Critics have questioned Margaret's largely passive role in the novel, although her inner strength and her unashamed sense of her identity is a significant marker of feminist energy and self-acceptance. Further, the depth of Margaret's spirit-driven artistry suggests mystical elements of great and almost uncontrollable power that overflows in the creation of her paintings.

However, feminist themes are also incongruent and contradictory as the two women characters vacillate between their competence and agency within professional space (s) and the romantic intrigues with Maru and Moleka. Margaret maintains a deep sense of her identity as a Masarwa that she asserts in bold terms when she arrives in Dilepe. When she allows herself to be swept away by Maru at the end, it bespeaks of maudlin sentiment that is uncharacteristic of a woman with her intelligence although she experienced a near death reaction to the marriage of Dikeledi and Moleka. Moreover, Dikeledi's status as an elite and powerful woman in Dilepi is contrasted with her unquestioning affair with Moleka, and the resulting pregnancy before she is married.

Head's portrayal of behaviors that run contrary to the otherwise strong feminist images of both women suggests that women's vulnerability to the power of romantic intrigue is somehow inevitable. Moreover, the ending of the novel has come under scrutiny because when Maru essentially abducts her, the absence of her voice in crafting a future outside Dilepe usurps her agency in charting her future. The idea of a female in distress being "rescued" by a male supports the fairy-tale quality of the ending where love conquers all.

The political ramifications of the novel's ending suggest the absence of substantial change in the status quo in Dilepe since Maru's abdication of the chieftaincy does not rid the society of racism. Maru is "dead" to his fellow Botswanans and the perception of the Masarwa remains unchanged. The ending suggests that the route to liberation for the Masarwa may only be achieved through the actions of the oppressed themselves, something that the Botswana people are as yet unaware. Critics have noted these ambiguities as a weakness in the novel, especially since the fairytale ending runs counter to the serious treatment of discrimination, inequality, and gender imbalance in society as expressed in the work. Despite the incongruent elements at play, the novel effectively renders the painful realities of intra-racism in Botswana as a mirror of her own experience that she presents to the world. The ending is a reflection of the author's romantic idealism and the hope that racial, ethnic, and political boundaries may indeed be bridged through our humanity expressed in the bonds of love. As a postcolonial novel, Maru unfolds discomforting truths about intra-ethnic conflict in Botswana and throughout the African continent that remains a major impediment to social transformation, progress, and stability in many nations in Africa.

Notes

1 *The Cardinals* was published posthumously in 1993.
2 Head's autobiography: *A Woman Alone*: Autobiographical Writings. 1990. Edited by Craig MacKenzie.
3 A derogatory name for the ethnic community indigenous to several countries across the southern region of Africa such as Namibia, Zambia, Angola, Zimbabwe, Lesotho, and South Africa. The appropriate name is the Khoisan.
4 The racial category in South Africa that consists of bi-racial people whose status was lower than Caucasians.

Works Cited

Abrams, Cecil. ed. 1990. *The Tragic Life: Bessie Head and Literature in South Africa*. Trenton. Africa World Press.

———. 2003. *Critical Essays on Bessie Head*. Westport, CT, London. Praeger.

Bazin, Nancy Topping. 1986. "Feminist Perspectives in African Fiction: Bessie Head and Buchi Emecheta". *The Black Scholar*. The Black Woman Writer and the Diaspora. March/April Vol. 17, No. 2. pp. 34–40.

Brown, Coreen. 2003. *The Creative Vision of Bessie Head*. Madison. Rosemont Publishing and Printing.

———. 2004. "Bessie Head's South Africa". *Emerging Perspectives on Bessie Head*. Trenton. Africa World Press. pp. 73–89.

Glover, Daniel. 1990. "The Fairy Tale and the Nightmare". *The Tragic Life: Bessie Head and Literature in Southern Africa*. Trenton. Africa World Press.

Eilerson, Gillian Stead. 1995. *Bessie Head: Thunder Behind Her Ears*. South Africa. David Phillip Publishers Ltd.

Fanon, Franz. 1963. *The Wretched of the Earth*. France. Presence Africaine.

Feilding, Maureen. 2003. "Agriculture and Healing: Transforming Space, Transforming Trauma in Bessie Head's *When Rain Clouds Gather*". *Critical Essays on Bessie Head*. Westport, CT, London. Praeger. pp. 11–24.

Head, Bessie. 1968. *When Rain Clouds Gather*. New York. Simon and Shuster.

———. 1971. *Maru*. London. Heinemann.

———. 1974. *A Question of Power*. London. Davis Poynter.

———. 1977. *A Collector of Treasures and Other Botswana Tales*. London. Heinemann.

———. 1981. *Serowe: Village of the Rain Wind*. London. Heinemann.

———. 1984. *A Bewitched Crossroad: An African Saga*. Johannesburg. Ad. Donker.

———. 1990a. *A Woman Alone: Autobiographical Writings*. ed. Craig MacKenzie. Oxford. Heinemann.

———. 1990b. "Social and Political Pressures that Shape Literature in Southern Africa". *The Tragic Life: Bessie Head and Literature in South Africa*. ed. Cecil Abrams. Trenton. Africa World Press. pp. 11–17.

———. 1990c. *The Tragic Life: Bessie Head and Literature in South Africa*. ed. Cecil Abrams. Trenton. Africa World Press.

———. 1993. *The Cardinals: With Meditations and Stories*. ed. M.J. Daymond. Cape Town. David Phillip Ltd.

Ibrahim, Huma. 1996. *Subversive Identities in Exile*. Charlottesville. University of Virginia Press.

Katrak, Ketu. 1995. "'This Englishness will Kill You': Colonialist Education and Female Subjugation in Merle Hodge's 'Crick Crack Monkey', and Bessie Head's *Maru*". *College Literature*. February Vol. 1, Third World Women's Inscriptions, pp. 62–77.

Kapstein, Helen. 2003. "'A Peculiar Shuttling Movement': Madness, Passing, and Trespassing in Bessie Head's A Question of Power". *Critical Essays on Bessie Head*. Westport, CT, London. Praeger. pp. 71–98.

Kemp, Yakini, 1988. "Romantic Love and the Individual in Novels by Mariama Ba, Buchi Emecheta, and Bessie Head". *Obsidian II*. Winter Vol. 3, No. 3. pp. 1–16.

MacKenzi, Craig. 1999. *Bessie Head*. New York. Twayne Publishers.

Quayson, Ato. 2014. *Oxford Street: City Life and the Itineraries of Transnationalism.* Durham and London. Duke University Press.

Rohleder, P. (2014). "Projection, Overview". *Encyclopedia of Critical Psychology.* ed. T. Teo. New York, NY. Springer. https://doi.org/10.1007/978-1-4614-5583 -7_415

Ogunyemi, Okonjo Chikweny. 2009. "Mapping a Female Mind: *A Question of Power* and the Unscrambling of Africa". *Twelve Best Books by African Women.* Critical Readings. ed. Chikwenye Okonjo Ogunyemi and Tuzyline Jita Adams. Athens. Ohio University Press. pp. 137–159.

Ogwude, Sophia O. 2002. "An Exile Writing on Home: Protest and Commitment in the Works of Bessie Head". *African Literature Today.* Vol. 22. London. James Currey.

Olaogun, Modupe O. 1994. "Irony and Schizophrenia in Bessie Head's *Maru*". *Research in African Literatures.* Winter Vol. 25, No. 4. pp. 69–87.

Palmer, Eustace. 2008. *Of War and Women, Oppression and Optimism.* Trenton. Africa World Press.

Sample, Maxine. 2003. "Artist in Exile". *Critical Essays on Bessie Head.* Westport, CT, London. Praeger. pp. 1–9.

Starfield, Jane. 1997. "The Return of Bessie Head". *Journal of Southern African Studies.* December Vol. 23. pp. 655–664.

Wilhelm, Cherry. 1983. "Bessie Head: The Face of Africa". *English in Africa.* May Vol. 10, No. 1. pp. 1–13.

3 Sisters of the Soil: Women's Resistance in Muthoni Likimani's

Passbook Number F.47927

Muthoni Likimani's *Passbook Number F.47927* (1985) is a work of historical fiction examined in Chapter 3. The nine stories that comprise the novel
highlight themes of women's solidarity, identity, and the important roles they
played in the Mau Mau revolution in Kenya.

Muthoni Likimani is a Kikuyu writer and activist whose works also
include her first novel *They Shall Be Chastised* (1974), followed by a narrative poem *What Does a Man Want* (1974). In addition, she has published
Women of Kenya in the Decade of Development (1985) and her autobiography, *Fighting Without Ceasing* (2005). Likimani's extraordinary career
spans several decades as one of Kenya's foremost public figures. Along with
her writing, she has worked as a broadcaster, politician, and actress. The
title *Passbook F.47927* represents Likimani's identification card during the
years of Mau Mau insurgence leading to Kenya's independence in 1963. Her
observations and experiences derive from first-hand accounts that convey
authenticity and insight into women's lives that are cast against Kenya's revolution against British colonial domination. Prominent themes in her writing
are the ways in which race and gender shape the lives of women, human
rights, politics, and religion. As a postcolonial novel, *Passbook F.47927* illuminates the colonial landscape of Kenya through the lens of gender. The
work is a multi-vocal collection that was published as part of the Women in
Society Series with an introduction by Jean O'Barr.[1]

Analysis of the novel augments the feminist themes that appear in other works
included in the volume by highlighting Kenyan women's strength, resilience, and
enormous sacrifices in support of the nationalist movement for independence
during the 1950s. Likimani has crafted nine fictionalized accounts that form a
composite sketch of female agency as women become social actors in defense of
their nation. The chapter elucidates Likimani's fictionalized accounts of Kenyan
women's solidarity, courage, and subversive strategies, during the anti-colonial
movement. The chapter penetrates the inner world(s) of women at war with
powerful forces of destruction that threaten themselves, their families and the
nation. In a 1986 interview with Adeola James, Likimani states:

> it can be said that *Passbook F.47927* indirectly answers the question:
> Did women contribute to the Mau Mau struggle? In all the previous

DOI: 10.4324/9781003350200-5

literature on the subject nobody ever focused on the contribution of women. We read about men in detention, but nobody said there was also a gang of women guerillas fighting, carrying guns, hiding and feeding the Mau Mau. Even the prostitutes incited the white soldiers and got their guns after getting their men to beat them. These women made their own contribution, and they were remarkable spies. Yet nobody talks about them.

(Likimani, 1990: 60)

Feminist perspectives take center stage in the work because women characters articulate gender inequality and patriarchy within their communities that parallel gender oppression meted out by the colonial authorities that invade and corrupt their society. Muthoni examines women's roles and status in Kenyan society that in some cases is advantageous, while in other instances, females were at great risk for their safety and survival during the period of Mau Mau resistance. The women featured in the novel evolve politically strategic solidarity through collective actions against the colonial power structure. In a review of the book in 1988, David Maughan-Brown asserts that the:

The strongest stories are those portraying life in Nairobi during the 1950's where the pass system so impinged upon the daily lives of women. Viewed through the eyes of a woman, the tinderbox atmosphere of the African locations of the city seems closer to fear and chaos rather than the struggle for power that has echoed through the work of many writers.

(1998: 355)

This observation may be understood within the context of women's personal narratives that probe a full range of emotional, cultural, historical, and politically charged recollections of a nation struggling to reclaim its sovereignty. These diverse and rich characteristics of women's narratives underscore the importance of unearthing their stories to celebrate women's voices of resistance alongside those of male writers.

Passbook F47927 is a chronicle of the brutality, disruption, and violence of the colonial enterprise that evokes elements of Nazi concentration camps, slavery, and genocide in human history. The authenticity of the novel is expressed through the authorial voice that introduces each story to provide the historical context of colonial policies, local cultures, gender roles, and customs and practices. The work is also a critique of divisiveness among diverse ethnic communities in Kenya and the ways in which the colonial intrusion exacerbated and exploited these tensions to the detriment of all Kenyan people as colonial subjects. *Passbook F.47927* represents the hitherto untold story of Kenya's women freedom fighters and their contribution to the Mau Mau rebellion. The fact that women's participation is largely missing from the historiography of the struggle for Kenya's independence is hardly surprising and is parallel to the occlusion of women's contribution to other resistance movements in the world. O'Barr contextualizes the work through Kenya's historiography, the Mau Mau revolt, women in Kenyan society, and the impact of Colonialism on the economic and political activities of women.

The Mau Mau[2] movement is a peasant revolt by the Kikuyu Land and Freedom Army that took place between 1952 and 1960 that initiated the State of Emergency[3] in the colony when African leaders such as Jomo Kenyatta were arrested. Mau Mau is known as Kiama Gia Ithaka na Wiyathi among Kenyans that were part of the rebellion. Evans Mwangi states that: "The Mau Mau War cost the lives of ninety-five Europeans (thirty-two settlers and sixty-three rebels), near two thousand Kenyan loyalists, and 11,503 Kenyans identified as rebels. About eighty thousand Mau Mau sympathizers and fighters were detained" (2010: 88). The rebellion was centralized in the forests of Mount Kenya, comprised of the Kikuyu, Meru, and Emba ethnic communities. As Kenya's largest ethnic group, the Kikuyu dominated the rebellion as they were most adversely affected by European colonial oppression. According to Louise White:

> It was said that 15,000 Kikuyu went into the forest, which they used as a staging ground for raids that were often ill-advised and, after mid-1953, were little more than attempts to secure food and ammunition. There is no narrative history of Mau Mau from 1952-1956, let alone one of the operations in the forest.
>
> (1990: 11)

Jean O'Barr, in the introductory essay of *Passbook F.47927*, describes the four major activities of the Mau Mau resistance:

> People demonstrated their allegiance to members of their ethnic groups and their opposition to colonial authority; this demonstration took the form of oaths and rituals, signifying solidarity of purpose. People resisted the economic and political institutions placed over them by attacking and destroying the most immediate manifestations of those institutions, for example, colonial farms and police stations. People promoted their evolving sense of consensus by forming organizations, usually based on indigenous ones in form, and by recognizing leaders who could articulate their goals. And finally, people reacted to the military attacks on them not only by counterattacks, but by creating support networks in as many places and with as many people as possible.
>
> (1985: 3–5)

Likiman's publication of *Passbook F.47937* represents the onset of knowledge about women's participation in the revolution for Kenya's independence from British colonial rule. According to Jean Barr, the treatment of women's roles in the rebellion is limited because: "In social science analysis, in the first-hand accounts and in Kenyan fiction, women emerge only as nameless supporting characters in a play dominated by men" (1985: 6). The early accounts were written by men who failed to discuss women's participation "beyond those of sexual partners and couriers" (O'Barr, 1985: 6). *Passbook F47927* presents women's voices narrating their truth as a corrective to the unexplored examination of their lives, roles in their families and communities, and their activism as freedom fighters for their nation. Likimani's rendering of women's experiences inaugurates feminist expression because their stories are told from a woman's point of view to ultimately become women's *herstories* as part of national discourses in Kenya. In this way, women's narratives usurp the male gaze and the idea that women's experiences have been presented by male writers only in relation to events surrounding men in their communities.

Finally, the significance of *Passbook F.47927* lies in the gendered representation of the Kenyan rebellion that becomes a (re)writing or (re)construction of the male-dominated literature in the social sciences as well as in fictional works about Kenya during the colonial period leading to independence in 1963. As a work of historical fiction, *Passbook F.47927* gives names and identities to the nameless and voiceless women whose support, sacrifice, and commitment to freedom were invaluable to the resistance movement. Likimani's commitment to foregrounding the experiences of females is a groundbreaking contribution to African women's literature, women's history, and feminist scholarship. *Passbook F.47927* contains only firsthand accounts of the struggle for independence by a woman.

In *Passbook F.47927*, Kenyan women display extraordinary solidarity to sustain and protect their families and communities during the Emergency. The second story in the collection is called "Forced Communal Labor," and the account describes how entire village communities were compelled to work without pay on government projects as part of the communal labor policy of the colonial administration. The majority of those forced to work were women because many men were in prison, detention camps, or in the forests as Mau Mau fighters. Likimani calls the forced communal labor a "deadly slavery" (1985: 60). The conditions under which people worked caused suffering, hunger, and brutality, with no pay for villagers who had to cater to their families, gardens, and livestock. The sheer strength and solidarity of the women allowed them to survive the terrible hardship. Likimani recalls:

> Many colonialists wondered how these Central Province women worked all day at communal unpaid work followed by a strict curfew, and yet still survived. The secret of everything was that traditionally these women were very hardworking, and with the emergency problems they had learned to survive.
>
> (Likimani, 1985: 61)

The conditions described bear a striking similarity to plantation life in the Americas during the Atlantic Slave Trade. Historical accounts credit women as the core of survival in the slave communities on plantations. In the story, villagers are summoned and commanded to begin work on constructing a road and bridge. The narrator notes that:

> It is very hard to understand how Kamuri people survived. Children being helped by their elders and at the same time sisters and brothers continuing to go to school. Women grew to like each other. There was no room for gossip, no room for backbiting, and no time to be wasted. People lost their selfishness, and the thought of hatred by women because they loved the same man disappeared. Care for others grew. Children were cared for communally, housework was done together. At five pm, when forced communal labor was finished, some women went to fetch water, others went for firewood, and yet others rushed to collect food from the gardens. All these activities were to be done between five and six.
>
> (Likimani, 1985: 73)

And so they survived, but the harsh conditions took a huge toll on women because they experienced severe weight loss while pregnant women miscarried, malnourished children developed kwashiorkor, and babies died because their mothers were unable to breastfeed them (Likimani, 1985: 74). Further, the author narrates the mistreatment of women by home guards, "and the way the women were forced to work no matter what their physical condition, whether feeding a baby, pregnant, or sick. But the glory of the women was continued" (Likimani, 1985: 61). This story is a harrowing account of the indomitable spirit of Kenyan women whose solidarity forms the bedrock of survival for their families and communities. The ending of the story presents horrible irony because colonial officers received promotions for "fostering such high communal spirit" (Likimani, 1985: 74). This is disturbing because of the human suffering, disease, and trauma experienced by Kenyan people in their own land.

The courage and unflinching spirit of women are also displayed in the story by a woman called Wambui when her son is badly wounded for violently resisting colonial officers. When he is beaten and thrown in prison, she challenges the guards by demanding to see her son. When she is rebuked:

> Wambui bent in front of these men, took hold of a handful of soil. She smelt it as if it was something precious, like a woman smelling a new perfume...Then she smelt the soil in her hands again, put it in her mouth and chewed it. Then said, "Whatever I go through, no matter how I suffer, I suffer for this soil. The soil is ours!"
>
> (Likimani, 1985: 70–71)

Moreover, Wambui threatens to strip naked as a form of a curse, described as "the nastiest abuse one can expect from a Kikuyu woman. It is the worst curse one can expect" (Likimani, 1985: 71). When she began stripping, the policemen ran away. Unfortunately, her son is detained for interrogation and Wambui simply departs for home.

The story is a vivid rendering of unity, sharing, and sacrifice in the interest of collective survival for people in the village of Kamuri. The communal nature of Kenyan and African societies was the basis for collective survival strategies during the state of emergency in the nation.

The third story in the collection is "Kariokor Location" in Nairobi and Likimani confirms the authenticity of this account that describes the people's vulnerability to the wrath of home guards who were loyal to the colonial government. The abuse of authority and power by home guards represents the colonial strategy of divide and rule that was effective with horrific consequences among communities in Kenya. Throughout the novel, home guards exhibit dishonesty, violence and brutality, personal revenge, and sometimes arbitrary actions against those suspected of Mau Mau loyalties. "Kariokor Location" is the story of Wanjiku who has a baby as well as the victimization of Nyamburu who had been helping her when she was in labor. Nyamburu is caught and questioned by the police for not having a passbook, breaking the curfew laws, and being caught in the wrong house. These "offenses" were punishable by prison or detention camp. This story is a painful account of how innocent people were brutalized and traumatized as their humanity is completely denied. A pregnant woman is crying out during labor, and when her husband leaves home to seek help from another woman, the home guards beat him up and question him. Nyambura is detained and falsely labeled a dangerous woman to be repatriated to her village. The treatment of both women displays their vulnerability to abuse because of the intersection of race, class, and gender. Wanjiku is sent to a maternity hospital and the events surrounding her labor are distorted in the news media.

Women's comradeship emerges when Eunice, the head midwife at the hospital, makes the decision to rescue Wanjiku. While observing Wanjiku's isolation:

> She remembered how that poor woman was brought in by the guards, the baby almost dropping out. There she was, not knowing where her husband was. Since she came to the hospital no one had brought her anything. Poor Wanjiku, she did not even know where her children were, neither did she know that her husband was in the news at lunch time; that he was awaiting interrogation. "Poor girl. And for me to allow her to get into more problems! Not me! I would rather die! I am not going to betray a woman like myself. And a mother, too-an African mother. Not me!"
>
> (Likimani, 1985: 89)

Eunice comforts Wanjiku, discloses her Kikuyu ethnicity, and says she will help her to escape:

So Wanjiku, listen. I want you to run away from here because these
people want you for questioning, and you know even if they don't find
anything wrong with you, some guards are never satisfied before they
lock you in.

(Likimani, 1985: 90)

Wanjiku is given clothing and successfully escapes although she does not
return to her home in Kariokor Location to see her children. In the darkness,
she walked with her baby to a place called Bahati, known as a site of Mau
Mau activities. Wanjiku disguises herself as a Muslim and remains there until
her husband is released. Eventually, she is reunited with her husband and
children at his village. This story evokes powerful confirmation of the self-
less behaviors of women through secrecy, sharing, courage, and sisterhood.
Feminist agency underpins their actions in the spirit of collective survival
and the cause of national liberation from colonial oppression. The family-
centered values of African culture act as a unifying strength of the communal
environment under siege from foreign control.

The last story in the collection is "Hero's Welcome," which vividly expresses
the power of women's concerted efforts to create a leader through sponsoring
education overseas for promising young males. "Hero's Welcome" portrays
a male protagonist although his mother Wanjiru and other women in the
village are exemplary in their cooperative efforts to promote and champion
him as a future leader of their community. Wanjiru looks forward to his
return from studying overseas. She expresses her spirit of resistance when
she rejects the Christian form of prayer in favor of the "God of her ancestors
who dwells not in heaven but in Mount Kenya" (Likimani, 1985: 187). The
narrator notes that:

Wanjiru decided not to pray to the God of that European teacher.
Instead, she put her open hands close and side by side, as if ready to
receive millet porridge. She then turned her face from the skies and
looked to the northern side to face Mount Kenya. Despite the missionary's harassing word, God took care of my son when he left, and I am
sure he will take care of him when he comes back.

(Likimani, 1985: 187)

Women are indeed the backbone of the local community, and Likimini
affirms that: "it was the women who initiated, planned, and organized the
raising of funds for those clever and promising young men-and later women.
Communities found that they could make future leaders this way" (Likimani,
1985: 185). Mama Rebecca is the leader of the women's group, and although
a large amount of money was intimidating:

She called together all the people of the village and explained the need
to educate their son overseas. For the fight we are fighting we need to

educate Joseph overseas. For the fight we are fighting we need to prepare one who will take the whites' places when they leave.

(Likimani, 1985: 189)

Through Mama Rebecca's leadership and ingenuity, funds are raised through
her solicitations from people in the community. She knew the political implications for nation-building and imagined the promise of education for future
leaders.

Kamau is sent abroad, and after four years, when he is expected to return
home, the women pool their efforts again to plan a huge welcome for him
and Mama Rebecca announces to the women:

We must plan a welcoming for Kamau our son. We must prepare an
African cloth for him, to be presented to him and be worn by him as
soon as he approaches the airport gate. We must give him a shield and
a spear to fight for our country and the shield to protect it. ... We shall
meet him in thousands as we sent him off.

(Likimani, 1985: 191)

The welcome activities are well planned and executed effectively.

The events in the remainder of the story center on Kamau and his re-entry
into his local community. The story takes an unfortunate turn when having
been away for four years Kamau returns to his village which in his absence is
completely transformed by the colonial government. His community is essentially a prison camp marred by restricted movements, identification cards, displacement, curfews, victimization, and violence by home guards and police.
Kamau is incredulous, and at every turn, he questions the draconian policies that he encounters. His presence creates mounting tension and suspicion
among the authorities, and eventually, he is summoned for questioning and
his home is searched by the home guards and police. When nothing is found,
Kamau is released. In the presence of Mama Rebecca, he states: "I must now
take that Mau Mau oath.[4] It is a shame that I never took one. I must be a real
Mau Mau" (Likimani, 1985: 207). The story illustrates women's leadership,
unity, and their capacity to imagine a future for their nation after independence. Nationhood and nation-building are salient themes of post-coloniality
expressed through the feminist agency of women committed to the creation
of effective leadership from a son of the soil.

In *Passbook F.47927*, Kenyan women's strength and solidarity emerge
through their identities as women, ethnicity, and their personal characteristics. The first story in the collection bears the same title that introduces the
fluid and shifting identities of women caught in the grip of repressive colonial policies. One of the most oppressive regulations was the requirement
of "passbooks" that were also used in South Africa during the Apartheid
era. These were identification cards mandated by the colonial government to

monitor and control the movements of suspected members of ethnic groups: namely, the Kikuyu, Meru, and the Embu because these groups belonged to or secretly supported the Mau Mau rebellion as a threat to the colonial authorities. Possession of a passbook conferred legal status that determined employment and legal documentation to remain in Nairobi. The story uncovers the ways in which gender determines a person's status, and the author notes that:

> Many women did not qualify for a passbook. They often turned for help to men whose own wives were living on farms. These city women would pretend to be wives to the single men, sharing the same houses. They became known as Passbook wives.
>
> (Likimani, 1985: 42)

The process for getting a passbook were long and tedious, and required an interrogation by the authorities. *Passbook F.47927* unfolds around a woman named Wacu who experiences the privilege of employment as a domestic worker in Nairobi. She had no passbook and had run away from her husband. Wacu reflects:

> living in Nairobi is impossible without a passbook. To get a passbook I have to get a letter from my employer or have a husband to sign for me. My employer is out of the country. A husband I don't have. And to go back to the village I would rather die.
>
> (Likimani, 1985: 50)

Time is running out for her to acquire the passbook, and in desperation, she approaches an old boyfriend, Irungu, for help. He assisted by allowing her to live in his house as his wife lived in his village. He promised to take her to apply for a passbook. She is successful after a long, tedious, and humiliating process.

The story takes an unfortunate turn when Wacu leaves her passbook inside the house while she is washing at the communal water tap. A policeman on patrol demands to see her passbook and accuses her of being one of the "Prostitutes who feed Mau Maus" (Likimani, 1985: 54). She is taken away with many others, but luckily, her new husband Irungu brought her passbook to the authorities, and she is released. The fact that she is helpless because of her gender underscores women's unequal status in society because their identity is subsumed under patriarchal authority which extends to legal documentation. Women's identity is thus defined in relation to males. In the twenty-first century, in Nigeria and some African nations, a woman needs her husband's permission to obtain a passport, to work or to travel. This is a violation of women's and human rights, and in *Passbook.F47927*, sometimes both women and men were detained by the colonial authorities and questioned even when they held passbooks. Women's inability to determine their legal status, move about freely, and maintain their autonomy in Kenyan society was exacerbated by the colonial government.

Passbook F.47927 also highlights increased security measures in the midst of rising tensions during the national Emergency because Mau Mau freedom fighters, perceived as "terrorists" by the colonial government, stage an attack on the home guards. In response, further draconian measures were taken against the Kikuyu, Meru, and Embu people such as requirements that they report their movements. In addition, these groups were forbidden to ride motorbikes and to ride together in a car. These conditions are similar to the slave codes that existed in the American south as methods to monitor and control the movements of enslaved people. Restrictions included written permission to leave the plantation, forbidding firearms, and preventing people from gathering in groups.

Komerera is another story in the collection that foregrounds the fluid nature of women's identity in response to oppression, severe hardship, and emotional trauma. Komerera is a Kikuyu word that means "lie low, keep out of trouble" (Likimani, 1985: 92). The term connotes a survival strategy encouraged by Kenyans during colonization when their lives were at risk.

The women portrayed in the story emerge as heroic figures because their actions disrupt the practice of "Komerera" in very dramatic ways. In this inspiring account, Likimani illustrates "the determination and cunning that women demonstrated during the revolt" (Likimani, 1985: 92). Like Wambui in the story, "Communal Labor," the women convey deep ties to the soil. Three women characters risk their lives, demonstrate enormous courage, and: "Yet out of each person's terror and frustration we see growing a sense of community, of the need to work for all if anyone was to survive" (Likimani, 1985: 93). The story describes the bitter conditions of forced communal labor where the women are separated from their menfolk, concerned about their children, and fearful for the Mau Mau freedom fighters in the forests. Moreover, Likimani conveys the emotional toll and decline in the women's overall health as a result of malnutrition and harsh working conditions carrying water for the home guards.

Nyakio, Njeri, and Nduta are distraught because they have not seen their husbands in years. They comfort each other, and more importantly, they devise a plan of escape to Nairobi. The journey is very dangerous, and they start walking barefoot, in search of their husbands through the forests and rough terrain for over one hundred miles. Likimani narrates their bravery and support for the Mau Mau fighters that they encounter in the forest, revealing that Nyakio has taken the oath and in the past had organized the delivery of food and medical supplies to the fighters. Nyakio was the leader of the *githeri* operation to support the Mau Mau movement. Kanogo describes women's contribution:

The collection of food and its delivery to the freedom fighters was a major logistical operation, necessitating centralized organization. A woman leader would gather information about the guerilla requirements either directly from the guerillas at pre-arranged meetings, or from her "field workers". With the help of assistants, the leader would mobilize "initiated women (those under oath) to collect food. After preparation, the food would be put into Kikuyu baskets (*Ciondo*) and water-pots (*Ndigithu*) and dispatched at pre-arranged times by appointed women. To avoid suspicion by home guards, they concealed the food by covering it with goat manure."

(qt. in Oduol, 1993: 172)

Throughout the dangerous and unpredictable journey, the women use their cunning, wit, and intelligence to get past the home guards, to receive assistance from villagers along the way, and to continue undetected through dangerous territory. Since they secretly support the rebellion, they use words and signs that are recognizable only to Mau Mau supporters. When they finally reach Nairobi by train, Nyakio learns that her husband died after a severe beating. Nyakio goes into hiding with a man and eventually becomes a passbook wife. Njeri learned that her husband was detained, and through lies and pretense, she finds her way back home. Nduta is reunited with her husband and, eventually, her son comes to live with them. The story unfolds the plight of women who suffer untold anguish, suffering, and dehumanization. Under these conditions, marriage and family life can barely survive and the fragments of emotional ties wear thin in the effort to survive. Emotional trauma became the norm among women who had little control over much of their existence as colonial subjects. Likimani recreates their voices to provide important insight into women's thoughts, feelings, and sheer determination to not only survive but to support and protect others who are trapped in the brutal and repressive machinery of the British colonial government. "Komerera" is a riveting story of women's remarkable courage in the midst of the national emergency period in Kenya's turbulent years prior to independence.

"Unforgotten Flames" profiles a woman named Mumbi who discovers Mau Mau fighters concealed in her vegetable garden. Her actions demonstrate women's identity during the rebellion through her inventiveness and resourceful behaviors. Her loyalty to the revolution compels her to hide them at the risk of her own safety. The fighters are planning an attack on the home guard post and require her assistance. When she offers to help, she is told:

This can be a very dangerous thing for you and your family too. If such a thing happens in this village, everybody will suffer the repercussions! Curfew will be added, and we shall be badly victimized...Now our first demand is that you shut your mouth about us, tell no one about us. Second, you must find us a hiding place and feed us, failure to help us will put you in the group of traitors.

(Likimani, 1985: 118)

Through Mumbi's assistance, the freedom fighters are safely hidden and fed in her mother-in-law's home. Likimani vividly describes how the attack on the home guards post was planned over several days and successfully executed. In retaliation, many homes were destroyed by the authorities, but Mumbi and her mother-in-law escape to safety with no one ever knowing it was they who hid and fed the freedom fighters. The significance of women's contribution is critical, and although the setting of this account is not a squatters' village in the White Highlands, the sentiments of the settlers vividly express the perception of women rebels in the struggle:

> The settlers worried not only about squatter men and their violence, but also about squatter women and the way they supported their men in the Mau Mau struggle. Not only did they act as go-betweens and carriers of food and firearms, but they also generally provided a brazen system of intelligence which was hard to keep eliminated.
>
> (Kanago, 1987: 143)

The strategies employed by the two women involve courage, secrecy, and cunning, and having taken the oath of loyalty, the women ensured the survival of the freedom fighters. Wilhemina A. Uduol confirms that:

> It is therefore not an exaggeration to say that the entire Mau Mau guerilla warfare would not have lasted as long as it did if women had not made various sacrifices to keep their men alive as they fought the oppressors.
>
> (1993: 172)

The story "Forgotten Flames" acknowledges the brave actions of women to support the Mau Mau rebellion that ended in the burning of their homes. The final words of the story are memorable: "Always with such pain, with such suffering, did the food for the fighters in the forest have safe delivery, and the soil remained ours" (Likimani, 1985: 131).

Nyokabi is the protagonist of "The Squatter's Tragedy" that narrates the unfortunate punishment of a woman whose unbroken spirit of resistance denotes her Kikuyu identity and support for the rebellion. The account unfolds a tale of displacement, trauma, and dehumanization inflicted by colonial authorities. One of the worst abuses of colonization was the appropriation of African lands by European settlers in diverse nations in Africa during the colonial era in the late nineteenth and early twentieth century. In Kenya, the Europeans settled in the most fertile areas known as the White Highlands. Likimani describes these vast landscapes that sometimes stretched for thousands of acres. Squatters were local people who lived and worked for low wages on these estates. During the state of emergency, Mau Maus attacked these farms, and to protect the Europeans, squatters were brutally rounded up and dumped into relocation camps. The method of collecting entire villages was dehumanizing as people were wrenched from their homes without warning as police swooped down on men, women, and children as if they were herding animals. Children were separated from their parents, while relatives and loved ones were lost amidst the mangled emotions and psychological trauma.

Nyokabi's untimely workday on the farm unravels a terrible fate for her because when she returns to her village, she is shocked to find it empty. After calling out for her children, she is distraught and tries to commit suicide. A watchman explains the events to her and informs the authorities that she was left behind. The story ends badly because home guards arrive to transport Nyokabi to join the others at camp. When she is questioned, she spits in the home guards' face screaming "Kill me! I don't want to live! Shoot me, you have your guns! Don't waste time!" (Likimani, 1985: 141). She is beaten and raped by four men and eventually taken to a detention camp, having been accused as a Mau Mau gang leader and described by a home guard as one of the most dangerous women ... She fights like an injured lioness (Likimani, 1985: 143). Although Nyokabi's fate is bleak and uncertain, her fighting spirit is remarkable under life-threatening conditions, and it demonstrates that she is not afraid to die.

Muthoni Likimani narrates the treatment and conditions of detained local people in the story called "The Interrogation Camp." The action centers on Githi, who is the husband of Njambi, and the story uncovers the strategies employed by the colonial authorities to track down people suspected of being Mau Mau supporters. The ruthless tactics used include arbitrarily rounding up men, checking for weapons, beatings, interrogation, castration, and torturing them to extract information about the Mau Mau revolt. They are asked whether they have taken the oath of loyalty to the rebellion. The story details the success of divide and conquer because loyalists to the colonial government could cause trouble for members of the Kikuyu, Emba, or Meru ethnic groups. Githii is tortured by being forced to sit on a red-hot wire, and seeking release from the pain, he makes up a confession to the soldiers. The story concludes on a dark note because he had no idea what the future held for himself or his family. The story of the "Interrogation Camp" represents only one type of detention site because under worsened conditions, epidemics break out and cause massive illness, suffering, and death among prisoners.

"Vanishing Camp" is a recollection of this deadly site of suffering as well as an account of the resourcefulness and courage of the female protagonist. Likimani recalls the similarities between characters in the story and her own life because she is a Kikuyu married to a medical doctor. In this story, Nyaruai is a midwife who has been working and living at Msambweni General Hospital with her husband Mwacharo. This location was considered dangerous as a site of strong Mau Mau presence. The colonial authorities detained many Kikuyu people at a place called Mitaboni Detention Camp under horrible conditions such as poor food, polluted water, and below-standard facilities. The narrator describes the terrible and life-threatening conditions of the detainees:

> The skin of many detainees became covered with blisters and sores particularly on those parts constantly exposed to the hot sun of the coast. They grew weak, their tongues and the corners of their mouths became swollen and sore; they suffered through days of diarrhea and vomiting. The detainees lost energy and hope. Their minds became confused and full of depression. They lay waiting for their fate-death-hopeless, emaciated, diseased, distraught, in the middle of a jungle surrounded by animals hungry, waiting to feast on their flesh.
>
> (Likimani, 1985: 163)

Nyaruai's husband is sent to the camp to improve conditions, and when she visits him, she learns of the life-threatening conditions of the diseased prisoners who are mostly Kikuyu like herself.

The highlight of the story is Nyaruai's ingenuity that results in letters being smuggled out to England, vast improvement and decrease in disease suffering, and the movement of freedom fighters out of the Detention Camp to a hospital. She convinces her husband to execute this plan so that eventually her husband Macharo: "ordered health checks of the entire camp. Many were declared healthy, but some were recommended for outside hospitalization" (Likimani, 1985: 182).

In this way:

> It was not long before the hospital was turned into a freedom fighters compound. The sick detainees started preaching their aims and objectives. The soil is theirs, it is high time they ruled themselves. Look at the discrimination; see your standard of living. Compare yours and that of your white masters. Compare your salaries, compare how you are housed and how they are housed. Listen to the stories of how these colonialists are killing and making our fellow African suffer. We need all of you. You must join the freedom fighters, support them morally and physically, contribute all you can. The sick detainees continued preaching until many people were convinced.
>
> (Likimani, 1985: 183)

Moreover, oath-taking ceremonies were held in Nyaruai's room, and with her support, letters were sent to England and to the media overseas exposing the horrible conditions at the camp.

As a Mau Mau stronghold, the detainees achieved a significant impact because of the improved conditions along with an investigation of the site by the colonial authorities. The narrator confirms that the Europeans remained unaware of the source of the leakage which was a successful covert operation. The story emphasizes the solidarity of colonized Kenyans as well as the agency of a woman whose ideas and strategies became the groundwork for concerted resistance among the detainees. Nyaruai's interventions ignited the efforts to mitigate human suffering among those detained in what became essentially a death camp.

In sum, Muthoni Likimani's *Passbook F.47927* animates the stories of women's contribution to the Mau Mau struggle in Kenya. The collection is a vivid rendering of the ways in which art is a mirror of life as expressed in the authentic accounts of women participants in the anti-colonial movement during the 1950s. Women's identity, solidarity, and courageous actions pervade the stories in the collection to explore the complexities of women's roles and status in the movement as well as in local communities. The work is a richly textured narration of Kenyan women's experiences in marriage, and as mothers and caregivers within local their environment that were distorted by the colonial intrusion. Especially poignant are the stories of mothers who lost babies or were separated from their children through displacement or detention. Women were forced to care for their children in the absence of their husbands who were detained, imprisoned, or dead. Jean O'Barr attests that: "*Passbook F.47927* both affirms the place of women in Mau Mau as it has been previously described by men and extends the analysis of women's involvement by documenting the diverse motivations women had and the numerous tasks they undertook" (1985: 30). The stories "Forced Communal Labor," "Kariokor Location," and "Komerera" highlight the difficulties and complexities of balancing communal work, childcare, and survival under the severe and inhumane restrictions by the colonial government. Moreover, along with women's everyday tasks was their assistance to the freedom fighters as portrayed in "Unforgotten Flames" and "Vanishing Camp." In "Hero's Welcome," women demonstrate that they are the backbone of their communities through the power of collective actions, and their solidarity illustrates their vision for Kenya's future after independence from Britain. Women were compelled to renegotiate their legal status and mobility by becoming passbook wives as a strategy for their survival in the lead story *Passbook F.47927* when the colonial government created passbook laws. Because of their gender, women's subordinate status made them vulnerable to being labeled prostitutes or repatriation to their villages.

As a work of historical fiction, *Passbook F.47927* is a corrective to the absence of women's recollections of their role in the Mau Mau revolt. It provides a composite profile of women's enormous contributions to the revolt as a testimony of their resilience, solidarity, courage, and intelligence as actors in defense of their nation during the Mau Mau era. The work is a postcolonial classic that is written from women's perspectives on gender, race, oppression, patriarchy, and national liberation. The words "the soil is ours" frame the patriotic sentiments of women who were fearless in their support for Mau Mau rebels in the anti-colonialist movement.

Notes

1 Jean O'Barr wrote the introductory essay of *Passbook F.47927* that provides a historical and political account of the anti-colonial movement. The Introduction highlights the social, economic, and political background of Kenyan women in society.
2 Official dates of the Mau Mau rebellion are 1952–1956. The insurrection included guerilla or forest fighters who stage attacks on colonial authorities and their Kenyan supporters such as the home guards.
3 The State of Emergency was declared on October 21, 1952, by the British colonial government in response to the insurrection that was termed terrorism. The government employed military and police forces against the Mau Mau movement.
4 Oath-taking was a ritual by Kenyan people who supported the Mau Mau anti-colonial movement. People who had taken the oath swore allegiance to the liberation of Kenya from colonial domination.

Works Cited

Kanogo, Tabitha. 1987. *Squatters and the Roots of Mau Mau*. London and Nairobi. James Currey Ltd.

Likimani, Muthoni. 1985. *Passbook F.47927*. London. Macmillan Publishers.

———. 1974a. *They Shall Be Chastised*. Nairobi. Kenya Literature Bureau.

———. 1974b. *What Does a Man Want*. Nairobi. Kenya Literature Bureau.

———. 1985. *Women of Kenya*. Nairobi. Noni's Publicity.

———. 1990. "Muthoni Likimani". Interview. *Their Own Voices*. ed. Adeola James. London. James Currey Ltd. pp. 58–62.

———. 2005. *Fighting Without Ceasing*. Nairobi. Noni's Publicity.

Maughm-Brown, David. 1988. "Mau Mau Facts and Fiction". *The Journal of African History*. Vol. 29, No. 2. pp. 354–355.

Mwangi, Evan. 2020. "The Incomplete Rebellion: Mau Mau Movement in Twenty-First Century Kenyan Popular Culture". *Africa Today*. Winter Vol. 57, No. 2. pp. 86–113.

O'Barr, Jean. 1985. "Introductory Essay". *Passbook F.47927*. London. Macmillan Publishers. pp. 1–37.

Oduol, Wilhemina. A. 1993. "Kenyan Women in Politics: An Analysis of Past and Present Trends". *Transafrican Journal of History*. Vol. 22. pp. 166–181.

White, Luise, 1990. "Separating the Men from the Boys: Constructions of Gender, Sexuality, and Terrorism in Central Kenya, 1939–1959". *The International Journal of African Historical Studies*. Vol. 23. pp. 1–25.

4 Postcolonial Disjunctures and Urban Spaces in Amma Darko's *Faceless*

Amma Darko's *Faceless* (2003) narrates a journey into the dark underbelly of urban Accra to uncover the complexities of female identity shaped by social, economic, and political forces of oppression in modern Ghana. This chapter highlights Darko's account of moral decay and sexploitation of children in modern Accra. The title of the novel expresses the tragic dimensions of commodification and violence against children trapped within an unforgiving environment that robs them of childhood innocence while eroding their humanity in society. Like Darko's earlier novels, women characters take center stage in ways that form a composite sketch of female subjugation across spatial boundaries that demarcate abandonment and neglect. Darko's fictional works include her debut novel *Beyond the Horizon* (1998) and *Housemaid* (1999) that firmly establish her as one of Ghana's most important writers. Her novels stand tall among the fictional works of Ghanaian female icons such as Efua Sutherland, Ama Ata Aidoo, and contemporary author Yaa Gyasi. Darko's works draw attention to pressing issues that arise in the post-independence landscape of Ghana from the late twentieth to the twenty-first century. According to Angsotinge, Dako, Denkabe, and Yitah:

> Amma Darko's writing reflects the angst in contemporary Ghanaian society-they echo the stories that we read daily in the Ghanaian press. The headlines scream of abandoned babies, brutalized and murdered women; wives, mothers, daughters, sisters, girlfriends of ritual executions, of incest and rape, of sale of children, of child labor and of a general degeneration of society into one of oppression and violence.
>
> (2007: 86)

In drawing the reader's attention to the glaring issue of sexploitation and abuse, Darko challenges the government, society at large, fathers, and mothers to live up to the commitment to provide a promising future for Ghana's children. Through the lens of gender, Darko narrates the plight of women that struggle to survive in the subaltern spaces of Accra that often become sites of crippling adversity and uncertainty for females and children.

The vivid portrayal of non-rural life in African literature is a reoccurring trope in postcolonial writing that examines the debilitating effects of urban

DOI: 10.4324/9781003350200-6

settings on people and communities, culture, values, and social and economic outcomes. Amma Darko's *Faceless* resonates intertextual elements
with early as well as twenty-first-century African writing through interrogation of the pernicious effects of urban life on African subjects. Salient among
the genre in the mid-twentieth century are Cyprian Ekwensi's *People of the
City* (1953) and *Jagua Nana* (1961). In these works, the Lagos city-scape
is the setting for all manner of unseemly behaviors among those seeking
new opportunities for upward mobility. Critical to understanding the complexity of Lagos in Nigerian novels is the conceptualization of the city as
a *dystopian landscape*, emerging in fictionalized accounts with the appearance of the city as almost a "character" in the works. Ekwensi's *People of
the City* unravels a tapestry of characters whose lives intersect against the
urban background of a bustling, disjointed, competitive, and debilitating
swirl of detrimental forces. The novel opens with the epigraph "How the
city attracts all types and how the unwary must suffer from ignorance of its
ways." The city is thus personified as an antagonistic site of uncertainty and
struggle to survive against all odds.

The work unfolds through the perceptions of the protagonist, Amusa
Sango, a journalist and musician. He makes a living as a crime reporter who
chronicles unsavory criminal activity in the dangerous but exciting environment of the city. Seen through Sango's experiences, the city is described as
a pulsating vortex of multifarious characters, seduced by the lure of fast
money, amenities, sophistication, and exuberance offered by Lagos life.
Sango must skillfully navigate numerous disappointments, setbacks, and dangerous encounters in the uncertain battle to subsist. The city is thus a breed-
ing ground for immorality, political corruption, and all manner of crooked
strategies to eke out a living. Faced with poverty, life in Lagos brings out
the worst human qualities as people cheat, lie, and steal to survive. Amma
Darko's *Faceless* echoes these negative perceptions through the behaviors
of both female and male characters who sink into moral depravity in the
quest for survival. Like the characters in Ekwensi's novels, Darko's *Faceless*
explores the depths of human depravity in the cruel environment of Accra
street life.

In the twenty-first century, leading female writers such as Chimamanda
Ngozi Adichie, in *Purple Hibiscus* (2003), Sefi Atta, in *Everything Good Will
Come* (2006) and *Swallow* (2008), continue to disprove the myth that urban
environments confer material success, wellbeing, and security in the global
age. Rather, African characters in these works experience new configurations of identity, challenges to survival, and abrasive realities of their status
as marginalized others. The unwholesome nature of the Lagos metropolis
draws the characters into spiraling confusion and uncertainty against the
backdrop of the Nigerian landscape fraught with social, economic, and political upheaval in the post-independence era. For instance, Adichie's *Purple
Hibiscus* (2003) contrasts the past and the present, tradition and modernity, and changing African values in the descriptions of village life in the

hometown of her family at Nsukka. The novel illustrates the stark differences between Lagos and Nsukka through the transformative energies of coming of age, the oppressive political climate, and the disconnection from cultural moorings for Kambili and her family.

Likewise, Sefi Atta describes the unfavorable environment of Lagos and the deleterious outcomes in the lives of young female characters coming of age in her award-winning and widely acclaimed debut novel *Everything Good Will Come* (2006). This novel vividly captures the complexities of gender and class dynamics for both middle-class females like the protagonist Enitan and her childhood friend Sheri Bakare whose background is less privileged. The Lagos environment poses many challenges to women's identity, autonomy, dignity, and ultimately their economic stability. Atta's second novel *Swallow* (2010) pairs two young Nigerian women in Lagos who are helpless in the face of sexual harassment in the male-dominated rat race to eke out a living in Lagos.

Both Tolani and Rose are employed in a bank, but gender inequality and sexual harassment create barriers to gainful employment, and they are faced with few choices to survive. The tragic dimension of the novel is highlighted when, unfortunately, Rose loses her life when she becomes a drug carrier at the urging of an unsavory male character. Drug-filled balloons burst inside her body, and she dies. A strong message in the novel is the suggestion that alternative sites of employment, survival, and empowerment are possible in a rural setting. Tolani returns to her village and is reconnected to her cultural moorings and to her family. Both works underscore the inherent dangers of modern metropolis settings that entrap young women with the potential to destroy their lives.

The vulnerability of female children living in modern African cities like Lagos is further illustrated in Chika Unigwe's award-winning *On Black Sisters' Street* (2009). This novel is a vivid rendering of societal forces in the postcolonial landscape that drive unsuspecting young women into the clutches of the international sex industry. From the diaspora setting as "sisters" in the sex industry in Belgium, the four female characters each unveil their troubled urban experiences of economic adversity, sexual abuse, and violence during childhood that undermine their opportunities for success. These harsh experiences become ripe soil for recruitment as prostitutes in the seamy underbelly of the red-light district in Belgium. As each woman recalls her life, a common feature of their experiences is family problems made worse by economic adversity during childhood. Three of the women narrate instances of sexual abuse, early pregnancy, and financial stress within urban spaces. One of the young women experiences gang rape, by soldiers during an ethnic conflict in her country. An important similarity to *Faceless* is the complicity of women in the exploitation and brutality meted out to prostitutes working for a "madam" who controls them for profit, and in *Faceless*, it is sadly a mother, Mama Tsuru, along with other women who profit from the sex work of her daughter.

NoViolet Bulawayo's *We Need New Names* (2013) is a penetrating account of neglected street children who are left to fend for themselves in Harare, the economic and politically ravaged capital of Zimbabwe during the 1980s. This highly acclaimed work closely parallels Darko's *Faceless* in the portrayal of the ways in which poverty distorts the lives of children and young women who are cornered in the margins of a failed society. Darling and her friends run the streets in search of food and in the process are exposed to harsh realities such as death, HIV Aids, and the failure of NGOs to provide solutions to their plight. One of Darling's friends is raped by her grandfather and is pregnant at age nine. Children represent the future in society, and both *We Need New Names* and *Faceless* depict a bleak outlook for many children who are Africa's most valuable resource for sustainable growth and development in the future.

Collectively, these fictional works provide insight into the dangers of urban life and the risks they pose for African girls and women. The latter years of the twentieth century ushered a dramatic increase in the numbers of street children worldwide that is well documented in the social sciences. In the introduction to *Faceless*, Kofi Anyidoho observes that:

> The phenomenon of street children has become one of the most widely discussed social tragedies of our time. We are witness to a deluge of talk about the plight of these children, from newspaper articles to radio talk shows, television documentaries and elegant academic discussions... Even Government claims to be doing its very best to tackle the problem. And yet, in spite of all these well-publicized efforts, the problem not only persists but also seems to be getting even more intractable.
>
> (Anyidoho, 2003: xix)

Moreover, in "Homes, Places, and Spaces in the Construction of Street Children and Youth,"[1] Judith Ennew and Jill Swart-Kruger document many social and economic factors that place added stress on already impoverished families as a cluster of underlying causes for the rise in street children in urban municipalities. In the twenty-first century, Georgina Yaa Oduro notes that for Ghana, the post-independence era has not realized the commitment to the welfare of children's rights and wellbeing articulated during the 1990s. According to Oduro:

> some Ghanaian youth find themselves living on the streets. Rapid urbanization, family breakdown and poverty contribute to the migration of many young people who move from impoverished rural areas to the city in order to try and make a living.
>
> (2012: 42)

Further, Oduro identifies two categories of street children in Ghana:

> children "of" the streets, refers to the "typical" Ghanaian street child who lives and works on the street, and has made the street their home.

The second, children "on" the street, comprise the urban poor children who survive daily on the street but still have family ties.

(2012: 42)

Faceless unfolds the disturbing experiences of Fofo and Baby T who are sisters and their relationship to their mother, as well as her complicity in their exploitation.

With reference to children's vulnerability to experience a range of unwholesome encounters as street children, West African countries like Ghana, along with Nigeria and Togo, represent a high incidence of abuse of children. Sossou and Yogtiba state that in 2007 the "Global Fund for Children identified West Africa as a site where "children are more likely to be raped, trafficked, beaten, or abused and are less likely to go to school, receive proper health care or be properly nourished" (2009: 1219). Mary Ellen Higgins notes that "The novel was published in the year after the Ghanaian NGO, The Center for Public Interest Law (CEPIL), called attention to over 30,000 squatters who were delivered an ultimatum to vacate their enclaves.[2] Such grim observations of displaced children living on the streets of Accra contextualize the urgent need for government intervention to tackle the complexities of urban poverty and the attendant social ills described in *Faceless*.

Mary Ellen Higgins recalls her 2003 interview with Darko where the author states that:

her stories are inspired from the Ghanaian media, in addition to research and her own imagination. She commented that her work is based "on the story of so many people. I mix them knead them and come out with my own story."

(2003: 112)[3]

Darko's realism, frequently expressed in journalistic fashion, creates the flavor of authenticism that pervades the work. Darko's creative imagination animates the novel's portrayal of postcolonial disjuncture through the interrogation of Ghana's failure to address the commitment to alleviate poverty of her citizens.

Although *Faceless* is a fictional work, Darko clearly implicates the failure of the Ghanaian government to address the urgent plight of the nation's most vulnerable citizens who are children and women. Sossou and Yogtiba conclude that:

The abuse and neglect of children in the West African sub-region is one of the most serious violations of social justice and an abuse of the rights of children. Irrespective of the prevailing socio-economic conditions in the sub-region, the best interests of all children should be the priority of West African governments through the provision of adequate resources to ensure the healthy development of children.

(2009: 1231)

Diverse perspectives of life in the city reveal postcolonial fractures within Ghana as a modern nation-state along with the social and economic liabilities for women and girls. Ato Quayson articulates the structure of *Faceless* through "spatial traversal"[4] of the characters whose movements denote socioeconomic divisions in the city (2014: 217). The contrastive sites in the novel are the slum called Sodom and Gomorrah, Kanda, a middle-class neighborhood, and Agbogbloshie Market. The work unfolds through the voices of two female protagonists, Fofo and Kabria, whose lives intersect across generational, economic, and social boundaries. The co-protagonists meet at Agbogbloshie Market as a site of new energies of collaboration, revelation, and hope for social transformation. The novel comprises three sections that cover twenty-five chapters. The work illuminates the potential for tragedy because a female child falls prey to the pitfalls that abound in spaces of economic deprivation and other social ills that endanger young lives with females at the greatest risk.

Fofo is at the center of the novel, and the postcolonial landscape of Accra exposes many layers of her life on the streets that are marked by movement from one space to another. Fofo shuttles between the Agbogbloshie marketplace and the squatters' enclave at Sodom and Gomorrah, and like the biblical appellation, it is a site of moral decay, violence, and dehumanizing experiences that plague the children who are victims of circumstances beyond their control. Quayson observes that "Sodom and Gomorrah invoke a set of ideas having to do with decadence, a raw netherworld energy, and even the potential doom and damnation that were the lot of its biblical namesakes" (2014: 254). Thus, Sodom and Gomorrah become sites of unbelonging as children suffer the effects of emotional and physical neglect from their parents and guardians. Darko describes Sodom and Gomorrah as a place of "Filth and sin, suffering and ignorance, helplessness and woes ruled the days. And caught in the middle of it all, were girls like Fofo who grew up never ever really experiencing what it means to simply be a child" (Darko 66).

Fofo and her cohorts are cast into the streets of Accra as part of a global trend in the twentieth and twenty-first centuries of rapid social, economic, and political transformation across Africa and the world. Life on the streets forces children to navigate a plethora of unwholesome and dangerous experiences such as rape, drug abuse, disease, and violence that sometimes may lead to tragic consequences as illustrated by the death of the protagonists' sister Baby T.

Darko effectively conveys the web of risk factors to children through the perceptions of Sylv Po on *Good Morning Ghana* who narrates:

> There is a lot of pain and hopelessness out there on the streets which many seek to deal with through drugs, sex, and alcohol. During a recent survey we conducted for a programme, all the girls we talked to out there were already very sexually active. And we also established that, for many of them, rape was their first sexual experience. And I

am talking about girls as young as seven. Many were child prostitutes. They had no idea at all about the extent of self- damage to themselves. Sex to them was just a convenient means of survival. Many were roaming about, oblivious to whether or not they were HIV positive, so.

(Darko, 2003: 32)

The social, emotional, and physical trauma inflicted on children by life on the streets shows the government's lack of political will to structure policies that benefit the burgeoning urban demographic that remains trapped at the bottom of the economic ladder.

Faceless opens with jarring realism that captures the precarious existence of adolescent street children in Accra. The young protagonist awakens after spending the night on a piece of flattened cardboard in front of a store at the Agbogbloshie market. Sleeping in the open is a survival strategy adopted as protection from an assault during the night. This is an added strain on the emotional and psychological wellbeing of children who must fend for themselves in the absence of parental care and security. The dysfunctional families of children like Fofo thrust them into dangerous exposure to adult life, and she recalls "Life on the streets made mixed-up persons out of children" (Darko, 2003: 21).

The narrator of *Faceless* observes that:

A part of Fofo was and would always remain the fourteen years that she was; but the harshness of life on the streets has also made a premature adult of part of her. She was both a child and an adult and could act like both; talk like both; think like both and feel like both.

(Darko, 2003: 22)

Noted critic Kofi Anyidoho, in the introduction to *Faceless*, asserts that:

In *Faceless*, as in *The Housemaid* we find the children thinking and speaking and acting above their age. This should not surprise us. Having been abandoned to the streets, each one of them has had to grow too quickly into the ways of the world in order to take up for themselves those responsibilities their parents have turned their backs on. For many of these children, thinking, talking, and indeed acting "grown up" is a necessary skill for survival in a ruthless world.[5]

(2003: xv)

Fofo's adult traits are displayed in the novel in the way that she speaks assertively to adults, especially to her mother, when she challenges her for her failed mothering, and complicity in the plight of her sister Baby T. An ironic twist of fate occurs when, in the heated exchange, Fofo assumes moral authority over her mother as a reversal of the natural order of parent and child relations. Anyidoho aptly notes that "for many of these children, thinking, talking, and indeed acting 'grown-up' is a necessary skill for survival in a ruthless world" (2003: xv). Moreover, Fofo's mature analysis of her situation is clear-eyed when she tells the NGO workers at MUTE that she wants to meet with "Government"! "I said government. I want government" (2003: 47).

These are not the ideas of a childish mind but rather the astute expression of a victim of poverty who identifies and challenges the political machinery of post-independent Ghana. Anyidoho observes that:

> Fofo, in her innocence, insists that she wants to see Government; she cannot think of anyone in her world to take up their case, especially the case of her sister Baby T. What she doesn't know is that Government itself has lost its priorities, its sense of direction; it has become dysfunctional and deaf to the cries of children abandoned or sold to the merciless street lords of the Poison kind, and their equally heartless female collaborators such as Maami Broni.
>
> (2003: xvii)

When the women at MUTE question Fofo about why she wants government, she responds, "because it is the government who had the power to make people do or stop doing certain things" (Darko, 2003: 79). The author's social commentary is especially poignant in the novel because the message is spoken by a child. Further, Fofo's heightened consciousness about the political dimensions of her plight illustrates an important feature of feminist consciousness/awakening. Thus, Darko's social critique serves a dual purpose in the novel; calling attention to the role of Ghana's government to ameliorate crushing poverty, and secondly, giving "voice" to a powerless female child who speaks out in ways that resonate feminist agency and expression.

Darko charts the starkly ironic ways in which *home* in the novel is the initial site of *unbelonging* for children like Fofo, her sister Baby T, and her friends in Accra. Home represents a space of love, nurturing, protection, security, and belonging. For the children in *Faceless*, home is a space fraught with uncertainty, rejection, neglect, abuse, and emotional fractures with parents, most notably, with mothers such as Maa Tsuru and her friend Odarley's mother who "sacks her like a fowl when she goes to see her" (Darko, 2003: 25). The idea that children are cast out of their homes by mothers displays the extent to which economic desperation is a catalyst for reprehensible neglect and maltreatment of children living in urban squalor and decay that is both material and emotional. The role of women and mothers unfolds the gendered complexities of poverty that ravage maternal care, moral responsibility, and the bonds of love. Early in the novel, Fofo visits her mother and recalls ambivalent feelings and emotional distress:

> She often pondered over whether what she deemed to be hatred was merely a desire to cushion the pain of her existence and to blame Maa

Tsuru whom she held responsible for dumping her into the world. Because that was exactly how she felt about herself. Dumped.

(Darko, 2003: 20)

Home is also a site of unbelonging and displacement through the intrusion of patriarchal hegemony of fathers, stepfathers, and other unsavory males that disrupt domestic space and victimize women and children. Toward the end of the novel, Fofo recounts how her father "entered mother's life and pushed us all out of it!" She began, "First my two older brothers, then Baby T, then me" (Darko 2003: 157). Further, Maa Tsuru is indeed to blame because of a series of events that causes emotional agony, sexual abuse, violence, and the death of her daughter Baby T. Patriarchal violence manifests in the person of Maa Tsuru's "husband," Kpakpo, who defiles Baby T. This is abominable, and the literature on the rape of children indicates that most often the rapist is a father, uncle, or male relative. Sadly, Baby T is also molested by a neighbor, affectionately known as Onko (Uncle). A brutal and vicious character appropriately named Poison is a pimp who quite literally beats Baby T to death and disfigures her face and body as well.

Moreover, home is a site of unbelonging for Baby T because Maa Tsuru sells her into prostitution from which she earns a profit. Quayson confirms the absence of normal familial bonds in Baby T's homelife because:

an older prostitute she is given to reside with prevents her from establishing any natural relationships with her family or friends. Her life is absolutely devoid of privacy, much less of the shared rituals that allow for the constitution of any forms of familiarity.

(2003: 223)

Essentially, the homelife of both Fofo and Baby T is dysfunctional on multiple levels, and out of fear that she may end up like her sister, Fofo runs away from home to the street as a perceived site of freedom from danger. Thus, for the children in *Faceless*, "unbelongingness" begins at home. The idea that the street offers young females some measure of safety from abuse in the domestic space connects to Saadawi's Firdaus (although she was age nineteen) in *Woman at Point Zero* (Saadawi, 1987). Firdaus runs away from home and into the streets several times in the novel to escape sexual violence and abuse by male characters. The street becomes an important motif as a representational site of safety.

Before Baby T's death is revealed, Fofo narrowly escapes being raped by the violent street lord named Poison, the same man who murders and mutilates her sister. Fofo spent the night in the open space in front of a shop and is awakened when she is molested. When she fights back, she is asked "You want to live?" (Darko: 200: 4). She successfully fends him off and fortunately escapes unharmed. This incident underscores that female children living on the streets are essentially in harm's way as they navigate strategies to remain safe.

Oduro's research sheds light on the inherent dangers of life on the street for females:

A major finding from the study was the extent to which sexual abuse, in the form of single and gang rapes, were common on the street. The lack of shelter, accommodation and parental figures had compelled many street youth to sleep in open places such as "lorry stations", "in front of shops", "by roadsides", "on school compounds" and at the "cold store".

(2012: 47)

A young woman named Odarley narrates the experience of renting a place to stay each night amidst adolescents like herself: "Boys and girls together, stripped together and did things with each other, many times under the influence of alcohol, wholly unconscious of what they were doing or with whom "(Darko, 2003: 5).

Kwaku Oppong Asante, Anna Meyer-Weitz, and Inge Peterson document findings from a study in Ghana in which over 54% of the homeless youth reported having exchanged sex for food, money, or even a place to sleep, with females more likely to engage in such behaviors than males (5).

Socio-economic divisions are sharply etched in *Faceless* as Fofo and her co-protagonist Kabria meet at the Agbogbloshie Market. Dressed as a boy, Fofo attempts to steal her bag but is caught by an angry mob, ready to punish her. Kabria intervenes, and the convergence of their lives outside of Sodom and Gomorrah materializes a promising future for Fofo. Kabria's professional life, domestic responsibilities, and her socio-economic status are juxtaposed against the battered existence of Fofo in what Ato Quayson aptly articulates as "spatial traversals" (2014: 217) when their paths meet across neighboring boundaries in the landscape of Accra. Kabria's environment is the middle-class neighborhood of Kanda. She works for MUTE, a non-governmental organization that specializes in the investigation of the status of women and children in Accra. The narrator describes MUTE as "just that: MUTE. As in silence. Not an acronym" (Darko, 2003: 38). Kabria's work entails investigative reporting about gender and children in Accra. Led by Kabria and her co-workers, MUTE forms a collaboration with a media broadcaster named Sylv Po who hosts a radio program called "Good Morning Ghana."

Darko's portrayal of Kabria's life is a compelling representation of gender inequality expressed when she is described as:

The mother, wife, worker, and battered-car owner that she was, no day passed that Kabria didn't wonder how come the good Lord created a day to be made up of only twenty-four hours, because from dusk, domestic schedules gobbled her up; office duties ate her alive. Her three children devoured her with their sometimes realistic and many times very unrealistic demands; while the icing on the cake, their father, needed do no more than simply be your regular husband, and she was in a perpetual quandary.

(Darko, 2003: 11)

Kabria's frustration with the challenges in her life is also evident when she asks her husband for money to repair her rickety and unreliable car. Her husband Adade asks sarcastically whether she receives a salary to which she replies: "If I had had the time to study further like you did, I would also have been reaping the benefits today in terms of a better salary. But I was busy making babies then. Remember?" (Darko, 2003: 15).

The visceral imagery of being "gobbled up," "eaten alive," and "devoured" conveys the burdensome nature of her multifaceted roles and responsibilities that frequently occurs in the lives of women in Ghana, Africa, and across the globe. As Kabria points out to her husband, gender inequality reinforces the imbalance of responsibilities and intensive labor experienced by women who must navigate childrearing and domestic tasks alongside their careers and/or employment outside the home.

These tensions and contradictions resonate in the novel *Changes* (1993) by the iconic Ghanaian feminist author Ama Ata Aidoo. Esi is the protagonist in *Changes* who expresses similar frustrations with her marriage and domestic roles that she feels are a barrier to her career and self-actualization. Although Kabria's situation and complaints to her husband is not identical to those of Esi, the idea that many married women working outside the home may experience an economic disadvantage through inadequate education, or opportunities to pursue their careers is pervasive in the lives of women in Africa and beyond.

Kabria negotiates the gendered spaces in her demanding life that includes dropping her children off at school, going to work, and to the market via her decrepit vehicle she calls "Creamy." The unpredictable and frequent breakdowns of the car provide opportunities to ruminate about the urban landscape, her life, and to her embarrassment, the poor condition of Creamy that causes fuming and exasperated drivers to insult her for stalling in traffic. To Kabria, the car takes on human qualities, and at one point, she ponders whether it has a "soul." The way that she speaks to and about Creamy personifies contentious and comic reflection on her challenges to fulfill multiple roles as a woman. Ato Quayson interprets a less obvious significance of Creamy in the novel:

> it is Creamy that foregrounds the essential precariousness of the intersection between class and gender in the novel, for the car provides the constant reminder that her passage from one point to another across the cityscape is also the interweaving of the distinctive yet overlapping roles of mother, wife, and worker.

(2014: 220)

The spatial traversal across class boundaries occurs the second time Fofo and Kabria meet at the Agbogbloshie market, and this time, sadly, Fofo has been badly beaten by Poison as a warning to silence her about the death of Baby T. Kabria and her co-workers at MUTE are deeply shocked as they learn the sordid details of Fofo's life on the streets.

In collaboration with Sylv Po through his radio talk show, they embark upon a two-pronged plan of action; to solve the mystery of Baby T's death and to rehabilitate Fofo. They plan to visit Maa Tsuru because Fofo refuses to divulge information out of fear for her safety. Dina, the director of MUTE, gives shelter to Fofo, and in the safety of Dina's home, Fofo dramatically narrates how she ended up on the streets. Her story details an inescapable cycle of hopeless poverty in the absence of her father in the home. Her mother is unable to sustain the household and both Fofo and her sister drop out of school and start to beg for food on the streets. In what is perhaps the most startling aspect of Fofo's "coming of age" to street life, she reveals that:

> Whatever money I made on the streets, I kept for myself. All of it. And I spent it as and when I wanted. The time I used to go home to sleep, mother used to take my money from me. See? So as soon as I made a friend and joined a gang, I left home for good.
>
> (Darko, 2003: 102)

As the novel unravels the mystery of Baby T's death, it acquires the flavor of a detective/crime investigation sparked by increased publicity by Harvest FM's provocative talk show, as well as the enthusiasm of Sylv Po whose interest in the case peaks during the later portion of the work. He began a series on street children based on Fofo's case. The commitment of MUTE in the investigation sustains public discourse on the endemic nature of children living on the streets. The tension is heightened by an unknown caller to the radio station who crudely suggests that Baby T is a *kayayoo* girl from Northern Ghana. These are girls who work as porters in the market.

The circumstances of Baby T's life as a prostitute are a complicated series of events leading to her entrapment by predatory male and female characters who exploit her for profit. All of the male characters in her young life rob her of her childhood, and her dignity that eventually leads to her violent and untimely death. While she is still in her mother's womb, her father Kwei tries to end her life. After brutally beating Maa Tsuru and making her bleed, he told everyone, "he had singlehandedly and very cost effectively terminated an unwanted pregnancy" (Darko, 2003: 124). Baby T survived, but as a young girl, her stepfather, Kpakpo, assaults her and later accuses Baby T of forcing herself on him because she is already sexually active. She is also raped by Onko, a man that everyone trusts as an "uncle." Finally, Poison, the pimp who ends Baby T's life, is feared by everyone, and Darko reveals his childhood of abuse by his stepfather as a cause of his violence to women and girls. Mary Ellen Higgins avers that "Poison personifies neocolonial exploitation and modern corruption; he views other humans only as a means to increase his wealth and power. He sees himself, above all other things, as a 'businessman'" (2007: 67). Darko's gripping portrait of Poison's brutality is indeed monstrous through his unbridled violence to women. Moreover, Edgar Nabutanyi contextualizes how in the post-1990 landscape, "deprivation and environment cohere to produce monsters in some African cities" (Nabutanyi 2014: 89).

Maa Tsuru's involvement in the commodification of her daughter's body is explicit when Onko offers her money earned from Baby T's sex work:

> Maa Tsuru stared long and hard at the thick wad of notes in her hand. There was a look of worry and hopelessness in her eyes and another not so easily discernable… Never once in her life had she held so much money in her hand.
>
> (Darko, 2003: 138)

She and Onko have a tense conversation as he urges her to accept the money with the promise of more to come. Eventually:

> Maa Tsuru rose abruptly. Onko's face fell. Then the corners of his lips stretched into a smile as Maa Tsuru untied her cover cloth around her waist; placed the wad of notes in one corner of it and proceeded to slowly tie it up.
>
> (Darko, 2003: 139)

In addition to Maa Tsuru's complicity in the neglect, abandonment, sexploitation, of Baby T, other older women play decisive roles in the girl's unfortunate life. She is sent to live with Mama Abidjan who sells girls into prostitution while pretending to recruit them as housekeepers. Baby T. ends up in a brothel, owned by Poison, and managed by Maami Broni an older prostitute. She accepts Baby T. into the brothel because she has been told by Kpakpo and Mama Abidjan: "She is already giving herself to men freely!… She even almost enticed her stepfather on one occasion. Poor man. He fought her off like she was the very devil" (Darko, 2003: 188). She introduces Baby T. to marijuana as "the 'devils weed'. It helped. Once Baby T began to use it regularly, carrying out her 'duty' with several men night and day became bearable. The men liked her. She was pretty and young" (Darko, 2003: 190). These actions by a mature woman are incomprehensible and disturbing, with broad implications for the breakdown of familial and cultural norms in modern urban sites of pervasive moral decay.

Notably, Darko crafts events that lead to Onko's suicide as symbolic punishment for defilement of Baby T. In "Images of Rape in African Fiction: Between the assumed fatality of violence and the cry for justice," Augustine H. Assah notes the rare instances of punishment of rapists in fictional works by African writers. The collusion of Maa Tsuru's complicity in the abuse and sexploitation of her daughter, and the fatal brutality of Onko, illustrates important features of crime fiction as posited by Assah:

from this tale of crime and punishment emerges a pattern of maternal inertia at the news of their daughters' defilement since no concrete steps are taken to dissuade rapists, still less initiate legal proceedings against them. The fate of prostitution to which mothers subject their daughters only serves to further estrange their children, worsen the victim's agony and precipitate their daughter's death.

(2007: 339)

In this context, Assah states that Darko must be commended because "In all the narratives studied, it is only in *Faceless* where civil society and due process combine to bring criminals to justice" (343). When his welding business fails, Onko hangs himself. Edgar Nabutanyi corroborates Assah's framing of *Faceless* as a crime novel: "The plot of *Faceless* is centered on the commission of crimes, their investigation and the symbolic punishment of the perpetrators" (2007: 80).

The headquarters of MUTE, the NGO appears as an important site in the novel because although it is not a neighborhood in the physical sense like Kanda, Sodom and Gomorrah, or the Agbogbloshie Market, its location in the lives of the co-protagonists engenders women's agency, collaboration, investigating the murder of Baby T., and Fofo's rescue from the streets. Kabria's movement and interactions with Fofo, Dina, and the other women form a collective effort in the interest of street children that derives from the goals of the NGO. The fact that it is an all-female organization speaks to the potential for women's empowerment at the grassroots level. Higgins corroborates this message in the novel: "Darko explores the potential for solidarity between women-for the balancing of loads -across economic and spatial divides, in addition to the prospects for collective action across gender lines" (2007: 59). Further, when Fofo and Baby T. are abandoned to the streets, it represents ruptured generational ties to parents who repudiate their roles as guardians and nurturers of children in their homes. Kabria and the other women thus represent the restoration of broken generational bonds of children to the adult world. Thus, MUTE is significant as a site of support, alliance, and consensus among women who are committed, intelligent, and actively engaged in tackling the plight of street children in urban Accra.

Amma Darko's fictional imagination has woven a tapestry of post-1990's Ghana in the throes of urban crisis as many children and youth have fallen into an abyss of poverty, and violence in the streets of Accra. The urban landscape is the setting of contrasting sites of socio-economic strata as the lives of the inhabitants intersect across boundaries that shape their lives in different ways. *Faceless* foregrounds the voices of female characters who speak their truths in ways that bridge the conventional barriers to communication between young and old, privileged, and poor, and the educated and unschooled sectors of Ghana's urban dwellers. Two female protagonists emerge as strong and resilient as they collaborate to solve the criminal investigation of the protagonists' sister who loses her life through maternal neglect, abuse, and sexploitation. In the process of unraveling the murder, Fofo paves the way for her own redemption from life on the streets to chart a promising future for herself. The concerted efforts of women disentangle the complexities of economic crises, failed government policies, and parental neglect in modern Ghana.

The structure of the novel unfurls divergent urban sites that situate the gendered nature of social and economic experiences in ways that pose challenges to survival for each of the co-protagonists. The spatial dimensions of the work foreground the sharp class divisions that wreak havoc on the urban underclass peopled by females and children as the most vulnerable citizens in Ghana. Kabria's life in a middle-class neighborhood of Kanda is juxtaposed with Fofo's precarious existence as she navigates Sodom and Gomorrah, and the Agbogbloshie Market where their lives converge. Darko's realism conveys women's inequality from multiple perspectives as Kabria navigates her role as mother and wife who must function professionally in her employment with MUTE.

Spatial elements highlight the domestic sphere as the initial site of unbelonging, neglect, and danger from predatory males for Fofo and her sister Baby T. who experiences sexual violence. Both sisters are rejected at home and end up on the streets through maternal complicity in sexploitation that ends Baby T's life and causes the disfigurement of her face and body. Life on the streets is a dangerous mix of unwholesome realities to which children are exposed as they negotiate ways to remain safe from sexual assault, hunger, neglect, and utter despair.

The Agbogbloshie Market represents the collision of alternate experiential realities for Ghanaian females as the setting for alliance between Kabria and Fofo across generational and class boundaries. MUTE represents a site of social transformation through feminist agency, activism, and investigative journalism that examine the lives of street children and child prostitution in Accra. Darko's social commentary is multifaceted through vivid rendering of the failure of Ghanaian government, society, and parents to protect children from violence, prostitution, and drugs, which disproportionately plague the lives of children left to fend for themselves in Accra and other African cities.

The solidarity exhibited by members of the all-female NGO represents Darko's belief in the potential for grassroots organizing, women's agency, and the plausibility of collusion across economic and social divisions in society. Such measures become the route to social progress in lieu of government's neglect of glaring economic disparities, social pathologies, and other dangerous ills in society. Through journalistic style, Darko effectively captures the urgent need to address the crisis of street children and child prostitution in the post-independence era in Ghana and other African cities.

Notes

1 See Special Issue of *Children, Youth and Environments*
2 See Mary Ellen Higgins, page 64
3 See Mary Ellen Higgins, page 64
4 Ato Quayson, Oxford Street. Ch. 7
5 See introduction to *Faceless* by Kofi Anyidoho

Works Cited

Adichie, Chimamanda Ngozi. 2004. *Purple Hibiscus*. Lagos. Farafina.

Angsotinge, Gervase, et al. 2007. "Exploitation, Negligence and Violence: Gendered Interrelationships in Amma Darko's Novels". *Broadening the Horizon: Critical Introductions to Amma Darko*. ed. Vincent O. Odamtten. Banbury. Ayebia Clarke Publishing Limited. pp. 81–99.

Anyidoho, Kofi. 2003. *Amma Darko's Faceless: An Introductory Essay*. Accra. Sub-Saharan Publishers. pp. ix–xxi.

Aidoo, Ama Ata. 1991. *Changes: A Love Story*. New York. The Women's Press.

Atta, Sefi. 2006. *Everything Good Will Come*. North Hampton. Interlink Books.

———. 2010. *Swallow*. North Hampton. Interlink Books.

Assah, Augustine H. 2007. "Images of Rape in African Fiction: Between the Assumed Fatality of Violence and the Cry for Justice". *Annales Aequatoria*. Vol. 28. pp. 233–355.

Asante, Kwaku Oppong, Anna Meyer-Weitz, and Inge Petersen. 2014. "Substance Use and Risky Sexual Behaviors Among Street Connected Children and Youth in Accra, Ghana". *Substance Abuse Treatment, Prevention and Policy*. http://www.substanceabusepolicy.com/conent/9/1/45

Bulawayo, NoViolet. 2013. *We Need New Names*. New York. Regan Arthur Books.

Darko, Amma. 2003. *Faceless*. Accra. Sub-Saharan Publishers.

Enew, Judith and Jill Swart-Kruger. 2003. "Homes, Places and Spaces in the Construction of Street Children and Street Youth". *Children, Youth and Environments*. Spring Vol. 13, No. 1. pp. 81–104.

Ekwensi, Cyprian. 1953. *People of the City*. London. Andrews Dakers Ltd.

———. 1966. *Jagua Nana*. London. Heinemann.

Higgins, Mary Ellen. 2007. "*Ngambika* and Grassroots Fiction: Amma Darko's *The Housemaid and Faceless*". Broadening the Horizon: Critical Introductions to Amma Darko. ed. Vincent O. Odamtten. Banbury. Ayebia Clarke Publishing Limited. pp. 58–70.

Nabutanyi, Edgar. 2014. "Documenting Child Prostitution in Amma Darko's *Faceless*". *English in Africa*. Vol. 41, No. 2. pp. 79–93.

Odamtten, Vincent O. ed. 2007. *Broadening the Horizon: Critical Introductions to Amma Darko*. Banbury. Ayebia Clarke Publishing Limited.

Oduro, Georgina Yaa. 2012. "Children of the Street: Sexual Citizenship and the Unprotected lives of Ghanaian Street Youth". *Comparative Education*. Vol. 48, No. 1, Special Issue (43): Youth, Citizenship and the Politics of Belonging. pp. 41–56.

Saadawi, Nawal El. 1983. *Woman at Point Zero*. New York. Zed Books.

Sossou, Marie-Antoinette and Joseph A. Yogtiba. 2009. "Abuse of Street Children in West Africa: Implications for Social Work Education and Practice". *The British Journal of Social Work*. Vol. 39, No. 7. pp. 1218–1234.

Quayson, Ato. 2007. "I No Be Like You": Accra in Life and Literature". *Modern Language Association Special Topic: Cities*. pp. 252–255.

———. 2014. "'The Lettered City': Literary Representations of Accra". *Oxford Street Accra: City Life and the Itineraries of Transnationalism*. Durham. Duke University Press. pp. 213–238.

Part II
Voices from the Diaspora in African Women's Fiction

5 Unveiling Women's Identities in the African Muslim Diaspora in Leila Aboulela's *The Translator* and *Minaret*

Leila Aboulela is a Sudanese author whose Anglophone works of fiction illuminate the lives of Muslims as they navigate matters of identity, religious faith, and class dynamics within transcultural spaces of the west. Her writing mirrors much of her own experiences as a transnational subject who has lived in diverse locales such as Sudan, Britain, Egypt, Indonesia, and Qatar. Like numerous African immigrant writers, Leila Aboulela writes with insight and realism drawn from years abroad. Her experiences of hybridity and *otherness* provided insight into diaspora angst as reflected in the Muslim female characters in her fiction. After completing her undergraduate degree in Khartoum, she earned a Ph.D. in Statistics from the London School of Economics and later migrated to Aberdeen with her family. As a cultural outsider, she faced the challenges of life as a Muslim beyond her native Sudan.

This chapter illuminates the ways in which religion becomes a focal point in reconfiguring identity in the Sudanese diaspora where the protagonist is exiled. The author unveils women's cultural space through the representation of a displaced Sudanese female as she moves beyond the challenges of racial otherness in Europe to experience new forms of hybridity through Islamic faith, unfulfilling relationships with males, and memory of home. These tensions pervade her difficult journey toward spiritual awakening within a transnational setting of fragmented identity and loss.

The Translator (1999) is Aboulela's first novel set in the Sudanese Muslim diaspora of Aberdeen, Scotland. Aboulela's fictional works include *Minaret* (2005), *Lyrics Alley* (2011), The *Kindness of Enemies* (2015), *Elsewhere Home* (2018), and *Bird Summons* (2019). Notably, she is the first winner of the Caine Prize for African Writing in 2000 for her diaspora story, *The Museum*, from her short fiction collection, *Coloured Lights* (2011). *The Translator* as well as her second novel *Minaret* form counter-narratives to western monolithic images and perceptions of women whose lives are enmeshed by the patriarchal structures of Islam. Aboulela skillfully subverts hegemonic discourses of women in Islam as a form of writing back to reshape contentious discourse about Islam that arose in the late twentieth century. Further, Abbas provides a broad context for Aboulela's works and frames them as religious novels. She asserts the author's didactic motivation for writing and states that *The Translator* and *Minaret* are:

DOI: 10.4324/9781003350200-8

Formally cautious and convention bound to their core, they are still genuinely intriguing. *The Translator* was published in 1999, at a moment when the Gulf War, the subsequent sanctions against Iraq, anti-Muslim feeling attendant upon the Rushdie affair, the increasing visibility of Europe's Muslim immigrants, and an American rhetoric of a coming clash of civilizations were already conspiring to turn Islam, *tout court,* into an anti-imperial token. The novel is clearly meant to be a response to these events.

(Abbas, 2011: 436)

Moreover, Samaa Abdurraqib contextualizes the gendered nature of the portrayal of Islam in immigrant fiction:

Immigrant narratives that focus on religion have the potential to follow the same patterns as normative immigration novels. However, when Muslim women are placed at the center of these oppositions, the patterns are revised. The oppositions become stauncher-and the divisions between "us and them" are relied upon more heavily. Islam becomes the religion of the "other" and the culture from which women need to be liberated.

(Abdurraqib, 2006: 56)

Aboulela's creative artistry disrupts foreign interpretations and narrative tropes of silenced Muslim women. Within a postcolonial framework, Aboulela's diaspora novels (re)envision the discourse of Islam from a woman's perspective, and Al-Karawi and Bahar aptly note that: "Aboulela's work, in showing the rootedness of religion, fills a gap in Western representations of Muslim women" (2014: 256). Emily Churilla corroborates the significance of Aboulela's literary interventions thus:

As current discussions of home and diaspora seems to revolve around the barb-wire borders of nation states and equally impermeable divisions of national identity and affiliation, it seems imperative to evolve out of the limited options available for forming one's identity.

(2011: 44)

Moreover, Aboulela's diaspora novels continue the literary traditions of first-generation African women writers who began writing in English during the mid-1960s with the publication of the classic *Efuru* (1966) by Flora Nwapa who is known as the "mother" of African women's Anglophone writing. In this, and other works by early African women authors like Ama Ata Aidoo, Buchi Emecheta, and Mariama Ba, the portrayal of women protagonists represents a (re)imagined image that counters prevailing perceptions that appear in male-authored texts.

Both *The Translator* and *Minaret* may appropriately be termed Islamic Feminist novels as posited by Shirin:

> Aboulela repeatedly rehearses details—Islamic prayers, the logic and explanation animating Islamic rituals, conscious activities such as fasting, and the observance of other Islamic habits—through which a Muslim woman expresses feminism first in her choice to trace her actions on an Islamic model and then to extend the Islamic inspiration to other aspects of her life, namely work, marriage, love, education, and relationships. This expressly Islamic feminist consciousness in choosing Islam as a way of life that Aboulela's female characters exemplify is also emphatically present in the Translator, where the main protagonist Sammar's feminism is markedly shaped by a consciousness of Islam. Not only does Aboulela's fiction describe the growth and development of an ostensible Islamic feminist consciousness: it also details the ways in which this Islamic consciousness impacts all aspects of their lives, thus characterizing Aboulela as an unmistakably Islamic feminist author.
>
> (2013: 62)

Islamic feminist expression is also underscored because the Muslim women protagonists in both *The Translator* and *Minaret* defy stereotypes of muted and subordinate women through their agency and their mobility as transnational subjects across multi-local spaces. Through her women characters, Aboulela speaks her truth about the centrality of her faith to ground her while navigating hostile spaces of the west in an interview titled "Keeping the Faith":

> There is this sense of alienation, that there is only you and God. That's what religion teaches, that life is a temporary thing which is going to dissolve one day…I can carry religion with me wherever I go, whereas the other things can easily be taken away from me.
>
> (2005)

Further, Shirin interprets that "For Aboulela, a personal, religious identity provides more stability than national identity" (2005).

As postcolonial works, *The Translator* and *Minaret* contribute to the growing body of diaspora fiction by African women writers that dominate the African literary landscape in the global age. Since the dawn of the twenty-first century, immigrant fiction by women chronicles the transformative energies of life beyond Africa through the lens of gender as a new trajectory of the African novel. Chimamanda Ngozi Adichie's bestseller *Americanah* (2013), Sefi Atta's *A Bit of Difference* (2013), Chika Unigwe's *On Black Sisters' Street* (2009), and NoViolet Bulawayo's *We Need New Names* (2013), among many others, are vivid and compelling novels of third-generation authors that have garnered critical acclaim. Igiaba Scego is a Somali-Italian author whose novel *Adua*[1] (2015) resonates themes of Muslim women's identity in the Somali-Italian diaspora. Cristina Ali Farah's *Little Mother*[2] (2011) also unfolds a Muslim woman's journey in Europe. This body of works by women is an enormous contribution to African literary history, and Sackeyfio emphasizes that: "The image of women protagonists in fictional works was forever changed through projection of strong, diverse, and complex characters that resist patriarchal oppression and barriers to their empowerment through their agency, strength and resilience" (2021:2). These and other fictional works represent the continuing emergence of women's voices to convey stories of their experiences and the complications of life in multi-local settings. Contemporary immigrant fiction is a lens to examine the complexities of mobility and life-changing circumstances in the global age of migration and mutability.

These works are connected through their exploration of women's shifting identities that translate new ways of telling the African story in the global age of social, economic, and political transformation. Each of these novels highlights the intersection of race, class, and gender for African women migrants in foreign lands where religion and ethnicity emerge as prominent themes that influence the lives of the female characters. These works are among an array of twenty-first-century fiction that forms composite portraits of cultural hybridity and the tensions that arise between local and global realities in the global age.

The challenge of negotiating Islamic faith in a foreign setting lie at the heart of Aboulela's diaspora novels, and her works explore religious faith as an uncommon theme in African immigrant fiction. The focus on Muslim religious identity in the African diaspora informs discourses of marginalization and subaltern status as cultural outsiders whose voices are largely unheard. Aboulela's novels are crafted from her perspective as a Sudanese Muslim who has lived in Europe for many years. Aboulela successfully navigated the delicate balance between her faith and the unwelcoming realities of Western life in Europe. In a 2005 interview with Anita Sethi of *The Guardian*, Aboulela says of her religion that:

> My faith was started off by my grandmother and mother and so I always saw it as a very private, personal thing. At the same time, they were very progressive. My grandmother studied medicine in the Forties, which was very rare in Egypt, and my mother was a university professor, so my idea of religion wasn't about a woman not working or having to dress a certain way; it was more to do with the faith.
>
> (Aboulela, 2005: 1)

The Translator is narrated by Sammar, a young widow who emerges from loneliness and alienation as she comes to terms with her transnational identity. She works as a translator of Arabic for a Scottish professor at a university that becomes the setting for a growing relationship that develops in her life. Important themes that unfold in the book are postcolonial elements, hybridity, spatio-temporality, and the power of memory to evoke personal growth and emotional balance in one's life. Sammar lost her husband and has never healed throughout a four-year period of mourning where she is alone in a clouded space of uncertainty. Similar to the protagonist in the second novel, *Minaret*, Aboulela explores the ways in which Muslim women living abroad adhere to religious faith as an intrinsic feature of their identity in their families and communities. The diaspora theme of religion, especially Islam, is underrepresented in African immigrant fiction, and Aboulela's novel is an insightful window into thoughts, feelings, and the inner world of a Muslim woman who narrates her experiences in life. In *The Translator*, Aboulela has infused sensitive matters of Muslim faith in ways that highlight the complexity and the gendered nature of a woman's personal commitment to her religion.

The two-part structure of the novel replicates the contrasting periods of Sammar's life in the past and present. And similar to other novels of African immigrant fiction, the division into two segments symbolizes a bifurcated identity in the lives of African characters as well as sites of dissimilar cultural identity in Africa and the diaspora of Europe or North America. In this way, spatio-temporal dimensions influence the fluid and shifting perceptions of identity. Sammar's memories are a haunting reminder of her pain and loss in the past because not only did she lose her husband, she left her son in Sudan with her mother-in-law when she returned to Aberdeen. In a moment of nostalgia, Sammar recalls: "She had lived for four years as if home had been taken away from her in the same way Tarig had" (Aboulela, 1999: 33). Leaving her son behind was difficult and the source of her inner turmoil because she wants to get married again.

Sammar thinks of what her life could become if she remained in Sudan:

> She imagined that what she wanted from life was simple, nothing grand, just to continue and live in the same place, be another Mahasen when she grew up. Have babies, get fat, sit with one leg crossed over the other and complain to life-long friends about the horrific rise in prices.
> (Aboulela, 1999: 26)

Muslim women's identity is often prescribed by conventional norms such as domestication and child rearing, and since Sammar is educated, this poses a challenge to her sense of womanhood in the future.

Sammar's loneliness is acute and the cold and gloomy environment in Aberdeen weighs heavily on her conscience. Aberdeen is frequently described as foggy and cloudy as a mirror of Sammar's conflicting emotions and blurred future. Her work as a translator is the springboard for her growing interest in Rae Isles, the Scottish professor who is a historian of Middle Eastern Affairs. Her mind flows back and forth in time to recall her life in Sudan, and when she thinks of Rae, she is reminded that "She felt separate from him, exiled while he was in his homeland, fasting while he was eating turkey and drinking wine. They lived in worlds divided by simple facts-religion, country of origin, race-data that fills forms" (Aboulela, 1999: 34). At the university in Aberdeen, Sammar's growing interest in Rae is marked by her steady descriptions, recollections of their conversations, and discussions with her only friend Yasmine, a Sudanese woman she works with. Sammar asks her friend:

Do you think he could one day convert?

That would be professional suicide.

Because no one will take him seriously after that. What would he be? Another ex-hippy gone off to join some weird cult. Worse than a weird cult, the religion of terrorists and fanatics. That's how it would be seen. He's got enough critics as it is: those who think he is too liberal, those who would even accuse him of being a traitor just by telling the truth about another culture.

A traitor to what?

To the West. You know, the idea that West is best.

Are you hoping he would convert so you could marry him?

This conversation lies at the heart of the issues examined in the novel as Sammar and Rae fall in love and their emotions are tested by matters of religious faith because Islam forbids marriage between non-Muslims. Sammar returns to Sudan and the romance unfolds through long phone calls, and when she is told he wants to travel with her to help her forget the past, she experiences conflict again over the prohibitions of her religion:

Once upon a time in another part of the world, were the fears *someone will see us together, alone together...a woman's reputation is fragile as a matchstick...a woman's honor...*Reputation was the idol people set up, what determined the giving, the holding back. A girl's honor...your father will kill you...your brother will beat you up...you will go to school the next morning as the bolder girls inevitably did, with puffy red eyes, unusually subdued.

(Aboulela, 1999: 57)

In Sudan, Sammar would have encountered these restrictions on her behavior and mobility, but the diaspora space offers her greater freedom of choice. With resolve, she puts the ideas behind her and agrees to go out with him in the future. This decision represents awakening feminist energies to plan her own life within a new space of freedom. The spatio-temporal shift that juxtaposes the past and present marks a subtle transformation in the protagonist's perceptions of herself in relation to the world around her. Aboulela employs positionality to uncover suppressed emotions that denote Sammar's evolving identity. These events suggest that diaspora spaces hold the potential for personal growth despite the alienation and hybridity that is common to African and other immigrants in foreign lands. Aboulela's second novel *Minaret* shares intertextual elements because Najwa's inner journey opens a path to happiness through her devotion to her faith while living in the unwelcoming environment of London.

Sammar's isolation is acute, and her apartment is described as a hospital room because of the sterile atmosphere. Everything is old, decaying, and moldy since she hadn't bought anything new for four years since her husband died. For Sammar, it seems as if time stopped and the ashes of her broken life settled over her mind to obscure her happiness, "as if there were a fog blocking her vision" (Aboulela, 1999: 67). One day she "looked around the hospital room and said to herself, 'I am not like this. I am better than this'" (Aboulela, 1999: 67). The Sharia stipulates a mourning period of four years and ten days for widows and now that it is over Sammar awakens to new possibilities, dreams, and hope for a better life. Her faith in Islam grounds her thinking: "My fate is etched out by Allah Almighty, if and who I will marry, what I eat, the work I find, my health, the day I die are as He alone wants them to be" (Aboulela, 1999: 73).

These thoughts are an affirmation of Sammar's faith that remains at the core of her life.

Sammar is planning to return home to Sudan and the author crafts a stunning turn of events when just before her departure Sammar asks Rae if he will commit to Islam and marry her:

> I imagined we could get married today. Her voice startled and bruised her, like sandpaper, like sea-salt. Now and I could go with you to Stirling. I don't want to go to Egypt...I thought Fareed could marry us and it would not be difficult to get two witnesses.
>
> (Aboulela, 1999: 125)

When Rae doesn't respond, "She thought, why isn't he saying anything, why isn't he talking to me? She thought, why am I numb, why am I not crying yet?" (Aboulela, 1999: 126). Sammar is in shock and thinks of the implications of her actions:

> It occurred to her now that she had come here to his office to ask him to marry her and he had not said yes. He had not said yes, and yet here she still sat, clinging. She had no pride. If she had pride she would go away now. Instead she was still sitting.
>
> (Aboulela, 1999: 127)

Within the precepts of Islam, Sammar's actions are unthinkable in a culture where extended family members are involved in marriage and approval is sought as well as other formalities. She made one final attempt, "If you say the *Shahadah* it would be enough. We could get married. If you just say the words" (Aboulela, 1999: 127). The heavy sadness is distressing and hurtful to Sammar and she tells Rae she wishes he had not begun a relationship with her, regrets trusting him, and begins to insult him with curses. Finally, Rae tells her to go away.

Her exit from Rae signals more than departure from Aberdeen. It opens a new chapter of her life when she returns to Sudan to reconnect with her son, her aunt, and her mother-in-law. Part II of the novel is set in her country where her feelings remain conflicted. Sammar expresses a deep love for her country despite the unexpected changes in the standard of living among her people. The Postcolonial factors that drive untold numbers of Africans to migrate abroad are vividly described in the novel. Sammar recalls the differences between her comfortable life in Europe and the economic depression in Khartoum. Her Aunt and her brother advise her to return to Aberdeen where her son will be better off. She tells her brother that living in Aberdeen wasn't a great success. He responds: "You're so fortunate. A good job, a civilized place. None of these power cuts and strikes and what not…What's the matter with you?" (Aboulela, 1999: 149). Sammar notes the irony of the situation because her brother is fed up with the lack of opportunities and the overall decline in the society and desperately wants to leave but cannot. She has a job already but does not want to leave Sudan.

Sammar convinces herself that in time she will forget about Rae and assumes he has moved on to another relationship. She recalls her new life of mixed realities of the postcolonial environment:

> Deprivation and abundance, side by side like a miracle. Surrender to them both. Poverty and sunshine, poverty, and jewels in the sky. Drought and the gushing Nile. Disease and clean hearts. Stories from neighbors, relations…A challenge just to live from day to day, a struggle just to get by. But there were jokes about the cuts, rationing and the government.
>
> (Aboulela, 1999: 161)

Sammar notes that:

> There was no water. In this land where the Nile flooded, no water. No water to have a shower with, flush the toilets with, cook drink… This was her life. Fighting malaria, penicillin powder on the children's cuts. The curfew at eleven.
>
> (Aboulela, 1999: 161–162)

These problems have arisen across many African nations in diverse urban sites because of failed government policies, political corruption, poor leadership, and global forces that undermine development in post-independent African states. Aboulela critiques these issues delicately, but the correlation between difficult living conditions and increasing migration is underscored, and like Sammar's brother stated, many African Muslims found more opportunities in Arab nations such as Saudi Arabia and Qatar.

Sammar veers back and forth in a depressed mental state but finally sends a letter of resignation to the university in Aberdeen. Eventually, she "found herself nostalgic for her old job, the work itself, moulding Arabic into English" (Aboulela, 1999: 164). The novel has a fairytale ending because she learns that Rae has converted to Islam and they are reunited when he arrives in Sudan. They plan to return to Aberdeen with her son and live happily ever after.

The Translator unveils a Muslim woman's transnational identity that evolves through her exposure to a foreign culture, way of life, and love for a European man. The novel explores a similar theme to Minaret about the ways in which religious faith is tested through the experience of love and loss against the backdrop of spatio-temporal realities. The portrayal of Islam usurps western images of oppressed Muslim women who are forced to veil themselves and remain subordinate to males. Aboulela's protagonist is educated, and her evolving consciousness demands that she charts her own future with a man on her own terms. This is illustrated when she asks a foreign man to marry her which is counter to the norms of her Sudanese Muslim society.

Leila Aboulela's *Minaret* (2005) is the second novel that explores Muslim women's identities in Africa and Europe to broaden the interrogation of transcultural spaces in the lives of African immigrant females. Similar to *The Translator* and unlike much of contemporary diaspora fiction that narrate experiences of racial otherness and hybridity in the west, Aboulela foregrounds the centrality of religion as a binding thread of women's experiences in the cosmopolitan space(s) of London. *Minaret* is a multilayered fictional account of postcolonial expression because the characters' lives unfold against the background of political and economic upheaval in Sudan that forces them to migrate abroad in search of a better life. Memories of Sudan and familial connections to home shape the hybrid identities of the women characters. Like her contemporaries, Aboulela has crafted compelling narratives that capture the realism of female journeys despite the challenges of liminality as women pursue happiness and success in foreign lands.

The portrayal of women characters in The *Translator* and *Minaret* also runs counter to female protagonists in classic works such as Nawal El Saadawi's *Woman at Point Zero*[3] (1975) and *God Dies by the Nile*[4] (1985). Saadawi is well known as a courageous Egyptian feminist whose literature and activism focus the status of women in the Arab Muslim world. In her iconic works of Arab women's fiction, women's lives are caught in the grip of rigid Islamic norms, expectations, and restricted roles in society, but Saadawi's female protagonists eliminate their male oppressors as expressions of feminist resistance. Susan Ardnt articulates such works as radical feminist writing in *The Dynamics of African Feminism: Defining and Classifying African Feminist Literatures* (2002). Leila Aboulela's artistry in *The Minaret* is a form of rebuttal to critiques of women in Islamic cultures because the protagonist embraces her faith as a liberating force in her life. Aboulela's depiction of women's identity in *Minaret* unveils diverse realities and circumstances in the lives of African Muslim women along with insight into the complexities of socio-economic status.

Minaret vividly uncovers the shifting identity of a displaced Sudanese woman in London. As a political refugee, Najwa is the female at the center of the work that moves back and forth through time to reconstruct the complexities of her life in Khartoum, and the transition to a dislocated existence in London. The novel opens in the mid-1980s and is divided into five sections that represent a fragmented life and hybrid identity. Along with the trauma of leaving Sudan, Najwa must navigate her marginalized status in London, challenges of survival, and the ultimate test of her faith in Islam. The chronological structure of the work is not linear, but rather marked by multi-temporal stages of development of Najwa's consciousness, sense of self, and (re) positioning of her identity through religious devotion.

In the prologue to the novel, Najwa is in London where she reflects on her new beginning while facing an uncertain future. In a brief moment, she notes the minaret of the mosque as a subtle foreshadowing of her journey back to her faith. Narrated in first person, Najwa's thoughts are that she "has come down in the world. I've slid to a place where the ceiling is low and there isn't much room to move" (Aboulela, 2005: 1). These ideas are repeated throughout her journey to discover her place in the world and restore her faith in Islam. These thoughts set the tone of the narrative voice by inserting positionality or spatio-temporality that reshapes her perspective in London.

Shifting between space and time, Najwa is haunted by her past life in Sudan where she is the pampered daughter of a wealthy businessman and politician. As a university student, she experiences privileged status and regularly enjoys expensive vacations in Paris and London where her family owns a flat. In her everyday life, she wears western designer clothes, drives a car, and enjoys a carefree social life of parties and entertainment. As part of the wealthy, educated elite, she revels in much freedom and her lifestyle reflects the trappings of the Sudanese bourgeoise for whom religious practice is minimal.

Recollections of her life as a non-practicing Muslim in Sudan foreground class differences that are vividly described, and upon reflection, she notes inner stirrings of ambivalence and puzzling emotions about Islam. Early in the novel, she is talking to her friend Randa about magazine photos of women in Iraq and Iran wearing chadors and being completely covered:

> "Totally retarded," she said looking at the picture and handing me a spoon. "We're supposed to go forward, not go back to the Middle Ages. How can a woman work dressed like that? How can she work in a lab or play tennis or anything?"...They're crazy, Randa said. "Islam doesn't say you should do that." "What do we know? We don't even pray." Sometimes I was struck with guilt.
>
> (Aboulela, 2005: 29)

The frivolous attitudes toward veiling, modesty among women, and fasting during Ramadan reflect the shallow nature of Najwa's life in Khartoum. From her perspective as a carefree student, she and her friend cannot imagine fasting in London because it would spoil all the fun. Najwa "looked down at the picture and thought of all the girls in university who wore hijab and all the ones who wore tobes. Hair and arms covered by our national costume" (Aboulela, 2005: 30). Class differences sharpen Najwa's perceptions of conventional Muslim women and accentuate inner feelings of guilt and self-doubt. She recalls seeing two girls at school:

> They were provincial girls and I was a girl from the capital and that was a reason we were not friends. With them I felt, for the first time in my life, self-conscious of my clothes; my too short skirts and too tight blouses. Many girls dressed like me, so I was not unusual. Yet these provincial girls made me feel awkward. I was conscious of their modest grace, of the tobes that covered their slimness-pure white cotton covering their arms and hair.
>
> (Aboulela, 2005: 14)

Minaret skillfully traces Najwa's latent spiritual awakenings that unfold through remembrance of the sound of the *azan* or morning call to prayers. Her return from all night partying is juxtaposed with inner longing of her spirit:

> I could hear the *azan*. It went on and on and now, from far away, I could hear another mosque echoing the words, tapping at the sluggishness in me, nudging at a hidden numbness, like when my feet went to sleep and I touched them.
>
> (Aboulela, 2005: 32)

Najwa's growing awareness of non-religious behaviors among the males in her life contrasts her perceptions of religious norms within her community. All of the men in her life disappoint her and fuel her spiritual growth and personal development. Her father is a minister in the Sudanese government. As a patriarch, he fails her when he is arrested after a coup and eventually executed for corruption. The next day she is forced to flee with her mother and brother to London as political refugees. These traumatic events signal a downward spiral into a clouded future that she expresses in the opening lines of the work: "she has come down in the world" (Aboulela, 2005:1). Her new life as an exile means displacement, loss of social status, interrupted education, and hybrid identity in London. This represents a crisis in her life that she never actually recovers from despite her spiritual journey.

When she and her family learn of her father's execution after being found guilty of corruption, her world falls apart:

> There are all kinds of pain, degrees of falling. In our first weeks in London we sensed the ground tremble beneath us. When Baba was found guilty we broke down, the flat filling with people, Mama crying, Omar banging the door, staying out all night. When Baba was hanged, the earth we were standing on split open and we tumbled down and that tumbling had no end, it seemed to have no end, as if we would fall and fall for eternity without ever landing. As if this was our punishment, a bottomless pit, the roar of each other's screams. We became unfamiliar to each simply because we had not seen each other fall before.
>
> (Aboulela, 2005: 61)

Her father's demise has many ramifications in Najwa's life because as the Muslim patriarch in her family, he is the moral center, holding the family's survival in his hands. Though emotionally distant, her father controls her destiny until she is married when she would submit to the authority of her husband. Her family is splintered further because after her mother dies, her situation worsens when she begins working as a maid, living in the shadows of the Muslim family that employs her. Her lower socio-economic status is a sharp contrast to the aristocratic background of her past as she gradually acquires the demeanor and behaviors of a downcast servant.

Najwa experiences a failed romantic relationship with Anwar who is a radical student activist while at university in Khartoum. He has rejected conventional Islamic practice, and as a Marxist, his political ideology and religious ideas frequently clash with Najwa. Although they are strongly attracted, he is always a thorn in her side because of his sharp criticism of Najwa's father as an example of the corrupt bourgeoisie in Khartoum. His campus speeches openly humiliate her and his irreligious comments are caustic and unkind. Later in London, she reads a newspaper article he has written about her father's trial where Anwar states: "justice would be met and nothing was a fairer punishment for corruption than sequestration and the noose" (Aboulela, 2005: 61).

When there is another coup in Sudan, Anwar seeks political asylum in Britain where he and Najwa renew their friendship. Unfortunately, it is a rocky relationship, fraught with conflict, but Aboulela has artfully woven postcolonial themes into the layered and problematic romance. Najwa asks Anwar:

> "What's wrong with us Africans?".
>
> (Aboulela, 2005: 165)

The London environment is cosmopolitan and multi-ethnic, and Najwa admits to herself that:

> She envies other nationalities in London and "wonders how it would feel to have, like them, a stable country. A place where we could make

future plans and it wouldn't matter who the government was-they wouldn't mess up our day-to-day life. A country that was a familiar, reassuring background, a static landscape on which to paint dreams. A country we could leave at any time, return to at any time and it would be there for us, solid, waiting".

(Aboulela, 2005: 165)

Najwa daydreams of marriage and returning to Sudan where she and Anwar would resume their lives. Conflict over religion stains their relationship along with disjointed exchanges about their hybrid status as postcolonial subjects, displaced by political instability in Sudan: Najwa imagines that whatever happens in her life:

London remained the same;...That was why we were here: governments fell and coups were staged and that was why we were here. For the first time in my life, I disliked London and envied the English, so unperturbed and grounded, never displaced, never confused. For the first time I was conscious of my shitty-coloured skin next to their placid paleness.

(Aboulela, 2005: 174)

These unsettling feelings nag her conscience as she questions the nature of her confusing existence. She feels guilty about sex with Anwar and he tells her she's been brainwashed about the importance of virginity in Arab society. Her acceptance of his ideas comes to the surface when she identifies with the majority of females in London whom she assumes are no longer virgins: "I was in the majority now, I was a true Londoner" (Aboulela 176). Anwar tells her: "I know you're Westernized, I know you're modern, ...that's what I like about you-your independence" (Aboulela, 2005: 176).

When Najwa realizes he is not likely to marry her, she ends the relationship while drifting closer to her faith.

The unfortunate plight of Najwa's brother Omar causes her shame and regret, and like Anwar, Tamer has rejected Islam. In London, he is imprisoned for fifteen years when he is caught by the police for selling drugs. When she visits him in prison, their discussions are frustrating because he is detached and unconnected to his cultural moorings and has little interest in returning to Sudan. All of these experiences take their toll and Najwa reflects:

It was becoming clear that I had come down in the world. I had skidded and plunged after my father's execution and through my mother's illness when I dropped out of college, then after Omar's arrest and through my relationship with Anwar. The process took so long, was mixed up and at times gave the illusion of better things.

(Aboulela, 2005: 239)

The idea of "coming down in the world" is a temporal marker of Najwa's difficult journey to find her identity while coping with the trauma of exile from her homeland.

The only male who treats her with respect is Tamer, the brother of the family she works for as a maid. He is many years younger than her and a student. Gradually they fall in love and she admires his devotion to Islam. Aboulela employs an effective narrative structure to unfold Najwa's spiritual path. In a conversation with Tamer, he shares his perceptions of religious identity:

> My education is Western and that makes me feel that I am Western. My English is stronger than my Arabic. So I guess, no, I don't feel very Sudanese, though I would like to be. I guess being a Muslim is my identity. What about you? I talk slowly. I feel that I am Sudanese but things changed for me when I left Khartoum. Then even while living here in London, I've changed. And now, like you, I think of myself as a Muslim.
>
> (Aboulela, 2005: 110)

He wants to marry her but sadly his grandmother Doctora Zenab vehemently rejects her because of her past. She offers a large sum of money to compensate Najwa and she accepts. The money seals her future as a path to a better life with the possibility of an education as well as to assist her brother Omar when he is released from prison. The relationship ends while Najwa makes a deeper commitment to her faith that includes a pilgrimage to the Hajj. She tells Tamer that when she returns from Mecca, she will have cleansed her sins to start a new life.

The traumatic events, failed relationships, and hybrid status propel the protagonist's spiritual journey. These experiences chart her path back to her "center" as a devout Muslim woman. Al-Karawi and Bahar highlight the representation of characters through a Muslim-centered lens:

> Aboulela provides her novel with the dichotomy of religious versus non-religious people. Almost all devout Muslim people in Aboulela's *Minaret* are represented as kind, sincere and selfless. It is the non-religious people who are represented as cruel, mean and shallow, generally providing a black-and-white picture. Anwar, Najwa's boyfriend and Omar, Najwa's brother are examples of non-religious people in the novel whose characters are endowed with negative traits such as opportunism, hedonism, and irresponsibility.
>
> (2014: 258)

The protagonist negotiates these unsettling realities and they ultimately help her to grow stronger, and this is especially evident when she ends her inappropriate relationship with Anwar. Her rejection of him signals an important shift toward religious principles as well as a step toward autonomy as an act of feminist expression. She tells him: "I can't live a life where I don't even know that Ramadan has started. I can't. I'm tired of having a troubled conscience. I'm bored with feeling guilty" (Aboulela, 2005: 244).

Similarly, Najwa's agency and strength to move past her relationship with Tamer, despite admiring him, is also a feminist choice. The money she is given by his mother on condition that she leaves him is an opportunity to renew her faith and fulfill her religious obligations. Thus, her religious commitment absolves her liminal status and yearning for spiritual awakening. Najwa's renewed faith is visible because she wears a veil, prays, and attends the mosque to study the Quran. The most important symbol of devout religious practice for Muslim women is wearing the veil or hijab and Najwa is transformed and at peace with herself:

> I wrapped the tobe around me and covered my hair. In the full-length mirror I was another version of myself, regal like my mother, almost mysterious. Perhaps this was attractive in itself, the skill of concealing rather than to offer.
>
> (Aboulela, 2005: 246)

Claire Dwyer conducted a study of Muslim women in Britain between 1993 and 1994 where she interviewed young Muslim women. The responses documented in the study mirror the ideas about women's religious practice as presented in Minaret. Dwyer notes:

> For a smaller number of young women these negotiations were part of the process of engaging with a more self-conscious religious identity – an engagement with a Muslim identity which was seen as distinct from the more ethnically inflected religious affiliations of their parents.
>
> (2008: 144–145)

This represents a critical juncture in Najwa's spiritual journey and provides a sharp contrast with her ambivalence toward religion in the past. To wear the veil confers respectability, morality, dignity, and piety as expressed in the Quran. Al-Karawi and Bahar confirm the significance of the hijab: "the veil is seen as a sign with multiple layers of meaning because voluntary veiling is believed to be an empowering tool of self-expression through which women increase their relationship with their own faith and culture" (2014: 256). Najwa wears the veil of her own accord, contrary to non-Muslim perceptions of the practice:

> Samaa Abdurraqib examines veiling as a formal validation of Muslim religious identity: The veil thus becomes the visual repository for the Muslim identity that is being preserved, and veiling shifts from being construed as somewhat normal behavior into an action that proclaims identity.
>
> (2006: 59)

In addition to wearing the hijab, regular attendance at the mosque is a stark contrast to Najwa's disjointed past both in the Sudan and in London. Further, the significance of Najwa choosing the veil is emphasized because: "the narrative makes normal Islam centered lifestyles and experiences where these representations of Muslim identity provide alternatives to contemporary discourse which suggest the veil is imposed on Muslim women". (Al-Karawi and Bahar, 2014: 256)

She accepts an invitation to attend classes and enters a community of women that creates a deep sense of belonging and a counter for her alienation.

She feels accepted among diverse Muslim women, some of whom are non-African converts. At the mosque, ideas of social class and nationality are thus subsumed within the religious gathering of women. The mosque becomes a space of sisterhood that renews Najwa's spirit. Shakir Mustafa highlights the significance of the mosque as a space of refuge and inner peace:

> *Minaret* presents the mosque as a locale endowed with much more than strictly religious significance. It becomes a substitute for home almost literally for Najwa who begins her religious transformation there soon after the Gulf war of 1991. She finds in the mosque unconditional acceptance without the repeated betrayals she suffers from her brother, other family members and later Doctora Zeinab, her employer.
>
> (Aboulela, 2005: 285)

By the end of the novel, Najwa is fully integrated into the sisterhood of the mosque, having formed secure and fulfilling friendships with other women. In the final scenes, she dreams of being ill in her bedroom, surrounded by her parents. As a connection to the past, present, and future, she imagines the room as "dark and cluttered, all the possessions that distinguish us in ruins. I am not surprised. It is a natural decay and I accept it" (Aboulela, 2005: 276). These perceptions conflate the spatio-temporal elements to mirror her journey to a different reality and the resolution of religious and cultural ambivalence, symbolized by her acceptance of the crumbling surroundings. According to Emily Churilla, "Najwa's narrations of the past are memories of a present that seems endless, and the narrations of the present are fragments of deferral and delay, and a past that is never quite past" (2011: 40).

In sum, *Minaret* is a vivid and compelling narrative of displacement, trauma, and the search for spiritual truth. Aboulela's novel unfolds the complexities of life in the Sudanese diaspora to interrupt the dominant narratives of women in Islam that are pervasive in the western world. As a religious work, themes of Muslim identity come into focus through the realism of the author's portrayal of spiritual awakening in response to cultural hybridity and un-belonging in London. *Minaret* is an important contribution to immigrant literature by African women writers in the global age of transformation and flux. Aboulela has given voice to a female perspective on Muslim identity within a contested space of hostility, distorted perceptions, and "single stories" of women in the Islamic faith.

Minaret may be understood through a postcolonial lens through examination of social, economic, and political realities in Sudan that wreak havoc in the lives of people. The novel illustrates that women are disproportionately vulnerable, regardless of socio-economic class and privilege. Aboulela uncovers the unfortunate consequences of political instability, corruption, and misplaced energies that compromise the future for young people in Africa and abroad. The political themes explored in *Minaret* resonate with the fictional works of other African women writers that foreground challenging circumstances for women that are caused by post-independence crisis in the nation-state.

Adichie's *Purple Hibiscus*, Atta's *Everything Good Will Come*, Bulawayo's *We Need New Names*, and Unigwe's *On Black Sisters' Street* are leading works among others that illustrate these ideas.

Aboulela's religious themes play out in the spatio-temporal nexus of Sudan and London, the past and the present, and a viable future crafted by the feminist vision of the female protagonist. The work conveys the idea that despite the patriarchal structures within Islam, women may evolve agency to chart their lives, rise above their obstacles and setbacks, and reconfigure their identities within diaspora spaces of otherness. Further, the novel highlights the empowering features of Muslim women's solidarity, support, and belonging as a counter to alienation and marginalization of African migrants. *Minaret* normalizes devout spiritual practice as a source of strength to weather challenges of exilic life. An important message of *Minaret* is that women's voices are authentic historical narratives of their truths that are written from a female perspective. These narratives uncover the transformative nature of African women's experiences abroad in ways that highlight women's potential for personal growth and fulfillment on their own terms. Aboulela is undisputedly a Muslim feminist author as exemplified by the portrayal of her female characters whose religious faith is a cornerstone of their identities as transnational subjects.

Notes

1 *Adua* (2015) is a novel about a Somali woman who migrates to Italy.
2 Christina Ali Farah's novel about Muslim women from Somalia who are refugees in Italy.
3 Nawal El Saadawi's iconic novel *Woman at Point Zero* describes oppressive images of Islam and the collusion with patriarchy to subordinate women in Egypt. She highlights religious hypocrisy of males in the novel.
4 Nawal El Saadawi's novel that highlights the ways in which religion is a tool of oppression with women as the most vulnerable to abuse.

Works Cited

Abbas, Sadia and Leila Aboulela, 2011. "Religion, and the Challenge of the Novel". *Contemporary Literature*. Fall Vol. 52, No. 3. pp. 430–461.

Abdurraqib, Samaa. 2006. "Hijab Scenes: Muslim Women, Migration, and Hijab in Immigrant Literature". *Melus, Arab American Literature*. Vol. 31, No. 4. pp. 55–70.

Aboulela, Leila. 1999. *The Translator*. New York. The Black Cat.

———. 2005. *Minaret*. London. Bloomsbury.

———. 2011. *Lyrics Alley*. New York. Grove Press.

———. 2015. *Kindness of Enemies*. London. Weidenfeld and Nicholson.

———. 2018a. *Coloured Lights*. London. Telegraph Books.

———. 2018b. *Elsewhere, Home*. New York. Telegraph Books.

———. 2019. *Bird Summons*. London. Weidenfeld and Nicholson.

Adichie, Chimamanda Ngozi. 2013. *Americanah*. Toronto. Alfred A. Knopf.

Al- Karawi, Susan Taha and Ida Baizura Bahar. 2014. "Negotiating the Veil and Identity in Leila Aboulela's *Minaret*". *GEMA Online Journal of Language Studies*. Vol. 14, No. 3. pp. 255–268. https://doi.org/10.17576/GEMA-2014-16.

Arndt, Susan. 2002. *The Dynamics of African Feminism: Defining and Classifying African Feminist Literatures*. Trenton. Africa World Press.

Atta, Sefi. 2013. *A Bit of Difference*. Northampton. Interlink Books.

Bulawayo, NoViolet. 2013. *We Need New Names*. Bulawayo, New York. Regan Arthur Books.

Churilla, Emily. 2011. "Coming Home: Communities Beyond Borders in Caryl Phillips' *The Atlantic Sound* and Leila Aboulela's *Minaret*". *Obsidian*. Vol. 12, No. 2. pp. 25–46.

Djebar, Assia. 1993a. *A Sister for Sherezade*. Trans. Dorothy Blair. Portsmouth, NH: Heinemann.

——— 1993b. *Fantasia: An Algerian Cavalcade*. Trans. Dorothy Blair. Portsmouth, NH: Heinemann.

Dwyer, Claire. 2008. "The Geographies of Veiling: Muslim Women in Britain". *Geography*. Vol. 93. pp. 140–147.

Edwin, Shirin. 2013. "(Un)Holy Alliances: Marriage Faith, and Politics in Leila Aboulela's *The Translator*". *Journal of Middle East Women's Studies*. Vol. 9. pp. 58–79.

El Sadawi, Nawal. 1975. *Woman at Point Zero*. London. Zed Books.

———. 1985. *God Dies by the Nile*. London. Zed Books.

Farah, Cristina Ali. 2011. *Little Mother*. Bloomington. Indiana University Press.

Mustafa, Shakir. 2009. "Defending the Faith: Islam in Post 9/11 Anglophone Fiction". *Religion and Literature*. Vol. 41, No. 2. pp. 281–288.

Sackeyfio, Rose. 2021. *African Women Writing Diaspora: Transnational Perspectives in the Twenty-First Century*. Lanham. Lexington Books.

Scego, Igiaba. 2015. *Adua*. New York. New Vessel Press. Trans. Jamie Richards.

Sethi, Anita. 2005. "Keep the Faith". *The Guardian*. June. https://www.theguardian.com/books/2005/jun/05/fiction.features2.

Unigwe, Chika. 2009. *On Black Sisters' Street*. London. Jonathan Cape.

6 Ruptured Spaces of the Self in *We Need New Names* by NoViolet Bulawayo

We Need New Names (2013) by NoViolet Bulawayo is a vivid rendering of the shattered innocence of Zimbabwean youth. The life of the female protagonist unfolds a bildungsroman experience that spans Zimbabwe and America. *We Need New Names* conveys postcolonial perspectives on the failed state of the nation during a period of political upheaval, the violence of poverty, and the unfulfilled dreams of a nation in turmoil. Against this landscape, Bulawayo weaves a coming-of-age tale of a young protagonist at the center of the novel who matures in America as the setting for her awakening to a new and conflicted identity. This chapter argues that childhood innocence is a casualty in the marginalized world of Robert Mugabe's Zimbabwe that is marred by social, economic, and political injustice. This chapter also demonstrates how childhood innocence gives way to a new form of splintered existence in America that juxtaposes the *divided self* of the protagonist.

We Need New Names is NoViolet Bulawayo's critically acclaimed first novel, which was shortlisted for the Man Booker Prize and winner of the Etisalat Prize for Literature in 2013. In 2011, her short story "Hitting Budapest"[1] won the Caine Prize and was later expanded to the successful novel, *We Need New Names*. Her second novel *Glory* (2022) is an allegorical work about the political landscape in her native Zimbabwe, which has also been shortlisted for the prestigious Booker Prize in 2022. The name she was given at birth was Elisabeth Zandile Tshele from her Ndebele ethnic community. The name she adopted as her pen name derives from the city of Bulawayo where she spent part of her childhood. Like other African writers that live in Europe or America, Bulawayo's work lends much insight into both the African experience and the diaspora novel to support the contention of Mukoma wa Ngugi that *"We Need New Names* is squarely an African, and at the same time a diasporic and American novel"* (Wa Ngugi, 2019: 172).

In Zimbabwe, the characters, both children and adults, are trapped in a web of chaotic and dehumanizing realities, dysfunctional behaviors, and oppression that erodes their dignity and humanity. At the center of the work, childhood perceptions mirror the challenge to survive as people struggle to make sense of their lives. The ugly realities displayed in the work mark the failure of Zimbabwe's independence to provide freedom and stability for

DOI: 10.4324/9781003350200-9

her people. The novel reveals the collusion of destructive forces from within and outside Zimbabwe during a time of political conflict and a reign of terror from the government. Despite expectations of successful nationhood and development, children are at the mercy of forces beyond their control as they respond to an outright assault on their humanity and the abject decay of their community. At age ten, Darling and her friends represent the future of a nation but the harsh encounters with death, HIV AIDS, poverty, and hunger; the failure of NGOs is a stark and painful contrast to normative experiences of childhood. Moji affirms that the novel "cleverly subverts the cliched tropes of childhood purity" (Moji, 2014: 184).

As a postcolonial novel, *We Need New Names* is important as a vivid and compelling examination of the dystopian environment in Zimbabwe during the twenty-first century through a gendered lens. The work is an authentic account of the destructive consequences of an oppressive and violent nation-state under Robert Mugabe. Zimbabwe gained independence in 1980 and like many African nations, the buoyant hopes of growth and development of the nation gave way to despotic rulers, economic frailty, and widespread political corruption. Mugabe ruled the nation for over 40 years, and by the mid-2000s, the nation sank into political and economic decline because of factors such as the world's highest rate of spiraling inflation at 8000%, massive unemployment, and human rights abuses.

In the midst of economic meltdown, thousands of people were displaced and NoViolet Bulawayo captures the ramifications of the situation on children, females, and families and communities. The brutality of their existence sharpens the political themes of the novel and is a "clear-eyed indictment" of government policies that crippled the nation's economy. According to D. Mutanda et al.:

> An honest assessment of the period 2000–2008 reflects on a decade of madness and extreme authoritarianism. The Mugabe regime valued political survival using violent tactics. Economic woes which reduced three-quarters of Zimbabweans to paupers were effectively ignored. The country's economy deteriorated from one of the continents strongest to the world's worst with the official inflation rate estimated at more than 1,000%in 2006....Hyperinflation, large scale retrenchments, unemployment and shortage of foreign currency resulted in a number of households living in poverty.
>
> (2016: 263)

Into this mix are a group of impoverished children struggling to survive in the capital city of Harare. Children are the nation's most vulnerable citizens, and the novel is a riveting account of their fractured lives as street children left to fend for themselves.

The novel unfolds through the voice of Darling, whose childhood is ruptured by brutal realities of survival on the streets, transition to adulthood, political conflict, and her uncertain future. In framing the dehumanizing experiences of children, Bulawayo uses appellative strategies to construct identities that disaffirm conventional experiences of childhood innocence and carefree existence. The structure of the novel illustrates the bifurcated and multilayered themes of duality in the spatio-temporal nexus of Zimbabwe and America, childhood and adulthood, the past and the present, and cultural hybridity experienced by Darling. Among many works of African immigrant fiction, these ideas foreground the spatio-temporal elements that parallel the dueling identities of the African characters. Mukoma wa Ngugi explains: "NoViolet Bulawayo's *We Need New Names* is rooted in Detroit and rural Zimbabwe and, ...shows us characters that live out the simultaneity of US, and Zimbabwean politics" (2019: 182).

Ato Quayson notes the ways in which fictional characters' subjectivities emerge as they move across spaces in their environment which he terms "spatial traversal" (Quayson, 2014: 214). In his book *Oxford Street* (2014), he examines the urban setting of Accra in Amma Darko's *Faceless* (2013) through analysis of characters' movement across spaces, the social implications of their encounters with others, and the shifting identities that occur within multiple sites of dislocation in the text. *Faceless* is Darko's classic rendering of the plight of street children and child prostitution in the slums of Accra in the mid-to late twentieth century. The novel shares intertextual elements with *We Need New Names* because in both works, destitute female children are the protagonists at the center of the novels and because of their unfortunate plight, they and their friends are exposed to dangerous experiences in the adult world such as death, sex, violence, and drugs. In their novels, both Darko and Bulawayo indict African governments for failed economic policies and lack of political will to stabilize their nations and provide for the masses, with women and children disproportionately vulnerable to extreme poverty.

Spatial traversal frames the structure of *We Need New Names*, and the book opens with movement:

> We are on our way to Budapest: Bastard and Chipo and Godknows and Sbho and Stina and me. We are going even though we are not allowed to cross Mzilikazi Road, even though Bastard is supposed to be watching his little sister Fraction, even though Mother would kill me dead if she found out; we are just going. There are guavas to steal in Budapest, and right now I'd rather die for guavas. We didn't eat this morning and my stomach feels like somebody just took a shovel and dug everything out.
>
> (Bulawayo, 2013: 1)

The furtive mobility of the children marks their entry into forbidden space that also crosses ethical boundaries because they plan to steal guavas out of sheer hunger.

Budapest is an affluent neighborhood, "not like Paradise, it's like being in a different country altogether" (Bulawayo, 2013: 6). Darling describes how she and her friends "can be better thieves" (Bulawayo, 2013: 6) by systematically moving down the streets as they steal to alleviate their hunger. Moji aptly notes that: "The children are trapped in a ceaseless quest for survival. Hunger is what prompts them to cross the border into Budapest, just as material lack prompts them to dream of escape and migration" (Moji, 2015: 184). Moji also highlights the children's escapism via migration that becomes a motif in the novel because Sbho imagines she will marry a rich man from Budapest, Bastard dreams of Johannesburg, and Darling's aunt Fostalina in America is an opportunity for her to leave Zimbabwe (Moji, 2014: 184). Thus, spatiality, real or imagined, is a correlative to the identities and experiences of the children.

Instead of real names, Darling and her friends are called by names that are puzzling such as Bastard, Chipo, Godknows, Stina, and Sbho. By creating such unusual and made-up names that jar the sensibilities, the author juxtaposes the past and the present to highlight the dehumanizing nature of the children's existence in the midst of chaos in Zimbabwe. Her friends' real names are Thamu, Josephat, Ncane, Verona, Maneru, and Mudiwa. In addition to the off-base and impudent names of her friends, the child at the center of the work is ironically called Darling and her environment is called *Paradise*. Early in the novel, it is clear that the children's neighborhood is actually anything but *paradise* and is in fact a *hellish* and thoroughly unwholesome existence for a child. In the past, Darling recalls:

> two homes inside her head: home one, before Paradise, and home two, inside Paradise, Home One was the best. A real house. Father and Mother having real jobs. Plenty of food to eat. Clothes to wear. Radios blaring every Saturday and everybody dancing because there was nothing to do but party and be happy. And then home two-Paradise, with its tin tin tin.
>
> (Bulawayo, 2013: 193)

The two homes not only represent the past and the present as temporal markers, it also denotes the downward spiral into chaos for family and other residents of Harare whose lives become a test of survival. Darling's recollection normalizes her earlier life in a real home with stability afforded by having two parents. The contrasting sites of her former homelife and the dislocation of Paradise is appalling as it narrates the literal destruction of her family and her neighborhood. Darling recalls the aftermath of bulldozing of homes that led to destitution, crushing poverty, and displacement of people in areas that did not vote for Mugabe in the elections of 2005. Darling describes how the police come with guns and baton sticks and start bulldozing while everyone is screaming. People are desperately grabbing anything they can salvage, from the houses: "plates, clothes, a Bible, food, just grabbing whatever they can grab" (Bulawayo, 2013: 68). The scene illustrates the agonizing attempt of Zimbabweans to collect the scattered pieces of their shattered lives from the rubble of chaos and destruction.

After the bulldozers leave, "everything is broken," and this represents the singular event in the novel that portends a downward spiral into poverty and decay for thousands of Zimbabweans in Harare and Bulawayo. It was called *Operation Murambatsvina*, a Shona[2] word that means "drive out the rubbish." The effects on citizens are catastrophic, and in an article called "Zimbabwe's Cleanup Takes a Vast Human Toll," Michael Wines reports that "the evicted are further crowding the overstuffed homes of relatives and neighbors, or sleeping in the open. Stories of suffering and death abound" (2005: 4). It is estimated that 700,000 people lost their homes and livelihoods in the mass evictions (Ray and Madzimbamuto 2007: 57).

In the dehumanizing attempt at piecing together their lives, Darling vividly recalls that people were:

> squatting to mark the ground like that, they appeared broken—shards of grass people...They appeared with tin, with cardboard, with plastic, with nails and other things with which to build, and they tried to appear calm as they put up their shacks, nailing tin to tin, piece by piece.
>
> (Bulawayo, 2013: 78)

These descriptions underscore the realistic dimensions of the novel that becomes historical fiction based upon real-life events.

Darling and her friends are further demeaned in one of the novel's most gripping accounts of the sporadic visits of NGO aid workers. The scene suggests controlled pandemonium when the children spot a lorry bringing gifts to the people. She and her friends want to rush to the lorry but recall that the last time they did so the NGO people did not like it and behaved as if they had committed a "crime against humanity" (Bulawayo, 2013: 53).

For the children, waiting for the NGO aid is painful and humiliating. The insensitive interaction with the workers is effectively conveyed when they start taking pictures. Darling says:

> they don't care that we are embarrassed by our dirt and torn clothing, that we would prefer they didn't do it.; they just take the pictures anyway, just take and take. We don't complain because we know that after the picture taking, comes the giving of gifts.
>
> (Bulawayo, 2013: 54)

The children are degraded further when the cameraman takes photos of Chipo who is pregnant, and Godknows' buttocks that show through the holes in his shorts. Finally, they are given gifts such as toy guns, tee shirts, sweets, and clothing. They are careful not to touch any of the NGO people, and Darling states that "we can see they do not want to touch us or for us to touch them" (Bulawayo, 2013: 56). When she politely says thank you to one of the workers, the woman does not respond and Darling says it feels as if she has just barked. The adults are given beans and sugar and mealie-meal. Bulawayo portrays the efforts of the adults to maintain a semblance of dignity as Darling describes them standing distractedly, pretending little or no interest, looking "embarrassed and disappointed" at the meager quantities. Eventually, they head back to the shacks, lives unchanged, their hunger unabated, their hopes dashed, and their families shattered. When people became desperate, Darling remembers that some-times, there were:

> stampedes when things started to fall apart and the stores were empty, how people would pour out onto the street and run like they were dying, chasing after trucks loaded with mealie-meal, sugar, cooking oil, bread, soap, and just about anything.
>
> (Bulawayo, 2013: 219)

This scene represents the intersection of local and global forces that fail to alleviate the horrific conditions on the ground. The proliferation of NGOs in many developing nations throughout the world symbolizes con-descension, arrogance, paternalism, cultural dissonance, and misplaced attempts to assist local people. Even the children can see through the charade by the five aid workers who create a scene that suggests poverty porn through the insensitive photographing: Chipo remarks: "They don't care that we are embarrassed by our dirt and torn clothing, that we would prefer they didn't do it; they just take the pictures anyway, take and take" (Bulawayo, 2013: 54).

The injustice of the Zimbabwean people's predicament forms the land-scape of dysfunctional family life, amoral behaviors, and unwholesome ini-tiation into adulthood as society continues to deteriorate. Darling says of the children, "they appeared empty, like their childhood had fled and left only the bones of its shadow behind" (Bulawayo, 2013: 78). These perceptions are expressed by a child, and vividly describe the devastation around them that alters the lives of entire families. Zimbabwe's children become helpless victims of human rights abuses as the most vulnerable citizens in the nation.

Moreover, childhood ends and the age of indignity begin as Darling and her friends are robbed of education, nurturing family life, and a carefree childhood. Their future, like the outlook for the country, is bleak and per-manently damaged with rippling effects on her friends, family, and the entire community. Darling and her friends come of age in the effort to quell their hunger and the quest for their own humanity within a marginalized world of degeneration and chaos.

With the collapse of normalcy around them since they no longer go to school, the children forage through neighboring communities (which they refer to as countries) searching for guavas to satisfy their hunger. Their dignity is assaulted by the indifference of a British woman they encounter who displays exotic perceptions of African children. She wants to take their pictures, including one of the girls who is pregnant at age eleven. The woman has no clue about the children's plight, and as they watch, she casually throws away food without offering them any. This makes them angry and they begin to insult her.

The children have their first experience with death as they stumble upon the body of a young woman who has hanged herself because she has HIV/AIDS. It is not surprising that a young Zimbabwean woman would commit suicide when learning she is infected. According to Sunanda Ray and Furai Madzimbamuto, in an article called "The HIV Epidemic in Zimbabwe: The Penalty of Silence," between 2001 and 2002, the prevalence of HIV disproportionately affected women at rates higher than South Africa, Zambia, Kenya, Burundi, Mali, and Niger. Chipo is:

> pointing ahead in the bush, and we see it, a tall thing dangling in a tree like a strange fruit. Then we see it's not a thing but a person. Then we see it's not just a person but a woman...The thin woman dangles from a green rope that's attached to a branch high up in the tree.
>
> (Bulawayo, 2013: 18)

For hungry children, survival becomes a matter of strategic actions to their advantage. As the children leave, Bastard draws attention to the young woman's shoes, which, if sold, could perhaps buy them a loaf of bread. In this instance, Bulawayo traces the corrupted values that evolve as the children's identities and behaviors are warped by their impoverishment and the need to survive. The desperate hunger they feel, and the absence of adult supervision and protection, defines their new identities as street children with names of "otherness" that convey the ravages of a dysfunctional society racked by poverty and destitution.

Darling has a close-up view of death because she loses her father to what is called "the sickness," because of the "culture of silence" that prevents people from naming the disease which is full-blown AIDS. Many others fall victim to the onslaught of the epidemic as there are continuous funerals in their community. Out of desperation caused by widespread unemployment, Darling's father, like scores of other men, goes to South Africa to find work, leaving in their wake, neglected families so that women and children are left vulnerable and desperate. To compound the irony, her father has a university degree, and in an angry exchange with Darling's mother, he wants them to leave Zimbabwe along with the droves of others who are fleeing the country. He asks if this is what they got independence for? He ends up leaving and Darling narrates how:

> her father comes home after many years of forgetting us, of not sending us money, of anything, vomiting and vomiting, Jesus, just vomiting

and defecating on himself, and it smelling like something dead in there, dead and rotting, his body a black terrible stick; unable to move.

(Bulawayo, 2013: 91)

Darling narrates other experiences of death from HIV/AIDS as funerals become more frequent and claim the lives of many young people. She remembers that:

> she used to be very afraid of graveyards, and death and such things, but not anymore. There is just no sense being afraid when you live so near the graves; If we are not watching funerals we sometimes walk around reading the names on the graves...She continues...when you know math's like me you can figure out the ages of the buried and see they died young...It's that Sickness that is killing them. Nobody can cure it so it just does as it pleases—killing—killing—killing, like a madman hacking unripe sugarcane with a machete.
>
> (Bulawayo, 2013: 135)

The failed system of healthcare compounded the onslaught of the AIDS pandemic that engulfed Zimbabwe's people. Mugabe's government can be held accountable for neglectful and counterproductive management policies that mandated silence about the disease. The reason it is called the "sickness" is because of the stigma and shame associated with the disease. In addition, the healthcare sector conveyed the message that "the infection was so bad, such a vile thing, that it should not be mentioned ... and that those who carry the stigma of HIV/AIDS are labeled shameful, as having done something bad, which must not be spoken of" (Ray and Madzimbamuto, 2007: 49). But for Darling and her friends, her father's return from South Africa and the discovery of his presence by her friends bring them face to face with the pandemic. Godknows remarks that they all know her father has "the Sickness," and Stina says flatly that: "It's like hiding a thing with horns in a sack...One day the horns will start boring through the sack and come out in the open for everybody to see" (Bulawayo, 2013: 102). Darling tries to hide her father's condition from her friends, but they eventually see him in a horrible and death-like condition.

In looking at the collusion of government and the health management system in Zimbabwe, Ray and Madzimbamuto confirm that: "one of the consequences of institutionalized political violence in Zimbabwe has been fear within the health system" (2007: 55). In addition, "At every level there has been poor leadership in responding to the HIV epidemic, especially with a human rights approach to HIV" (Ray and Madzimbamuto, 2007: 46). Furthermore, the political establishment refused to acknowledge the severity of the disease (Ray and Madzimbamuto: 2007: 46). To compound the situation:

> The denial of fundamental human rights in countries like Zimbabwe is closely linked with the reasons the HIV epidemic has raged there

for the past 15 years or so. The epidemic thrives on secrecy, stigma, gender inequity economic disempowerment, poor accountability, and monopolies of knowledge.

(Ray and Madzimbamuto, 2007: 45)

The complexity of the situation in Zimbabwe is broad and far-reaching in scope so that Darling and her friends are enmeshed in a web of destructive forces that is almost incomprehensible and certainly cannot be processed by children.

The end of childhood ushers the age of indignity within multiple sites that the children traverse throughout the novel. The breakdown of normalcy exposes Darling and her friends to sex. For example, Chipo, at age eleven, is raped by her grandfather in the absence of a conventional family environment and the breakdown of society in general. Although she plays with her friends, when they question Chipo about how she became pregnant she does not speak. Bulawayo juxtaposes the idea that while Chipo is in fact pregnant, neither she nor her playmates actually have knowledge of sex or the birth process. They have conversations where they ask each other "where does a baby come from? Where does a baby come out? Much later in the novel, it is revealed that when the adults were away, Chipo was assaulted by her grandfather. Darling is also exposed to sex when she overhears her mother with a lover whose face she has never seen because "all he does is just come in the dark like a ghost and leap onto the bed with Mother" (Bulawayo, 2013: 66). The absence of Darling's father in South Africa creates emotional and psychological stress on family relationships that are already in varying stages of estrangement.

Another site of alterity in the novel occurs when visiting a construction site operated by Chinese developers; the children see Zimbabwean women and a Chinese man leaving from a dark tent, suggesting that the women are sex workers. Unwholesome experiences such as these are inappropriate encounters that result from unsupervised and dysfunctional family life in Harare. The social and cultural borders between childhood and adulthood are broken and crossed leaving children vulnerable to socially unacceptable behaviors. The children are trapped in a society that is crumbling around them as they struggle to survive.

As Zimbabwe sinks into hopelessness, a mass exodus sweeps the nation, as escape from the country becomes the logical path to survival. Darling notes that things have fallen apart in her homeland as the setting of the novel abruptly changes to America. She continues her journey into confusion in the alienating spaces of the Midwest. Bulawayo's play on words captures the spirit of this new and problematic environment. The coming-of-age motif is sharply etched, and the challenges of the immigrant experience take shape for Darling in *DestroyedMichygen* a new environment of conflicting realities and splintered identity. One of the paradoxical realities that emerge is that although America offers new opportunities for education and success, alienation, clash of cultures, and splintered identity suggest the inevitability of broken American dreams. Moreover, Darling no longer faces hunger and debilitating poverty, but the ravages of growing up in America take their psychological and emotional toll as she gets older. The spatio-temporal locus of the novel shifts to *DestroyedMichygen* that suggests another dystopian site that shapes the life path of Darling as a newly minted immigrant. As this section of the novel unfolds, Darling's character and her perception of herself are markedly different in ways that illustrate the power of "place" to mediate identity.

Moji emphasizes the new challenges that Darling encounters in America:

> The cognitive dissonance created by the change from childhood ignorance to more adult knowledge, becomes apparent in the second half of the novel. Darling develops a greater consciousness of the categories of being—gender, race, and nationality—which are used by others to define her within the American social matrix. Dubois iconic work *The Souls of Black Folk*, (1903) highlights the ways in which double-consciousness is a link to black subjectivities and to ways of seeing and being seen by others.
>
> (2013: 187)

Thematic engagement with blackness in America and other transnational sites of hybridity is a reoccurring trope in African immigrant fiction. Darling's abrasive experiences mirror Adichie's vivid accounts of "Learning to be Black" that contextualize the nature of racialized identities. These discomforting realities constitute an initiation into the hierarchy of race and ethnicity that is part of America's dark history of slavery and racial oppression.

Darling begins a journey into *otherness* when she arrives in Washington, DC and recalls that she:

> just wanted to die. The other kids teased me about my name, my accent, my hair, the way I talked or said things, the way I dressed, the way I laughed. When you are being teased about, something, at first you try to fix it so the teasing can stop but then those crazy kids teased me about everything, even the things I couldn't change, and it kept going and going so that in the end I just felt wrong in my skin, in my body, in my clothes, in my language, in my head, everything.
>
> (Bulawayo, 2013: 167)

These perceptions mirror the nature of African immigrant experiences that assault their sense of African cultural identity in foreign lands. Abrasive encounters like these are common and are vividly illustrated in the fictional works of leading contemporary African diaspora women writers. For example, Chimamanda Ngozi Adiche's *Americanah* (2013) and stories in her collection *The Thing Around Your Neck* (2009) are important works that also explore the complexities of fractured lives of young African women living in the west. In *Americanah*, Ifemelu, the protagonist, recollects that she begins to change her speech patterns after an uncomfortable incident with a white person because of her accent. She narrates that: "in the following weeks, as autumn's coolness descended, she began to practice an American accent" (Adichie 135). Further, Adichie examines cultural hybridity in "The Arrangers of Marriage" from her short story collection *The Thing Around Your Neck*. These works share intertextual elements of cultural confusion and alienation in transcultural spaces abroad. All of the works display insightful presentation of the ways that women navigate disjointed lives in alien landscapes of the west. For dislocated Africans, the idea that ethnic features, speech, and behaviors are ridiculed and denigrated is a painful coming-of-age reality that is all the more difficult as characters navigate a maze of incongruent experiences, and a clash of cultures within transnational spaces.

For Darling, and many immigrants, the best way to survive is to sound American and she acquires an accent as a coping mechanism. These attempts are realistically conveyed as she struggles, very successfully by watching TV and gradually adopting the nuanced American speech patterns she observes around her. She thinks to herself that: "I don't know why Aunt Fostalina doesn't think to learn American speech like this, seeing how it would make her life easier so she wouldn't have to have a hard time like she is right now" (Bulawayo, 2013: 186). Her mother calls from Zimbabwe and remarks that America has taught her to speak English with an accent that makes her sound white.

Darling becomes aware of jarring differences in the American way of life, and incomprehensible situations that startle her sensibilities. When she was back in Zimbabwe, she would taunt her friends about the wonderful life she would live with her aunt in Detroit. Like many immigrants from Africa and other parts of the world, America is a mirage of mostly impossible dreams and hopes for a life of comfort that captures the imagination. When Darling writes to her friends in the early months after her arrival, she leaves out descriptions of the stark contrasts and disappointments of her new environment:

> I didn't tell them how in the summer nights there sometimes was the bang bang of gunshots in the neighborhood and I had to stay indoors, afraid to go out, and how one time a woman a few houses from ours drowned her children in a bathtub, all four of them, how there were poor people who lived on the streets, holding up signs to beg for money. I left out these things, and a lot more, because they embarrassed me, because they made America not feel like My America, the one I had always dreamed of back in Paradise.
>
> (Bulawayo, 2013: 190)

Another rude awakening to American life is the possibility of random violence when in middle school, one day a boy brings a loaded gun to class and panic spreads throughout the school. Teachers and students are screaming and running and the whole campus is shut down.

As the novel unfolds, Bulawayo skillfully interweaves recollections of Zimbabwe that parallel Darlings disjointed experiences in Detroit. For example, similar to the condescending and unflattering perceptions of NGO workers in *Paradise*, she has an uncomfortable encounter at a wedding she attends with her family. A white woman approaches her in the bathroom as if she is a wounded animal who must be pitied. The woman describes CNN stereotypes of glaring poverty, rapes, and killings in the Congo:

> Africa is beautiful, She says, going on with her favorite word. But isn't it terrible what's happening in the Congo? Just awful…Tell me about it. Jesus, the rapes, and all those killings! How can such things even be happening?
>
> (Bulawayo, 2013: 177)

The woman tells her that her niece joined the Peace Corps and went to Rwanda and to South Africa to teach at an orphanage: "And, oh, she took such awesome pictures. You should have seen those faces!" (Bulawayo, 2013: 178). The comments hurl Darling's mind back to Zimbabwe: "Then I'm seeing myself in this woman's face, back there when we were in Paradise when the NGO people were taking our pictures" (Bulawayo, 2013: 178–179). The woman is filled with emotion and sorrow that is perplexing to Darling so that "her brain is scattering and jumping fences" (Bulawayo: 2013: 177) in the attempt to make sense of the comments.

This encounter captures the intersection of local and global disparities, the western gaze on Africa that conjures the exotification of poverty, and the feigned sympathy that veils western feelings of superiority.

In addition, Darling becomes aware of dysfunctional family life in America in ways that mirror the chaos in Zimbabwe. Her aunt Fostalina has an empty marriage to a man from Ghana and has an extramarital affair. Her husband succumbs to depression and becomes an alcoholic. All the relationships in her new family in America are superficial and dysfunctional so that Darling does not receive much guidance and is mainly urged to do well in school and to choose a professional occupation. Bulawayo's portrait of immigrant family life in America is bleak, fragmented, and unfavorable, and resonates with other fictional works by African women such as characters in America and London in Adichie's *Americanah* (2013), Nigerian immigrants in Atta's *A Bit of Difference* (2013), Gyasi's *Transcendent Kingdom* (2020), and Chika Unigwe's *Better Never than Late* (2020) among others. The descriptions of hyphenated lives of dislocated Africans that reoccur in immigrant fiction display the complexities and the re-negotiation of the African *self* within transnational environments that demand adjustment in order to survive.

Bulawayo skillfully interrogates the conflicting notions of *home* that puzzle Darling's recollection of her life path and the political history of Zimbabwe:

There are three homes inside Mother's and Aunt Fostalina's heads: home before independence, before I was born, when black people and white people were fighting over the country. And then the home of things falling apart, which made Aunt Fostalina leave and come here. Home one, home two, and home three....When somebody talks about home, you have to listen carefully so you know exactly which one the person is referring to.

(Bulawayo, 2013: 193–194)

Darling's analysis is seemingly childish and simplistic, but on a deeper level, she examines the ways in which positionality and subjectivity play out within the spatio-temporal dimensions of her life that are driven by forces beyond her control. Darling has unwittingly identified the core of diaspora angst (at least for her) because the fragmented and splintered contexts of *home* that she narrates disrupt cultural moorings and a sense of continuity that are predictably stable and life-affirming. If her notions of *home* are splintered, it follows that her sense of identity with her home-land is problematic and conflictual.

As Darling matures, Bulawayo interrogates identity conflict after years of assimilation begin to wear on Darling's character. One day she is rummaging through old storage boxes where she discovers:

a medium sized clock in the shape of a map of our country. There is a drawing of a giraffe in the center, reaching above some trees where the hands of the clock meet. The time is stuck at six o'clock, and the long hand is broken. And last, I find this weird mask; it's split in the center, one half white, the other black. The black half is split further in numer-ous crazy patterns that I can't figure out.

(Bulawayo, 201: 285)

She thinks the mask is looking at her, as if it is trying to tell her something that will take years for her to comprehend. Her confusion speaks to an important message in the novel about the ways that assimilation into foreign life may cause Africans to become disconnected and to lose appreciation for their cultural heritage. The black half of the mask being split mirrors her own ruptured identity and it is like she is looking at herself. The symbol-ism of the mask is reminiscent of Fanon's classic work, *Black Skin, White Masks* (1952). This seminal work explores the idea of the *divided self* when Africans become disconnected from their culture. In the twenty-first century, the challenge to remain connected to cultural moorings is a complex real-ity within cross-cultural spaces. In the global environment that is charac-terized by increased mobility, cultural exchange, and rapid transformation, new configurations of identity surface for Darling and for other immigrant populations outside Africa.

The author poses this dilemma more sharply when Darling is speaking to her childhood friend who lives in Harare. In a conversation with Chipo, she is challenged in harsh tones about whether Zimbabwe is really her country. She is asked:

> What are you doing *not* in your country right now? Why did you run off to America…If it's your country, you have to love it to live in it and not leave it. You have to fight for it no matter what, to make it right.
>
> (Bulawyo, 2013: 288)

Darling is incredulous and basically has no clue when Chipo tells her: "you left the house burning and you have the guts to tell me, in that stupid accent that you were not even born with, that doesn't even suit you, that this is your country?" (Bulawayo, 2013: 288). Darling has no answer to these questions and in her anger throws her laptop at the mask. She knows she cannot return home and the novel's conclusion does not resolve her predicament. Cobo-Pinero underscores this point: "Dispossession permeates the new identity of a displaced Darling, who has no words to describe how she feels. Such nascent transnational identities need new inclusive names that tear down physical and imaginary walls" (2018: 22). The novel's message prioritizes the significance of place-making through the subjectivities of African migrants who take on new identities they cannot fathom. Thus, *We Need New Names* is perhaps Bulawayo's meditation on ruptured spaces of the self and the need for "new names."

The ending of the novel suggests that not only is Darling lost to her people back in Zimbabwe, she is also lost in America, and unlikely to recover her footing. This underscores the important parallels in the structure of the novel and juxtaposes layers of awareness and experiences of conflicting realities. The questions asked by Darling's friend who still lives in Zimbabwe highlight a critical dilemma about the responsibility for Africa's development. Since the early twentieth century, many African nations have experienced a steady brain drain of human capital which is the continent's greatest resource for development. The novel poses the question of moral commitment to change Africa's trajectory in the new millennium. The work counters Afropolitan aesthetics articulated by Taiye Selasi in her controversial essay, "Bye Bye Babar":[3] "Bulawayo distances herself from the depiction of a cosmopolitan privileged experience. She creates instead a bleak fictional space that conjures up a postcolonial picaresque, where precarity and vulnerability are the connecting threads capable of weaving together diasporic identities" (Cobo-Pinero, 2018: 22). It is unfortunate that many of Africa's youth may encounter barriers to success in local spaces because of economic malaise and political uncertainty that encourages migration to more advanced sites of opportunities in western nations. It is clear that the protagonist has no answer to these burning questions of potential contribution to changing the future of her nation. This suggests that despite material gains and opportunities in the west, African immigrant populations pay a price for Africa's future both individually and collectively.

In conclusion, *We Need New Names* is an indictment of the failed government of Zimbabwe through the destructive political and economic policies that dehumanize people, violates human rights, and destroys the lives of her citizens. The novel chronicles the ways in which the breakdown of family life and society makes children the victims of myriad experiences of brutality, and dysfunctional behaviors that portend a bleak future. The loss of innocence of Darling and her friends reflects the chaos and violence of life around them to disrupt normative childhood experiences. The novel is honest, with clear and penetrating insight into the impact of relentless oppression on both children and adults who are systematically brutalized.

Regarding the question of whether the novel conveys childhood's end or the age of indignity, the logical conclusion is that both themes resonate clearly, and succinctly capture the postcolonial ruptures in Zimbabwe. Poor leadership has turned the hopes of independence into a nightmare for millions of people. Although Darling escapes to America to live with her aunt, she is haunted by the past and becomes disconnected from her culture and the friends she left behind. Although she comes of age to diverse forms of oppression and ugly realities in Zimbabwe, in America she experiences yet another transformation as she becomes Americanized as a dislocated African. *We Need New Names* succinctly illustrates that people are products of their environment, and for children like Darling, it is unsettling to imagine the period of childhood as a journey through hunger, indignity, poverty, and uncertainty. Children are unlikely to reach their full human potential without the soil of stability, love, and nurturing family life. Despite America's image in the world as a symbol of freedom and land of opportunity, for many immigrants it may pose difficult questions of their transnational identity and unforeseen challenges to success. The twenty-first century is an age when more than ever, spatial mobilities of African, and other émigré's compels them to negotiate the complexities of their multi-local identities and a sense of belonging. *We Need New Names* takes the reader on a journey into the uncertain future of generations of Africa's youth who traverse the borderless world of transformative energies within national, linguistic, and ethnic spaces beyond Africa as homeland.

Notes

1 Hitting Budapest is a short story about hungry children in Zimbabwe who forage through an affluent white neighborhood to steal guavas. The story is the basis for the novel, *We Need New Names*.
2 Shona is a language spoken by an ethnic community bearing the same name in Zimbabwe and neighboring countries in the region.
3 Taiye Selasi's 2005 essay in LIP magazine articulates an elitist, privileged, cosmopolitan description of African immigrants that has stimulated debate because it ignores masses of immigrants whose lives do not reflect her descriptions.

Works Cited

Adichie, Chimamanda Ngozi. 2013. *Americanah*. Toronto. Alfred A. Knopf.

———. 2009. *The Thing Around Your Neck*. Toronto. Alfred A. Knopf.

———. 2014. "*Americanah* Author Explains Learning to be Black in The US". *NPR*. http://www.npr.org/2014/03/07/286903648/americanah-author-explains -learning-to-be-black-in-the-u-s.

Assah, Augustine. 2007. "Images of Rape in African Fiction: Between the Assumed Fatality of Violence and the Cry for Justice". *Annales Aequatoria*. Vol. 28. pp. 333–355.

Sefi, Atta. 2010. *News from Home*. North Hampton. Interlink Books.

———. 2013. *A Bit of Difference*. Northampton. Interlink Books.

Bulawayo, NoViolet. 2013. *We Need New Names*. New York/London. Bay Books.

Bulawayo, NoViolet. 2022. *Glory*. New York. Viking Press.

Cobo-Pinero, M. Rocio. 2018. *From Africa to America*. Atlantic. Vol. 40, No. 2. pp. 11–26.

Darko, Amma. 2003. *Faceless*. Accra. Sub-Saharan Publishers.

Dubois, W.E.B. 1903. *The Souls of Black Folk*. New York. Barnes and Noble.

Fanon, Franz. 2008. *Black Skin, White Masks*. New York. Grove Press.

Gyasi, Yaa. 2020. *Transcendent Kingdom*. New York. Penguin/Random House.

Moji, Polo Belina. 2015. "New Names, Translational Subjectivities: (Dis)location and (Re)Naming in Bulawayo's *We Need New Names*". *Journal of African Cultural Studies*. Vol. 27, No. 2. pp. 181–190.

Mutanda, Darlington, et al. 2016. "Women and State Violence in Zimbabwe, 2000–2008". *Introduction to Gender Studies in Eastern and Southern Africa: A Reader*. ed. James Etim. Netherlands. Sense Publishers. pp. 257–275.

Quayson, Ato. 2014. *Oxford Street: City Life and the Itineraries of Transnationalism*. Durham. Duke University Press.

Ray, Sunanda and Farai Madzimbamuto. 2007. "The HIV Epidemic in Zimbabwe: The Penalty of Silence". *Zimbabwe in Crisis: The International Reponse and the Space of Silence*. ed. Ranka Primorac and Stephan Chan. New York. Routledge. pp. 45–64.

Selasi, Taiye. 2005. "Bye-Bye Babar". *The LIP Magazine*. https://thelip.robertsharp .co.uk/category/lip5/.

Unigwe, Chika. 2020. *Better Never Than Late*. Abuja. Cassava Republic Press.

Wines, Michael. 2005. "Zimbabwe's Cleanup Takes a Vast Human Toll". *New York Times*. June 11. pp. 1–6.

Wa Ngugi, Mukoma. 2019. *The Rise of the African Novel: Politics of Language, Identity and Ownership*. Ann Arbor. University of Michigan Press.

7 Black Venus Dreams and the Migrant Body in Igiaba Scego's *Adua*

Igiaba Scego's *Adua* (2015) is a vivid and poignant novel about other-ness and hybridity in the Somali diaspora of Italy. Scego's artistry emerges through a lucid and compelling account of the ravages of diaspora life for an African woman migrant. This chapter engages the multi-vocal narration of the transnational encounter in Italy to frame the postcolonial discourse of the twentieth century into the global age. Scego's artistic vision chroni-cles the challenging experiences of a Somali immigrant woman in search of fame and success abroad. Local and global tensions erect barriers to legal status and the Italian Somali journeys unfold marginalized identities, failed dreams, and uncertainty.

The spatio-temporal elements of the novel span the early twentieth century to highlight contemporary perspectives on Somali diaspora sojourn in the global era. Scego privileges the female narrator's voice, and while the work unfolds a woman's life story, the voice of her father juxtaposes the patri-archal gaze as her parent, and later his life-threatening experiences in Italy during the colonial period. The novel is comprised of 30 alternating chap-ters that include "Adua," "Talking-To" (told in first person by her father), and "Zoppe" (third person) and is narrated from each of their perspectives. Spatio-temporality commands the structure of the work that moves back and forth in time as a form of (re)membering to reconstruct the postcolonial dimensions of life in Somalia, and in Italy for Adua and her father as trans-national subjects. Adua migrated to Italy in the mid-1970s, and by the end of the novel, she is a middle-aged woman recollecting her life.

Spatio-temporality informs the complexities of identity in immigrant fic-tion, and Ato Quayson notes that in the diasporic novel, "the question of identity—who am I?—is necessarily entangled with that of place" (Quayson, 2013: 148). In *Adua*, Somali identity is mediated by race, class, and gender dynamics that force the characters to negotiate their status as marginalized subjects in the Somali-Italian diaspora-scape of hyphenated existence. Scego writes in Italian and her fiction is informed by the lived experience of an African woman born to Somali parents in Rome. The author's perspective is expressed through her experience as a transnational subject created by intersecting cultures of Somalia and Italy where Scego and her family were educated. Political themes pervade the work that draws upon her family

DOI: 10.4324/9781003350200-10

background. Scego's father was an ousted politician during the 1969 coup of Siad Baare[1] in her Somali homeland that caused them to flee their nation.

The English translation of *Adua* by Jamie Richards resonates with other works of fiction by leading African women authors who write from the African diaspora perspective. Scego lends her voice to a growing body of African female authors whose works explore female subjectivity in foreign spaces of western landscapes. Alessandra Di Maio's "Black Italia, Contemporary Migrant Writers from Africa" avers that Scego's fiction is a notable contribution to the evolving field of Black European Studies. Women's writing from *Black Italia* is especially timely in the twenty-first century in light of the dominance of Anglophone European works that began during the late twentieth century when Buchi Emecheta published her iconic London novels, *In the Ditch* (1972), *Second Class Citizen* (1974), and *Head Above Water* (1986). Emecheta is the first African woman to write from the diaspora, and her novels are a defining moment in the development of African literature. Her works launched a genre that inspires new vision in the literary imagination of contemporary African authors. The creative artistry of a new generation of transnational female artists has increased dramatically since the turn of the century. Global mobility across national, geographic, ethnic, and linguistic boundaries has shifted the trajectory of African literary texts to feature immigrant fiction and the success of prominent female writers.

Most notable among these is Chimamanda Ngozi Adichie's sweeping epic *Americanah* (2016), Chika Unigwe's *On Black Sister's Street* (2009), NoViolet Bulawayo's *We Need New Names* (2016), and Sefi Atta's *A Bit of Difference* (2013). This evolving genre of African women's immigrant fictional works also includes Taiye Selasi's *Ghana Must Go* (2010) and Yaa Gyasi's *Homegoing* (2016) and *Transcendent Kingdom* (2020). Since 2018, Nana Oforiatta Ayim is among other emerging women writers from the African diaspora, and her debut novel, *The God Child* (2019), is set in Germany and Ghana. British-based novelist Bernadette Evaristo's novel *Girl, Woman Other* (2019) explores the lives of African-British females in the United Kingdom and the book is the winner of the 2020 Man Booker Prize. Somali British poet Warsan Shire's graphic poem "Conversations about Home: at the Deportation Center" echoes the thematic focus on recollections of home, exile, otherness, and war. The flavor of the poem conveys a female perspective on displacement in the unwelcoming space(s) of Italy in eloquent, and gripping imagery of the fluid and shifting mobility of the Black female body. Spatiality frames the poetic expression as the protagonist recalls her flight from war-torn Somalia to experience racialized identity, rejection, and uncertainty in the Italian diaspora-scape. The poem is an excerpt from the collection, *Teaching My Mother How to Give Birth* (2016).

The early forerunner of Somali-Italian women writers is Gabriella Ghermandi whose novel *Queen of Pearls and Flowers (Regina di fiori e perle)* (2007) is a finely sketched chronicle of memory and identity expressed through a woman's voice as a young girl sings the ancient songs of her people passed down to her from older generations of storytellers. Alongside the songs of the *griot*,[2] the work also draws heavily on African orality through the multi-vocal narration of both females and males, and according to Vivan, "The novel creates a new space for all those who have been dislocated, muted, or destroyed and are now reinstated and, through writing, awarded a new voice in the Italian language". Nurrudin Farah's classic *Yesterday Tomorrow: Voices of the Somali Diaspora* (2000) shares intertextual elements with Ghermandi's novel through the choral expressions of displaced Somali refugees in ways that recreate experiences, memories, and collective identity. Igiaba Scego's recent novel *Beyond Babylon/Otre Babilonia* (2019) is also a female-centered work of diaspora fiction that connects to *Adua* through the transformative energies of women's identity in the past and the present. Originally published in Italian in 2008, *Otre Babilonia* is described by Itala Vivan as "a novel that charms the reader with its postmodernist wit and the tenderness of its gaze on life and the world but also, thanks to the distant memory of a Somalia, full of songs and stories" (2011: 131). This work explores the mother–daughter relationship through the lives of four women characters that migrate to Italy.

Prior to the twentieth century, literary studies and research on the African diaspora in Italy are minimal. Over several decades, the African immigrant population has swelled in response to global forces generated by economic, political, and social transformation. Displacement resulting from war, and conflict sites such as Ethiopia, Somalia, and Eritrea in the Horn of Africa, has driven the movement of East Africans into Italy and other nations in Europe. As a former colony of Italy, Somalians have sought asylum and new opportunities for success through migration.

Di Maio confirms that:

> the existence of a postcolonial community…and indeed, some of the most powerful voices from the younger generation in Italian letters belong to Somali Italian women writers, whose spectrum of voices offers a choral representation of Italy's oldest and youngest connections with Africa-more specifically with East Africa.
>
> (2009: 120)

As a mirror of life, Somali Italian literature conveys the realities and challenges of the hyphenated lives of women and men ensnared in the complexities of identity formation within a multi-ethnic landscape. Igiaba Scego and Ubax Cristina Ali Farah have emerged as talented and bold women writers "who tell their often-inconvenient truths" (Di Maio,2009: 136). Like Scego, Cristina Ali Farah was born in Italy and in 2007 published *Madre piccola* (Little Mother), a novel about Somali refugees in Italy.

Cristina Ali Farah's *Little Mother* is a collage of memories retrieved within a polyphonic rendering as each of the three characters tells their story. Through vivid recollections of the past in Somalia, and multiple journeys in

Italy and throughout Europe, the characters reconnect to each other to forge a community through the bonds of love, trauma, loss, and other remembered experiences that reinscribe their Somali cultural identities. Beginning in the 1970s, the stories of female cousins, Domenica Axad and Barni, dominate the narrative to privilege women's accounts of their gender identity in the work. Ali Farah's characters evoke Somalian identity and a sense of collective history among themselves through memory, healing, and sutured relationships. The novel speaks to the potential of women's solidarity to meet the challenges of survival and the restoration of a shared sense of Somali cultural identity. *Little Mother* renders a kaleidoscopic portrait of life in Somalia and Italy through a patchwork of experiences of love and hate, life and death, war and trauma, abandonment and forgiveness, sisterhood, and sacrifice. The novel is a richly textured chronicle of human experience that ends on a note of hope.

The narrative structure of *Adua* channels the voice of the protagonist, her father, Mohammed Ali Zoppe, and in sections called "Talking To," "father to daughter" lectures to Adua. The novel unfolds much like a memoir when Adua, now an older woman, recalls her past that is riddled with ambiguity, trauma, and dislocation since her mother died in childbirth. During the 1960s, she and her sister are raised as nomads, in the Somali hinterland which marks a happy period in her life because of her sense of freedom. The father-daughter binary shapes Adua's identity in her family, mostly through the negative interventions of her overbearing father, Zoppe. Benedicty-Kokken notes the significance of Adua's name as a cultural marker of spatial origin and ethnic identity as a norm among African people:

> Adua's name refers to the Battle of Adwa, fought on March 2, 1896, in which the Kingdom of Ethiopia fought the Italian colonial power and technically the Kingdom of Italy. The battle took place near the city of Adwa in the Tigray region.
>
> (2021: 173)

During her childhood, Adua's identity is shaped by cultural practices, her father's overbearing parenting, and a range of unsatisfying experiences. The first chapter opens with an assertion of a hyphenated identity: "I am Adua, daughter of Zoppe" (Adua, 2015: 1).

In the most harrowing "talking to" session, Zoppe tries to convince Adua of the necessity and wisdom of female circumcision. Here, women's identity, acceptance, and status in Somali society are prescribed through this rite of passage, called *gudniinka*. Zoppe tells Adua to stop crying because:

> Now you're free, Adua, just think about that. You don't have that damned clitoris that makes all women dirty. Snip, it's gone, finally! Thanks be to God. The pain will pass...Later you will have only the happiness of being pure, finally closed as God commands. Your sex

won't dangle anymore, Adua. It's beautiful to be pure…Think of what a nice life you'll have without that nasty knocker hanging obscenely between your legs, as if you were a man. I've seen women with it, and I'll tell you it's not a pretty sight. They're repulsive, they're hungry for flesh, violent. Noisy. You've been spared, Adua from this shame. Now you're closed, clean, beautiful. You're like my mother, like my mother's mother, and like all the women worthy of esteem in this big family of ours. Your mother Asha, that fool was against the practice, imagine. She said, "No one will touch my daughter, no one will infibulate her". Luckily she's dead. And now you're saved, closed, without that filthy clitoris reminding you you're a woman.…I'll give you away to the best of men. When you're older you'll thank me.

(Scego, 2015: 84–85)

This passage painfully conveys the layered meanings, complexity, and brutality of the patriarchal gaze, infused with misogynist sentiment and destructive ideas about women's bodies and the perceived dangers of their sexuality. Infibulation is the most dramatic and invasive type of genital surgery that may sometimes lead to infection and other health issues related to menstruation and childbirth as well as psychological trauma among girls and women. In addition to Adua's transition to Somali womanhood, her father's celebratory tone is actually an indictment of women's sexuality, personhood, and autonomy. The vilification of her mother for speaking out against infibulation fuels his disdain and motivates his negative comments since her untimely death in childbirth. The idea that Adua's clitoris is a "filthy," reminder of her womanhood is a reprehensible comment that defies logical reasoning, beyond the cultural boundaries of Somalia. Zoppe's triumphal tone resonates with the deeply rooted practice in Somali communities, which prepares Adua to be given away in marriage by her father. The idea that Adua and other Somali girls and women have little or no control over their bodies or sexuality is a marker of women's identity and social acceptance in the past as well as the present. Essentialist interpretations of male support for female genital cutting are very tempting, but Zoppe's mention of Adua's Aunt Fardosa and a midwife reveals the role of older African women to continue the practice that is widely documented by research on the practice (Farida and Ortensi, 2014: 114).

In the African cultures that maintain the custom, the rite is a pre-condition for marriage that will confer status and socio-economic security in the family and the community. Further, Zoppe tells Adua that good girls do not cry and sharply compares her to her sister Malika who "didn't even shed one tear" (Scego, 2015: 84). Trivializing the pain of infibulation refutes research on the surgery that documents personal accounts of excruciating pain that lasts for several weeks. Elise Johansen in "Pain as a Counterpoint to Culture: Towards an Analysis of Pain Associated with Infibulation in Norway" documents the experiences of Somali women. Although the study was completed in Norway, among Somali immigrants, the findings are valid among Somali females in Italy, especially since the practice is widespread among nomadic communities. The surgery is usually performed when the girls are between five and eight years old and is an important marker of cultural identity among Somali communities (Grasivarro and Abdisamed, 1985: 312).

During extensive interviews of Somali women, the respondents had vivid recollections and most of them stated that "their circumcision had been the most painful experience in their lives, something they could never forget... They are cutting your flesh" (Johansen, 20002: 313). Women overwhelmingly recalled the pain as "being like a 'heavy burden' ...or a 'darkness' in their lives" (Johansen, 2002: 313). Interviews revealed that: "Many women expressed the lasting effect of their circumcision and the associated pain as a sense of loss in both body and soul" (Johansen,2002: 313). One of the women says of infibulation: "It is pain three times. It is the pain when infibulation is done, the pain when it has to be opened again at marriage, and the pain when it has to be further opened when giving birth" (Johansen, 2002: 316). Igiaba Scego's portrayal of patriarchal authority conveys a sterilized description of the traumatic process to Adua as she is compelled to remain voiceless to question or to object. Her subjectivity commands absolute obedience and submission to her father and the conventions of Somali society.

As nomads, Adua and her sister are essentially rootless until their father takes them to the city of Magalo, and her early perceptions of herself reveal a deep attachment to the land "that had become part of her bones" and she "didn't want to be rooted" (Scego, 2015: 39). Removal from the land begins the displacement that drastically alters her sense of identity. To compound Adua's trauma, being motherless creates a terrible void in her spirit, and the new urban life only deepens her frustration, severed cultural moorings, and profound sense of loss. Socially, urban life is unsatisfying in the absence of nurturing parental guidance, not fitting in with her peers, and the universal angst of adolescence. Adua's attachment to the land connects to postcolonial perspectives of African identity, cultural moorings, place of origin, ancestral roots, and lineage history. Adua's connection to the land resonates with the women and men in Muthoni Likimani's *Passbook F.47927* (1985) in Kenya where, as an act of resistance against the colonial government, people would actually eat the soil. Adua recalls that it was "hate at first sight between me and Magalo" and she thinks will be "the end of a life, an ominous change of destiny" (Adua, 2015: 53). Indeed, Adua's sentiments foreshadow a dark period in her life as she comes of age to the disjointed urban life where her identity and her future is ambiguous and clouded. Adua's coming-of-age experience is disheartening because of difficulties with her sister and her father's relentless scolding. She is told that like her mother she is a "pain in the neck"...and he says of women that they are "impossible"...Creatures from hell. "I can't stand you" (Scego, 2015: 121). Zoppe's misogyny is destructive to Adua's self-perception in ways that are fertile soil for self-hatred and rejection, and ultimately the pursuit of foreign images of women as more desirable.

As a naïve child, Adua's maturation takes an unwholesome turn through the cultural and political onslaught of the Italian colonial agenda. Under Mussolini's fascism, the Italian propaganda machine introduced Hollywood films to capture the imagination of the Somali people. Despite Somalia's independence in 1960, as former colonial subjects, people consumed these *en masse*, driven by escapism that Adua calls "manna from heaven" (Scego, 2015: 64). The Italian community remained highly visible in Magolo, coupled with lavish and enviable lifestyles that attracted the admiration of the locals. Adua is young, impressionable, and completely unaware of the political nature of the Italian presence propaganda, or colonialism. Adua recalls that there was no one to:

> educate us. To explain to the little people of Magalo that the value of our land lay in us, African citizens, architects of our own destiny. No one had ever told us that colonialism was the problem. Even those who knew the truth said nothing. My father for example said nothing...I was a little girl, I didn't think about political matters.
>
> (Scego, 2015: 66)

Like so many females in Magalo, Adua is seduced by the dreamlike images of the Hollywood screen. Captivated by the glamour, and lure of celebrity glitz, Adua's girlhood imagination romanticizes movie stars like Marylin Monroe and Audrey Hepburn, and looking back, she admits that she:

> wanted to be like Norma Jean. I didn't care about the rest. I wanted the lights, the makeup, the awards, the red carpets, the passionate kisses...I wanted to dream, dance, fly. I wanted to escape. Italy was kisses, holding hands, passionate embraces. Italy was freedom. And so I hoped it would become my future.
>
> (Scego, 2015: 66)

She describes the jealousy felt by herself and her fellow Somalians who envied the polished lives of Italians living in Magalo: "We were jealous. I admit it. And more than one dreamed of marrying an Italian when she grew up" (Scego, 2015: 66–67). Lost in Hollywood fantasy, her evolving identity is molded by unreality and illusory projections of a future beyond Somalia.

As a young girl, Adua's confused identity also stems from the absence of her mother in her life. In sections of the novel called "Talking To," the patriarchal voice of her father's criticism and lack of affection plant the seeds of rebellion, and eventual estrangement throughout her life. These sections of the work preclude parental and cultural grounding as a foundation for healthy self-image, esteem, and a sense of belonging in her community. Early in the work, Zoppe reminds Adua that her mother, Asha the Rash, died in childbirth and essentially is a "good for nothing...a whore...and heathen... who went and died on me" (Scego, 2015: 6). He tells Adua how much she resembles her mother and warns her of impending punishment. These perceptions bear a striking similarity to the short story *Girl* (1978) by Jamaica Kincaid. In this work, the mother figure is the speaker, addressing her daughter with a barrage of caustic advice that is meant to help and scold at the same. Like Kincaid's mother figure, Zoppe controls the one-way communication to admonish Adua in ways that are overbearing and insensitive. To illustrate, he warns her about manners, good behavior, and her speech, in clearly misogynistic tones. She is told not to be a fool like her mother.

The effect of her father's "parenting" is that Adua becomes a voiceless female in ways that shape the nature of her life in the diaspora. Like the daughter in Kincaid's *Girl*, Adua cannot explain herself or ask a question. Her *silencing* is emblematic of women's status in patriarchal Somali society. Moreover, her father's "talking to" sessions communicate the precepts and norms for females as well as to preserve the "honor" of her family. "Traditional" expectations require that Somali women are socialized as submissive and muted figures in their families and communities, unable to craft their own destinies beyond marriage and motherhood. Adua, now seventeen, is filled with the desire to escape Somalia for Italy. She meets Omar Genale, an unsavory figure who is known to "traffic in all sorts of items"…and someone who "knew how to navigate the intricate network of illegal trade" (Scego, 2015: 96). He arranges her passage to Italy, but Adua's future darkens in the grip of Italians who, unknown to Adua, only wish to exploit her beauty and sexuality. "Adua feels like she is in "seventh heaven"…and naively thinks the Italians would turn her into a "Marilyn Monroe"…, to become "immortal"… she'd leave that sewer Magalo forever" (Scego, 2015: 96–98). She tells no one of her secret plans and recalls how "in silence I let myself be swallowed up by an Alitalia Boeing with a stopover in Addis Ababa" (Scego, 2015: 113).

Adua's journey unfolds in the Somali diaspora of Italy where her identity is circumscribed by the complexities of race, class, and gender. This disturbing stage of her life is recounted in flashback many years later as an older woman. She encounters racist and exploitative Italians who inflict sexual violence and degrading experiences to make a pornographic film. "During the flight, the Italians tell her she will make them rich, and to celebrate, they sang "*Faccetta Nera,*" the 1930's fascist anthem about an Abyssinian girl being taken to Rome after the invasion of Ethiopia" (Scego, 2015: 113).

Spatio-temporality links the colonial perceptions of the black female body to the post-independence image that lingers in the Italian conscious during Adua's life and experiences in Italy. Although many of Adua's challenges are common to many female immigrants, Sandra Ponzanesi accurately construes the colonial and postcolonial Italian imagination of the sexualized African body described as "exotic native women who were depicted through photographs, advertisements, and literary accounts as Veneri Neri-Black Venuses: beautiful, docile, and above all, sexually available" (2015: 158).

When she arrives in Italy, she becomes a victim, similar to trafficked African women at the mercy of their captors in Chika Unigwe's *On Black*

Sisters' Street. She has no documents to legalize her status and no control over her body or her sexuality. At seventeen, she is unaware of the precarious situation she has unwittingly chosen. What follows is a period of sexual objectification, and commodification of the black female body that also resonates with features of the Atlantic Slave Trade, when enslaved women's bodies were essentially chattel, vulnerable to sexual exploitation, violence, and degrading acts in the service of the slave master. To the Italians who *own* Adua, she is essentially "an icon of sexualized beauty" (Ponzanesi, 2012: 56).

In Italy, Adua is duped by an Italian couple called Arturo and Sissi who brutalize, manipulate, and deceive her and in horrible irony, Adua thinks of them as "benefactors" to whom she is grateful. Adua expects to be given a script but learns that the character she is to play "undressed completely and gave her herself away to men like a dog in heat" (Scego, 2015: 114). She rationalizes her objectification as the price to pay to become Marilyn and remembers thinking "I would have paid anything to become Marilyn", she let herself be touched, groped, and smelled (Scego, 2015: 116).

Arturo and Sissi get her drunk and begin to molest her as a way of "teaching" her how to perform sexual acts on screen. She wonders whether she would:

> have the guts to go from fellatio to fellatio to reach [my] dream? She is too drunk to figure this out and when she is naked, they notice the stitches that bore the mark of infibulation. Arturo, remarks "it looks like she's run through with barbed wire."
>
> (Scego, 2015: 118)

They demand that she explain and, after being slapped repeatedly, she tells them:

> They do it for all the girls in my country. They cut our *siil*, the part that hangs down. They cut off other stuff down there too. Of course, it hurts, but then you get a bunch of gifts and it's nice. I got a shell. Then they sew us up. That way we remain pure, we're virgins. And we stay that way until our wedding day, when someone loves us and opens us up with his love.
>
> (Scego, 2015: 119)

Through these experiences, Adua plummets to a new low, subject to the bestiality and depravity of her film "director" and his wife who use a pair of scissors to "open her up" to deflower her. She wonders whether the same thing happened to Marilyn.

Under these conditions, the black female body is a text of pain and trauma, through dehumanizing acts of exotification. In the novel, the image of the Somali female body is narrated as a testimony of marginalized identity in the dark underbelly of Italian cinema. Casting Adua as a porn star echoes the colonial obsession with the black female body. The exhibition of an African woman in public space began in Europe in 1810 when Saartjie Baartman, a Khoikhoi woman from South Africa, was taken to London and who was known as the *Hottentott Venus*. She was told she could earn a lot of money by exhibiting her body to Europeans. This infamous case is a stark illustration of "European representations that portrayed colonial Africa and Africans, women in particular, as objects available for use, abuse and refuse…The Black body has been viewed as the object of denigration, primitive and exotic 'other'" ('Pro' Sobopha, 2005: 120). Further, with reference to the colonial state of Apartheid South Africa:

> The black female body endured the most degradation, functioning as an 'icon' in the construction of the apparently innate difference between the civilized and the uncivilized white and black, male, and female. While the white body has always been seen and represented as pure, holy, and civilized, the black female body has been viewed as impure, savage, and embodied evil. These racist, sexist, and negative images of the black body were profoundly exercised by the colonial West as can be observed in the humiliating stereotypes attributed to Sartjie Baartman.
>
> ('Pro' Sobopha, 2005: 120)

Adua's life continues a downward spiral into sexual exploitation that makes her feel "dirty and empty" with "disgust for herself" after oral sex with an Italian film magnate who is 40 years her senior (Scego, 2015: 130). He calls her Arturo's *Negress* and promises to make her a star. She is humiliated by Italian media headlines such as "Burning Hot Black Hole," Steamy Kiss from the Abyssinian Abyss," and "Black Venus." Her porn film exploits go horribly downhill and she ends up "penniless, drained dry, and duped like a dunce" (Scego, 2015: 151).

Adua's life in Italy is (re)membered through the fractured remnants of her failed acting career. As a child and young adult, Adua is voiceless, but eventually she subverts the constraints of patriarchy when, as an older woman, she marries a much younger Somali refugee. The act of choosing her own husband displays her agency and control of her sexuality. She calls him Titanic although his real name is Ahmed. She describes how he had "risked drowning at sea to come here…He needed a house, a teat, a bowl of soup, a pillow, some money, hope, any semblance of relief" (Scego, 2015: 21). Sadly, in summing up Titanic's needs to survive, Adua interprets her ill-fated and blighted life as a "mama, a *hooyo, a whore, a woman, a sharmutta, me*" (Scego,2015: 21). The novel brings to light the plight of immigrants who risk precarity for a better life in Europe. Salah Hassan, in "Rethinking Cosmopolitanism: Is Afropolitanism the Answer," evokes:

> Tragic images of African youth, men and women who have perished trekking through the deserts of North African countries in transit to Europe, and of thousands of others who have drowned, (sometimes deliberately left to face such a tragic destiny) while journeying on make-shift boats across the Mediterranean Sea to Europe. Those who have

made it alive have encountered a new fortress of draconian laws in a continent that has devoted its energies and legislation to its security-read curbing immigration as felt on a daily basis by Africans living in Europe or the USA.

(2012: 4)

Hassan's grim description is torn from reoccurring headlines of African immigrants lost at sea in the Mediterranean in the twenty-first century. Within a postcolonial framework, Cenedese points to Scego's infusion of multidirectional and intersectional memory through the juxtaposition of the old and new diasporas through Adua's rescue of Ahmed:

In fact, the novel's multidirectional and intersectional tendencies, with their motion to resist competitive singularity, are further evidenced by the connection that Scego makes between the old and new diasporas, and in turn to present-day and future social and political discourse…Their individual migration stories-their respective motivations for escaping Somalia, the means of escape, and the outcomes-are acknowledged as different, yet they are linked by Scego's act of narrative solidarity that highlights shared experiences of racism, vulnerability, precariousness, and oppression.

(2018: 109)

Adua rescues Ahmed from destitution in the street, takes him, and marries him out of convenience, not love, and she knows it will not last. He is an undocumented immigrant and in her role as an older woman, Adua controls the relationship, subverting patriarchy again since her young husband depends on her for everything: money, food, and emotional security. Adua assumes a new status as a married woman who assumes the conventional expectations for females in her Somali community.

The diaspora has become a space for self-discovery in lieu of her sordid past. Ahmed eventually sees the porn film she made and is horrified.

At the end of the novel, he does leave and gives Adua a video camera as a parting gift. He wants her to tell her story and to share her feelings. At their parting, she realizes that he loved her after all.

In reflecting on her past, she regretfully alludes to a life of "drugs, alcohol, cigarettes, fried food and men who wanted only my body" (Scego, 2015: 151). These recollections haunt Adua, who regrets her Italian odyssey into hybridity and shame. After her father's death, she contemplates moving back to her home, Labo Dhegax in Magalo. Her sentiments are nostalgic and filled with speculation of what it would actually be like to experience her homeland since she has been away for over thirty years. Itala Vivan notes that for immigrants like Adua:

the return of the migrant to his or her homeland is a compulsive step in the pattern of migration and must be accomplished either metaphorically

or materially in order to confront the many facets of one's own identity
and personal history.

(Scego, 2015: 125)

Adua contemplates returning home through conversations with her friend
who has departed Italy. Further, Vivan asserts that "The migrant's return
to his or her African home is linked to a need for retracing historical events
and facts that characterize the past and present history of the country of
origin and seeing them with new eyes" (Scego, 2015: 125). Adua's friend Lul
tells her that her father's house is "worth its weight in gold…about a mil-
lion dollars" (Scego 149). Lul is like a guardian spirit that Adua wishes had
been around in 1977 to guide her away from many unwholesome behaviors,
alienation from her Somali cultural heritage, and most of all, prevented her
from making that "movie with Arturo, that ugly, obscene movie" (Scego,
2015: 154).

The European assault on the black migrant body is a motif in the novel
through the juxtaposition of Adua's denigration with the brutality suffered
by her father in Italy where he is imprisoned and beaten by Italian soldiers.
His encounters with Italians occur during the mid-1930s colonial era under
Mussolini. He is a translator for the Italians and he suffers torture, constant
verbal abuse, and near starvation. His crime is his blackness that provokes
relentless abuse from sadistic officers who delight in their power over him.
The officers take turns thinking of ways to assault his body, such as burning
his feet, breaking his nose, or poking out his eyes, all to the tune of racial
slurs. His Somali identity is racialized in aggressive ways such as being spat
at, called n----r. The guards admit that the brutal beating is just for fun, and
the stream of racial insults convey their hatred. While in prison, his condition worsens, and he is given slop with prickly worms. Zoppe is valuable to
them as a highly skilled translator, speaking Arabic, Somali, Amharic, and
Tigrinya, which is why he is not killed by the soldiers.

The novel highlights the vulnerable psyche of colonial subjects to unwit-
ting seduction of colonial spaces that confer opportunities for mobility and
status. When Zoppe learned he would visit Rome, "he thought it was a mira-
cle. A Negro in Rome? Him?" (Scego, 2015: 13). In striking irony that parallels Adua's fascination with Italy years later, "Rome was his dream" (Scego,
2015: 13). He thought of himself as a linguistic ambassador, that is very similar to Adua's illusion of fame and success as an actress. Both Zoppe and his
daughter imagine new identities abroad that will transcend the African self.

In *Adua*, the innocent dreams of father and daughter, as colonized subjects in foreign spaces, are the cannon fodder of racial oppression and violence meted out to them and that ultimately alter the lives of marginalized
African migrants. Zoppe is arrested because he attempted to break up a fight
between two Italian men. Zoppe's dreams are brutally shattered, similar to
events in the autobiographical novel *Immigrato* (1990) by Tunisian born
Salah Methnani, who narrates: "finding out that the country of his dreams

more often than not is that of his nightmares" (qtd. in Dimaio,2009: 126). Scego's novel presents a finely sketched portrait of assault on migrant black bodies, their battered lives, and fractured psyche to memorialize their pain in the past and present.

Further, Sun Lee elucidates the nature of identity in relation to spatiality:

> But identity is not determined by spatial location in any simple manner. Space and place are themselves extraordinarily complex, as we have seen: divided, layered, unmappable. Through the pressures of diaspora, other social wholes undergo a similar stretching and distortion. As nations and families are spread apart, the question of belonging becomes both urgent and difficult to ascertain. In the host nation, class undergoes a reshuffling, and unfamiliar categories of racial difference make themselves impossible to ignore. Identities are sometimes assigned to you, and just as often denied. Belonging to a larger whole, cannot be taken for granted. In these novels, identity emerges as something radically contingent on performance, on performing certain types of acts, gestures or styles.
>
> (2018: 198)

Thus, Sun Lee's discussion accounts for the multilayered contingencies that act upon transnational subjects that inhabit the Somali-Italian diaspora. Both Adua and her father's experiences are mediated by the colonial perceptions of Black bodies viewed through the Italian gaze, and the appropriation of these bodies for exploitation and abuse.

In sum, Igiaba Scego's *Adua* is a journey through the shattered hopes and failed dreams of a Somali woman in Italy. The diaspora perspective unfurls the interrogation of the colonial gaze and the postcolonial ruptures of the nation state inscribed on the bodies of women and men. The novel untangles the web of confusion for Adua, generated by patriarchal authority in the absence of maternal love and guidance. Raised on the corrosive stream of her father's misogyny, the protagonist imagines an escapist adventure into foreign spaces where her Somali identity is subsumed in the degrading status of the African female *other*. The novel speaks to the violence inflicted on the female body during rites of passage that marks the beginnings of womanhood and the control of sexuality for girls and women in Somali society. In the search for a new identity modeled on foreign illusions that are unattainable, Adua's transnational identity is a debilitating and regrettable experience. Torn between the past and the present, Somalia and Italy, Adua's evolution illustrates the dangers of migratory energies for both women and men. Women's subjectivity presents challenges both at home and abroad but the power of European influence equally threatens males during colonization as well as the post-independence era in Italy. Paradoxically, the Italian diaspora materializes the space for the evolution of women's agency and self-discovery in re-shaping broken lives. For the protagonist, silence is no longer an option or a compelling behavior as a mature woman. Adua assumes control over her sexuality and her status as a woman in ways that disrupt the patriarchal order of her Somali cultural origins and the trappings of sexualized identity. *Adua* conveys the lessons of the past, endured through physical and mental suffering of African women and men who surrender their bodies in alien lands of racial oppression, exploitation, and loss of dignity.

Local and global forces frame the spatio-temporal arc of the work over a thirty-year period in Italy for Adua. The choice to return to her homeland of Somalia represents a new journey into uncharted spaces linking the past to the present, Africa to Europe, and the hybrid nature of diaspora identity. The novel illustrates the potential for healing and reconciliation of regretful mistakes, and outright failures in the past. As a mature woman, Adua comes to terms with a new sense of her identity within her Somali community. *Adua* is a significant contribution to African literature, women's writing, and diaspora studies in the twenty-first century. Finally, the novel raises questions about the price that African immigrants pay in the search for economic opportunities, survival, and freedom from sites of conflict in their homelands in the global age.

Notes

1 Said Baare is the former president of Somalia from 1969 to 1991.
2 griot is an oral historian, poet, story teller, musician throughout many African cultures.

Works Cited

Ali Farah, Cristina. 2077. *Little Mother Madre piccolo*. Milan: Frassinelli.

Adichie, Chimamanda Ngozi. 2013. *Americanah*. Toronto. Alfred A. Knopf.

Atta, Sefi. 2013. *A Bit of Difference*. Northampton. Interlink Books.

Ayim, Nana Offoriatta. 2019. *The God Child*. Oxford, New York, New Delhi. Bloomsbury Press.

Benedicty-Kokken, Alessandra. 2021. "Italy, Somalia, and the Black Mediterranean, or reading Igiaba Scego's Adua alongside Ba, Mbembe, Waberi, and Somali praise poetry". *Transnational Africana Women's Fictions*. ed. Cheryl Sterling. London. Routledge. pp. 169–187.

Bulawayo, No Violet. 2013. *We Need New Names*. Bulawayo, New York. Regan Arthur Books.

Cenedese, Marta-Laura. 2018. "Instrumental Narratives of Postcolonial Rwmomory: Intersectionality and Multidirectional Memory". *Storyworlds: Journal of Narrative Studies*. Vol. 10, No. 1–2. pp. 95–116.

Curti, Lidia. 2007. "Female Literature of Migration in Italy". *Feminist Review*. No. 87. Italian Feminisms. Vol. 87. pp. 60–75.

Di Maio, Alessandra. 2009. "Black Italia, Contemporary Migrant Writers from Africa". *Black Europe and the African Diaspora*. ed. Darlene Clark Hine, Tricia Danielle Keaton, and Stephen Small. Illinois. University of Illinois Press. pp. 119–144.

Emecheta, Buchi. 1972. *In the Ditch*. London. Heineman.

———. 1974. *Second Class Citizen*. New York. George Braziller

————. 1986. *Head Above Water*. London. Fontara.

Evaristo, Bernadine. 2019. *Girl, Woman, Other*. New York. Grove Press.

Farah, Nuruddin. 2000. *Yesterday, Tomorrow: Voices from the Somali Diaspora*. London and New York. Cassell.

Farina, Patrizia and Eliza Ortensi. 2014. "The Mother to Daughter Transmission of Female Genital Cutting in Emigration Evidenced by Italian Survey Data". *Genus*. May–December Vol. 70, No. 2–3. pp. 111–137. Women, Marginalization and Vulnerability.

Feathers, Lori. 2019. Book Review. *Beyond Babylon, a Novel*. On the Seawall. https://www.ronslate.com/on-beyond-babylon-a-novel-by-igiaba-scego-translated -from-italian-by-aaron-robertson/.

Ghermandi, Gabriella and Cristiana Lombardi-Diop. 2007. *Queen of Pearls and Flowers Regina di Fiori e perle*. Roma: Donzelli.

Grasivarro, Pia and Marian Abdisamed. 1985. Female Circumcision in Somalia: Anthropological Traits. *Anthropologisher Anzeiger*. Jahrg. 43, H4 December. pp. 311–326.

Gyasi, Yaa. 2017. *Homegoing, a Novel*. New York. Vintage Books.

Hassan, Salah M. 2012. "Rethinking Cosmopolitanism: Is 'Afropolitan' the Answer?" http://www.princeclausfund.org/files/docs/5_PCF_Salah_Hassan_Reflections _120x190mm5DEC12_V.

Itala, Vita. 2011. "From AfricaMix to Babilonia: The African Voice in Writing Italian". *Global South*. Vol. 5, No. 2, Special Issue, Indigenous Knowledges and Intellectual Property Rights in the Age of Globalization. pp. 121–138.

Johansen, R. and B. Elise. 2002. "Pain as a Counterpoint to Culture: Towards an Analysis of Pain Associated with Infibulation in Norway". *Medical Anthropology Quarterly, New Series*. September Vol. 16, No. 3. pp. 312–340.

Kincaid, Jamacai. 1978. *Girl. New Yorker Magazine*.

Lee, Sun Yoon. 2018. "The Postcolonial Novel and Diaspora". *The Routledge Diaspora Studies Reader*. ed. Klaus Stierstorfer and Janet Wilson. London. pp. 196–200.

Methnani, S., with M. Fortunato. 1990. *Immigrato*. Rome-Naples. Theoria.

Ponzanesi, Sandra. "The Color of Love: Madamismo and Interracial Relationships in the Italian Colonies". *Research in African Literatures*. Summer Vol. 43, No. 2. pp. 155–172.

'Pro' Sobopha, Mycineni. 2005. "The Body: Gender and the Politics of Representation". *Agenda: Empowering Women for Gender Equity*. Vol. 2,2 No. 63, African Feminisms, Sexuality and Body Image. pp. 117–130.

Quayson, Ato. 2013. "Postcolonialism and the Diasporic Imaginary". *A Companion to the Postcolonial Novel*. ed. Ato Quayson and Girish Daswani. London. Cambridge University Press. pp. 140–159.

Scego, Igiaba. 2015. *Adua*. New York. New Vessel Press. Trans. Jamie Richards. *Beyond Babylon a Novel*. 2019. *Oltre Babilonia*. Trans. Aaron Robertson. San Francisco. Two Lines Press.

Selasi, Taiye. 2013. *Ghana Must Go*. New York. Penguin Press.

Shire, Warsan. 2011. *Teaching My Mother How to Give Birth*. London. Flipped Eye.

Unigwe, Chika. 2009. *On Black Sisters Street*. London. Jonathan Cape.

Vivan, Itala. 2011. "From AfricaMix to Babilonia: The African Voice Writing Italian". *The Global South*. Vol. 5, No. 2, Special Issue: Indigenous Knowledges and Intellectual Property Rights in the Age of Globalization, pp. 121–138.

8 Afropolitan Energies in the Twenty-First Century

Immigrants, Dreamers, and Marginalized Others in *Americanah* by Chimamanda Ngozi Adichie

In the contemporary era, a new generation of African writers is crafting literature that chronicles the experiences of African émigrés in transnational spaces. Increasingly, the lives of African migrants in the global age span diverse cultures, ethnic entities, and ideological boundaries of Africa, Europe, and America. The dynamic realities of the livelihoods of African émigrés have been articulated as a new way of being in the African Diaspora through the lens of *Afropolitanism*, understood by some writers and scholars as a phenomenon that represents a unified and universalistic assimilation into western life for African immigrants. This chapter argues that these constructs of *Afropolitanism* are not universalistic, because they reflect the lived experiences of a particular sub-set of African Diasporans that collapses the multiple, diverse, and contested spaces of other African subjectivities into a singular narrative. Chimamanda Ngozi Adichie's *Americanah* (2013) is a successful fictional work that refutes the assertions of Afropolitanism.[1] The novel captures the complexities of immigrant experiences through a gendered lens. The portrayal of conflicts, hybridity, and marginalization of female characters is realistic and oppositional to glossy descriptions of success, acculturation, and globalized identities across national boundaries in Europe and America.

For the more privileged and hybrid characters explored in *Americanah*, the diverse and frequently paradoxical experiences denote transnational spaces of otherness and unbelonging. The spatio-temporal geographies of "place-making" that immigrants encounter compel the re-negotiation of race, class, gender, and other social/political configurations. Many immigrants from elite backgrounds carry the aura of sophistication, multi-linguistic advantage, education, and professional advantages that confer high-powered lifestyles as described by Selasi in "Bye Babar" in 2005.

For this class of African immigrant, movements across international boundaries does in fact represent many Afropolitan elements; although paradoxically, even privileged migrant subjects must grapple with unfavorable and unwelcoming energies such as racialized identities. Yet for other African subjects, particularly those who do not represent urbane and cosmopolitan lifestyles, *Afropolitanism* ignores the underprivileged masses and fails to

DOI: 10.4324/9781003350200-11

capture the dynamics of their subjectivity. Chielozona Eze concurs when he notes "the more damning weakness of the term, as has been pointed out by many critics, is in its exclusivity and elitism" (2014: 240).

Taiye Selasi's life models *Afropolitanism's* mobility and cultural hybridity because she was born in London to Nigerian, Ghanaian, and Scottish parents, raised in Boston, and studied at Yale and Oxford. She has lived in New Delhi, Accra, Rome, and Berlin, and in "Bye Babar," she defines *Afropolitanism* lifestyles in glowing terms that project the experiences of successful immigrants who are:

> African young people working and living in cities around the globe, they belong to no single geography, but feel at home in many. They, [(read we]) are Afropolitans-the newest generation of African emigrants, coming soon or collected already at a law firm/chemlab/jazz lounge near you.
>
> (Selasi, 2005: 2)

Selassie says of Afropolitans: "you'll know us by our funny blend of London fashion, New York jargon, African ethics, and academic successes" (Selasi, 2005: 2). Though colorful and self-assured, her descriptions are exclusionary, drawing sharp criticism from writers and scholars that describe the term as elitist posturing. Despite ethnic mixes within successful migrant populations, connecting threads of Afropolitan identity emerge when Selasi claims that:

> there is at least one place on the African Continent to which we tie our sense of self: be it nation-state (Ethiopia), a city (Ibadan), or an auntie's kitchen. Then there's the G8 city or two (or three) that we know like the backs of our hands.
>
> (Selasi, 2005: 2)

Selasi's ideas that celebrate cultural hybridity omit the experiences of masses of immigrant populations that form the bulk of the African Diaspora presence across Europe and North America. More appropriately, the term can be defined as "cosmopolitanism with African roots" (Gehrmann, 2016: 61), but these perceptions are reductionist and narcissistic and suggest a single-storied reality derived from elitism that is born of socioeconomic status and privilege.

Although Simon Gikandi echoes positive expressions of *Afropolitanism* in the foreword to *Negotiating Afropolitanism: Essays on Borders and Spaces in Contemporary Literature and Folklore* (2011), he acknowledges the negative consequences of transnationalism such as alienation, conflicting behaviors, and fragmented identities when Africans traverse geographical and linguistic boundaries (2010: 11). Gikandi's elucidation is a sound response to swirling debates around *Afropolitanism's* viability, and certainly his ideas illuminate class dynamics and offer the caveat to avoid essentialist expressions of the term. This is certainly accurate and timely within a global context where rapid changes impact social transformation and mobility in modern societies and provide new spaces that compel diaspora subjects to re-imagine what it means to be African.

The flawed representations of *Afropolitanism* are underplayed and removed from the context of race, class, and gender dynamics within a growing political climate in the west that is clearly anti-immigrant as reflected in sweeping political upheaval within recent elections, and right-wing extremism driven by xenophobia throughout western nations. Social, economic, and political landscapes of Europe and North America are presently the stage for discriminatory immigration policies and exclusionary paradigms of otherness and marginalization of populations perceived as a threat. However, long before nativism, parochialism, and populist sentiments became widely politicized over the past ten years, significant numbers of African immigrant populations have consistently experienced racial barriers in Europe and increasing political resistance in the United States as migrants traverse geographical, linguistic, and ethnic boundaries. Although globalization has engendered a new world of possibility and opportunity for masses of African migrants, anti-Muslim sentiments and ethnic divisions fester, as western nations erect new boundaries in an age of racial discord, xenophobia, and economic and political uncertainty.

Afropolitanism, as articulated by Selasi in "Bye Bye Babar" (2005), fails to address the problematic features of African Diaspora life such as the rude awakening to racial barriers, alienation, and conflicting relationships with Africa as "home-space." Selasie's descriptions of *Afropolitans* render a saucy flavor of buoyant exuberance in the glossed-over conflation of smartly packaged lifestyles of globetrotting Africans. In stark contrast, the sad and disturbing realities of ill-fated efforts to escape conflict zones in Africa sharpen the gulf between Selasi's cool and sleek representations of the new African elite who embody fluidity and mobility across foreign spaces. For example, Salah Hassan, in "Rethinking Cosmopolitanism: Is Afropolitanism the Answer," evokes:

> Tragic images of African youth, men and women who have perished trekking through the deserts of North African countries in transit to Europe, and of thousands of others who have drowned, (sometimes deliberately left to face such a tragic destiny) while journeying on makeshift boats across the Mediterranean Sea to Europe. Those who have made it alive have encountered a new fortress of draconian laws in a continent that has devoted its energies and legislation to its security-read curbing immigration as felt on a daily basis by Africans living in Europe or the USA.

> (2005: 4)

These "truths" harbor the dark side of border-crossing so that Africans flee-ing the continent in desperation and crisis are driven by the need to escape and survive. These realities contradict the discourse of naming and framing cosmopolitan identities in delusive terms. Ignoring the unfavorable politi-cal environments within contemporary western spaces becomes an exercise in self-congratulatory sentiments of elitism with reference to affluent and mobile immigrant communities. Moreover, Simon Gikandi articulates the requisite that *Afropolitanism*:

> consider the negative consequences of transnationalism, the displace-ment of Africans abroad, the difficulties they face as they try to over-come their alterity in alien landscapes, the deep cultural anxieties that often make diasporas sites of cultural fundamentalism and ethnic chauvinism.
>
> (2010: 1)

Nevertheless, Selasi successfully captures the flavor of a segment of African émigré populations who are indeed a privileged lot, educated, well-traveled, and seemingly at home in multi-local spaces. Selasi says of *Afropolitans*:

> You'll know us by our funny blend of London fashion, New York Jargon, African ethics, and academic successes. Some of us are eth-nic mixes, e.g., Ghanaian, and Canadian, Nigerian, and Swiss; others merely cultural mutts: American accent, European affect, African ethos. Most of us are multilingual: in addition to English and a Romantic or two, we understand some indigenous tongue and speak a few urban vernaculars....We are Afropolitans: not citizens, but Africans of the world.
>
> (Selasi, 2005: 2)

The exhilarating descriptions have garnered harsh critique among scholars, and Emma Dabiri warns of essentialist thinking because:

> The problem is not that Afropolitans are not privileged *per se* – rather it is at a time when poverty remains endemic for millions, the narratives of a privileged few telling us how great everything is, how much oppor-tunity and potential is available may drown out the voices of a majority who remain denied basic life chances.
>
> (Dabiri, 2014: 7)

These declarations suggest the danger of yet another single story pervad-ing the public imagination that contributes to the complexity of discourse about Africa and her Diaspora. Further, Dabiri cautions that: "while Afropolitanism may appear to offer an alternative to the single story, we run the danger of this becoming the dominant narrative for African success" (Dabari, 2014: 6). Gikandi offers a more nuanced articulation of Taiye Selasi's viewpoints when he asserts that African identities may be thought of: "as both rooted in specific local geographies but also transcendental of them." He emphasizes that:

> To be *Afropolitan* is to be connected to knowable African communities, nations, and traditions: but it is also to live a life divided across cultures, languages, and states... to embrace and celebrate a state of cultural hybridity – to be of Africa and of other worlds at the same time.
>
> (Gikandi, 2010: 2)

To be fair, *Afropolitanism* succeeds in subverting time-worn tropes of victimhood and crisis such as disease, war, poverty, aid dependence, and political corruption in the western projections of Africa, past and present. Miriam Pahl asserts that with reference to *Afropolitanism*, "the phenomenon appears as an alternative to 'Afropessimism' and the representation of Africa determined by deprivation and misery" (2016: 77). The term articulates a re-imagined sense of African identity within a globalized world of possibilities and opportunities. These ideas disrupt pejorative images of Africa and represent perhaps the best measure of *Afropolitanism's* merits within the cultural discourse.

In the mid to late twentieth century, the first postcolonial generation of Anglophone African writers began to examine African Diaspora life in Europe. Buchi Emecheta's autobiographical work *In the Ditch* (1994) and Ama Ata Aidoo's *My Sister Killjoy or Reflections of a Black-Eyed Squint* (1998) introduce readers to harsh realities and the difficulties of displacement in foreign spaces. The most recent publication by Ama Ata Aidoo, *Diplomatic Pounds* (2012), is a collection of short stories about Ghanaian women living in London. The female characters develop troubled relationships with their homeland and with their loved ones, and some of them never want to return to Ghana. The fictional works illustrate a common thematic exploration of cultural hybridity, dislocation, and marginalization in foreign lands. Ironically, some of the women characters achieve a measure of success and material comfort although, in the process, they become estranged from their families, and exhibit problematic relationships with Ghana.

A growing number of Diaspora-based African writers in the twenty-first century energize the literary imagination to represent a range of possibilities and multiple (re)constructions of identity for the new African Diaspora that are complex and oppositional to elitist representations posited by *Afropolitan* constructions. Since the turn of the century, an impressive cadre of African Diaspora writers is producing critically acclaimed works that form a genre of immigrant fiction that will be examined further in this chapter. Contemporary works by African writers mirror new configurations of identity and capture tensions between the local and the global, the past and the present, tradition and modernity, assimilation, and displacement.

Contemporary African writers use their creative artistry to capture new tropes of identity formation, mobility, and fluid perceptions of the self as a mirror of their lived experiences since almost all of them reside in the west. These works include Adichie's *Americanah* (2013) and her collection of short stories *The Thing Around Your Neck* (2009). Sefi Atta's *A Bit of Difference* (2013) and stories in her short fiction collection *News from Home* (2009) examine diaspora life through a gendered lens. Akachi Adimora Ezeigbo's *Trafficked* (2008) exposes the unfortunate experiences of trafficked women entangled in the sex industry between Europe and West Africa. As a new writer from Zimbabwe, NoViolet Bulawayo has crafted a compelling portrait of the disruptive elements of Diaspora life in *We Need New Names* (2013). Brian Chikwava, also from Zimbabwe, published *Harare North* (2009), set in London. Taiye Selasie's *Ghana Must Go* (2013) examines Diaspora conflicts that span Ghana, Nigeria, and the United States. Teju Cole's *Open City* (2011) and Dinaw Mengetsu's *The Beautiful Things That Heaven Bears* (2007) have received critical acclaim for the portrayal of Diaspora discontent in New York and Washington, DC, respectively. Chris Abani's *Becoming Abigail* (2006) and Okey Ndibe's *Foreign Gods* (2013) add to this array of recent publications by writers who live in the west. Finally, E.C. Osondu's short fiction collection *Voice of America* (2010) examines a range of African migrant experiences within multi-local settings. The works represent compelling and realistic experiences that reveal the dark underbelly of global mobility across transnational borders of Africa and the west. These works refute reductionist and one-dimensional expressions of Afropolitanism because they capture diverse and nuanced representations of cultural dissonance, alienation, and failure to achieve their dreams of success and happiness.

An important feature of new Diaspora literature in the global age is the reconfiguration of race and identity that redefines *blackness* among troubled immigrant communities. In the seminal work, *Modernity: An Introduction to Modern Societies,* Stuart Hall (1996) succinctly articulates the inevitable development of multiple identities when people traverse geographical, political, and cultural boundaries of Africa and the west. In framing Diaspora life in modern urban settings, he asserts that the intersection of multiple and diverse localities generates bifurcated identities as individuals are torn between the demands of antagonistic realities and the clash of cultures in transnational settings. Highly visible and successful works of leading African writers bear out these projections through realistic narratives of discontent and disjointed spaces in the lives of African immigrants in ways that clearly challenge the assumptions of Selasi's glowing descriptions of *Afropolitan* lifestyles. Literary postmodernism examines the tensions and contradictions that surface in the lives of African immigrants within modern societies that are transformed by displacement, social flux, and incongruent realities of marginalized status.

Chimamanda Ngozi Adichie's *Americanah* represents an important work of African Diaspora literature that resonate *Afropolitan* elements within a larger framework of failure to achieve the American dream or the European equivalent. The characters in *Americanah* portray an emerging demographic of Diaspora subjectivity within a globalized arena. As a highly celebrated book in recent years, it vividly conveys unsavory experiences of alterity as African identities are distorted by crippling barriers to acceptance in the west. The diaspora landscape as portrayed in *Americanah* is a counter-narrative to images described by Selasie in "Bye Bye Babar" in which *Afropolitans* are: "African young people working and living around the globe, they belong to no single geography, but feel at home in many" (2005: 2). Critics of *Afropolitanism* note the failure to address the dynamics of class differences, and in contemporary immigrant fiction, few, if any of the African characters, feel at home in the harsh, racially polarized environments of Europe and America.

Broadly speaking, the growing body of fictional works by African writers that live abroad has re-defined African writing in the global age in ways that re-conceptualize African literature as a genre. Multi-local settings, cultural hybridity, and new relationships with Africa represent fresh perspectives that challenge *Afropolitanism's* claims to an all-consuming reality of savvy, sophisticated, and cosmopolitan lifestyles. Contrasting views of cultural identity and socially incompatible behaviors are conveyed in works that command readers' attention and illuminate contemporary challenges of life in the African Diaspora. For example, shifting identities, marginality, and splintered consciousness translate into postmodern elements of the social and cultural landscape in the body of works by Adichie and numerous African writers in the global age.

Further, *Afropolitanism* is neglectful of the ways in which the reconfiguration of race and identity redefines *blackness* among troubled immigrant communities. The transformative experiences of new African émigrés in *Americanah* resonate with the African American experience of the *divided self* that is chronicled by W.E.B. Dubois in the early twentieth century. In "Revisiting Double-Consciousness and Relocating the Self in *Americanah* by Chimamanda Ngozi Adichie," Sackeyfio (2017) notes that in 1993, Paul Gilroy published his classic, *The Black Atlantic: Modernity and Double Consciousness* where he re-visits the concept within the spatio-temporal locus of marginalized Black immigrants in Europe. "Contemporary expressions of double-consciousness is an important theme within Diaspora studies because of the didactic elements, and potential to connect the past to the present through interrogation of the new as well as the old African diaspora" (2017: 15–16). Within this context, *Afropolitanism* is re-conceptualized as inadequate to capture the complexities and multiple forms of alienation for African people who traverse geographic, linguistic, and national boundaries.

Chimamanda Ngozi Adichie is arguably Africa's most successful and well-known contemporary writer. She has won critical acclaim for all her works that include *Purple Hibiscus* (2003), *Half of a Yellow Sun* (2006), a collection of short stories called *The Thing Around Your Neck* in 2009, and

Americanah (2013). Her recent publication is a collection of essays called *We Should All Be Feminists* (2016). Among Adichie's many distinguished awards are the MacArthur Fellowship (2008), The O. Henry Prize (2003), The Commonwealth Writer's Prize (2005), and The Orange Prize in 2007. In April 2017, Adichie was inducted into the National Academy of Arts and Letters for her distinguished contributions to literature. Her fiction introduces new perspectives in African and postcolonial writing, and Women's and World Literature in new and exciting ways. As a voice for third-generation postcolonial African writers, Adichie's creative artistry connects Nigerian culture and history in ways that interrogate social, economic, and political realities for African and African Diaspora people in the global age. The late Chinua Achebe stated that: "We do not usually associate wisdom with beginners, but here is a new writer endowed with the gift of ancient storytellers... Adichie came almost fully made." Achebe's tribute to Adichie's talent symbolizes her importance as a writer whose influence spans the boundaries of Africa and the west.

In *Americanah*, Adichie's presentation of multiple perspectives underscores the paradoxical nature of Diaspora discontent and the intersectionality of multiple sites of alienation and shifting identities. The broad scope of the novel explores the ways in which multi-local environments of transnationality in the African Diaspora forms the backdrop of ambiguous and problematic identities that refute *Afropolitanism* as a universal phenomenon. The novel confirms the broad spectrum of subjectivities and experiences that is shaped by the intersection of race, class, and gender dynamics among African immigrants in America and the United Kingdom. The complexities of life in western nations echo the influence of globalization, migration, and change. The work also reveals that education and material comfort is not a singular measure of success and well-being in contemporary society. *Americanah* explores the lives of Nigerian and other African immigrants as they grapple with acceptance and belonging outside Africa as a *homespace*. For many immigrants, the longing for emotional connection to people, places, and remembered experiences of their homelands denotes a fragmented sense of their existence. These sentiments heighten prevailing tensions between local and global realities in the lives of African subjects.

Ifemelu, the female protagonist, is at the center of a complex and enigmatic journey to find herself in America as she pursues education and success. When she departs Nigeria, she leaves behind her boyfriend Obinze and their lives follow different paths across three continents. The novel juxtaposes African immigrant life in America and London through experiences that project Diaspora tensions and distress among all the African characters in the work. A compelling feature of *Americanah* is the homodiegetic narration that underscores hybridity as a controlling theme that unfolds against the backdrop of a love story between Ifemelu and Obinze. The work is narrated through the voice of Ifemelu who begins her journey into *otherness* by adopting an American accent. Of all the dislocated Africans in the work, she emerges as the only character that embodies some *Afropolitan* qualities in its conventional sense, but this evolves much later in the novel. Through self-discovery, she finds her way home to Nigeria to embrace her identity, cultural moorings, and reconnection to Nigerian womanhood. Unlike the educated and sophisticated Africans described by proponents of *Afropolitanism*, Ifemelu had never been abroad before although some of her friends in secondary school had passports, travel with their parents, and their privileged status enables them to float seamlessly into foreign spaces.

Unlike her schoolmates, her parents are not rich, but are teachers and civil servants, who took the bus around town and did not have drivers (Adichie, 2013: 66). She is offered a scholarship for college in America and her experiences capture a gendered tale of poverty, depression, and Diaspora angst. Like many African writers, Adichie's fiction mirrors fragments of her own life as a Diaspora subject. In an interview with Michael Ondaatje, Adichie recalls her experiences with "culture shock" – a de-centering of herself that turned her into an "entirely different person," which resonates the complexities of *Afropolitan* sensibilities. Early in the novel, Ifemelu experiences severe depression because of her inability to find employment and she narrates multi-layered experiences of *otherness* because of her Nigerian accent. After an abrasive encounter with a white woman, she makes a conscious choice to change her speech so that: "in the following weeks, as autumn's coolness descended, she began to practice an American accent" (Adichie, 2013: 135). Like many African immigrants, acquiring an American accent represents what Samir Dayal refers to as "diasporic double-consciousness" (1996: 47).

In 1903, W.E.B. Dubois coined the term "double-consciousness" in his seminal work *Souls of Black Folk* to describe the psychological impact of racism and alienation among African Americans. Double-consciousness "is a theoretical framework that elucidates the splintered psyche of African Americans that are cast as the *other* within the racially polarized environment of America" (2017:215). Important parallels emerge in the ideas of Dubois and Franz Fanon who crafted the classic *Black Skin White Masks* (1967). T. Owens Moore explores the strong similarities in "A Fanonian Perspective on Double-Consciousness" (2005) where he confirms that: "Dubois' double-consciousness sounds as though it is echoed in Fanon's first book" (Moore, 2005: 754). Fanon succinctly captures the essence of hybridity when he asserts that: "Subjectively, intellectually, the Antillean conducts himself like a white man. But he is a Negro. That he will learn once he goes to Europe" (1967: 48). These conflicting behaviors resonate among contemporary African Diaspora subjects, who exhibit new expressions of duality that are common, because an African accent is a tangible barrier to assimilation, to finding a job, and to climbing the ladder of success. Elliot P. Skinner confirms these ideas in the assertion that: "Generations of African peoples experienced the onus of seeing themselves through the eyes of others. As 'bastards' of the West, they always sensed that in many subtle and obvious ways they were illegitimate" (1999: 29). Themes of alienation and awkward attempts to overcome *otherness* are pervasive in the growing body of African diaspora literature.

Americanah vividly portrays the ways in which African immigrants assimilate new forms of double-consciousness when they are burdened with the legacy of America's racialized history, environment, lingering racial stereotypes, and social injustice in the lives of many African Americans. These encounters starkly contrast with Selasi's descriptions of successful African immigrants that are comfortable in foreign spaces. In the novel, Ifemelu's perceptions of her *blackness* begin to sink in, and in a blog that she authors, she explores ideas about racial dynamics in the context of American history. According to Miriam Pahl, "the blog Adichie creates for Ifemelu...exhibits a strong political and social commitment. It negotiates the hierarchization of cultures and criticizes the "white-centerdness of the US environment depicted in the novel, and chronicles everyday incidents of racism" (2016: 78). The dichotomy between African and African American identity is explained by Louis Chude-Sokei who affirms that novels by contemporary African writers portray characters that:

> dangle between Africa and America – the old and the new, tradition and modernity – in truth, the space between nations and continents is rendered secondary in these fictions to the newly discovered racialized spaces *within* the country in which they have arrived.
>
> (2014: 113)

In the blog, Ifemelu addresses African immigrants:

> Dear Non-American Black, when you make the choice to come to America, you become black. Stop arguing. Stop saying I'm Jamaican or I'm Ghanaian. America doesn't care. So what if you weren't "black" in your country? You're in America now. We all have our moments of initiation into the Society of Former Negroes. Mine was in a class in undergrad when I was asked to give the black perspective, only I had no idea what that was. So I just made something up. And admit it—You say "I'm not black", only because you know that black is at the bottom of America's race ladder. And you want none of that. Don't deny now. What if being black had all the privileges of being white? Would you still say "Don't call me Black, I'm from Trinidad"? I don't think so. So you're black baby".
>
> (Adichie, 2013: 122)

These perceptions underscore the pervasive nature of African immigrants' reckoning with skin color as the marker of identity as opposed to ethnicity and national origin in Africa. In an interview in 2013, called "Learning to Be Black in America," Adichie explains that she had to learn to navigate race and expresses her discomfort with the idea of ignoring America's history. Although Adichie, like other African immigrants, may recoil from being labeled *black*, distancing oneself from racial dynamics suggests complicity with the status quo that marginalizes African Americans. Louis Chude-Sokei states that: "What confronts Africans in America is certainly racism but also the expectation that they share a collective response to it" (Adichie, 2013: 113).

Moreover, Sackeyfio illuminates the nature of the dichotomy among Africans and African Americans in "Negotiating identity and Pan-African aesthetics in *Americanah* by Chimamanda Ngozi Adiche":

> "The absence of historical context, either by African immigrants, Caucasians, or diaspora people themselves, illustrates the great chasm among communities of color caused by ignorance, bias, and historical amnesia". Adichie admits her ignorance before migrating to America and in another interview called "Race doesn't occur to me" with Aaron Bady, she describes how she 'learned' to be black in America. She recalls that even though she had not been in the country long, she already knew that to be "black" was not a good thing in America, and she did not want to be "black".
>
> (Adichie, 2014: 7)

According to the precepts of Afropolitanism, neither racialized identities nor the historical fissures among Africans and African diaspora communities is addressed in Selasi's elaborate perceptions of successful African migrants. In the global mix of transnational mobility and shifting identities, an awareness of the ways in which spatiality and positionality mediate identity is key to understanding the complexities of skin color as perceived in western spaces. Perhaps the most favorable outcome of Adichie's exploration of racial dynamics in America is her avowed allegiance to Pan-Africanism.

As noted by Sackeyfio:

> Whether or not African immigrants chafe against being identified as black, the reality of their *perceived* blackness by the majority race is inescapable and certainly shapes their experiences in the west. Thus, Adichie's Pan-Africanist stance is clear in her recognition of historical contexts and the attendant realities of racism.
>
> (Sackeyfio, 2021: 55)

Finally, the importance of acknowledging racialized identities is critical to achieve meaningful discourse among diverse communities of color. In *Americanah*, Adichie explores these possibilities early in the novel when Ifemelu is getting her hair braided in a salon where there are women from Senegal and Mali. Ifemelu expresses feelings of solidarity; however, the women are not Afropolitan characters because of their socioeconomic status. Also, when Ifemelu is in college, she encounters other African students from a diverse array of nations. Because they are students, they cannot embody the exciting, globe-trotting lifestyles described by Selasi although future success is implied because they will be educated. They come together in a spirit of unity that parallels many university campuses that support African Student Associations.

In addition to the female protagonist, *Americanah* presents a host of immigrant characters that struggle with issues of identity and Diaspora angst. Ifemelu's Aunty Uju and her son Dike display familiar patterns of disquieting behaviors in the attempt to forge a sense of belonging, acceptance, and success. Ifemelu's aunt has worked for years to become a medical doctor and wades through Diaspora confusion and ineffective parenting of her son Dike. Ifemelu recalls that after passing her exams for a medical license her aunt tells Ifemelu:

> I have to take my braids out for my interviews and relax my hair ...If you have braids, they will think you are unprofessional. I have told you what they told me. You are in a country that is not your own. You do what you have to do if you want to succeed. There it was again, the strange naiveté with which Aunty Uju had covered herself like a blanket. Sometimes, while having a conversation it would occur to Ifemelu that Aunty Uju had deliberately left behind something of herself, something essential, in a distant and forgotten place.
>
> (Adichie, 2013: 120)

One of the most important features of Nigerian identity that Aunty Uju has left behind is her language. She forbids her son to speak Igbo and is unaware of his difficulties in coping with racial profiling and splintered identity. In what is perhaps the most harrowing episode in the novel, Dike is so deeply alienated that he attempts suicide. In "Back to Africa: Second Chances for the Children of West African Immigrants," Bledsoe and Sow document the vulnerability of the children of African immigrants to a range of dangerous pitfalls. These include delinquency, drugs, lack of respect for parental authority, and apathy toward academic achievement among others (Bledsoe and Sow, 2913: 753). Yet, Selasi's brand of *Afropolitanism* ignores such difficult realities of race, class, and cultural dissonance in ways that suggest seamless assimilation and acceptance within mainstream society. The body of literature by contemporary African diaspora writers almost speaks with one voice about rude awakenings to race and class and the ways in which individuals navigate new spaces that re-configure their identities.

The experiences of Nigerian immigrant characters in London parallel the downward spiral into *otherness* experienced by Ifemelu and others in America. Obinze, Ifemelu's former boyfriend, migrates to London when his mother unlawfully arranges a six-month visa. When it expires, he becomes desperate and he encounters a broad range of Africans, mostly Nigerians, whose lives are fragmented and who exist within a landscape of sketchy and fluid identities. Obinze meets Nigerians whose lives are marked by loosely connected pieces of their Nigerian culture. They speak with phony British accents and their lives abroad are superficial and empty. The African characters he meets in London are functioning in a world of pretense, inhospitality, and disconnection to Nigeria as homeland.

The new identities of his fellow Nigerians consist of shady business deals, and deceitful attitudes and their relationships with each other are often tenuous and frequently questionable. Obinze approaches several of them for assistance with employment, accommodation, and the National Insurance Card that would allow him to be employed legally in London.

As a newcomer, he is naïve to the sub-culture of fake marriages, flimsy promises, and the seamy underworld of undocumented status. Obinze must interact with what is essentially a web of illegal business deals to create a fake identity when he meets a man who will arrange a phony driver's license. Men from Angola promise to help him with an arranged marriage to a European woman in order to legalize his status.

Obinze has a crushing experience when he calls his friend Emenike because he:

> had imagined foolishly, that Emenike would take him in, show him the way. He knew of the many stories of friends and relatives who, in the harsh glare of life abroad, became unreliable, even hostile versions of their former selves. But what was it about the stubbornness of hope, the need to believe in tour own exceptionality, that these things happened to other people whose friends were not like yours?
>
> (Adichie, 2013: 249)

He has nowhere to turn since no one would help him and he ends up cleaning toilets. Obinze recalls that back in Nigeria:

> everyone joked about people who went abroad to clean toilets, and so Obinze approached his first job with irony: he was indeed abroad cleaning toilets, wearing rubber gloves and carrying a pail, in an estate agent's office on the second floor of a London building.
>
> (Adichie, 2013: 238)

This is especially disturbing because Obinze has a college degree. He quits the job because he finds it repulsive "all for three quid per hour" (Adichie, 2013: 238).

Obinze sinks into a lonely and dejected state and his situation is magnified by the unwelcoming political climate in London regarding fears of potential terrorism, ethnocentrism, and racism. When he read newspapers, he "only skimmed the British ones because there were more and more articles about immigration, and each one stoked new panic in his chest. *Schools swamped by Asylum Seekers* (Adichie, 2013: 258). He lives in fear and his alienation penetrates his thoughts because "he lived in London invisibly, his existence like an erased pencil sketch: each time he saw a policeman, or anyone in uniform, anyone with the faintest scent of authority, he would fight the urge to run" (Adichie, 2013: 259). Sadly, Obinze "thought of his mother and of Ifemelu, and the life he had imagined for himself, and the life he now had, lacquered as it was by work and reading, by panic and hope. He had never felt so lonely" (Adichie, 2013: 258). His story gets worse because he is using a fake identification card with someone else's name that allows him to work at a better job. In desperation, he seeks an arranged marriage of convenience in order to legalize his status. He is unsuccessful and ends up being arrested and deported back to Nigeria.

Adichie's portrayal of Obinze in London mirrors many immigrant narratives of educated people working at menial jobs. Okey Ndibe created a similar character in his novel *Foreign Gods Inc.* (2014) in which a Nigerian man earned a Bachelor's degree, having graduated at the top of his class from Amherst University in the USA. The man was driving a taxi for thirteen years because his Nigerian accent prevented him from getting a job.

Obinze's unfortunate experiences in London do not support Afropolitan aesthetics but rather reveal a dark side of African immigrant life, riddled with an unwholesome rat race to survive, and to beat the system if not legally, then by illegal means. The harsh circumstances and legal barriers faced by migrants push them to unlawful behaviors and to unsympathetic behaviors among their fellow Africans.

Conclusion

In sum, Adichie's *Americanah* captures the challenges of Diaspora life through a gendered lens. As a theoretical framework, *Afropolitanism* fails to address issues of race, class, and gender dynamics within transnational boundaries as these become the markers of difference, marginality, and alienation. The novel forms a tapestry of the African Diaspora setting that is marred by broken dreams, fractured identity, and displacement for many African immigrant characters. Adichie's *Americanah* portrays a female protagonist who emerges as strong and resilient through her personal development, intelligence, and agency. She illustrates African women's potential to re-claiming their identity from the margins of *otherness* and uncertainty. Ifemelu's ability to re-negotiate her identity is a central tenet of *Afropolitanism* through the existence of a range of *possibility* and opportunities. Ironically, the novel's ending suggests that the route to self-acceptance is to maintain cultural linkages as a foundation to navigate the rigors of life they may face when they depart from Africa. Ifemelu's journey vividly renders women's experiences of local and global tensions that are reflected in their evolving relationships with Nigeria and Africa. An important theme in Diaspora fiction is memory and longing for one's homeland alongside feelings of unbelonging and displacement in foreign lands.

Adichie's portrayal of a woman's decision to return to Nigeria is thus an important statement about the value of reconnection, identity, and belonging for female migrants in search of greener pastures within transnational spaces.

As a postcolonial text, *Americanah* succinctly engages and expands conventional themes of postcolonial critique in new ways that compel our attention. The metaphorical dimensions of the term "Americanah" contextualizes notions of migration and "return" to Africa for transnational subjects in the global age. An older theme that appears in early fictional works of postcoloniality is Ama Ata Aidoo's iconic *Our Sister Killjoy* where the female protagonist leaves and returns to Ghana. The racialized identities of Africans in the London novels of Buchi Emecheta such as *Second Class Citizen* and *In the Ditch* among others are vivid narratives of Africans living abroad. Since the 1980's downturn in Nigeria's economic and political trajectory, the nation has experienced a steady exit of many citizens to western spaces in the global north as well as many other nations throughout the world. The economic and political landscape in Nigeria has created uncertainty among youth such as rising unemployment, political repression, spiraling inflation, and lack of opportunities for university graduates. These conditions set the stage for the protagonist and the myriad Nigerian characters in the novel to search for greener pastures abroad. Against the backdrop of Nigeria's difficulty to offer viable futures for talented youth, Adichie has woven a tapestry of the disjointed lives that immigrants carve out for themselves in the Nigerian diaspora-scape.

Another postcolonial theme is the tenuous relationship of Nigerians to the country itself, and fortunately, the idea that the protagonist charts a new life for herself by returning to Nigeria is a powerful statement. The idea of "return" migration renders Nigeria's and Africa's potential for development as reflected in the talent, innovative energies, intelligence, and agency of young people like Ifemelu. Adichie seems to suggest that Nigeria and Africa have and will continue to produce promising young people who can achieve success at home in Africa, despite economic difficulties.

Along with postcolonial motifs that appear in *Americanah*, feminist aesthetics emerges in very compelling ways through the protagonist's evolving consciousness, her astute critique of and interaction with Nigerian and other diaspora people, as well as with non-black Americans. The protagonist journeys through depression, alienation, and hybrid mental states to achieve self-acceptance, professional success, and a "voice" that she shares through her blog. Ifemelu's "voice" is a commanding one, informed with knowledge and insight into issues of racial identity and historical perspectives on "blackness." Her agency to carve out a new path and to recover her "Nigeria identity" speaks to the potential of "rooted transnationalism" in place of Afropolitan terminology as discussed by Mukoma wa Ngugi in *the Rise of the African Novel* (2019). Although it is evident that Afropolitan aesthetics as described by Selasi does exist in *Americanah,* as a text, the work defies this monolithic conceptualization through presentation of primarily unfavorable experiences in the Nigerian diaspora as a counter-narrative.

Americanah skillfully chronicles experiences of class differences as immigrants wade through disparate environments of depression, marginal status, and adversity. *Afropolitanism*, as articulated by Taiye Selasi, fails woefully to represent the African immigrant experience in all its nuanced and diversified contexts of diaspora life in the global age. Though elitist in flavor, at best, *Afropolitanism* dictates new ways of being African in the world, devoid of tropes of victimhood and stereotypes of poverty, war, and disease in Africa. This is laudable, refreshing, and an authentic view of many immigrants who certainly embody Afropolitan energies and transnational identities.

Fictional works by Chimamanda Ngozi Adichie and other writers of the new generation of creative artists is a testimony of the ways in which art mirrors life. Mythic dimensions of *Afropolitanism* suggest that diasporic spaces inhabited by a generation of mobile, savvy, and globe-trotting African émigrés could become a new *single story* in the absence of critical engagement with the complexities of migration in the twenty-first century. This premise is easily defeated by a cursory look at the existence of refugee communities along with the vast majority of African immigrants that do not represent privileged elites.

Finally, as the abundance of African immigrant fiction illustrates, their collective experiences of *otherness* convey the dark side of globalization that generates flows of migrants across ethnic, linguistic, geographical, and national boundaries into new spaces of marginalization. The complexities of survival, difference, and assimilation in western environments resonate deeply as a feature of global migration and social transformation. Contemporary African fiction interrogates these dynamics, and *Americanah* successfully connects readers to an insightful exploration of what it means to be African at home and abroad in the twenty-first century.

Note

1   Afropolitanism is a popular but highly contested term articulated by author Taiye Selasi in LIP Magazine in 2005. The term asserts descriptions of a cosmopolitan elite, transnational African who is educated, privileged, multi-lingual, and mobile. The term has been criticized for its essentialist, monolithic perceptions of the African immigrant experience.

Works Cited

Abani, Chris. 2006. *Becoming Abigail*. New York. Akashic Books.
Adichie, Chimamanda Ngozi. and Aaron. Bady. 2013. Interview. Salon. *Boston Review*.   https://www.salon.com/2013/07/14/chimamanda_ngozi_adichie_race_doesnt_occur_to_me_partner/.

Adichie, Chimamanda Ngozi and Michael Ondaatje. 2007. "In Conversation: Chimamanda Ngozi Adichie, and Michael Ondaatje". *Brick*. Vol. 79. pp. 38–48.

Adichie, Chimamanda Ngozi. 2004. *Purple Hibiscus*. Lagos. Farafina.

———. 2007. *Half of a Yellow Sun*. Toronto. Alfred A. Knopf.

———. 2009a. *The Thing Around Your Neck*. Toronto. Alfred A. Knopf.

———. 2009b. "The Danger of a Single Story". *Ted Talk*. https://www.ted.com/talks /chimamanda_adichie_the_danger_of_a_single_story.

———. 2013. *Americanah*. Toronto. Alfred A. Knopf.

———. 2014a. "*Americanah* Author Explains Learning to be Black in the US". *NPR*.　http://www.npr.org/2014/03/07/286903648/americanah-author-explains -learning-to-be-black-in-the-u-s.

———. 2014b. *We Should All Be Feminists*. Fourth Estate Pub. Co. New York.

Aidoo, Ama Ata. 1977. *Our Sister Killjoy: Or Reflections of a Black-Eyed Squint*. New York. Longman.

———. 2012. *Diplomatic Pounds& Other Stories*. UK. Ayebia Clarke Publishing Co. London.

Atta, Sefi. 2010. *News from Home*. North Hampton. Interlink Books.

———. 2013. *A Bit of Difference*. Northampton. Interlink Books.

Bledsoe, H. Caroline and Papa Sow. 2013. "Back to Africa: Second Chances for the Children of African Immigrants". *The International Handbook on Gender, Migration and Transnationalism*. ed. Laura Odo and Natalia Ribas Mateos. Global and Development Perspectives. Spain. Universidade da Caruna. pp. 185–207.

Bulawayo, NoViolet. 2013. *We Need New Names*. New York. Regan Arthur Books.

Chikwava, Brian. 2009. *Harare North*. London. Vintage Books.

Chude-Sokei, Louis. 2014. "What Is Africa to Me Now?" *The Newly Black Americans*. MA. Indiana University Press, Bloomington. pp. 52–71.

Clifford, James. 1994. "Further Inflections Toward Ethnographies of the Future". *Cultural Anthropology*. Vol. 9, No. 3. pp. 302–338.

Cole, Teju. 2011. *Open City*. New York. Random House.

Dabiri, Emma. 2014. "Why I'm Not an Afropolitan". http://africasacountry.com /2014/01/why-im-not-an-afropolitan/.

Dayal, Samir. 1996. "Diaspora and Double Consciousness". *Journal of the Midwest Modern Language Association*. Spring Vol. 29, No. 1. pp. 42–62.

Dubois, W.E.B. 1903. *The Souls of Black Folk*. New York. Barnes and Noble.

Eze, Chielozona. 2014. "Rethinking African Culture and Identity: The Afropolitan Model". *Journal of African Cultural Studies*. Vol. 26. pp. 234–247. http://dx.doi .org/10.1080/13696815.2014.894474.

Ede, Amatoritsero. 2016. "The Politics of Afropolitanism". *Journal of African Cultural Studies*. Vol. 28, No. 1. pp. 88–100. http://dx.doi.org/10.1080/13696815 .2015.11326222016.

Emecheta, Buchi. 1972. *In the Ditch*. London. Barrie and Jenkins.

Ezeigbo, Akachi-Adimora. 2008. *Trafficked*. Lagos. Lantern Books.

Fanon, Franz. 1967. *Black Skin, White Masks*. New York. Grove Press.

Gehrmann, Susanne. 2016. "Cosmopolitanism with African Roots. Afropolitanism's Ambivalent Mobilities". *Journal of African Cultural Studies*. Vol. 28, No. 1. pp. 61–72. http://dx.doi.org/10.1080/13696815.2015.1112770.

Gikandi, Simon. 2010. "Foreword on Afropolitanism". *Negotiating Afropolitanism: Essays on Borders and Spaces in Contemporary African Literature and Folklore*. ed. Jennifer Warwrzinek and J.K.S. Makokha. Amsterdam. Rodopi. pp. 9–11.

Gilroy, Paul. 1993. *The Black Atlantic: Modernity and Double Consciousness*. MA. Harvard University Press.

Goyal, Yogita. 2014. "Africa and the Black Atlantic". *Research in African Literatures*. Vol. 45, No. 3, Africa and the Black Atlantic (Fall 2014), pp. v–xxv.

Hall, Stuart. 1996. et. al. *Modernity: An Introduction to Modern Societies*. Oxford: Blackwell Publishers. pp. 596–632.

Hassan, Salah. M. 2005. "Rethinking Cosmopolitanism: Is 'Afropolitan' the Answer?" http://www.princeclausfund.org/files/docs/5_PCF_Salah_Hassan_Reflections _120x190mm5DEC12_V.

Mbembe, Achille and Sarah Balakrishnan. 2016. "Pan African Legacies, Afropolitan Futures". *Transition*, No. 120. You Are next. pp. 28–37.

Mengetsu, Dinaw. 2007. *The Beautiful Things That Heaven Bears*. New York. Riverhead.

Moore, T. Owens. 2005. "A Fanonian Perspective on Double Consciousness". *Journal of Black Studies*. Vol. 35, No. 6. pp. 751–762.

Ndibe, Okey. 2014. *Foreign Gods Inc*. New York. Soho Press.

Osondu, E.C. 2010. *Voice of America*. New York. Harper Collins.

Pahl, Miriam. 2016. "Afropolitanism as Critical Consciousness: Chimamanda Ngozi Adichie's and Teju Cole's Internet Presence". *Journal of African Cultural Studies*. Vol. 28. pp. 173–87. http://dx.doi.org/10.1080/13696815.2015.1123143.

Sackeyfio, Rose A. 2017. Revisiting Double-consciousness and Relocating the Self in '*Americanah*'. *A Companion to Chimamanda Ngozi Adichie*. ed. Ernest Emenyonu. Martlesham: Boydell and Brewer. pp. 213–228.

Selasi, Taiye. 2005. "Bye-Bye Babar". *The LIP Magazine*. https://thelip.robertsharp .co.uk/category/lip5/.

———. 2013. *Ghana Must Go*. New York. Penguin Press.

Skinner, Elliot P. 1999. "The Restoration of African Identity for a New Millennium". *The African Diaspora: African Origins and New World Identities*. ed. Isidore Okpewho, Carol Boyce Davies, and Ali Mazrui. Bloomington. Indiana University Press. pp. 28–45.

Unigwe, Chika. 2009. *On Black Sisters Street*. London. Jonathan Cape.

Conclusion
Narrating African Women's Lives in Africa and the Diaspora

African Women Narrating Identity: Local and Global Journeys of the Self is a celebration of the rich outpouring of creative writing by African Women in the twentieth and twenty-first centuries. The fictional works in the volume convey the significance of women's experiences within Africa's complex cultures and transformative historical junctures. Gendered landscapes and regional diversity are the soil for an evolving literary tradition among successful women writers from across the continent who, in crafting their fiction, reveal their own truth to the world. The volume brings together some of Africa's most powerful and compelling women authors to form a cross-generational nexus of feminist and postcolonial writing. The female authors explored in the book raise issues that are central to African women's place in the world in ways that assert women's identities within and beyond the African continent. *African Women Narrating Identity: Local and Global Journeys of the Self* is a comprehensive analysis of the diverse perspectives of African women's lives across regional, ethnic, linguistic, generational, and religious boundaries that span the past and the present. An important feature of the broad scope of fictional representation is the emergence of connecting themes and tropes that unite women's voices through *herstories* of African women's literary expression. Despite spatio-temporal boundaries, the works are deeply connected through salient themes of feminist expression, patriarchal structures, customs and traditions, marginalization, hybridity, and post-coloniality, among others.

Part I examines the perspectives of women writers that live on the continent and represent the earlier generation of African women writers whose works span the early to mid-1970s beginning with Nawal El Saadawi's signature novel *Woman at Point Zero* and *God Dies by the Nile*. Also, Bessie Head's *Maru* was published in 1971 and Muthoni Likimani's *Passbook F.94727* in 1985. The intersection of feminist and postcolonial perspectives in Part I becomes the central focus of the literary engagement of the female authors. Overall, these iconic works are linked through a postcolonial lens that uncovers the intersection of gender, race, and class in an African setting during the colonial period. *Maru* and *Passbook F.47927* narrate the impact of the colonial intrusion on the lives of female protagonists in ways that illustrate African women's strength and resilience. Margaret Cadmore's identity

DOI: 10.4324/9781003350200-12

in the novel is shaped by a white missionary of the same name who ensures that she is educated to uplift her people in the future. The novel skillfully shifts to the strength of Margaret's identity as a highly intelligent Masarwa female who boldly asserts her membership in the outcast group in Dilepe society. Through the interpersonal dynamics of romance, power, gender, and caste discrimination, Head's *Maru* critiques the brutality of life in Botswana that mirrors the oppression meted out by Europeans during the colonial era.

The novel resonates autobiographical elements drawn from Head's own life because in South Africa and later in Botswana, she, like Margaret, was marginalized and shunned because of her ethnicity and her gender. The work interrogates the ill effects of displacement, and what is essentially slavery that exists in the society in Dilepe. Through graphic descriptions of the Masarwa who are perceived as filthy and subhuman, the novel raises ethical and moral questions about man's inhumanity to man, the nature of power, and the route to dismantle social and political stratification. The novel integrates romantic intrigue in the structure of the work although many critics have asserted this as a weakness in the novel. The romantic ending whereby Maru abdicates his role as paramount chief and marries an outcast woman may be read as the author's vision of political and social transformation across ethnic and gender boundaries.

Maru conveys messages of the critical need for equality and the ending suggests that the oppressed Masarwa will achieve their own liberation by violent means.

The strength of *Maru* also lies in the portrayal of strong women characters that surmount the barriers of gender to make their presence known in society. Feminist energies are present in the novel despite the puzzling actions of Margaret who is passive and silent when she is abducted by Maru at the novel's end. Instead of charting her own future, she allows herself to be rescued as a damsel in distress in fairytale style. However, the fact that she and Dikeledi are both educated and self-sufficient undeniably runs counter to conventional images of women characters who remain in the background as mere appendages to males. Feminist elements are more evident through Dikeledi's outspoken character, when she stands up to sexist males in power, and the assumption of a leadership role. The strength of *Maru's* message to readers lies within the interconnecting themes of postcolonial and feminist perspectives expressed through the women characters. The political structure of the village is effectively undermined with hope for a better future although an immediate end to discrimination against the outcast Masarwa is not forthcoming. Bessie Head's life became a template for her fictional works, and in *Maru*, the pain and human suffering caused by ethnic hatred and discrimination are juxtaposed alongside the brutality of European domination. The work unfolds the author's insight into the experiences of otherness and marginalization from a woman's perspective.

In 1985, Muthoni Likimani renders a powerful feminist narrative of Kenyan women's resistance to colonial domination in *Passbook F.47927.*

Women actors take center stage through their participation in the Mau revolt during the 1950s. Like Bessie Head, much of Likimani's fictional re-creations of women and events in her native Kenya are drawn from personal experience and observations in her society. Likimani has unsilenced women's voices to form a collective portrait of the diverse ways that women displayed their commitment to independence from Britain, the task of nation-building, and the preservation of their families. Likimani's female characters exhibit agency, courage, sacrifice, and collective political will during the anti-colonialist movement that was occluded in historical narratives written by males.

Many critics and historians acknowledge that without the support of women, the Mau Mau freedom fighters in the forests could not have survived without the food and supplies delivered to them by women. The accounts of the actions of women in the resistance movement bear the mark of authenticity as readers enter the world of brutalized, traumatized people who are fighting for the survival of themselves, their families, and their nation.

As the stories of women unfold in the text, the postcolonial perspectives are skillfully woven into the fabric of their experiences and two stories are vivid examples: *Passbook F.47927* and *Komerera* narrate the early period of the State Emergency in Kenya when the colonial government instituted the passbook laws to control and monitor the movements of the Kikuyu, Emba, and Meru communities. Likimani demonstrates the collusion of patriarchy and the ways in which draconian measures of the colonial authorities disproportionately affected women whose legal status could only be determined in relation to males, as in the term "passbook wives." Women were designated into two categories: wives and prostitutes, and to obtain the important "passbook" identification card, unmarried women were forced to relinquish their autonomy through liaisons with males. This became a form of commodification in the sense that women surrendered their bodies in exchange for protection, mobility, and documentation in Nairobi. The story emphasizes the imposition and power of the colonial machinery to determine Kenyan women's identities because of their gender.

The author narrates the desperation of women caught in precarious, and dangerous situations who faced limited choices because of gender subordination in their local communities along with the impositions of the colonial government. These realities underscore the fluid nature of women's identities determined by spatial proximity to males and the emotional stress of keeping safe from the home guards and colonial authorities. Perhaps the most significant role played by women during the Mau Mau revolution was the support of freedom fighters in the forests. Women risked their lives to hide men and to supply food and medicine as portrayed in "Unforgotten Flames" in which women make sacrifices to shield the Mau Mau fighters in clever ways.

Likimani's observations are realistic accounts that interrogate larger issues of gender inequality in Kenya, re-enforced by the British authorities to further disenfranchise women's status and role in society. Moreover, women were frequently left to fend for themselves and their children in the absence of husbands who were in detention, in prison, among the forest fighters, or deceased. The extreme hardship, poverty, and misery are vividly depicted as families were torn apart and displaced. Despite the extreme conditions, women characters found ways to survive and still care for their families. "Forced Communal Labor" captures the desperation of people trapped within a slave-like system of communal work on government projects that caused massive suffering. The everyday lives of women, and the strategies they developed to simply survive, reveal their vulnerability because of their gender. Despite working from sun-up to sundown, women farmed, cooked, and cared for their families through collective support. The inspirational flavor of the stories emerges through the women's resilience and solidarity in the effort to survive. Likimani highlights the strength of indigenous African cultural values as the basis of strength in unity to survive during the period of revolt.

Other memorable stories from the collection are "Kariokor Location," in which women secretly assist a new mother who has been separated from her husband while giving birth during a night-time raid. The woman is cared for and hidden by nationalist supporters whose real identities remain concealed. Women are also depicted caring for other women's children if they are left unattended. Again, such behaviors represent the strength of communal bonds as women faced daunting challenges to maintain some semblance of family life and care for loved ones under life-threatening conditions.

As the work unfolds, the diverse and complex roles of women in the Mau Mau rebellion come to light, and in "Vanishing Camp," a Kikuyu nurse goes to great lengths to relieve the suffering of Mau Mau detainees who are maltreated under dangerous conditions. Further, themes of nation-building in the wake of looming independence are explored in "Heroes' Welcome" when women work collectively to send a promising young man abroad for education. The women foresee the need to nurture a capable leader in an independent Kenya as females emerge as defenders of the soil alongside men. In some of the stories, women take the oath of loyalty to the Mau Mau revolt as well as ritualistic eating of soil, accompanied by the mantra, "the soil is ours." This practice is laced throughout the text as a symbol of undying support and love for their nation in the grip of colonial domination. The collective portrait of diverse contributions of women is expressed as a powerful testimony of feminist engagement rooted in the anticolonial struggle. The women's actions represent forms of indigenous feminist activism with specific political aims for independence along with social and economic transformation in the future. The postcolonial and feminist themes intersect within a framework of women's identities measured in strength, courage, and resilience in the Mau Mau rebellion against colonial domination. In the introductory essay by Jean O'Barr, she states unequivocally that:

Kenyan women's bravery and support, as freedom fighters, couriers, and mainstays of their communities during the revolt, is praised as a significant contribution to the struggle. Women like Field Marshal Muthoni (no relative to the author of this book) have a prominent place in Kenyan memories of Mau Mau; the leadership she provided along with Dedan Kimathi and General Mathenge in the fighting in the Aberdare Mountains is cited to extol women's participation in the struggle. Nonetheless, the form of those contributions was essentially traditional and the innovative behaviors, attitudes, and ideas which women contributed are noted but were not built upon generally in the before and after Mau Mau.

(1985: 27)

These ideas contextualize the nature of Kenyan women's participation, and O'Barr notes that after independence, women were unable to assume positions of leadership in substantial numbers and males were disproportionately credited for their diverse roles to support the anti-colonial movement.

(1985: 29–30)

Nevertheless, *Passbook F.47927* succeeds as an authentic narration of the critical support of women that reconfigures early historical publications about the anticolonial struggle by male authors. The rewriting of *history* about the Mau Mau period in Kenya parallels the pioneering West African fictional works of the first generation of women writers like Flora Nwapa, Buchi Emecheta, Ama Ata Aidoo, and Mariama Ba whose literature in the mid-1960s disrupted the poor image of women that appeared in male-authored texts by iconic male writers like Achebe, Soyinka among others. In this way, the full scope of the resistance movement is recorded with greater clarity and understanding of women's and men's enormous contributions.

African Women Narrating Identity: Local and Global Journeys of the Self highlights the linkages between Muslim women's identity in Egypt in Part 1 and the Sudanese Muslim Diaspora in the United Kingdom in Part 2. Nawal El Saadawi's iconic *Woman at Point Zero* and *God Dies by the Nile* are signature works of fiction created by one of the world's greatest writers and advocates for women's equality. In the twenty-first century, Leila Aboulela's writing extends themes of Muslim women's identity beyond North Africa to the United Kingdom. Saadawi's and Aboulela's novels represent generational intersections framed by spatio-temporal contingencies that surround the female protagonists.

The publication of *Woman at Point Zero* is a landmark in African women's fiction, and the impact of this work is a defining moment in the exploration of women's identity in the annals of literary studies. Both Saadawi's and Aboulela's novels bring to bear postcolonial elements as these continue to influence the imposition of Islamic religious practice on the lives of women in Egypt and the United Kingdom. Further, larger issues of transnationalism and hybridity that play out in the Sudanese diaspora create a nexus of interlocking themes that infuse Muslim women's religious faith both within and outside their communities. Also, in both Saadawi's and Aboulela's fiction, feminist synergy drives the inward search for identity in relation to religious faith experienced by the female protagonists.

Saadawi's *Woman at Point Zero* is a work of transformation as the author charts Firdaus's journey to radical feminist agency as a focal point of the book. The social, cultural, and religious environment of the protagonist is a catalyst for the evolution of feminist consciousness despite the tragic dimensions at the novel's ending. Saadawi, in presenting a woman's extreme response to toxic patriarchy and sexual exploitation, uncovers the plight of women who must survive within interlocking forms of oppression that mute the emergence of female identity. Since many women's roles and status in Egyptian society derive from conventional roles as wives and appendages to males, the idea of women defining themselves outside these parameters is not the norm. Saadawi's life is a case in point because in her autobiography, she recalls her brother being favored because of his gender. Her parents believed in the value of education for females and supported her educational goals. In the twenty-first century, there is a marked increase in literacy and education for women although the mandate to marry is still a cultural norm.

Radical feminist expression illustrates the strength of the novel through the vivid presentation of harsh and destructive cultural norms and practices like female circumcision, arranged marriage to older men, verbal and physical abuse, and complete subordination to male authority enforced by religion and patriarchal structures in Egyptian society. These prevailing norms in the treatment and status of women, as presented by the author, are painful realities that harden the protagonist's emotional responses. Radical feminist energy is illustrated in Firdaus's newly awakened consciousness when she develops a deep and penetrating analysis of the nature of her oppression by all the males in her life. Firdaus's feminist awakening is the springboard for her self-assertion, violent self-defense, and the courage to face the consequences of her actions. Firdaus's death is a form of freedom, and her identity illuminates the restrictions of Egyptian society that held the power to suffocate women's autonomy and silence their voices in society. Susan Ardnt avers that the novel does not end on an optimist note:

> For one thing, Firdaus is killed, and her development is unique within the context of the novel. There is no other woman who is as courageous and rebellious as Firdaus. In addition, the novel offers little optimism that the number of women like Firdaus will increase (in the near future). For another, the novel does not describe the woman-to-woman discrimination as likely to be overcome. The belief in women's solidarity is guarded, too. Any kind of collective resistance is considered as a utopia.
>
> (Ardnt, 2002: 163–164)

Although optimism for meaningful social transformation and equality for women is absent, in the novel, women's potential to awaken their consciousness is the first step to women's empowerment and their agency to change their lives.

God Dies by the Nile is also effective as a radical feminist text of sexual exploitation, moral corruption, and abuse of women and girls. The collusion of religion and patriarchy in the society of Kafr El Teen is presented more succinctly than in *Woman at Point Zero* that profiles the life path of a woman primarily through her sexuality. In contrast, Saadawi provides a skillfully nuanced sketch of religious hypocrisy through a number of powerful male figures, the leader of which meets his death at the hands of a woman. The title *God Dies by the Nile* aptly conveys the elevated status and religious authority of male leaders who are essentially a power unto themselves, and they are accountable to no one because of their gender. Females in the community have little or no status so that young girls and women are mere commodities of sexual objectification. Social class confers privilege since the male ruling elite are wealthy which further consolidates their power. The town is led by the mayor, and Saadawi interrogates the inner world of his tyranny along with other men through their use of fear and manipulation as mechanisms of control of the peasant population. Zakeya is the moral center of the novel, and she has witnessed the terrible loss of family members at the hands of the mayor. Like Firdaus, she kills the male oppressor and feels no remorse. The impact of the violent ending suggests that women are the only ones who may liberate themselves from the emotional and physical violence inflicted by males whose immoral acts unveil religious hypocrisy and inhumanity. The mayor is treated like a God in the village, and Zakeya's actions disrupt male power to transform the society in Kafir El Teen. Susan Ardnt's framing of radical feminist literature by African women serves as a lens to interpret Saadawi's novels.

Amma Darko's *Faceless* completes Part 1 of the volume's exploration of African women's perspectives while residing in their homeland. As one of Ghana's leading writers, Darko unveils the life experiences and challenges that Ghanaian women face in the twenty-first century. *Faceless* uncovers the failure of postcolonial Ghana to implement social, economic, and political policies to avert massive poverty for the nation's urban underclass, disproportionately represented by children and women. The novel vividly portrays the consequences of poverty and neglect as women children and young girls are trapped in a vicious cycle of poverty that drives them to engage in prostitution while living on the streets. The author draws upon her own observations in Accra, and during the late twentieth century, Ghana and other urban sites across the continent witnessed alarming numbers of children driven from their homes as urban poverty rates skyrocketed. Themes of intergenerational solidarity converge to subvert violence and commodification of adolescent girls when an NGO worker intervenes when a young girl is brutally murdered. Women come together to investigate the crime as well as to rescue her sister. The novel highlights sexual exploitation and violence against females who fall prey to men who employ them for profit. Spatial traversal frames the events in the novel when the two female protagonists cross into spaces that demarcate their social and economic status.

The novel also critiques parental neglect because mothers are depicted as complicit in the plight of their daughters because they "sell" their daughters, push them into the streets as well as profit from their earnings either from begging or from male clients. The novel provides insight into the experiences of mothers who are desperately poor and unable to nurture and protect their children. Further, the role of the media along with an all-female NGO is woven into the novel as the way forward to social transformation and the rehabilitation of girls who were forced to live on the streets. The title of the novel evokes the brutal defacement of the murdered girl, Baby T. so that she is unrecognizable. The book conveys a dark-themed message because, for the children in the novel, life remains uncertain on the margins of society. The novel depicts the severe emotional toll of life on the streets where children are vulnerable to drug abuse, sexual assault, and violence by gang members, and predatory figures of the shadowy underworld of the streets.

Moreover, the events that unfold in *Faceless* suggest that until Ghanaian society addresses the plight of the nation's disenfranchised urban youth, Ghana's future is suspended as children represent the greatest asset to one of the continent's most promising developing nations. *Faceless*, like Darko's other novels, probes the social and economic challenges and barriers experienced by females in society. As the most vulnerable demographic in society, women and girls must navigate barriers in society such as women's inequality, patriarchy, economic adversity, and government policies that cloud their futures in the global arena. Many children throughout Africa's urban environments have been robbed of a normal childhood because they are prematurely thrust into the adult world and forced to fend for themselves. The characters and events in *Faceless* are drawn from actual headlines in Accra during the 1990s, and Darko's creative artistry has fashioned a work of penetrating insight into a prevailing social problem in modern Ghana and other African urban settings.

Finally, the four novels examined in Part 1 provide a kaleidoscopic rendering of African women's lives within diverse regional settings. Postcolonial perspectives inform the authors' engagement with a broad range of issues such as anticolonial resistance, ethnic marginalization and discrimination, patriarchal structures, religious identity, gender inequality, and child prostitution. With the exception of Darko's *Faceless* that was published in 2003, the works represent the late twentieth-century landscape in Africa. The setting of Head's *Maru*, Likimani's *Passbook F.47927*, and Saadawi's novels is the colonial period which displays the local forces that shape women's lives against the background of foreign intrusion that worsened the status of women all over the continent. In all the works, patriarchal structures and gender inequality collude with racial otherness in ways that mediate women's diverse experiences in *Maru*, and in *Passbook F.47927* because of oppression by the British colonial government.

Moreover, the authors of all the works have projected strong feminist energies of resilience and strength among females despite the sometimes dangerous and life-threatening challenges they encounter. Saadawi's exploited women characters make the ultimate sacrifice to free themselves from their male oppressors. Likimani's Mau Mau supporters risk their lives in the struggle for independence. In *Maru*, women are educators and leaders who assert their identities that disrupt male power. In Darko's *Faceless*, women exhibit agency and solidarity to rescue and protect a young girl and to seek social justice for a murder. These characteristics are notable given the problematic images of women in male-authored texts since the inception of African writing by male writers in English during the mid-1950s. Women's writing in the novels examined in this book uncovers the full humanity of female actors through exploration of their inner world; thoughts, feelings, hopes, and fears as narrated by the women themselves. In this way, women writers are (re) writing history by making their voices heard through the power of their literary imagination. Nawal El Saadawi, Bessie Head, Muthoni Likimani, and Amma Darko's fictional works form a bridge between the first generation of African women writers who began writing in the mid-1960s and the new generation of writers who now command the African literary stage in the global age.

The literary works in Part II transports African women far beyond the regional, ethnic, linguistic, and geographical borders of the continent to enter new worlds of difference abroad. In the global north as well as other spaces in the world, African women migrants are thrust into diverse environments that test their resolve to maintain their identities and connection to their homelands. Since the new millennium, the literary world has witnessed a dynamic explosion of fictional works written from the diaspora perspectives of women writers that reside outside the African continent. Indeed, the African novel in the twenty-first century represents a resurgence of creative expression that is invigorating the genre. The last two decades have witnessed a dramatic shift in the African novel from conventional post-independence themes that address the European intrusion and the attendant fissures within the nation-state. One pivotal development has been the increased prominence of women writers expounding the complexities of race, class, and gender. African fiction of migration, too, mirrors the existential collisions, fractures, and challenges of global mobility and the way they mediate identity and belonging among African subjects. The literature of current African writers engages with a globalized world fraught with incongruent energies of cultural dissonance, while African subjects reconfigure new ways of being African in the world.

In addition to the growing body of African writing that explores diasporic settings, contemporary African female authors also appraise local issues that intersect with global influences: environmental devastation, international drug and sex trafficking, political corruption, and economic and political upheaval, thereby presenting new forms of postcolonial critique. A constellation of successful twenty-first-century African writers is reconfiguring African literary history and among them is the work of Chimamanda Ngozi Adichie, Sefi Atta, Chika Unigwe, NoViolet Bulawayo, Igiaba Scego, and Leila Aboulela. In their fiction, these and other contemporary authors investigate a broad range of contemporary themes, extending and reconstructing salient issues of postcoloniality in the labyrinthine spaces of the globalized world. The works examined in Part II engage new issues and challenges in the scope and trajectory of the African novel in addition to the interrogation of fluid and shifting identities in the hyphenated spaces of the African diaspora. Analysis of the novels in Part II explores the social, economic, and political valences of the global environment that reshapes the lives of African migrants in a world of transformation and flux.

Part II of *African Women Narrating Identity: Local and Global Journeys of the Self* engages new trajectories of the African novel and the ways in which conventional themes of post-independence writing are recast in the global age. Further, women's immigrant fiction in the volume uncovers the ways in which African literature written in the global age transcend new frontiers of postcolonial perspectives such as Afropolitan Aesthetics, Feminism, Transnationalism, Pan-Africanism, Afrofuturism, and Diaspora Studies among many others. Diaspora fiction in the volume unfolds the complexities of race, class, and gender as these are mediated within transcultural spaces of racial *difference*. Moreover, African diaspora fiction interrogates notions of *home* and *return* for African identities in transit as well as explores relationships between African immigrants and African-descended peoples within transcultural settings.

Part II includes the novels of Leila Aboulela, NoViolet Bulawayo, Igiaba Scego, and Chimamanda Ngozi Adichie. Their fiction has received critical acclaim in the literary world with Adichie as unarguably the most celebrated contemporary writer from Africa. The diversity in the settings of the works creates a richly textured background that investigates a broad range of diaspora experiences and themes. The fictional works of Leila Aboulela strengthen the exploration of immigrant fiction in the volume through the inclusion of her two novels about Sudanese Muslim women living in Europe. Her works deserve more attention because of the importance of Islam in the global arena where increasing religious diversity is the subject of public and academic discourse in a rapidly changing world. Islam is the world's fastest-growing religion because of increased migration of Muslims into the Global north.

Chapter 5, "Unveiling Women's Identities in the African Muslim Diaspora" in Leila Aboulela, analyzes *The Translator* and *Minaret*. Aboulela's second novel, *Minaret*, highlights a woman's search for meaning and religious faith in London. The author skillfully weaves postcolonial themes through the examination of the protagonists' past in Sudan. Spatio-temporal elements illustrate the shifting identity of Najwa as the protagonist who grapples with her new identity as a marginalized other mediated primarily through religious affiliation rather than racial otherness. The unwelcoming environment of London demands that she navigate religious practice, unbelonging, and alienation determined by her new status among the less privileged Sudanese underclass in London. Her experience of hybridity is complicated because of the search for belonging to a religious community, and she is separated from her family and remains unmarried. Aboulela's portrait of a lonely Sudanese woman is different from other narratives of immigrant angst because within Islamic practice, much of women's identity is subsumed under the codes of behavior, practices, and status in the home and in society. Islam is a patriarchal religion that subordinates women in society, and *Minaret* illustrates the ways in which norms, dress codes, religious faith, and a sense of community are renegotiated as a way to cope with isolation and create a sense of belonging in London. In this way, the novel is a chronicle of place-making and belonging for a Sudanese woman reconnecting with her cultural moorings in which religion is central to her life. Aboulela's *Minaret* is linked to Saadawi's *Woman at Point Zero* and *God Dies by the Nile* through divergent representations of Muslim women's identity, and in both of Saadawi's works, patriarchal structures have an iron grip on everyone in the novel with young girls and women being most vulnerable.

Aboulela's novels demonstrate that despite marginalization in the United Kingdom, women have greater freedom to reconfigure their identities. *Minaret* is a counternarrative to stereotypical presentations of women in Islam, and like all the women authors in Part II, Aboulela vividly crafts a narrative that unveils the thoughts and emotions of a displaced female immigrant struggling to reclaim herself by piecing together fragments of her past life in Africa.

Spatio-temporality juxtaposes the past and the present, unsuccessful romantic relationships, and the longing for home in Sudan. *Minaret* addresses authentic and contemporary discourses about the difficulties of assimilation into western nations by Muslim immigrants. The past two decades of social, economic, and political upheaval have driven increasing migration into Europe and America from North African nations with Muslim populations. The postcolonial landscape of North Africa has remained unstable, and Sudanese refugee communities have increased. In *Minaret*, Najwa was formerly from a wealthy family because her father was a businessman and politician. In Sudan, Najwa led a life of luxury as a university student who enjoyed elite status in Sudanese society. A military coup disrupts her life, and she must flee Sudan as an exile.

Life in London is a challenge as she copes with her isolation.

The novel is significant because it displays a woman embracing her faith as a refuge from the difficulties and stresses of unbelonging in London. Aboulela's literary imagination crafts a vision of a Muslim woman's journey beyond otherness to develop her religious practice that will ground her sense of selfhood and self-affirmation. This perspective is uncommon although

Cristina Ali Farah's *Little Mother* is a contemporary work that illuminates Muslim women's experiences in the Somali-Italian Diaspora. In addition, Somali-Italian writer Igiaba Scego's *Adua* brings important insight into diaspora narratives of transformation beyond Africa's borders.

Eventually, Najwa becomes part of a Muslim sisterhood to study the Koran as an expression of her spiritual awakening. The support, friendship, and solidarity with other Muslim women in the Sudanese diaspora illustrate the feminist energies conveyed in the structure of the novel. It is ironic that in the Sudan, the protagonist experienced ambivalence toward religious practice, but later in London when she must cope with the trauma of displacement, she renews her faith as a source of inner strength and resilience to weather her new life of *otherness*. Aboulela's treatment of the religious theme is uncommon in the context of diaspora fiction and herein lies the salience of the work. Not only does Aboulela's engagement with Islamic practice reconfigure the notion of an immigrant woman's inner journey, the novel goes further to disrupt the monolithic non-Muslim image of Islam as a religion embroiled in controversial discourse and critique.

Much of the discourse about gender roles in the Islamic faith interrogates the place of women within the parameters of codes of behavior, social restrictions, and dress codes. Conventional perceptions of Islamic patriarchal structures dominate the portrayal of the religion wherein women's voices are silenced and their agency in shaping their identities is muted and restricted. Aboulela's insightful disruption of this gaze deserves greater attention as an inventive theme of immigrant fiction by women authors. This is especially evident when the protagonist chooses to wear the Hijab, attends the mosque, and begins to pray regularly, not because she is compelled by anyone but through her own agency. Further, as part of her feminist awakening, she rejects her inappropriate and unsatisfying relationships with males in her life in London. Her commitment to deepen her religious faith includes plans to complete the Hadj as a milestone of Islamic practice. These actions confirm the renewal of her faith as both an inner journey and the creation of her membership in a religious community of women. It may be argued that *Minaret* does, in fact, succeed as a feminist novel, although events in the work appear understated. Aboulela has crafted a contemporary work of fiction through a woman-centered perspective as yet a new way of telling the African story in the global age.

Leila Aboulela's first novel *The Translator* is a multilayered work whose romantic elements infuse religious faith, cultural hybridity, spatio-temporal modalities, and postcolonial perspectives to create a haunting tale of a Sudanese woman's quest for a sense of her identity.

Her birthplace in London and estrangement from Sudan are the backdrop of her difficult path to happiness. The structure of the novel unfolds through memories that flow from the past to the present to form a vivid rendering of her life. Like *Minaret*, Aboulela's literary imagination foregrounds Islamic faith as a focal point of the protagonists' journey to self-acceptance and happiness. Important events in the novel serve as historical markers of the postcolonial landscape colored by politically charged perceptions of Islam, terrorism, and religious extremism in North Africa and the Middle East during the late twentieth century. In both *Minaret* and *The Translator*, Aboulela aims to subvert common distortions in the portrayal of Islam by the West and both works successfully achieve a more balanced and informed presentation of Islamic practice by ordinary people. In *The Translator*, a westernized Sudanese woman living alone is tormented for years by the loss of her husband in Aberdeen. Her grieving flavors the narration of her life, told in flashback and infused with powerful imagery that belies her unsettled and clouded mind. She has left her son in Sudan, and the events in the novel reveal a tangle of conflicting emotions about her marriage, hybrid existence in Aberdeen, and the prospect of romance with a Scottish professor for whom she works as a translator.

NoViolet Bulawayo's *We Need New Names* was received with critical acclaim in 2013 as the author's first novel. Chapter 6 explores "Ruptured Spaces of the Self" that represent the fractured life of the protagonist in the work which is a coming-of-age tale among an array of diaspora-themed works in the global era. The work traces the journey of ten-year-old Darling from the streets of Harare to Detroit Michigan as a transformative experience of hybridity and confusion, which reoccurs as a mirror of life for many immigrants when they leave Africa. The novel captures the complexities of postcolonial Zimbabwe that wreak havoc on the lives of children as the nation's most valuable asset in the post-independence era. The work is a compelling critique of the postcolonial landscape of Zimbabwe in the aftermath of politically motivated and deleterious policies of former president Robert Mugabe in the mid-twentieth century. His brutal dictatorship resulted in the deaths of thousands of innocent Zimbabweans and plunged the nation into economic collapse and political chaos. Into this mix, Zimbabwean women and children became the worst and most vulnerable victims as depicted in the ravaged slums of Harare where Darling and her friends are forced to fend for themselves. *We Need New Names* shares intertextual elements with Amma Darko's gripping novel of street children and child prostitution in *Faceless* described in Chapter 4. In both works, children are robbed of a wholesome childhood because they fall prey to hunger, sexual assault, drug abuse, and violence. Like *Faceless*, *We Need New Names* is an indictment of the government's failure to enact policies that ensure economic and political stability in the post-independence era. The postcolonial ruptures in Zimbabwe may be understood beyond the impact of social, economic, and political upheaval because the lives of individuals may also be affected in ways that are disjointed and unrewarding. The problems and challenges experienced by the masses in Zimbabwe held far-reaching implications, especially on the economic stability of families as highlighted in the novel.

Although the child protagonist escapes from Zimbabwe to the United States, she enters another stage of uncertainty and disjuncture caused by the hybrid nature of her existence; hence, the book is framed as immigrant/ diaspora fiction. As an adolescent coming of age in America, Darling struggles with unbelonging and unbalanced homelife with her aunt and uncle, and longing for her homeland. For the protagonist, the postcolonial ruptures resonate in struggles with her fragmented identity in America as she tries to make sense of the world around her. Toward the end of the novel, Bulawayo's symbolic image of a black and white mask represents the bifurcated identity of the protagonist of which she is dimly aware on a deeper level. An important event in the novel that underscores the postcolonial themes is an abrasive conversation between Darling and her childhood friend who challenges her on her Zimbabwean identity and commitment to the future of her nation. The novel's ending does not suggest a resolution of these tensions, and the reader is left to ponder the future of immigrants who leave Africa for new spaces of uncertainty and disconnection from their former lives in Africa.

The novel raises more questions than it answers about the erosion of cultural moorings among those who migrate beyond Africa in search of opportunities in the global North. An important issue posed by the enigmatic ending is the question of conflicted African identity and heritage through assimilation to western life. In addition, the novel interrogates the problem of commitment to Africa's future that is best achieved when people remain on the continent and lend their energies to nation-building in the post-independence era. There are no easy answers to complex issues such as these, but the work conveys compelling messages for a generation of immigrants and African-descended peoples in the twenty-first century.

"Black Venus Dreams and the Migrant Body in Igiaba Scego's *Adua*" is examined in Chapter 7. Somali-Italian author, Igiaba Scego writes from the diaspora setting of Italy to uncover the nations' colonial engagement with Somalia and the far-reaching impact on a woman's journey to find happiness and success. Chapter 7 examines the inner turmoil of displacement, coming-of-age angst, and the lure of foreign shores, which fuel the naïve protagonist's hopes for stardom and fame as a Hollywood film star. Her immigrant dreams of a magical life abroad fuel her imagination beyond the war-torn and precarious environment of her homeland from which she longs to escape. Scego's fictional work shares intertextual elements with Christina Ali Farah's *Little Mother*, and Warshan Shire's poetic rendering, *Conversations about Home*, narrates the discomforting experiences of females that migrate to Italy as refugees seeking escape from ethnic conflict in Somalia. Like many novels about the experiences of immigrants, the structure of the novel shifts from the past to the present in ways that highlight the contrasting periods of life that reconfigure their identities as migrant subjects in the postcolonial era. In addition, the structure of *Adua* presents two narrators, Adua and her father Zoppe, whose combined perspectives on the past and the present, gender dynamics, and generational modalities project a compelling account of immigrant life in Italy.

Adua's coming-of-age narration includes descriptions of her rites of passage ritual that she is compelled to submit to by her father. Although the ordeal is painful, it marks her transition to womanhood in her society. She misses her life as a nomad in the rural landscape, and ironically, she is firmly grounded to the land itself in ways that connect to Kenyan women's allegiance to the soil in Likimani's *Passbook F.47927*. When she is uprooted by her father and sent to the city of Magalo, her maturation unfolds severe unhappiness and dissatisfaction with her family and essentially everything around her.

The postcolonial gaze on life in Somalia reveals a glaring disruption of cultural moorings through the colonial intrusion of Mussolini's fascist agenda. Like many others in Somali society, Adua is enraptured by the propagandized Hollywood imagery that draws her imagination into foreign dreams of herself as a film star in the Italian cinema. Desperate to escape her homeland, she ends up in Italy, but unfortunately her dream of stardom becomes a nightmare journey into the seamy underworld of pornographic Italian Cinema. She is degraded, sexually assaulted, and commodified by an Italian director who casts her as "Black Venus."

After years of humiliation and degradation and abuse of drugs and alcohol, she is left penniless and riddled with shame and guilt. This period of her life is narrated in a flashback as an older woman. The contemporary theme of longing for home and return migration haunts Adua's memories of her unsatisfying life in Italy.

The male voice on the novel is her father Zoppe who also suffers at the hands of Italian police when he is arrested. His only crime is his blackness when he was beaten, tortured, and nearly starved. Scego foregrounds the European assault on the black body as a motif in the novel through the portrayal of Somali immigrants as mere tools of exploitation. Zoppe is not killed by the soldiers because he is useful to them as a translator. The novel ends on an uncertain note because although Adua considers moving back home, readers are never certain that she departs Italy.

The novel is a poignant recollection of failed hopes and shattered dreams for both Adua and her father and Italy becomes a space of pain trauma and an indictment of the postcolonial landscape abroad. Scego chronicles the unfortunate life of a female from her youth to maturity that parallels Bulawayo's Darling, through the uncertain futures they face. Finally, Adua's journey in Italy expresses the vulnerability of immigrants, especially women to the lure of easy success in foreign lands where they may encounter the barriers of race, class, and gender within unwelcoming spaces of western nations.

Chapter 8 demonstrates the ways in which Chimamanda Ngozi Adichie's Ifemelu fares better than the women protagonists featured in *We Need New Names* and in *Adua*. The success of Adichie's *Americanah* (2013) lies in the complexity of themes that emerge in stories of African migration in the twenty-first century alongside the powerful perspectives on race in America.

The book is epic in scope, and in this volume, "Afropolitan Energies in the Twenty-first Century: Immigrants, Dreamers, and Marginalized Others" investigates hybridity which is perhaps the most significant theme of contemporary diaspora studies. Chapter 8 also demonstrates the flawed conceptualization of *Afropolitanism* as a lens to interpret the characters in Adichie's award-winning novel. Granted, the concept is indeed meaningful and compelling in its broad application to a range of immigrant demographics in the global environment of transformation and flux. However, the less fortunate outcomes for some if not most of the characters in the novel do not represent the gleaming qualities of Afropolitan aesthetics as defined by Taiye Selasie in her well-known essay in 2005: "Bye Bye Babar."

The difficulty with Afropolitanism is not that it is invalid, but that it ignores glaring diversity in the ways that immigrants from Africa experience new identities within new spaces of western nations. In *Americanah*, Ifemelu's Nigerian boyfriend Obinze and his fellow Nigerians in London, Auntie Uju, and her son Dike are among immigrant characters whose identities are mangled in the sites of unbelonging and confusion in London and America. The economic woes and stressful emotions that spiral into depression are a counter-narrative to the celebratory claims of Afropolitan identities. Racial *otherness* is a leading barrier to happiness and a sense of belonging for significant numbers of African immigrants in the past and the present. Since the mid- to late twentieth century, many African writers engage these realities in their iconic fiction set in the African diaspora. Ama Ata's *Our Sister Killjoy* and the London novels of Emecheta like *In the Ditch* and *Second Class Citizen* vividly capture these unfortunate but realistic experiences.

Along with the portrayal of Nigerian characters who struggle to succeed in the west, Adichie cleverly deconstructs America's dark history of slavery, racial exclusion, and identity politics as well as the relationship among Africans and African Americans in the novel. On a lighter note, the book succeeds as a beautiful love story that symbolizes Ifemelu's having come full circle by returning to Nigeria and to the man she loved in secondary school. Ifemelu's feminist energies animate the work through her intelligence, agency, and independent spirit that shines through her commanding voice in her blog. Her decision to refashion her future in Nigeria is uncommon in diaspora fiction, and by the end of the novel, her character is a fully realized Nigerian whose American dream has been achieved and rejected when she returns home. These actions may be contrasted with other protagonists like Bulawayo's Darling and Scego's Adua who remain uncertain about how to negotiate their future in relation to their homelands from which they fled.

African Women as Transnational Subjects

In sum, the novels discussed in Part II shed light on diverse experiences and life stories of African women living in foreign spaces of the west. Spatio-temporality frames the discursive engagement with a range of successful texts that uncover new ways of being African in the global age. As African women immigrants migrate abroad for diverse reasons, they ultimately experience racialized identities as marginalized others in Europe and America. In this volume of critical essays, women's potential to adapt, assimilate, return to Africa, or to simply transform their identities is a shared response to their engagement with *difference*. The works explored provides an intimate view of postcolonial trajectories as many challenges on the African continent shape the lives of women for better or worse. Through their novels about African female migrants, Igiba Scego, Chimamanda Ngozi Adichie, NoViolet Bulawayo, and Leila Aboulela illuminate vivid and authentic perspectives on the ways in which race, class, and gender transform their identities in the multi-local spaces of the African diaspora. The narrative voices of the four authors are speaking in unison through the use of memory, African cultural identity, postcolonial disruptions, and their expectations for new lives beyond their homelands.

An important feature that the novels share is the backward glances to the past that includes recollections of their families, communities, milestones in their lives, coming-of-age memories, and romantic attachments that define their identities and essentially their place(s) in the world. As human beings, our sense of belongingness is rooted in the collective experiences we acquire throughout our lives. African experiences of cultural heritage, ethnic origin, religion, way of life, and all the variegated expressions of our cultural moorings are what African subjects carry with them when leaving the African continent. Cultural collisions are inevitable and form a normative feature of life in the global north where race, class, and gender mediate notions of identity in the perceptions of non-Africans and African subjects themselves.

The extent to which African female immigrants adapt, assimilate, or reject new ways of being African in a globalized world is skillfully rendered by Scego, Adichie, Bulawayo, and Aboulela. The female protagonists created by the authors are a mixed bag of immigrants whose lives in Europe and America display the human capacity to (re)invent themselves, draw from their inner strength, develop their potential, question themselves, and most often move beyond the restrictive expectations, norms, and stereotypical representations of African womanhood. Sometimes, the backward glances to the African past have not allowed each of the protagonists in the novels examined to evolve beyond their difficult experiences. This is realistic because people respond to life's challenges in different ways. This idea is frequently projected in disaster movies when a group of characters tries to survive a life-threatening event. Typically, all of them will simply not make it while other characters exhibit a powerful will to survive all odds based upon their personal qualities. As a mirror of life, the diaspora-oriented authors in Part II have used their artistry to shed light on women's inner lives to reveal a broad range, of responses to the harsh realities, adversity, and marginalization they face in Europe and America. Fortunately, women's choices are overwhelmingly positive, inspiring, and inventive as expressions of feminist agency and self-determination.

Bulawayo's Darling in *We Need New Names* is the female character that displays the least appealing changes in her self-perception, decisions, and consciousness of her subjectivity and path in life. When she contemplates the dysfunctional family that she lives with in "DestroyedMychigan," she asks herself hard questions about the motivation for the odd behavior of her relatives, emotional disconnections in her aunt's marriage, her cousin's puzzling behavior, and the environment in America. She constantly makes comparisons between the past and the present, celebrating that she is better off in America and at least no longer hungry. Because of her youth, she is unable to make coherent sense of her life in Zimbabwe, her new life in America, or her relationship to her country. Perhaps Bulawayo is suggesting that for some immigrants, they never quite make the balance between the old and the new, the past and the present. Neither are some immigrants able to form meaningful relationships with people or the communities they left behind.

Thus, Darling's consciousness remains fixed in a liminal space, displayed by her silence when she is asked pointed questions by her friend, Chipo, who is still in Zimbabwe. She is unable to grasp the significance of questions about Africans that leave home and never return abandoning their potential contribution to Africa's development. Further, when she looks at the black and white mask and gets angry, she doesn't know why. However, she knows she cannot return to Zimbabwe. Darling's predicament resonates with the clueless children in Sefi Atta's novella *News from Home*. Additionally, Aunty Uju's son Dike in Adichie's *Americanah* is another illustration of a confused young African who receives no guidance to make sense of his identity in America. Bulawayo's examination of these issues speaks to the effect of migration on young people in the global age who are products of migration in search of themselves, and a promising future elsewhere. *We Need New Names* is thus a story of incalculable loss of identity and self-knowledge in the splintered spaces of the American Midwest.

The female protagonist in Adichie's *Americanah* is exemplary in the evolution of her feminist consciousness, agency, and personal and professional growth. Not only does she stop using the phony American accent that she acquired as a coping mechanism, she is educated and shares her ideas and perspectives publicly about racial dynamics in America. Very importantly, she expresses her understanding of the African American experience of *blackness* and the dichotomy between Africans and African diaspora people created by the Atlantic Slave Trade. These ideas are uncommon in literary texts by African writers and remain sources of tension among both communities in America and on the African continent.

The idea of return migration is a compelling one that was raised by Bulawayo as well, and it illustrates the ways in which the authors are in conversation about this pressing issue. Adichie's Ifemelu has come full circle, and she emerges unscathed by the diaspora experience in America. It appears that for Ifemelu, her sojourn in America is a chronicle of a woman's self-discovery outside of her cultural comfort zone where she is cast as the *female black other*. It seems that despite early experiences of discomfort, depression, and marginalization, Ifemelu's consciousness emerged from somewhere deep inside her to create a self-realized African woman who is comfortably Nigerian, while she is also a transnational individual. In many ways, Ifemelu's character mirrors Adichie's life because as the most success-ful and visible African writer in the twenty-first century, she divides her time between Nigeria and America and makes substantial contributions in the form of publishing, mentoring, offering writing workshops among other activities that support emerging writers. An important feature of feminist consciousness in *Americanah* is the protagonist's ability to deconstruct the nature of her experiences and to articulate the social, economic, and politi-cal forces that determine her subjectivity through the lens of race, class, and gender.

Leila Aboulela's Najwa and Sammar also exhibit Ifemelu's feminist agency within the European diaspora. Both characters are strong and resilient as displayed by their embracing Muslim women's identity in the global arena. Religion or religious faith is the underlying theme in both *The Translator and Minaret*, and the author's narration is an original and significant contribu-tion to an under-represented subject in literary texts by women. The women characters have demonstrated a new way of being African in the world that is timely and necessary. The problematic, stereotypical and monolithic percep-tions of Islam and the role of women in religious practice deserve increased attention and analysis so that Aboulela's intervention is a significant contri-bution to literary studies. Both Najwa and Sammar are deeply connected to Sudan, and to echo the ideas of the author, religious faith is something that one can take anywhere. Very importantly, the women characters exhibit free choice and autonomy in charting their lives which is a critical measure of feminist consciousness.

Finally, Adua is able to contemplate returning to Somalia because she inherited her father's home after his death. The most important action that unfolds her evolution in the Somali-Italian diaspora is her choice to rescue and marry an undocumented Somali immigrant. The old and the new dias-pora meet and forge a new life together although he eventually leaves her.

Adua has at least come to terms with the trauma of her early years in Italy and admits that she had no guidance, and essentially no clue to the social, economic, or political forces at work in Somalia, Italy, or in her own life as a sexually objectified immigrant. Her insight at the end of the novel is the result of her middle-aged perspective that is realistic, unlike Darling, who for the most part still has no clue about the larger forces that have influenced her path in the diaspora. The four novels studied in Part II are indeed in conversation about identity, hybridity, and the diverse ways in which they are motivated to cope with these challenges. As transnational subjects, the protagonists have, through self-discovery, forged new identities in the trans-formative world of the global age.

Works Cited

Aboulela, Leila. 1999. *The Translator*. New York. The Black Cat.

———. 2005. *Minaret*. New York. The Black Cat.

Adichie, Chimamanda Ngozi. 2007. *Americanah*. New York. Alfrd. P. Knopf.

Adichie, Chimamanda Ngozi. 2013. *Americanah*. Toronto. Alfred. A. Knopf.

Aidoo, Ama. 1998. "The African Woman Today." *Sisterhood Feminisms & Power From Africa to the Diaspora*. Trenton. Africa World Press. pp. 39–50.

Ardnt, Susan. 2002. *The Dynamics of African Feminism: Naming and Classifying African Literatures*. Trenton. Africa World Press.

Bulawayo, No Violet. 2013. *We Need New Names*. New York. Regan Arthur Books.

Darko, Amma. 1993. *Faceless*. Accra. Sub Saharan Publishers.

Head, Bessie. 1971. *Maru*. London. Heinnemann.

———. 1974. *A Question of Power*. London. Heinnemann.

Likimani, Muthoni. 1974. *Passbook F47927. Women and Mau Mau. In Kenya*. Nairobi, Houndmills and London. Mac Millan Publishers.

O'Barr, Jean. 1985. "Introductory Essay". *Passbook F.47927: Women in Mau Mau*. New York. MacMillan.

Saadawi, Nawal El. 1974. *God Dies by the Nile*. Trans. Sherif Hetata. London and New York. Zed Books.

———. 1983. *Woman at Point Zero*. Trans. Sherif Hetata. London and New York. Zed Books.

Scego, Igiaba. 2015. *Adua: A Novel*. Trans. Jamie Richards. New York. New Vessel Press.

Selasi, Taiye. 2005. "Bye Bye Babar". *The LIP Magazine*. https://thelip.robertsharp. co.uk/2005/03/03/bye-bye-barbar/

Wa Thiongo, Ngugi and Micere Mugo. 2013. *The Trial of Dedan Kimathi*. Long Grove. Waveland press.

Index

For Product Safety Concerns and Information please contact our EU
representative GPSR@taylorandfrancis.com
Taylor & Francis Verlag GmbH, Kaufingerstraße 24, 80331 München, Germany

www.ingramcontent.com/pod-product-compliance
Lightning Source LLC
Chambersburg PA
CBHW071112100726
47908CB00008B/2352

* 9 7 8 1 0 3 2 3 9 5 4 0 1 *